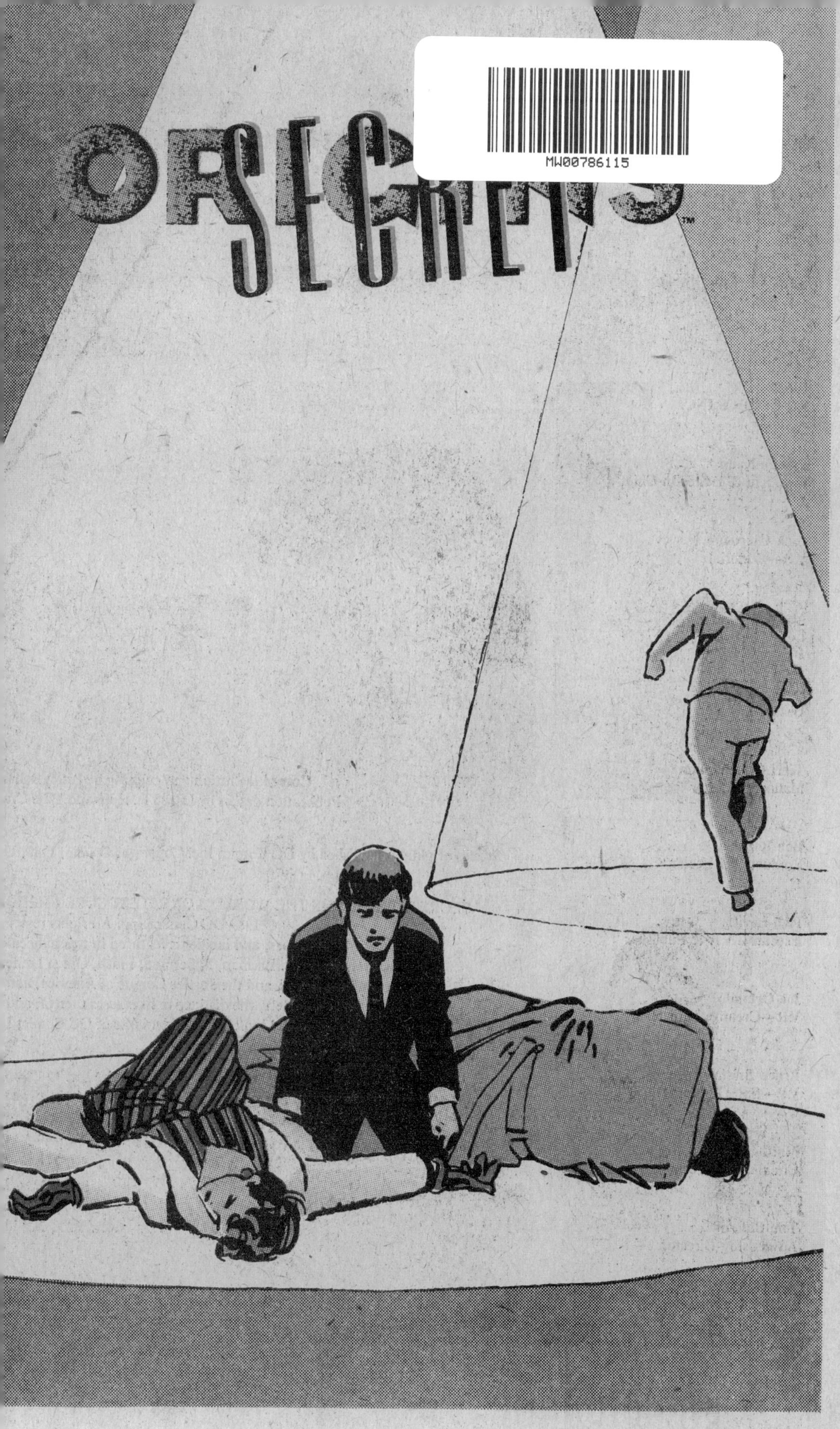
SECRETS™

DC COMICS INC.

Jenette Kahn
President & Editor-In-Chief

Dick Giordano
V.P.—Editorial

Mark Waid
Editor

Richard Bruning
Design Director

Terri Cunningham
Managing Editor

Bob Rozakis
Production Director

Paul Levitz
Executive V.P. & Publisher

Joe Orlando
V.P.—Creative Director

Bruce Bristow
V.P.—Sales & Marketing

Matthew Ragone
Circulation Director

Tom Ballou
Advertising Director

Patrick Caldon
V.P.—Controller

Cover illustration and coloring by Brian Bollar
Publication design by Eileen R. Hoff and Dale Cra

Stories originally published by DC Comics Inc. Copyright © 1986, 1988, 19

DC Comics I
666 Fifth Ave
New York, NY 10

A Warner Bros. Inc. Compa
First Prin
ISBN 0-930289-5

TABLE OF CONTENTS

LEGENDS

DC Comics' great strength lies in its characters—the best-known, most original, and most popular Super-Heroes of all time. And each of those heroes has his own unique origin . . . a tale carved in stone, immutable in detail, iron-clad and never-changing throughout the march of time.

Sort of.

Okay, not really. Because there's a certain science—or magic—or circus act not unlike juggling fragile china plates—to keeping thirty- to fifty-year-old characters alive and contemporary. And judicious—*judicious*—changes are a part of that act. That's something we've learned from experience, and something evidenced by the stories in this volume.

Take Superman, for example. The Man of Steel, of course, is the seminal super-hero—the first and the most legendary. But just as legends are refined and redefined for new generations, so has the Metropolis Marvel been subtly altered since his debut in ACTION COMICS #1 (June, 1938). When we first met Superman, he could "merely" leap an eighth of a mile . . . lift tremendous weights—outrace a locomotive . . . and withstand any assault short of a bursting shell. And, no, we're not leaving anything out—those were his powers . . . and they were enough.

For a while, anyway. But Superman's success brought forth a slew of super-powered imitators. Before the end of the decade, dozens of comics publishers were running adventures of tough, longjohned do-gooders who could have taken Superman in two falls out of three . . . had not the Krypton Kid been in heavy training himself. Gradually, Superman's abilities had evolved. His senses became ultra-acute, as he began peering through walls with his x-ray eyes and listening to whispered conversations with his super-hearing. His strength and stamina increased to the point where bursting shells were no more dangerous to him than cap pistols. And most marvelously, he developed the power to defy gravity, to fly at super-speed to any destination on this earth—or beyond.

Throughout the 1940s and 1950s, Superman's super-powers were forever on the increase. His writers, always looking for a new angle, continually topped themselves by giving the Last Son of Krypton new abilities: infra-red vision; super-intellect; super-ventriloquism; the list went on. By the 1960s, Superman was juggling planets and igniting dead suns with his heat vision.

And something more was going on. Superman's writers had re-discovered Krypton . . . and re-discovered it . . . and re-discovered it . . . *ad infinitum*. The rich historical lore of the doomed planet Krypton was a continual source of story material. Lost artifacts and lost survivors from Krypton became a mainstay in Superman stories. A *constant* element. School-age Superman fans were deluged with enough information about the fictional planet Krypton to eclipse anything they might be learning over in social studies class about *real* countries and places.

WHEN MATURITY WAS REACHED, HE DISCOVERED HE COULD EASILY:

LEAP 8TH OF A MILE; HURDLE A TWENTY-STORY BUILDING . . .

RAISE TREMENDOUS WEIGHTS . . .

. . RUN FASTER THAN AN EXPRESS TRAIN . . .

AND THAT NOTHING LESS THAN A BURSTING SHELL COULD PENETRATE HIS SKIN!

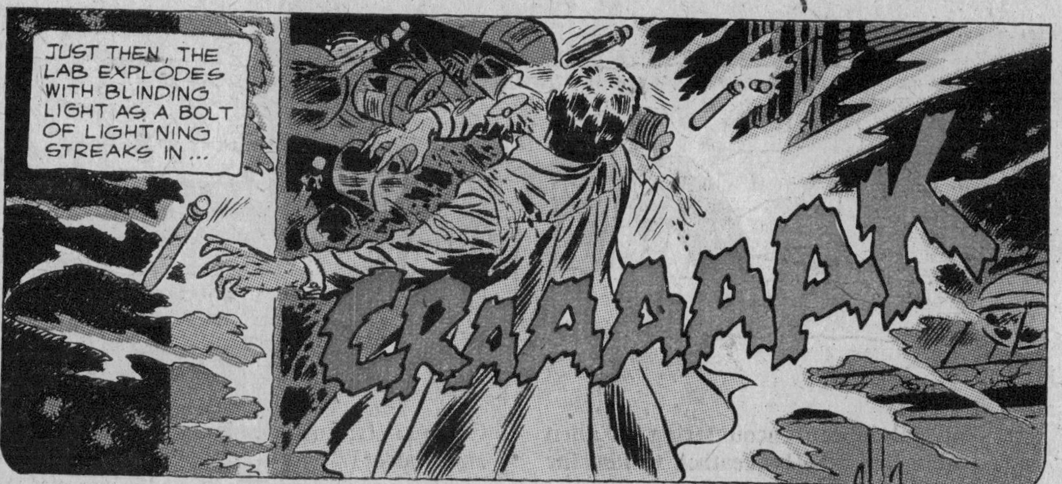
JUST THEN, THE LAB EXPLODES WITH BLINDING LIGHT AS A BOLT OF LIGHTNING STREAKS IN ...
CRAAAAK

What's more, Superman was no longer alone in the DC Universe. As DC's stable of Super-Heroes increased, the pressure to retain Superman's status as the first and greatest got completely out of hand; in other words, whether you were Flash, Green Lantern, Wonder Woman, or a lord of time and space, whatever you could do, Superman could—and had to—do better.

Well. Something snapped after nearly fifty years of escalation. In 1986, DC decided to wipe Superman's slate clean, to start him anew with a more modern bent, slightly more controlled powers, and no "baggage" tying him to previous Superman continuity. He was the same, only different; most significant, as shown to great effect in the story chosen for this volume, his ties to the planet Krypton were all but severed. Though he was still a stranger from another planet, his home . . . his *only* home . . . was Earth.

The changes Superman has endured have often been sweeping. By contrast, his contemporary—and the only comics character who might tie Superman for world-wide visibility—has enjoyed very little "tinkering" over the years. The Batman first appeared in DETECTIVE COMICS #27 (May, 1939), less than a year after Superman made his debut, though the revelation of his origins waited another six months, until DETECTIVE #33. There, readers first learned of Batman's parents, who were gunned down by a cheap hood and whose death inspired the Dark Knight to dedicate his life to avenge the victims of crime. Unlike Superman's Krypton, which has changed substantially over the years, the deserted street corner where the Waynes were killed has changed not a whit in fifty years—but other facets of the Batman's origin have been examined during that time, by asking such questions as where Bruce Wayne learned his skills, or why a bat served as such a riveting inspiration; those revelations have been distilled into the all-new Batman story in this book.

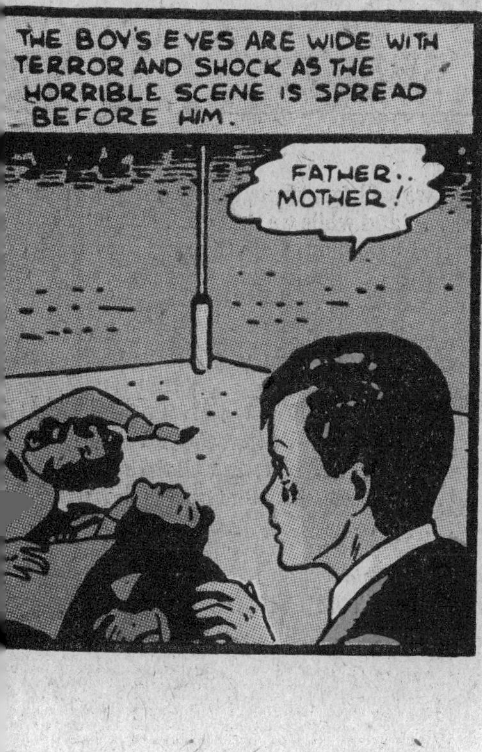
THE BOY'S EYES ARE WIDE WITH TERROR AND SHOCK AS THE HORRIBLE SCENE IS SPREAD BEFORE HIM.
FATHER.. MOTHER!

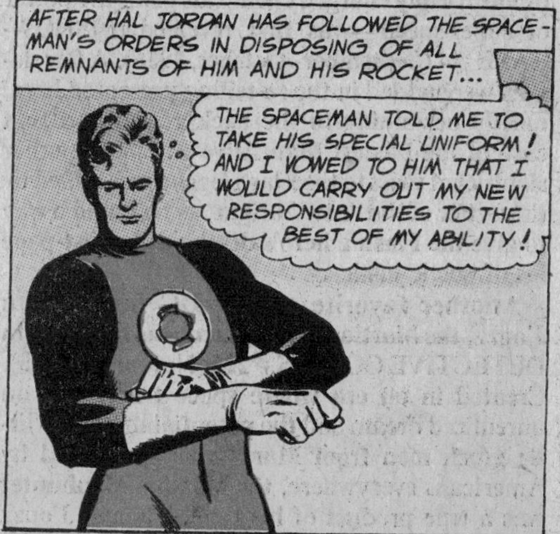
AFTER HAL JORDAN HAS FOLLOWED THE SPACE-MAN'S ORDERS IN DISPOSING OF ALL REMNANTS OF HIM AND HIS ROCKET...
THE SPACEMAN TOLD ME TO TAKE HIS SPECIAL UNIFORM! AND I VOWED TO HIM THAT I WOULD CARRY OUT MY NEW RESPONSIBILITIES TO THE BEST OF MY ABILITY!

If you've never read our new Green Lantern origin, you may find that GL isn't exactly the man he used to be, though he's every bit the hero. His origin story in SHOWCASE #22 (September–October, 1959) began and ended with

"AFTERWARD, WE HELD AN IMPROMPTU GET-TOGETHER AND DECIDED THAT SINCE TEAM-WORK ALONE HAD ENABLED US TO DEFEAT THE METEOR-BEINGS, IT MIGHT BE WISE FOR US TO UNITE..."

WE OUGHT TO FORM A CLUB OR SOCIETY...

A LEAGUE AGAINST EVIL! OUR PURPOSE WILL BE TO UPHOLD JUSTICE AGAINST WHATEVER DANGER THREATENS IT!

test pilot Hal Jordan encountering an alien named Abin Sur, who bequeathed to him the Green Lantern ring and uniform that made Jordan a super-hero. But it wasn't for many issues of GREEN LANTERN comics that Jordan learned the limitations of the ring's powers, or about the intergalactic squad of Green Lanterns, or about their bosses, the Guardians of the Universe. As a further twist to the origin, it has recently been revealed that the ring itself may have made Jordan the "man without fear" he has always been known as; whether this development will become an official part of the Green Lantern mythos remains to be seen.

The origin of the Flash—a police scientist hit by electrically charged chemicals gains the power of super-speed—was first revealed in SHOW-CASE #4 (September–October, 1956). A few details were added in the re-telling presented here, mostly pertaining to the background and first case of the Fastest Man Alive . . . but another significant twist to the Flash legend was added by the writer of the "new" origin, as he found a way to give the Flash a hero's death with a last-page bit of poetic justice.

Another favorite among DC fans, J'onn J'onzz, the Martian Manhunter, was first seen in DETECTIVE COMICS #225 (November, 1955). Created in an era where space travel was an unrealized dream and the potential threat of "little green men from Mars" was speculated by Americans everywhere, the Martian Manhunter was a true product of his time. Though J'onzz was originally depicted as a humanoid inadvertently plucked from among a thriving race of Martians, in recent years (not coincidentally, as real-world travel to the planet Mars has become reality), we've learned that he is humanoid only by choice, and that he was plucked through time as well as space—his people are long dead.

His new family on Earth became the Justice League of America—the stars of this volume's final tale. The League's origin was revealed in JLA #9 (February, 1962), but when the DC editors decided to reprise that story, some alterations had to be made. According to the original version, the five charter JLAers were Aquaman,

Green Lantern, Flash, Martian Manhunter . . . and *Wonder Woman*, who, under recently revised DC history and continuity, had *never met* the Justice League of America! An eleventh-hour editorial decision brought Black Canary into the group in place of the Amazon Princess. Nevertheless, the fundamental story, involving would-be alien conquerors, remains as was.

FOR LONG MOMENTS, THE ROBOT BRAIN CRACKLES AND BUZZES -- THERE IS A VIVID FLASH -- AND A STRANGE, AWESOME FIGURE...

THE ROBOT BRAIN... LOOK WHAT IT BROUGHT-- AN ALIEN BEING!

I READ YOUR MIND WELL, EARTHMAN-- AND I UNDERSTAND YOUR EVERY THOUGHT AND WORD!

As we said, our strength is in our great characters . . . and while we find ourselves subtly altering their trappings from time to time in order t keep them contemporary, their basic origins al ways have—and always will—remain true. A long as there is a DC Comics, you can rest as sured that Superman will always be a strang visitor from another planet; that The Batman will forever have been born out of the senseles death of his parents; that the adventures of th Flash, Green Lantern, and all their compatrio will reflect the history that made them what the are: Legends.

—*Mark Waid*
Editor, SECRET ORIGINS

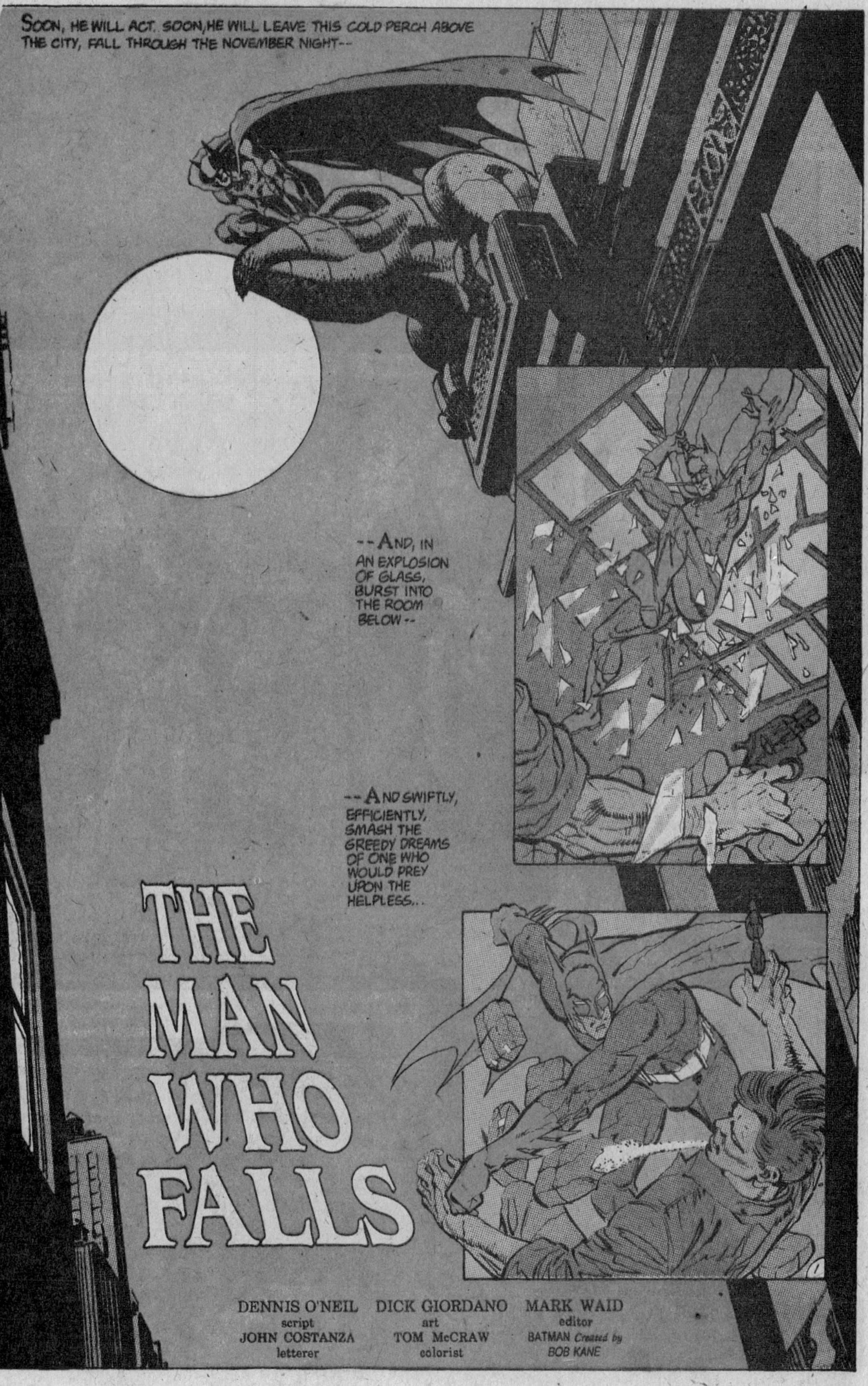
SOON, HE WILL ACT. SOON, HE WILL LEAVE THIS COLD PERCH ABOVE THE CITY, FALL THROUGH THE NOVEMBER NIGHT--
--AND, IN AN EXPLOSION OF GLASS, BURST INTO THE ROOM BELOW--
--AND SWIFTLY, EFFICIENTLY, SMASH THE GREEDY DREAMS OF ONE WHO WOULD PREY UPON THE HELPLESS...
THE MAN WHO FALLS
DENNIS O'NEIL script
DICK GIORDANO art
MARK WAID editor
JOHN COSTANZA letterer
TOM McCRAW colorist
BATMAN Created by BOB KANE

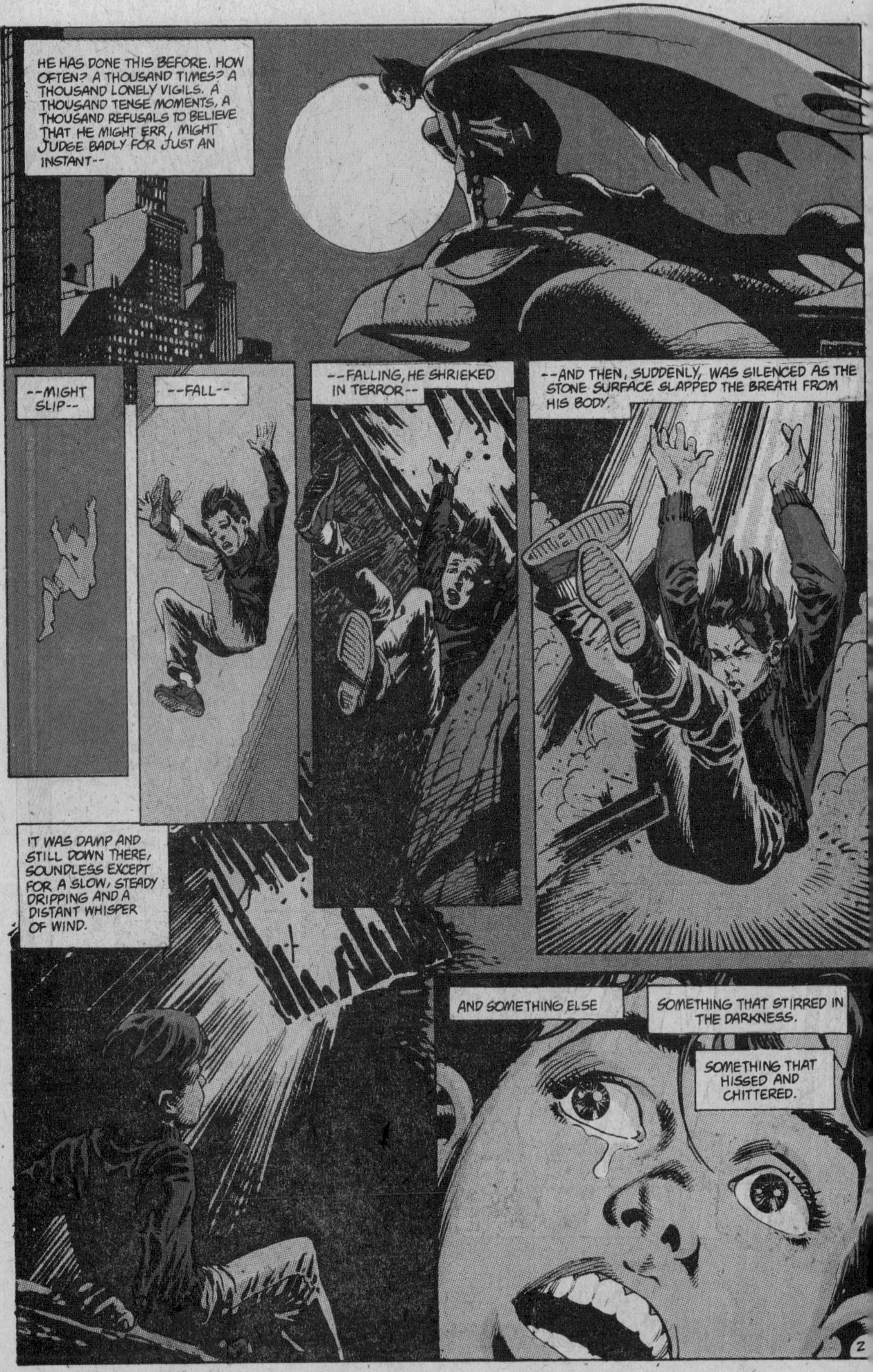
HE HAS DONE THIS BEFORE. HOW OFTEN? A THOUSAND TIMES? A THOUSAND LONELY VIGILS. A THOUSAND TENSE MOMENTS, A THOUSAND REFUSALS TO BELIEVE THAT HE MIGHT ERR, MIGHT JUDGE BADLY FOR JUST AN INSTANT--
--MIGHT SLIP--
--FALL--
--FALLING, HE SHRIEKED IN TERROR--
--AND THEN, SUDDENLY, WAS SILENCED AS THE STONE SURFACE SLAPPED THE BREATH FROM HIS BODY.
IT WAS DAMP AND STILL DOWN THERE, SOUNDLESS EXCEPT FOR A SLOW, STEADY DRIPPING AND A DISTANT WHISPER OF WIND.
AND SOMETHING ELSE
SOMETHING THAT STIRRED IN THE DARKNESS.
SOMETHING THAT HISSED AND CHITTERED.
2

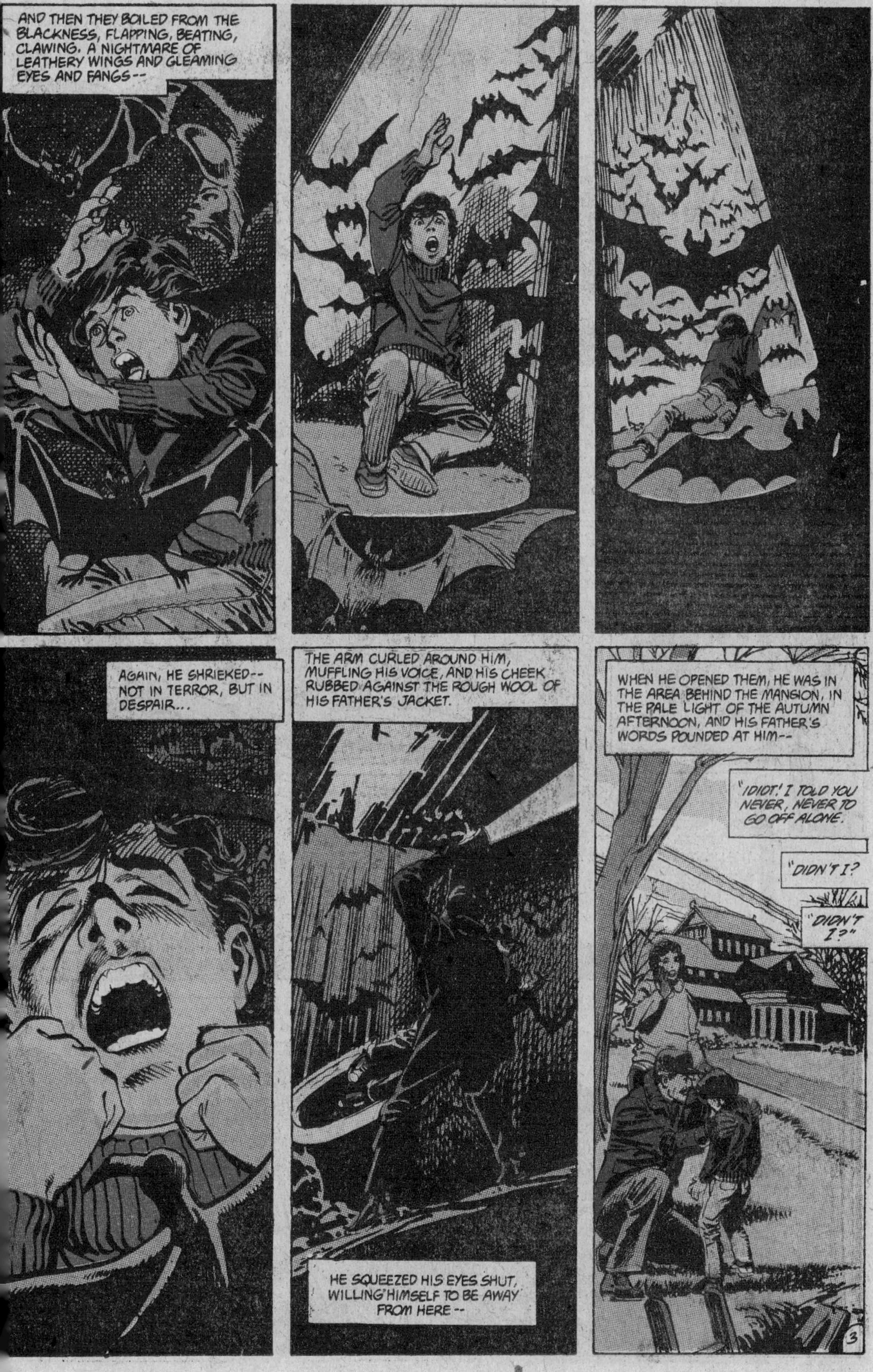
AND THEN THEY BOILED FROM THE BLACKNESS, FLAPPING, BEATING, CLAWING. A NIGHTMARE OF LEATHERY WINGS AND GLEAMING EYES AND FANGS--
AGAIN, HE SHRIEKED--NOT IN TERROR, BUT IN DESPAIR...
THE ARM CURLED AROUND HIM, MUFFLING HIS VOICE, AND HIS CHEEK RUBBED AGAINST THE ROUGH WOOL OF HIS FATHER'S JACKET.
HE SQUEEZED HIS EYES SHUT, WILLING HIMSELF TO BE AWAY FROM HERE--
WHEN HE OPENED THEM, HE WAS IN THE AREA BEHIND THE MANSION, IN THE PALE LIGHT OF THE AUTUMN AFTERNOON, AND HIS FATHER'S WORDS POUNDED AT HIM--
"IDIOT! I TOLD YOU NEVER, NEVER TO GO OFF ALONE.
"DIDN'T I?
"DIDN'T I?"
3

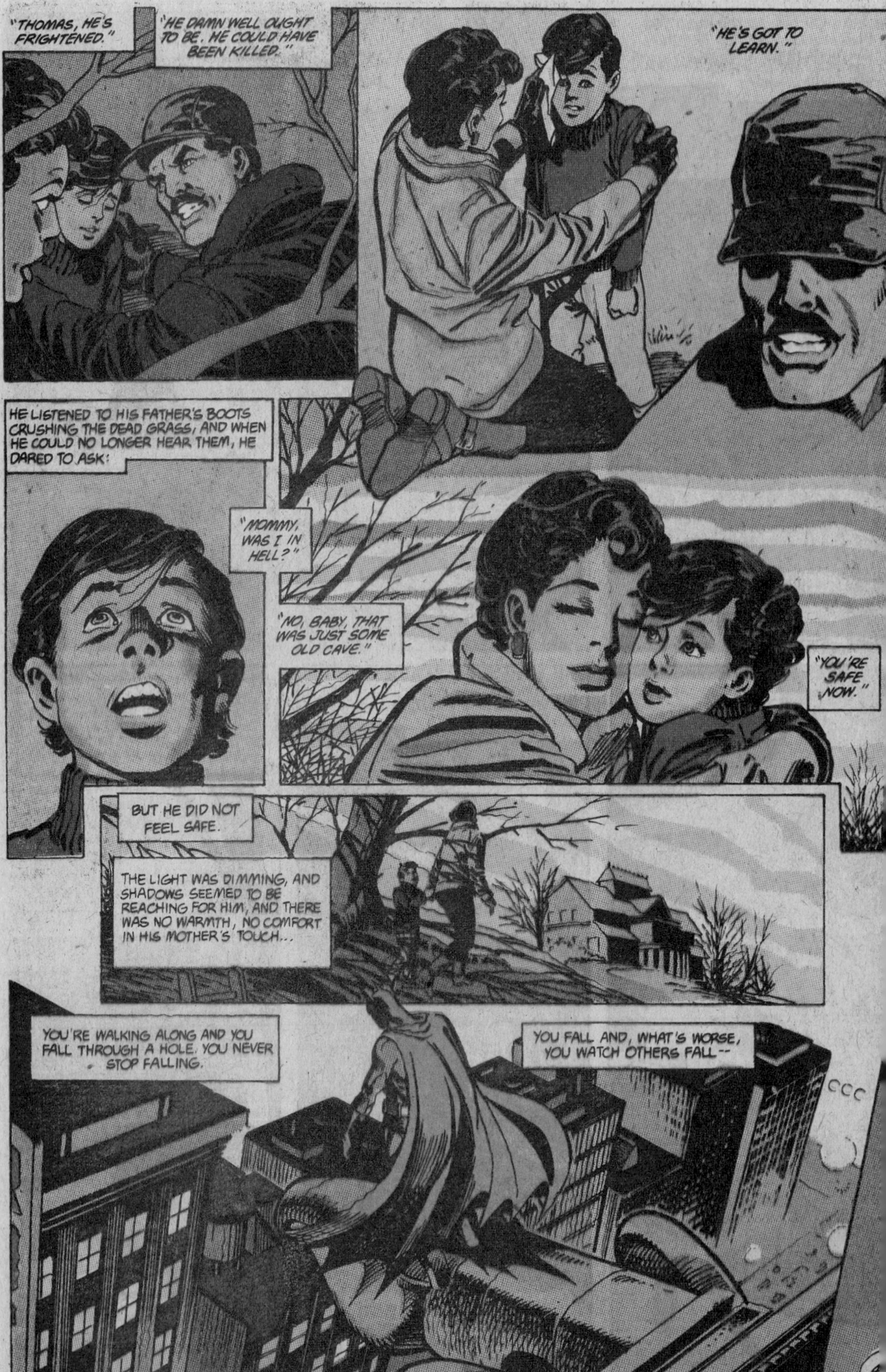
"THOMAS, HE'S FRIGHTENED."
"HE DAMN WELL OUGHT TO BE. HE COULD HAVE BEEN KILLED."
"HE'S GOT TO LEARN."
HE LISTENED TO HIS FATHER'S BOOTS CRUSHING THE DEAD GRASS, AND WHEN HE COULD NO LONGER HEAR THEM, HE DARED TO ASK:
"MOMMY, WAS I IN HELL?"
"NO, BABY, THAT WAS JUST SOME OLD CAVE."
"YOU'RE SAFE NOW."
BUT HE DID NOT FEEL SAFE.
THE LIGHT WAS DIMMING, AND SHADOWS SEEMED TO BE REACHING FOR HIM, AND THERE WAS NO WARMTH, NO COMFORT IN HIS MOTHER'S TOUCH...
YOU'RE WALKING ALONG AND YOU FALL THROUGH A HOLE. YOU NEVER STOP FALLING.
YOU FALL AND, WHAT'S WORSE, YOU WATCH OTHERS FALL--
CCC
4

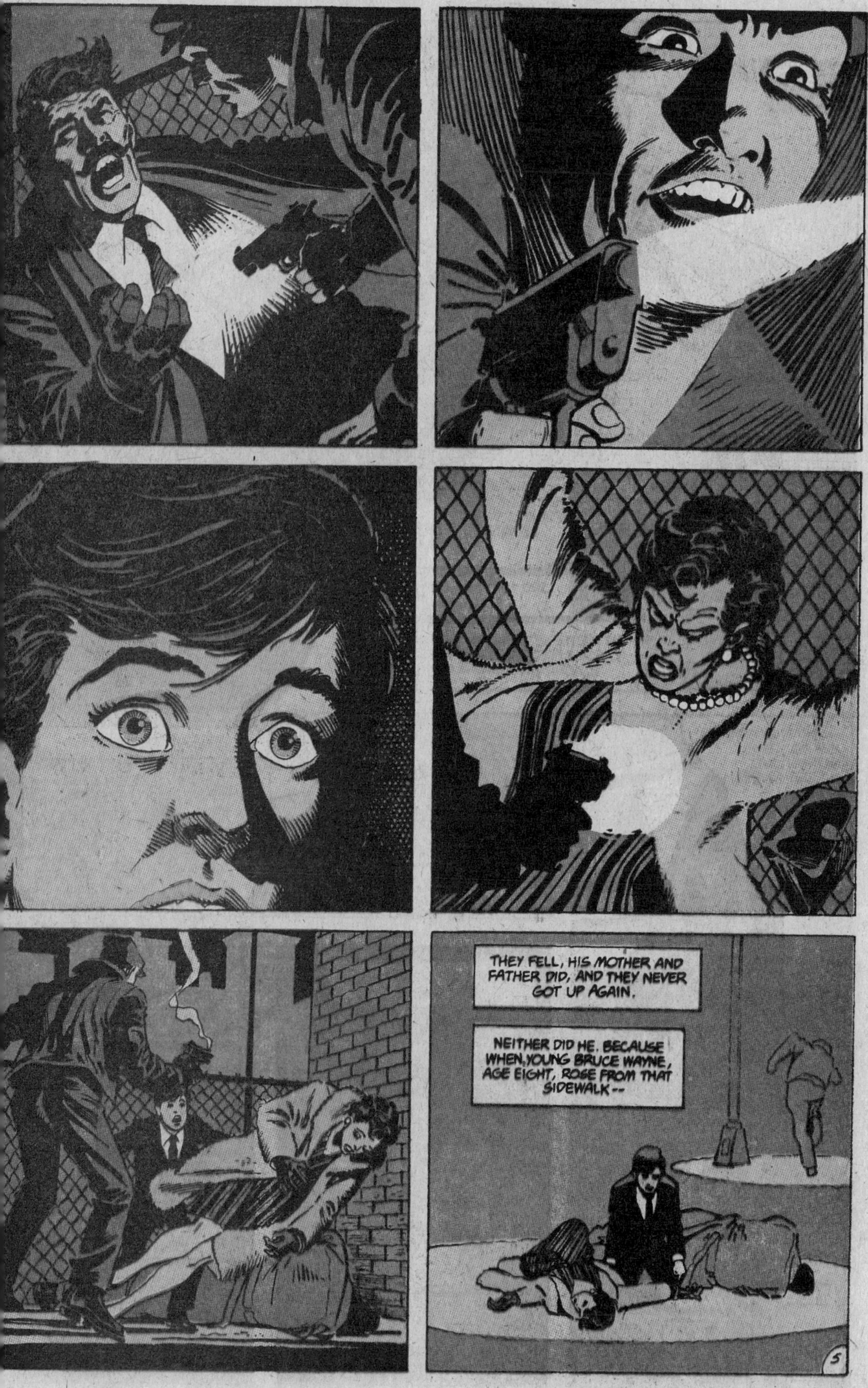

THEY FELL, HIS MOTHER AND FATHER DID, AND THEY NEVER GOT UP AGAIN.
NEITHER DID HE. BECAUSE WHEN, YOUNG BRUCE WAYNE, AGE EIGHT, ROSE FROM THAT SIDEWALK--

— HE WAS ALREADY BECOMING WHAT HE WOULD EVENTUALLY BE.

HE HAD A PURPOSE. NOW HE NEEDED A DIRECTION.

HE NEEDED OTHER THINGS, TOO -- KNOWLEDGE AND SKILLS.

AND TO GET THOSE, HE NEEDED CUNNING. HE HAD TO THWART ALL THE WELL-MEANING PEOPLE WHO WANTED TO *CARE* FOR THE POOR ORPHAN.

AND THE POOR ORPHAN'S FORTUNE.

HE WROTE LETTERS THAT WEREN'T EXACTLY FORGERIES AND WEREN'T EXACTLY ANYTHING ELSE --

-- AND THEY ENABLED HIM TO LEAVE GOTHAM CITY AT AGE 14 AND BEGIN A GLOBAL QUEST FOR WHAT HE WANTED TO KNOW.

HE VISITED MANY CAMPUSES --

-- AND MANY *OTHER* PLACES OF LEARNING --

-- BUT HE NEVER STAYED LONG.

"THE WAYN[E] BOY'S BRIGHT," T[HE] PROFESSOR[S] WOULD SAY "BUT HE'S G[OT] NO DISCIPLI[NE], HE SKIPS AROUND, HE WON'T DECID[E] ON A MAJO[R]

6

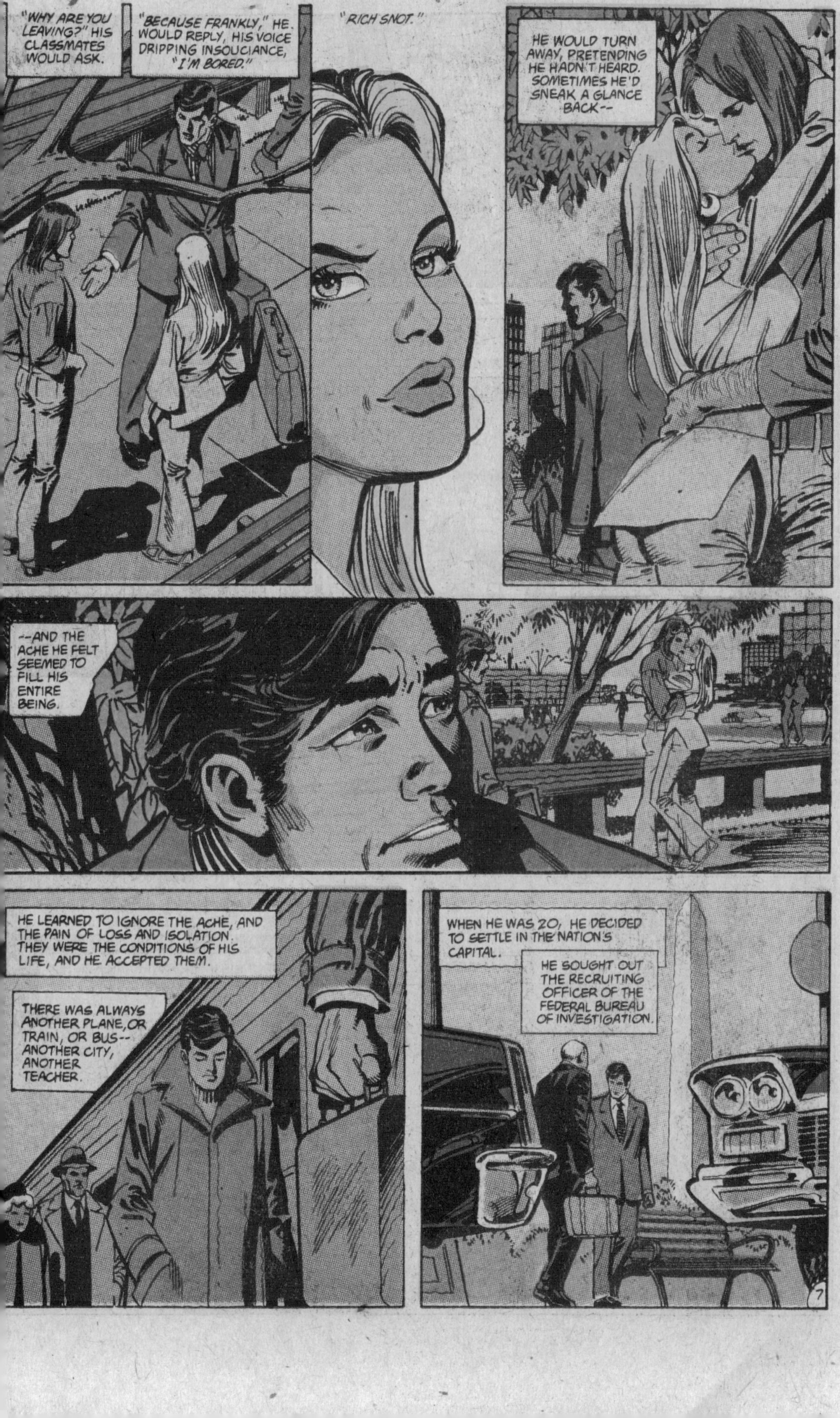
"WHY ARE YOU LEAVING?" HIS CLASSMATES WOULD ASK.
"BECAUSE FRANKLY," HE WOULD REPLY, HIS VOICE DRIPPING INSOUCIANCE, "I'M BORED."
"RICH SNOT."
HE WOULD TURN AWAY, PRETENDING HE HADN'T HEARD. SOMETIMES HE'D SNEAK A GLANCE BACK--
--AND THE ACHE HE FELT SEEMED TO FILL HIS ENTIRE BEING.
HE LEARNED TO IGNORE THE ACHE, AND THE PAIN OF LOSS AND ISOLATION. THEY WERE THE CONDITIONS OF HIS LIFE, AND HE ACCEPTED THEM.
THERE WAS ALWAYS ANOTHER PLANE, OR TRAIN, OR BUS-- ANOTHER CITY, ANOTHER TEACHER.
WHEN HE WAS 20, HE DECIDED TO SETTLE IN THE NATION'S CAPITAL.
HE SOUGHT OUT THE RECRUITING OFFICER OF THE FEDERAL BUREAU OF INVESTIGATION.
7

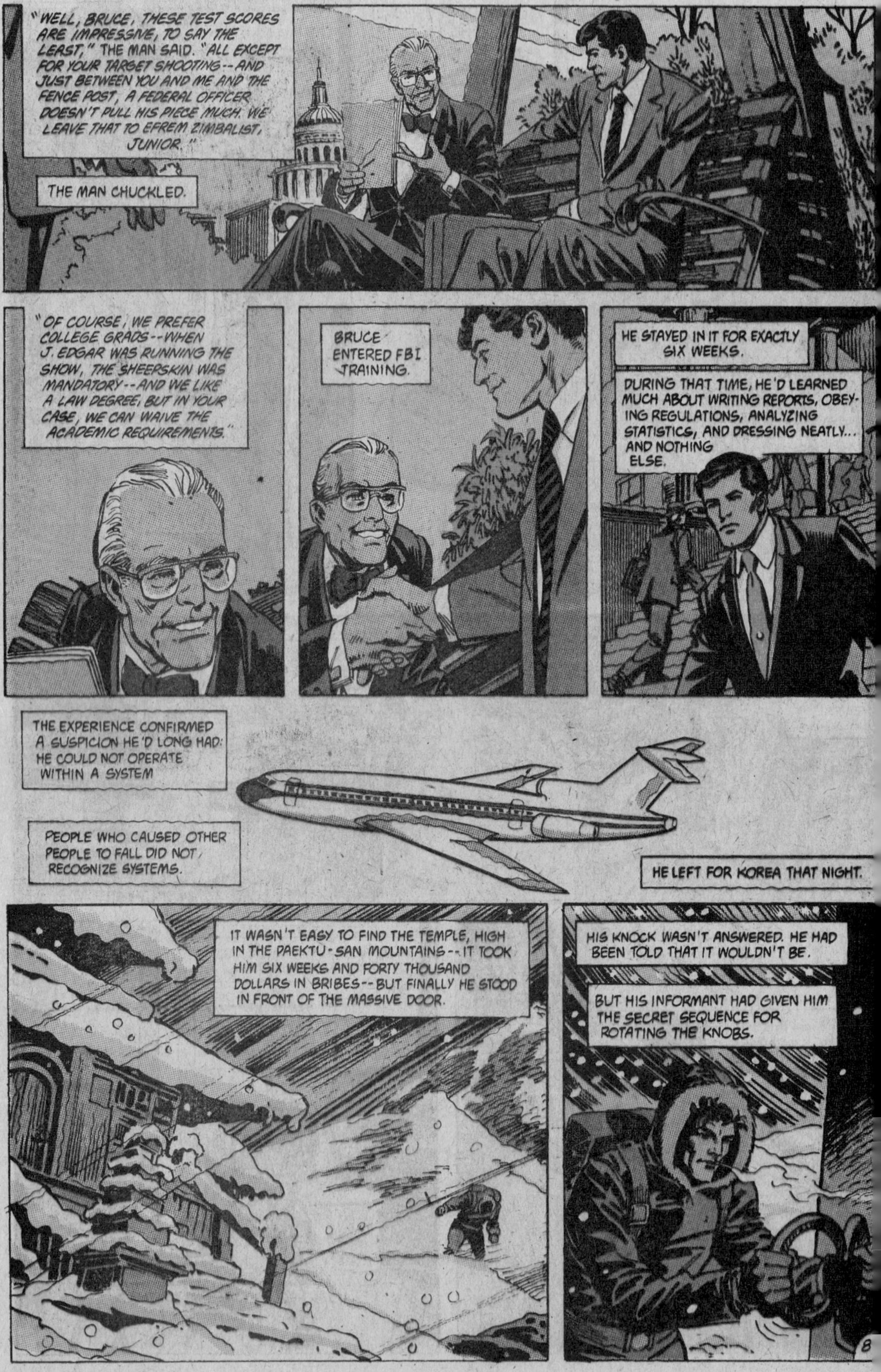
"WELL, BRUCE, THESE TEST SCORES ARE IMPRESSIVE, TO SAY THE LEAST," THE MAN SAID. "ALL EXCEPT FOR YOUR TARGET SHOOTING-- AND JUST BETWEEN YOU AND ME AND THE FENCE POST, A FEDERAL OFFICER DOESN'T PULL HIS PIECE MUCH. WE LEAVE THAT TO EFREM ZIMBALIST, JUNIOR."
THE MAN CHUCKLED.
"OF COURSE, WE PREFER COLLEGE GRADS--WHEN J. EDGAR WAS RUNNING THE SHOW, THE SHEEPSKIN WAS MANDATORY--AND WE LIKE A LAW DEGREE. BUT IN YOUR CASE, WE CAN WAIVE THE ACADEMIC REQUIREMENTS."
BRUCE ENTERED FBI TRAINING.
HE STAYED IN IT FOR EXACTLY SIX WEEKS.
DURING THAT TIME, HE'D LEARNED MUCH ABOUT WRITING REPORTS, OBEYING REGULATIONS, ANALYZING STATISTICS, AND DRESSING NEATLY... AND NOTHING ELSE.
THE EXPERIENCE CONFIRMED A SUSPICION HE'D LONG HAD: HE COULD NOT OPERATE WITHIN A SYSTEM
PEOPLE WHO CAUSED OTHER PEOPLE TO FALL DID NOT RECOGNIZE SYSTEMS.
HE LEFT FOR KOREA THAT NIGHT.
IT WASN'T EASY TO FIND THE TEMPLE, HIGH IN THE PAEKTU-SAN MOUNTAINS--IT TOOK HIM SIX WEEKS AND FORTY THOUSAND DOLLARS IN BRIBES--BUT FINALLY HE STOOD IN FRONT OF THE MASSIVE DOOR.
HIS KNOCK WASN'T ANSWERED. HE HAD BEEN TOLD THAT IT WOULDN'T BE.
BUT HIS INFORMANT HAD GIVEN HIM THE SECRET SEQUENCE FOR ROTATING THE KNOBS.

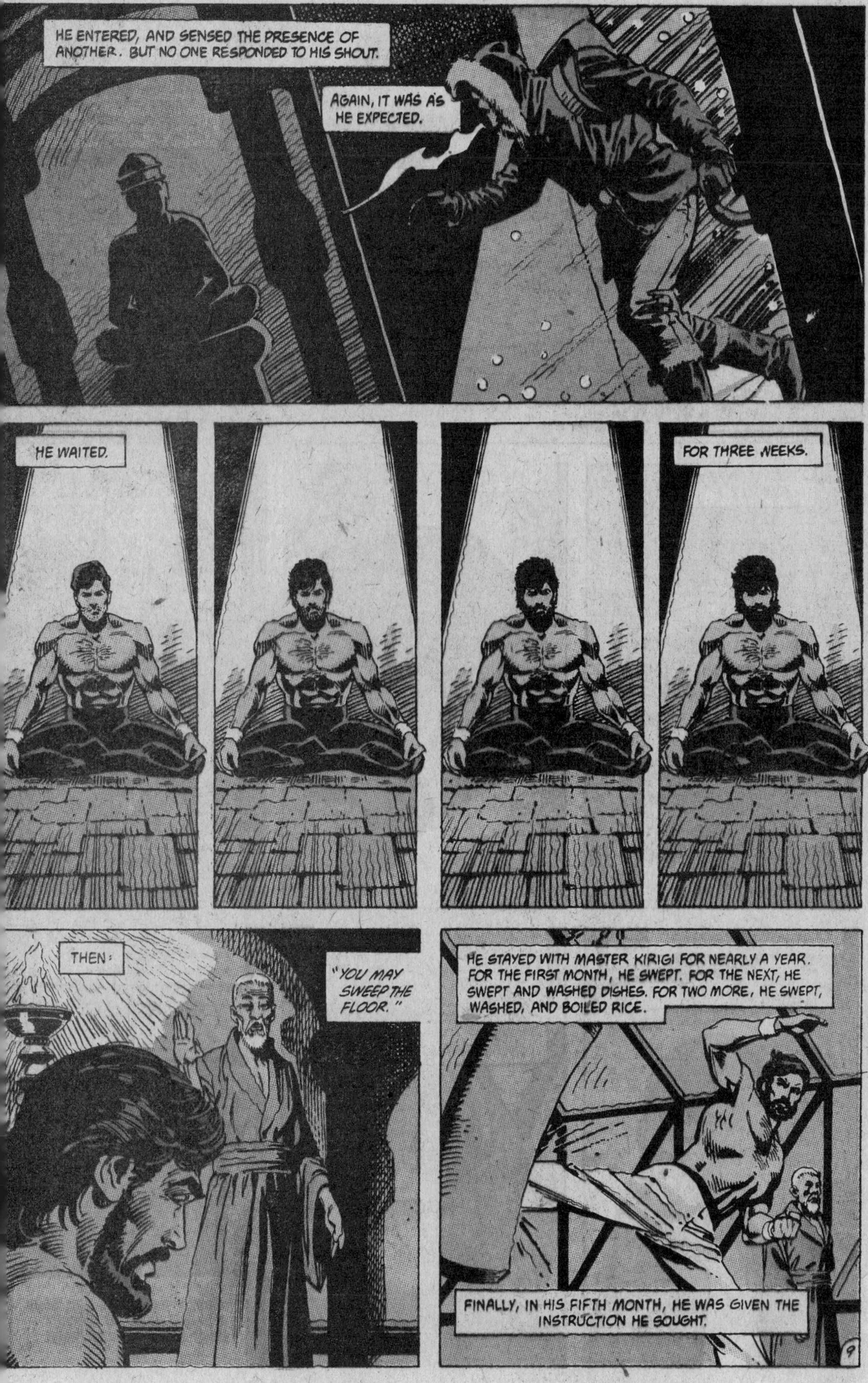
HE ENTERED, AND SENSED THE PRESENCE OF ANOTHER. BUT NO ONE RESPONDED TO HIS SHOUT.
AGAIN, IT WAS AS HE EXPECTED.
HE WAITED.
FOR THREE WEEKS.
THEN:
"YOU MAY SWEEP THE FLOOR."
HE STAYED WITH MASTER KIRIGI FOR NEARLY A YEAR. FOR THE FIRST MONTH, HE SWEPT. FOR THE NEXT, HE SWEPT AND WASHED DISHES. FOR TWO MORE, HE SWEPT, WASHED, AND BOILED RICE.
FINALLY, IN HIS FIFTH MONTH, HE WAS GIVEN THE INSTRUCTION HE SOUGHT.
9

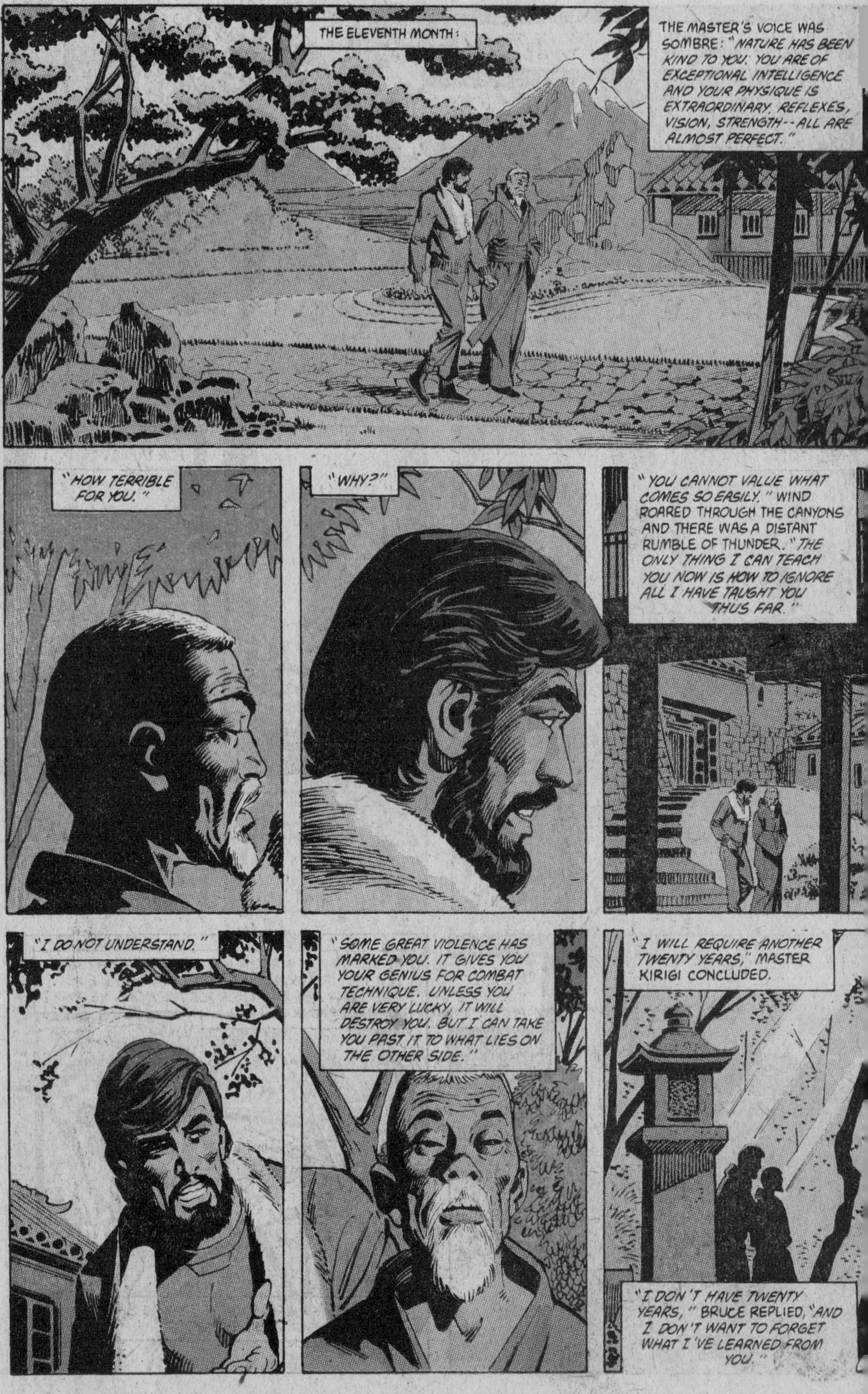
THE ELEVENTH MONTH:
THE MASTER'S VOICE WAS SOMBRE: "NATURE HAS BEEN KIND TO YOU. YOU ARE OF EXCEPTIONAL INTELLIGENCE AND YOUR PHYSIQUE IS EXTRAORDINARY. REFLEXES, VISION, STRENGTH--ALL ARE ALMOST PERFECT."
"HOW TERRIBLE FOR YOU."
"WHY?"
"YOU CANNOT VALUE WHAT COMES SO EASILY." WIND ROARED THROUGH THE CANYONS AND THERE WAS A DISTANT RUMBLE OF THUNDER. "THE ONLY THING I CAN TEACH YOU NOW IS HOW TO IGNORE ALL I HAVE TAUGHT YOU THUS FAR."
"I DO NOT UNDERSTAND."
"SOME GREAT VIOLENCE HAS MARKED YOU. IT GIVES YOU YOUR GENIUS FOR COMBAT TECHNIQUE. UNLESS YOU ARE VERY LUCKY, IT WILL DESTROY YOU. BUT I CAN TAKE YOU PAST IT TO WHAT LIES ON THE OTHER SIDE."
"I WILL REQUIRE ANOTHER TWENTY YEARS," MASTER KIRIGI CONCLUDED.
"I DON'T HAVE TWENTY YEARS," BRUCE REPLIED, "AND I DON'T WANT TO FORGET WHAT I'VE LEARNED FROM YOU."

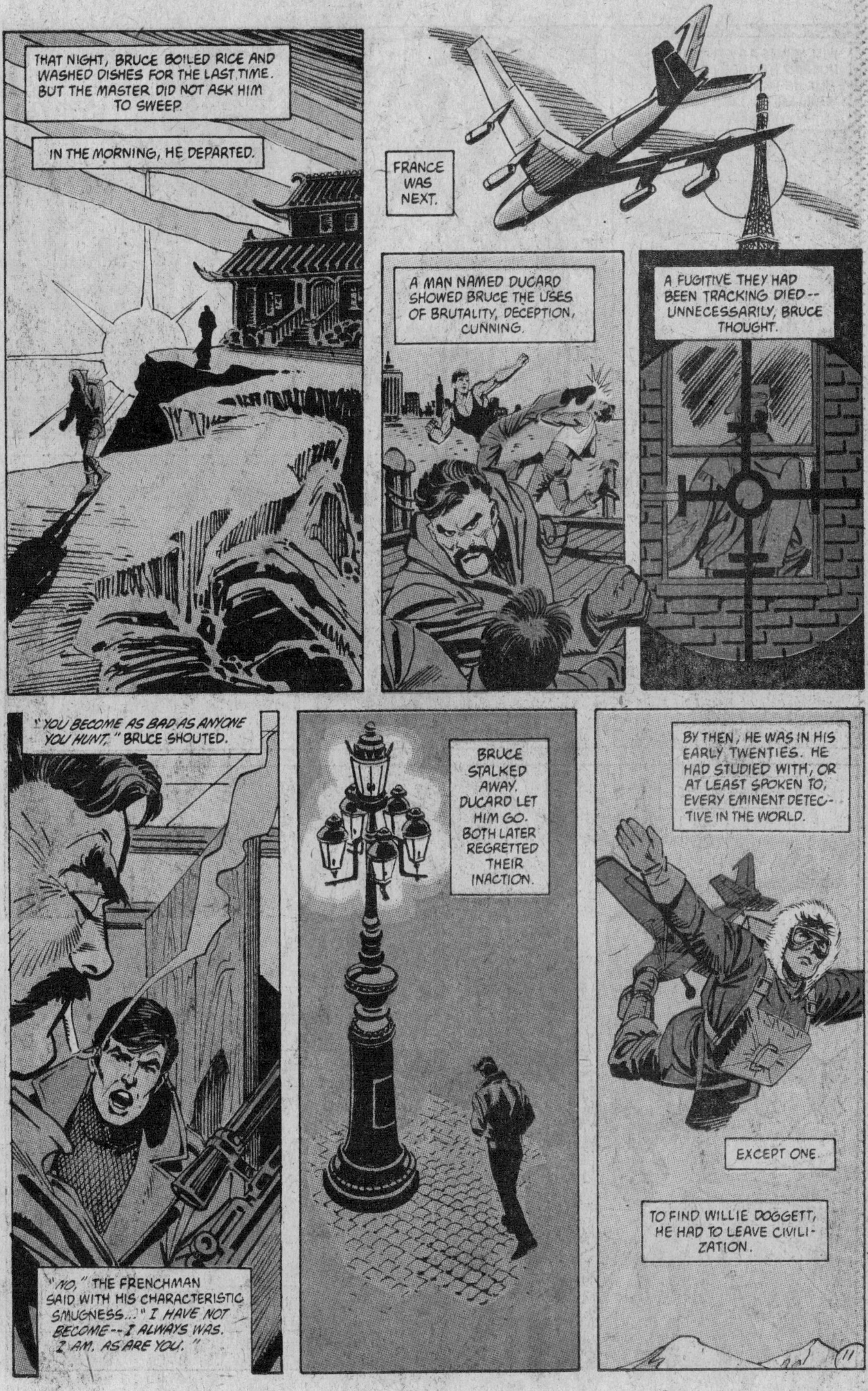
THAT NIGHT, BRUCE BOILED RICE AND WASHED DISHES FOR THE LAST TIME. BUT THE MASTER DID NOT ASK HIM TO SWEEP.
IN THE MORNING, HE DEPARTED.
FRANCE WAS NEXT.
A MAN NAMED DUCARD SHOWED BRUCE THE USES OF BRUTALITY, DECEPTION, CUNNING.
A FUGITIVE THEY HAD BEEN TRACKING DIED-- UNNECESSARILY, BRUCE THOUGHT.
"YOU BECOME AS BAD AS ANYONE YOU HUNT," BRUCE SHOUTED.
"NO," THE FRENCHMAN SAID WITH HIS CHARACTERISTIC SMUGNESS..." I HAVE NOT BECOME-- I ALWAYS WAS. I AM. AS ARE YOU."
BRUCE STALKED AWAY. DUCARD LET HIM GO. BOTH LATER REGRETTED THEIR INACTION.
BY THEN, HE WAS IN HIS EARLY TWENTIES. HE HAD STUDIED WITH, OR AT LEAST SPOKEN TO, EVERY EMINENT DETECTIVE IN THE WORLD.
EXCEPT ONE.
TO FIND WILLIE DOGGETT, HE HAD TO LEAVE CIVILIZATION.
11

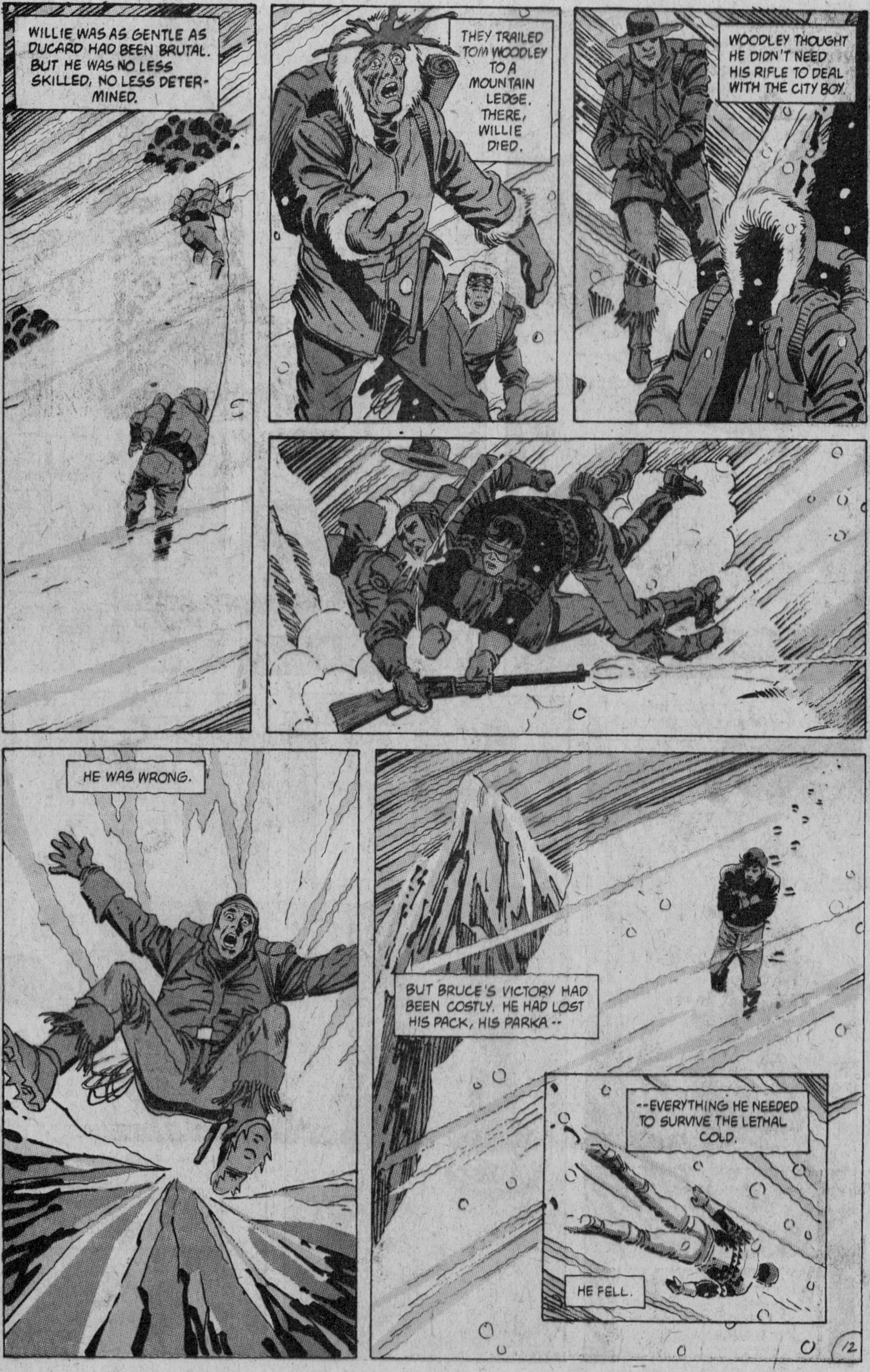
WILLIE WAS AS GENTLE AS DUCARD HAD BEEN BRUTAL. BUT HE WAS NO LESS SKILLED, NO LESS DETERMINED.
THEY TRAILED TOM WOODLEY TO A MOUNTAIN LEDGE. THERE, WILLIE DIED.
WOODLEY THOUGHT HE DIDN'T NEED HIS RIFLE TO DEAL WITH THE CITY BOY.
HE WAS WRONG.
BUT BRUCE'S VICTORY HAD BEEN COSTLY. HE HAD LOST HIS PACK, HIS PARKA--
--EVERYTHING HE NEEDED TO SURVIVE THE LETHAL COLD.
HE FELL.
12

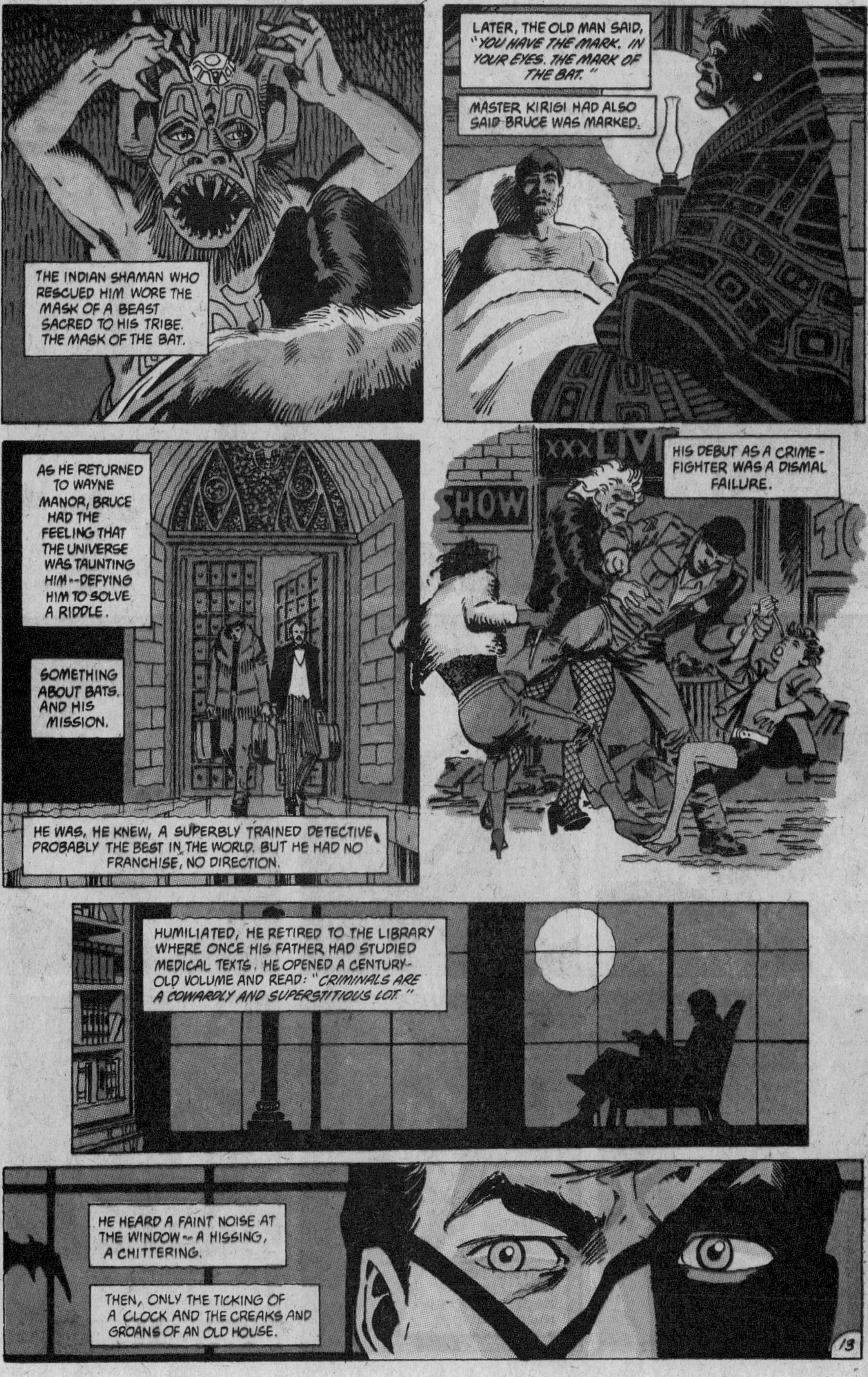
THE INDIAN SHAMAN WHO RESCUED HIM WORE THE MASK OF A BEAST SACRED TO HIS TRIBE. THE MASK OF THE BAT.
LATER, THE OLD MAN SAID, "YOU HAVE THE MARK. IN YOUR EYES. THE MARK OF THE BAT."
MASTER KIRIGI HAD ALSO SAID BRUCE WAS MARKED.
AS HE RETURNED TO WAYNE MANOR, BRUCE HAD THE FEELING THAT THE UNIVERSE WAS TAUNTING HIM--DEFYING HIM TO SOLVE A RIDDLE.
SOMETHING ABOUT BATS. AND HIS MISSION.
HE WAS, HE KNEW, A SUPERBLY TRAINED DETECTIVE, PROBABLY THE BEST IN THE WORLD. BUT HE HAD NO FRANCHISE, NO DIRECTION.
XXX LIVE
SHOW
HIS DEBUT AS A CRIME-FIGHTER WAS A DISMAL FAILURE.
HUMILIATED, HE RETIRED TO THE LIBRARY WHERE ONCE HIS FATHER HAD STUDIED MEDICAL TEXTS. HE OPENED A CENTURY-OLD VOLUME AND READ: "CRIMINALS ARE A COWARDLY AND SUPERSTITIOUS LOT."
HE HEARD A FAINT NOISE AT THE WINDOW--A HISSING, A CHITTERING.
THEN, ONLY THE TICKING OF A CLOCK AND THE CREAKS AND GROANS OF AN OLD HOUSE.

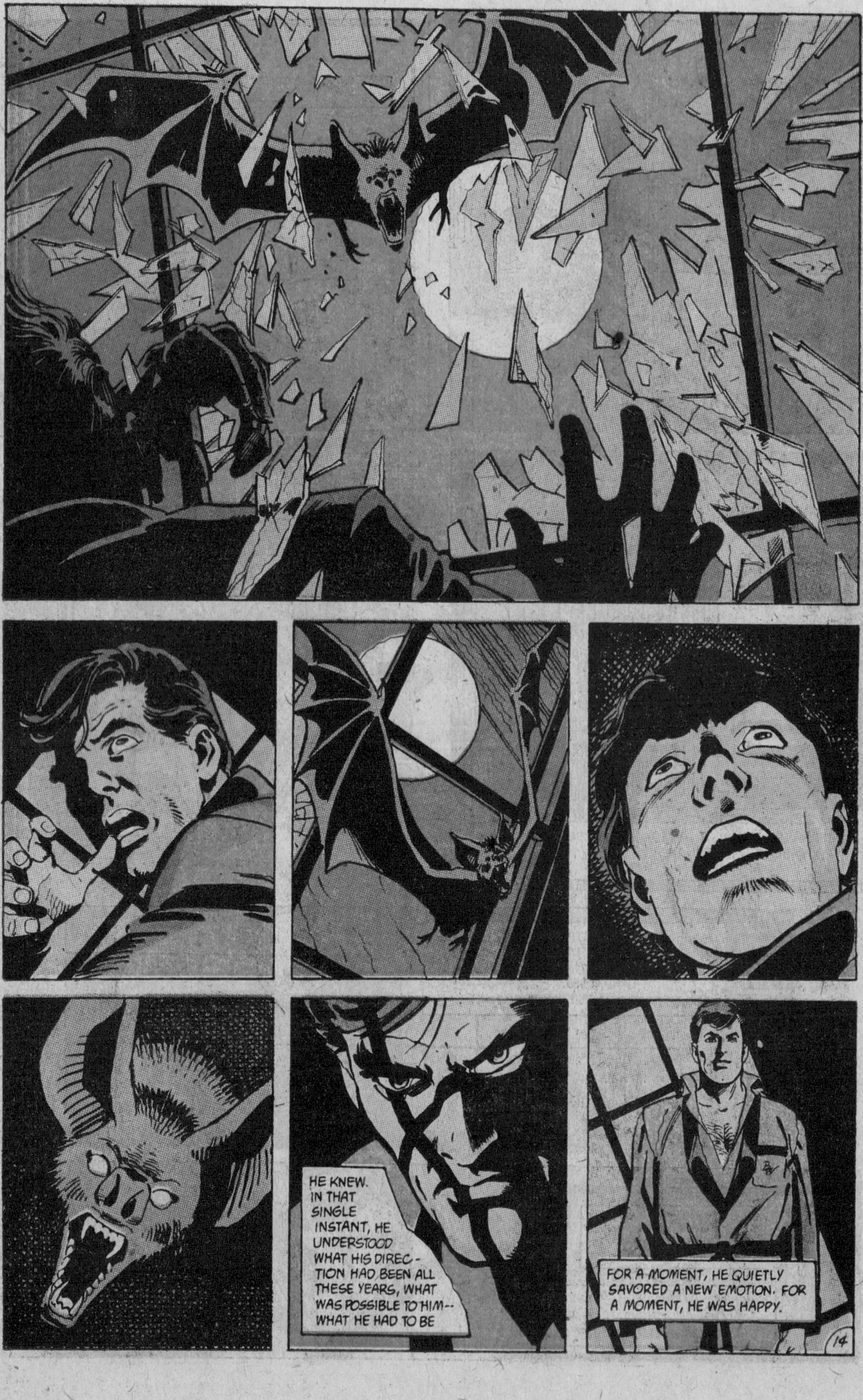
HE KNEW. IN THAT SINGLE INSTANT, HE UNDERSTOOD WHAT HIS DIRECTION HAD BEEN ALL THESE YEARS, WHAT WAS POSSIBLE TO HIM-- WHAT HE HAD TO BE
FOR A MOMENT, HE QUIETLY SAVORED A NEW EMOTION. FOR A MOMENT, HE WAS HAPPY.
14

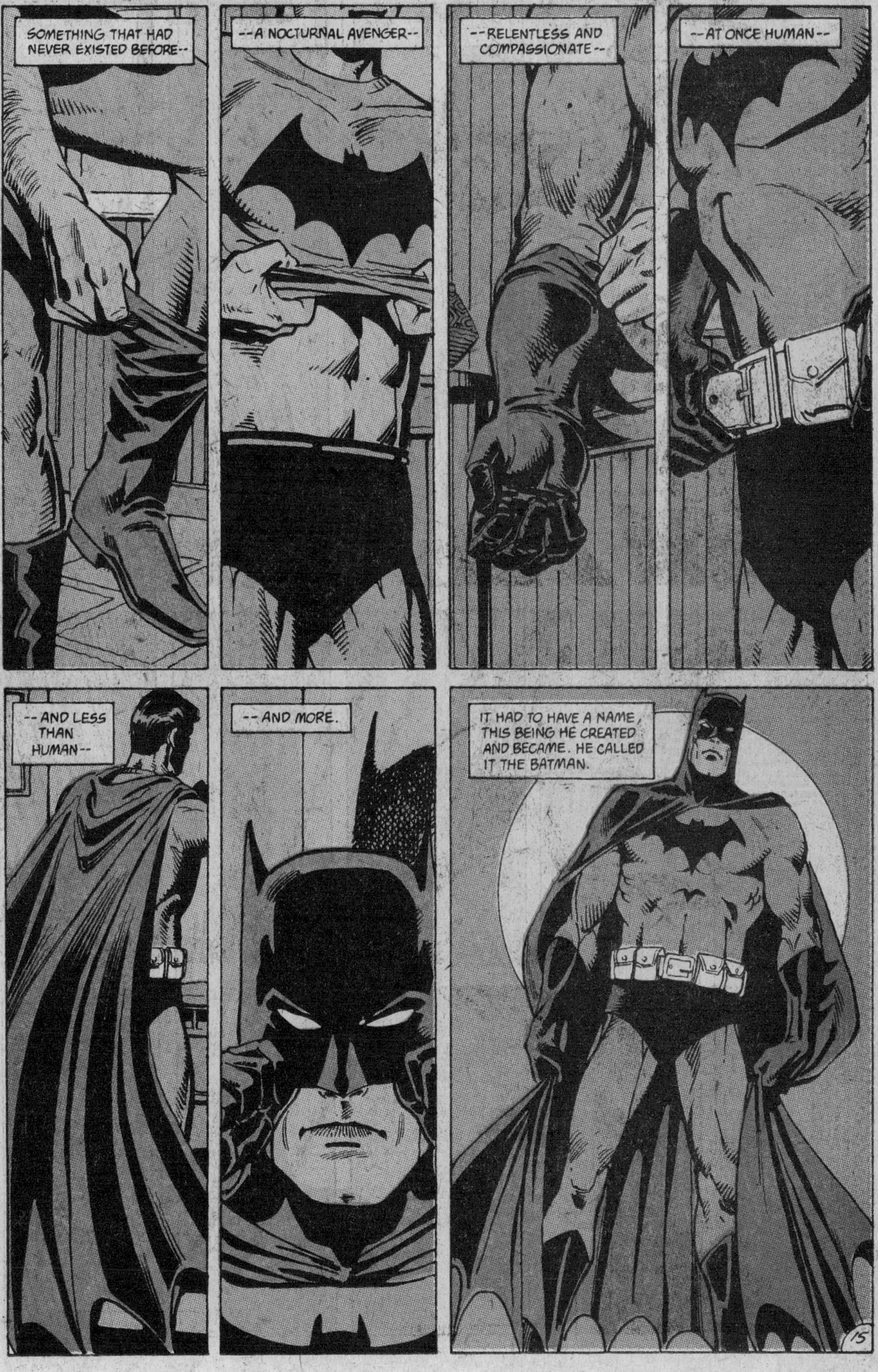
SOMETHING THAT HAD NEVER EXISTED BEFORE--
--A NOCTURNAL AVENGER--
--RELENTLESS AND COMPASSIONATE--
--AT ONCE HUMAN--
--AND LESS THAN HUMAN--
--AND MORE.
IT HAD TO HAVE A NAME, THIS BEING HE CREATED AND BECAME. HE CALLED IT THE BATMAN.
15

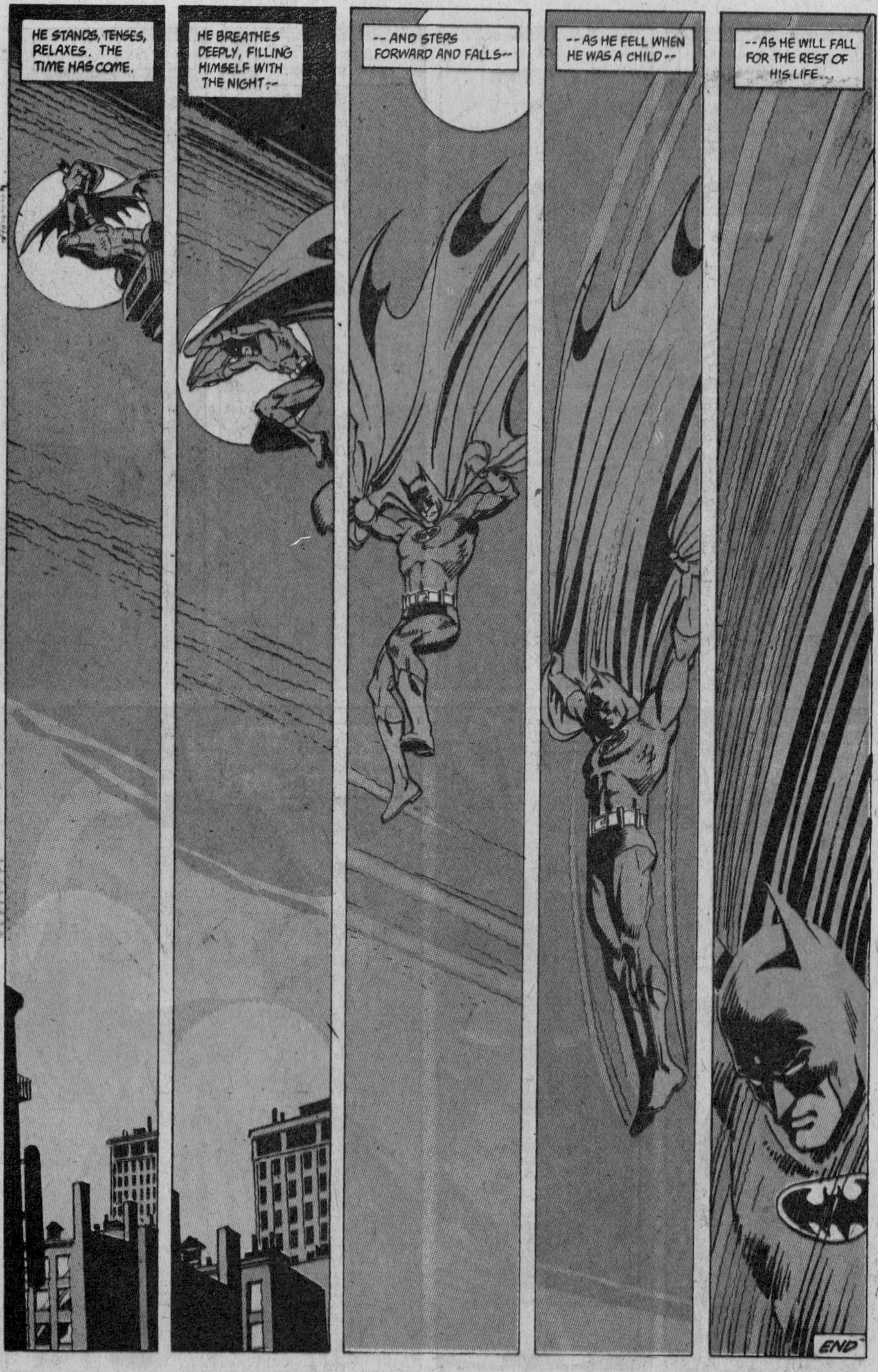
HE STANDS, TENSES, RELAXES. THE TIME HAS COME.
HE BREATHES DEEPLY, FILLING HIMSELF WITH THE NIGHT;-
--AND STEPS FORWARD AND FALLS--
--AS HE FELL WHEN HE WAS A CHILD--
--AS HE WILL FALL FOR THE REST OF HIS LIFE...
END

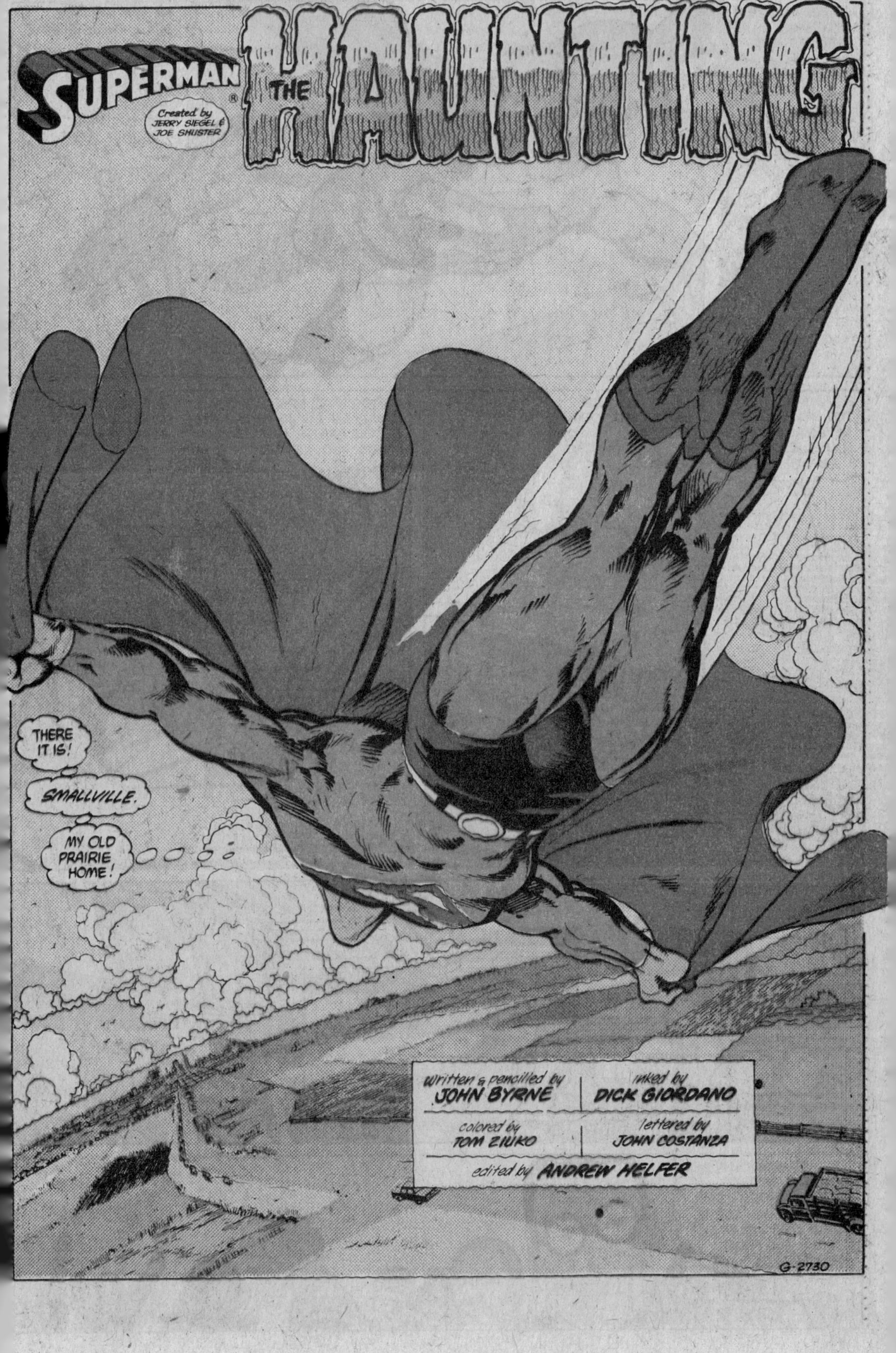
SUPERMAN
THE HAUNTING
Created by JERRY SIEGEL & JOE SHUSTER
THERE IT IS!
SMALLVILLE.
MY OLD PRAIRIE HOME!
Written & pencilled by JOHN BYRNE
inked by DICK GIORDANO
colored by TOM ZIUKO
lettered by JOHN COSTANZA
edited by ANDREW HELFER
G-2730

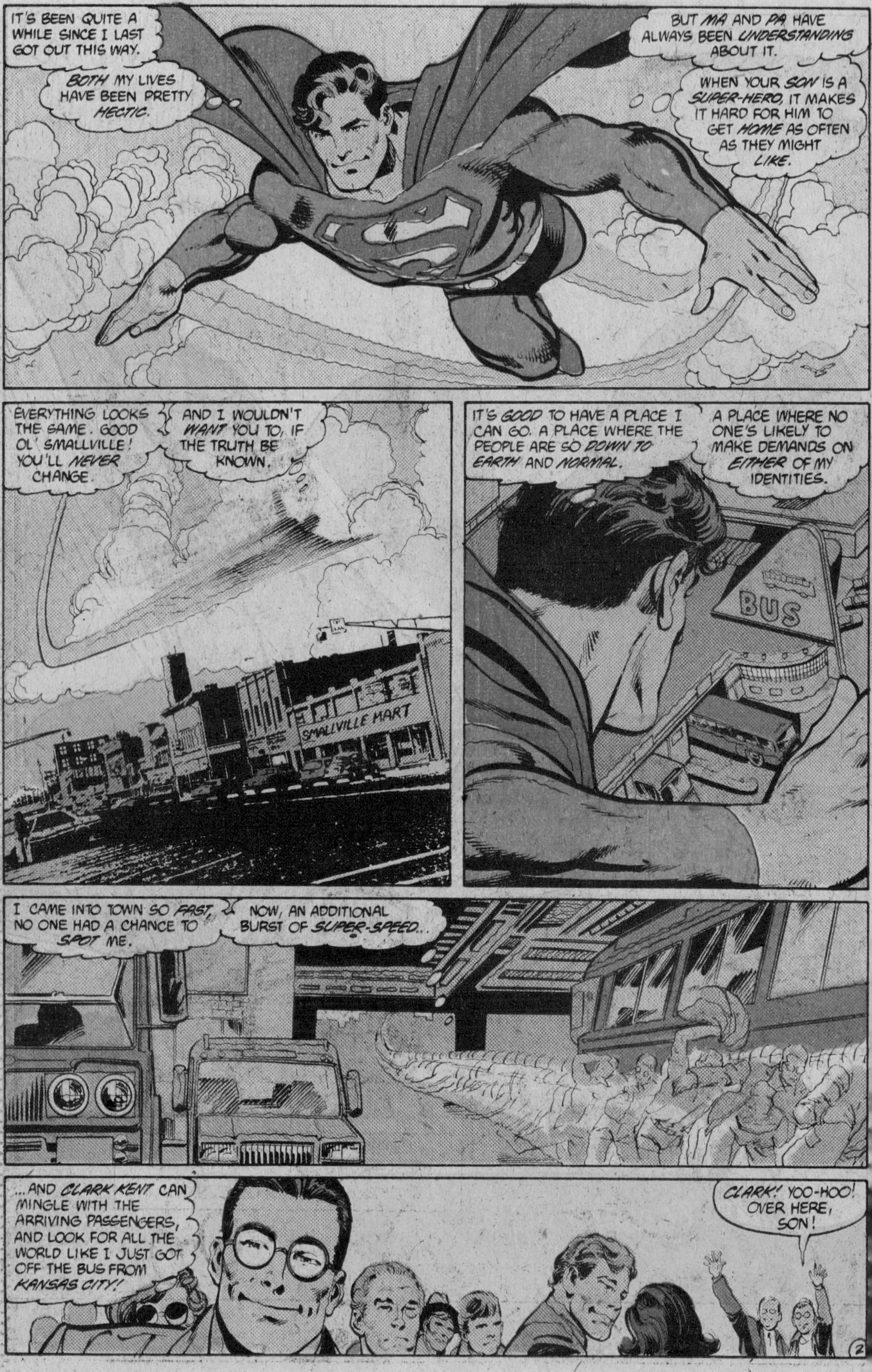
IT'S BEEN QUITE A WHILE SINCE I LAST GOT OUT THIS WAY.
BOTH MY LIVES HAVE BEEN PRETTY HECTIC.
BUT MA AND PA HAVE ALWAYS BEEN UNDERSTANDING ABOUT IT.
WHEN YOUR SON IS A SUPER-HERO, IT MAKES IT HARD FOR HIM TO GET HOME AS OFTEN AS THEY MIGHT LIKE.
EVERYTHING LOOKS THE SAME. GOOD OL' SMALLVILLE! YOU'LL NEVER CHANGE.
AND I WOULDN'T WANT YOU TO, IF THE TRUTH BE KNOWN.
SMALLVILLE MART
IT'S GOOD TO HAVE A PLACE I CAN GO. A PLACE WHERE THE PEOPLE ARE SO DOWN TO EARTH AND NORMAL.
A PLACE WHERE NO ONE'S LIKELY TO MAKE DEMANDS ON EITHER OF MY IDENTITIES.
BUS
I CAME INTO TOWN SO FAST, NO ONE HAD A CHANCE TO SPOT ME.
NOW, AN ADDITIONAL BURST OF SUPER-SPEED...
...AND CLARK KENT CAN MINGLE WITH THE ARRIVING PASSENGERS, AND LOOK FOR ALL THE WORLD LIKE I JUST GOT OFF THE BUS FROM KANSAS CITY!
CLARK! YOO-HOO! OVER HERE, SON!
2

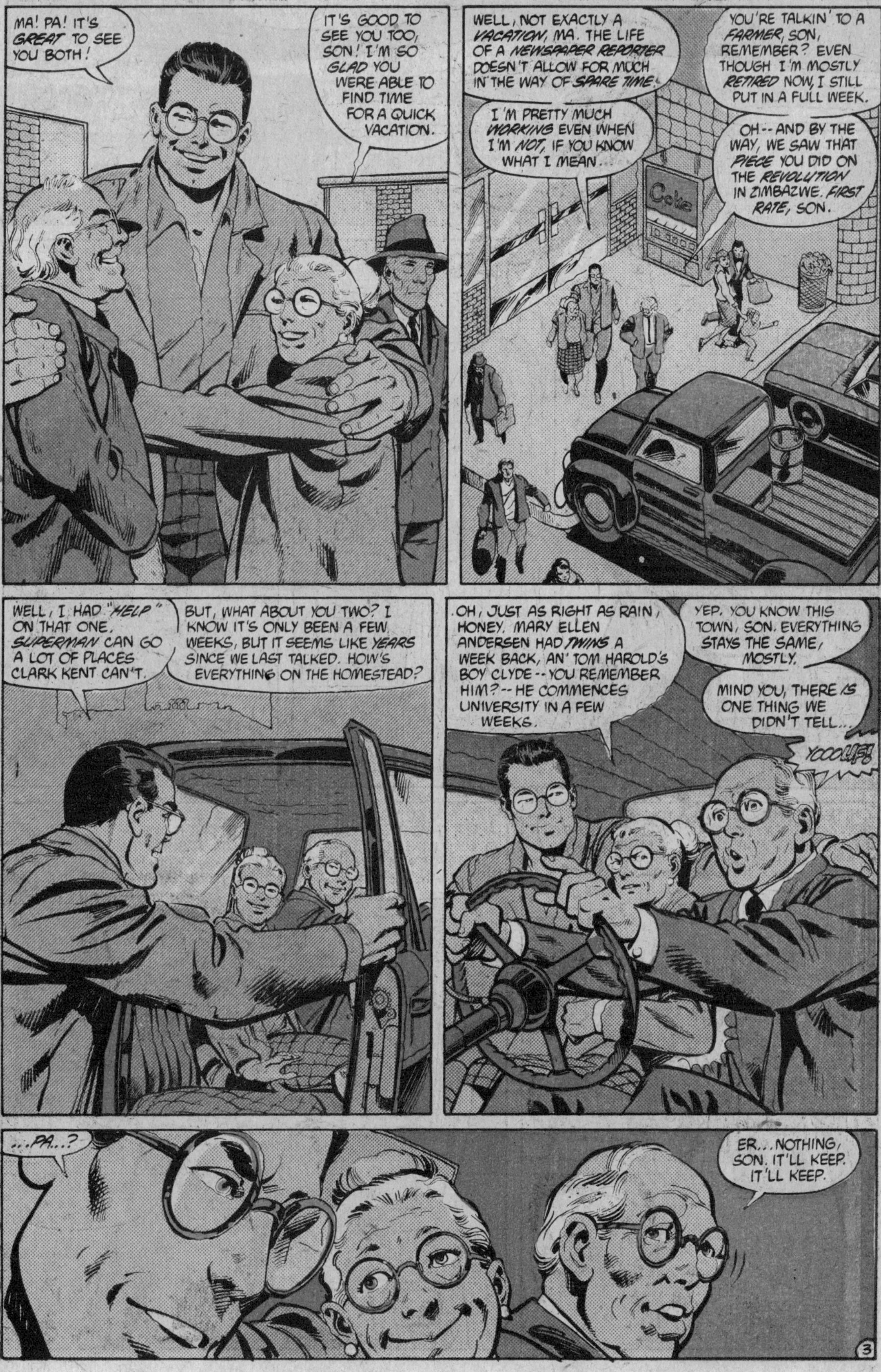
MA! PA! IT'S GREAT TO SEE YOU BOTH!
IT'S GOOD TO SEE YOU TOO, SON! I'M SO GLAD YOU WERE ABLE TO FIND TIME FOR A QUICK VACATION.
WELL, NOT EXACTLY A VACATION, MA. THE LIFE OF A NEWSPAPER REPORTER DOESN'T ALLOW FOR MUCH IN THE WAY OF SPARE TIME.
I'M PRETTY MUCH WORKING EVEN WHEN I'M NOT, IF YOU KNOW WHAT I MEAN.
YOU'RE TALKIN' TO A FARMER, SON, REMEMBER? EVEN THOUGH I'M MOSTLY RETIRED NOW, I STILL PUT IN A FULL WEEK.
OH--AND BY THE WAY, WE SAW THAT PIECE YOU DID ON THE REVOLUTION IN ZIMBAZWE. FIRST RATE, SON.
Coke
WELL, I HAD "HELP" ON THAT ONE. SUPERMAN CAN GO A LOT OF PLACES CLARK KENT CAN'T.
BUT, WHAT ABOUT YOU TWO? I KNOW IT'S ONLY BEEN A FEW WEEKS, BUT IT SEEMS LIKE YEARS SINCE WE LAST TALKED. HOW'S EVERYTHING ON THE HOMESTEAD?
OH, JUST AS RIGHT AS RAIN, HONEY. MARY ELLEN ANDERSEN HAD TWINS A WEEK BACK, AN' TOM HAROLD'S BOY CLYDE--YOU REMEMBER HIM?--HE COMMENCES UNIVERSITY IN A FEW WEEKS.
YEP. YOU KNOW THIS TOWN, SON. EVERYTHING STAYS THE SAME, MOSTLY.
MIND YOU, THERE IS ONE THING WE DIDN'T TELL...
YOOOUFF!
...PA...?
ER... NOTHING, SON. IT'LL KEEP. IT'LL KEEP.
3

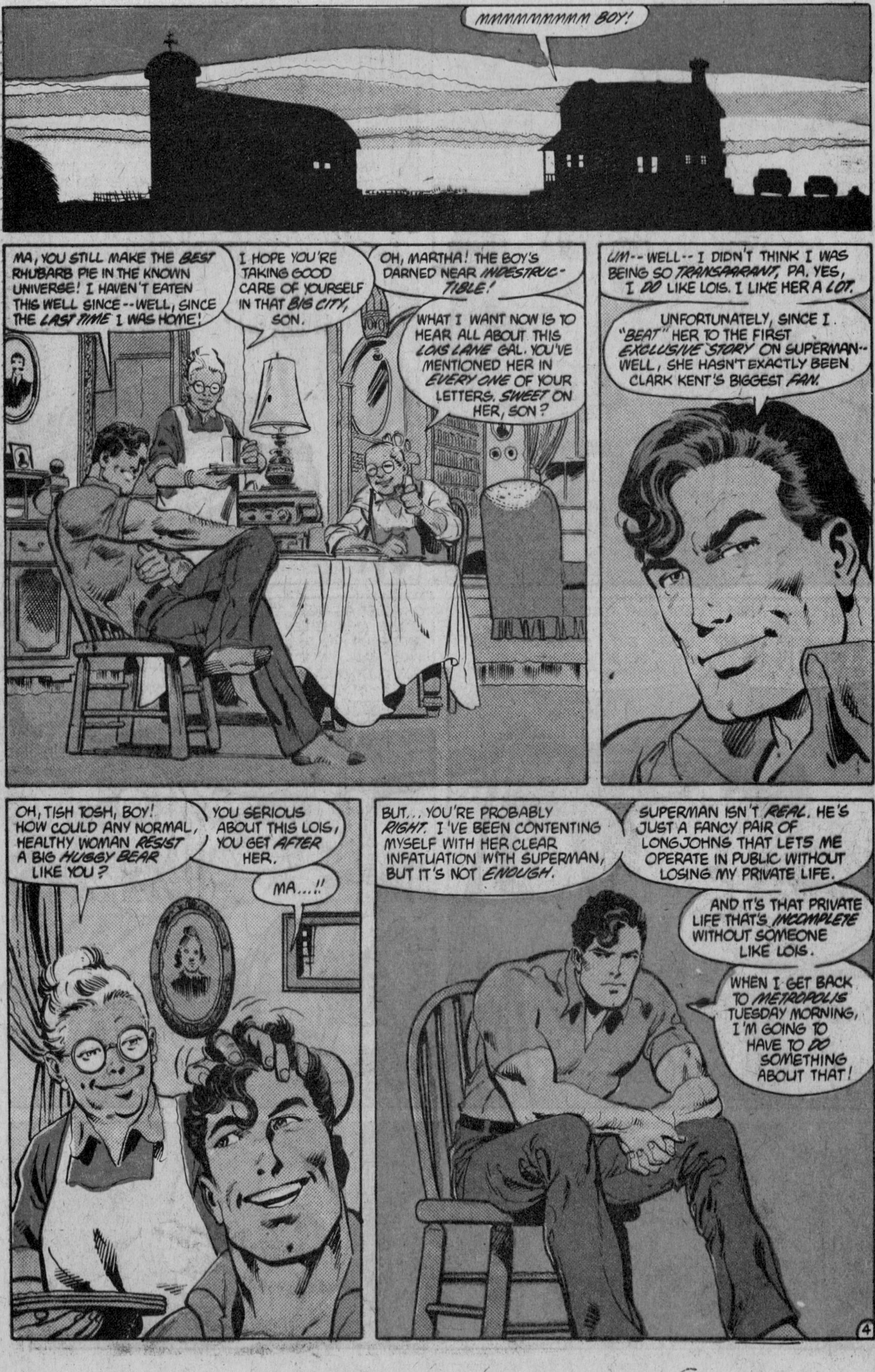
MMMMMMMMMM BOY!
MA, YOU STILL MAKE THE BEST RHUBARB PIE IN THE KNOWN UNIVERSE! I HAVEN'T EATEN THIS WELL SINCE--WELL, SINCE THE LAST TIME I WAS HOME!
I HOPE YOU'RE TAKING GOOD CARE OF YOURSELF IN THAT BIG CITY, SON.
OH, MARTHA! THE BOY'S DARNED NEAR INDESTRUCTIBLE!
WHAT I WANT NOW IS TO HEAR ALL ABOUT THIS LOIS LANE GAL. YOU'VE MENTIONED HER IN EVERY ONE OF YOUR LETTERS. SWEET ON HER, SON?
UM--WELL--I DIDN'T THINK I WAS BEING SO TRANSPARANT, PA. YES, I DO LIKE LOIS. I LIKE HER A LOT.
UNFORTUNATELY, SINCE I "BEAT" HER TO THE FIRST EXCLUSIVE STORY ON SUPERMAN--WELL, SHE HASN'T EXACTLY BEEN CLARK KENT'S BIGGEST FAN.
OH, TISH TOSH, BOY! HOW COULD ANY NORMAL, HEALTHY WOMAN RESIST A BIG HUGGY BEAR LIKE YOU?
YOU SERIOUS ABOUT THIS LOIS, YOU GET AFTER HER.
MA...!!
BUT... YOU'RE PROBABLY RIGHT. I'VE BEEN CONTENTING MYSELF WITH HER CLEAR INFATUATION WITH SUPERMAN, BUT IT'S NOT ENOUGH.
SUPERMAN ISN'T REAL. HE'S JUST A FANCY PAIR OF LONGJOHNS THAT LETS ME OPERATE IN PUBLIC WITHOUT LOSING MY PRIVATE LIFE.
AND IT'S THAT PRIVATE LIFE THAT'S INCOMPLETE WITHOUT SOMEONE LIKE LOIS.
WHEN I GET BACK TO METROPOLIS TUESDAY MORNING, I'M GOING TO HAVE TO DO SOMETHING ABOUT THAT!
4

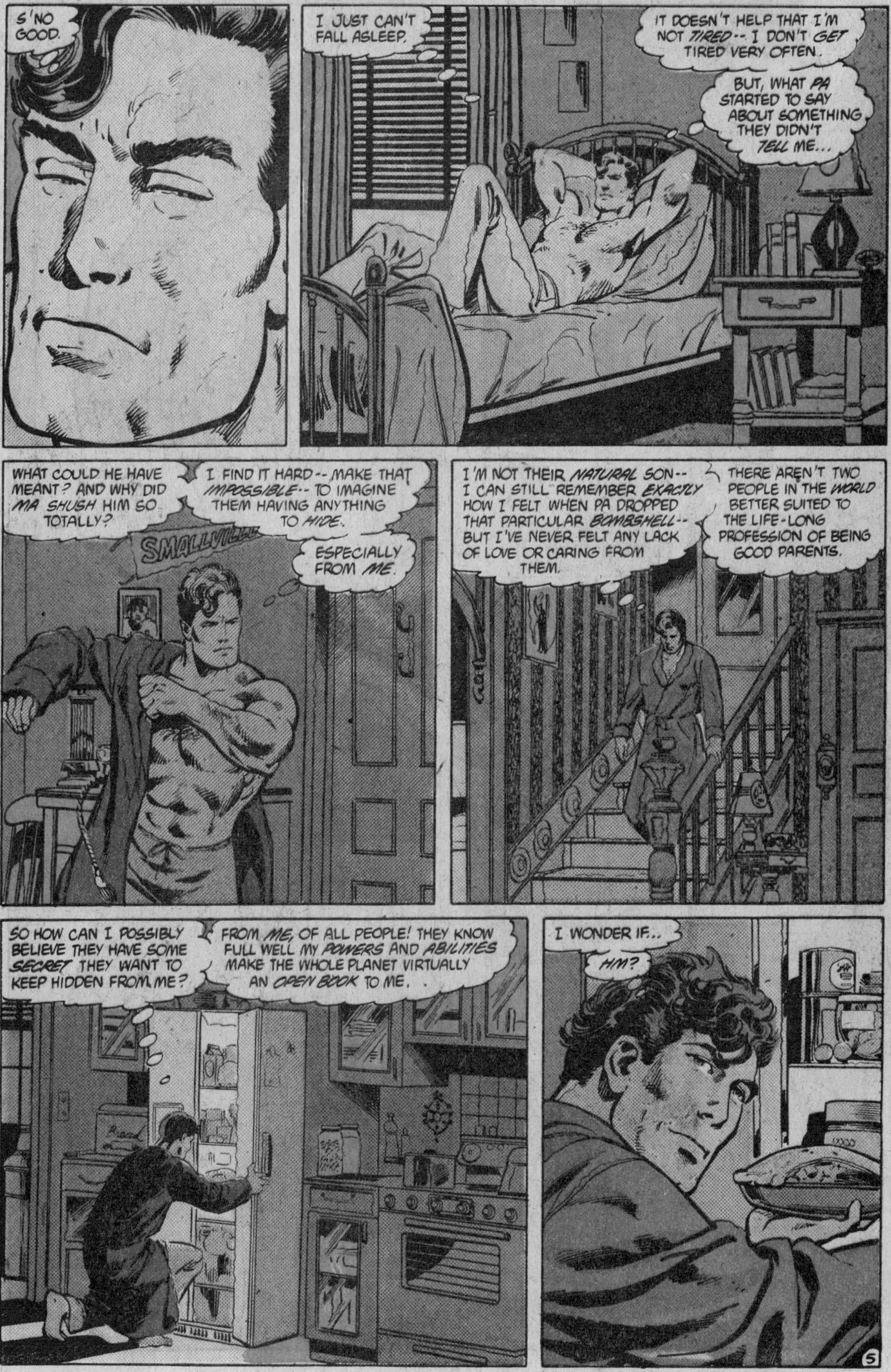
S'NO GOOD.
I JUST CAN'T FALL ASLEEP.
IT DOESN'T HELP THAT I'M NOT TIRED-- I DON'T GET TIRED VERY OFTEN.
BUT, WHAT PA STARTED TO SAY ABOUT SOMETHING THEY DIDN'T TELL ME...
WHAT COULD HE HAVE MEANT? AND WHY DID MA SHUSH HIM SO TOTALLY?
I FIND IT HARD-- MAKE THAT IMPOSSIBLE-- TO IMAGINE THEM HAVING ANYTHING TO HIDE.
ESPECIALLY FROM ME.
SMALLVILLE
I'M NOT THEIR NATURAL SON-- I CAN STILL REMEMBER EXACTLY HOW I FELT WHEN PA DROPPED THAT PARTICULAR BOMBSHELL-- BUT I'VE NEVER FELT ANY LACK OF LOVE OR CARING FROM THEM.
THERE AREN'T TWO PEOPLE IN THE WORLD BETTER SUITED TO THE LIFE-LONG PROFESSION OF BEING GOOD PARENTS.
SO HOW CAN I POSSIBLY BELIEVE THEY HAVE SOME SECRET THEY WANT TO KEEP HIDDEN FROM ME?
FROM ME, OF ALL PEOPLE! THEY KNOW FULL WELL MY POWERS AND ABILITIES MAKE THE WHOLE PLANET VIRTUALLY AN OPEN BOOK TO ME.
I WONDER IF...
HM?
5

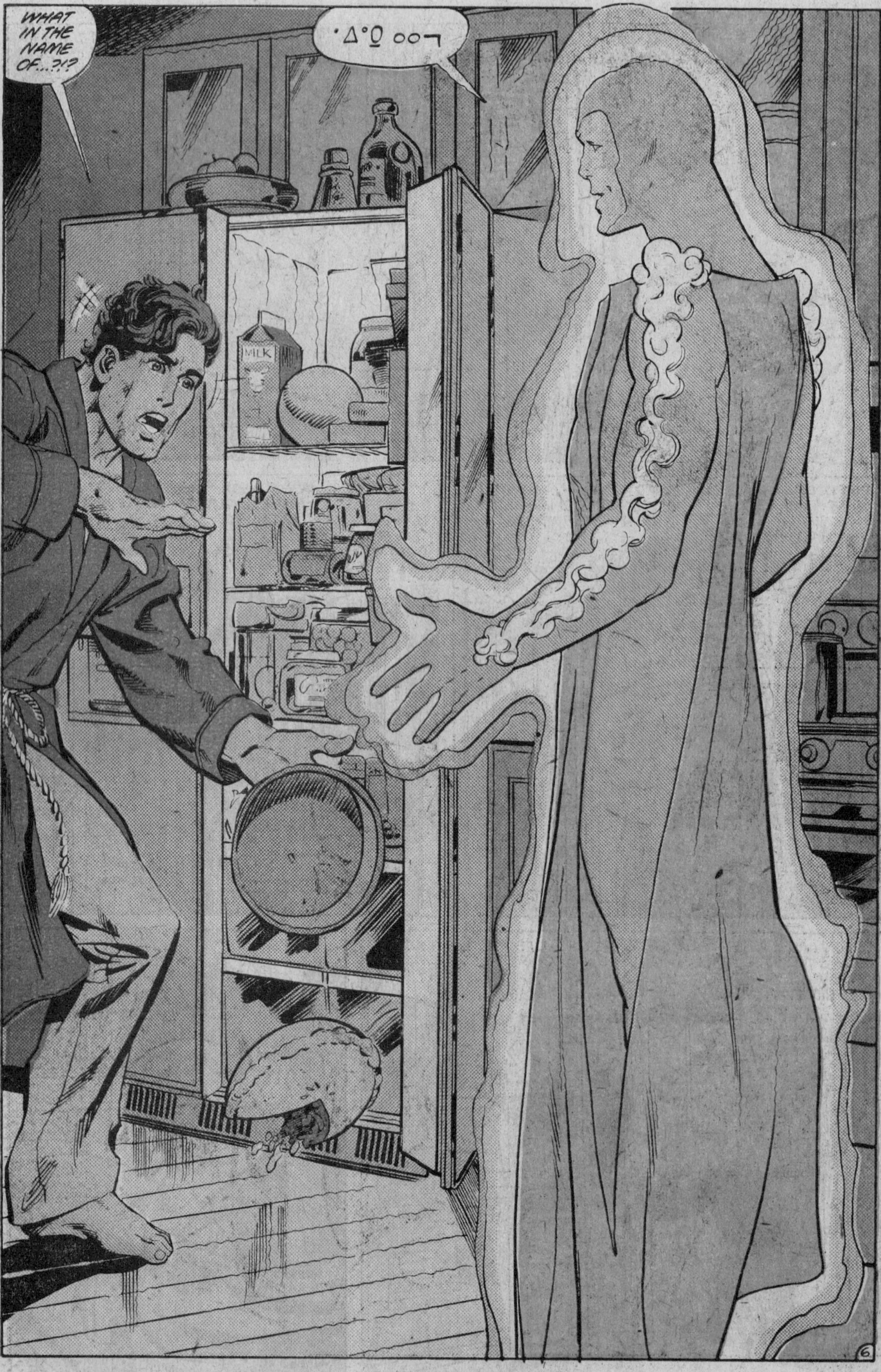
WHAT IN THE NAME OF...?!?

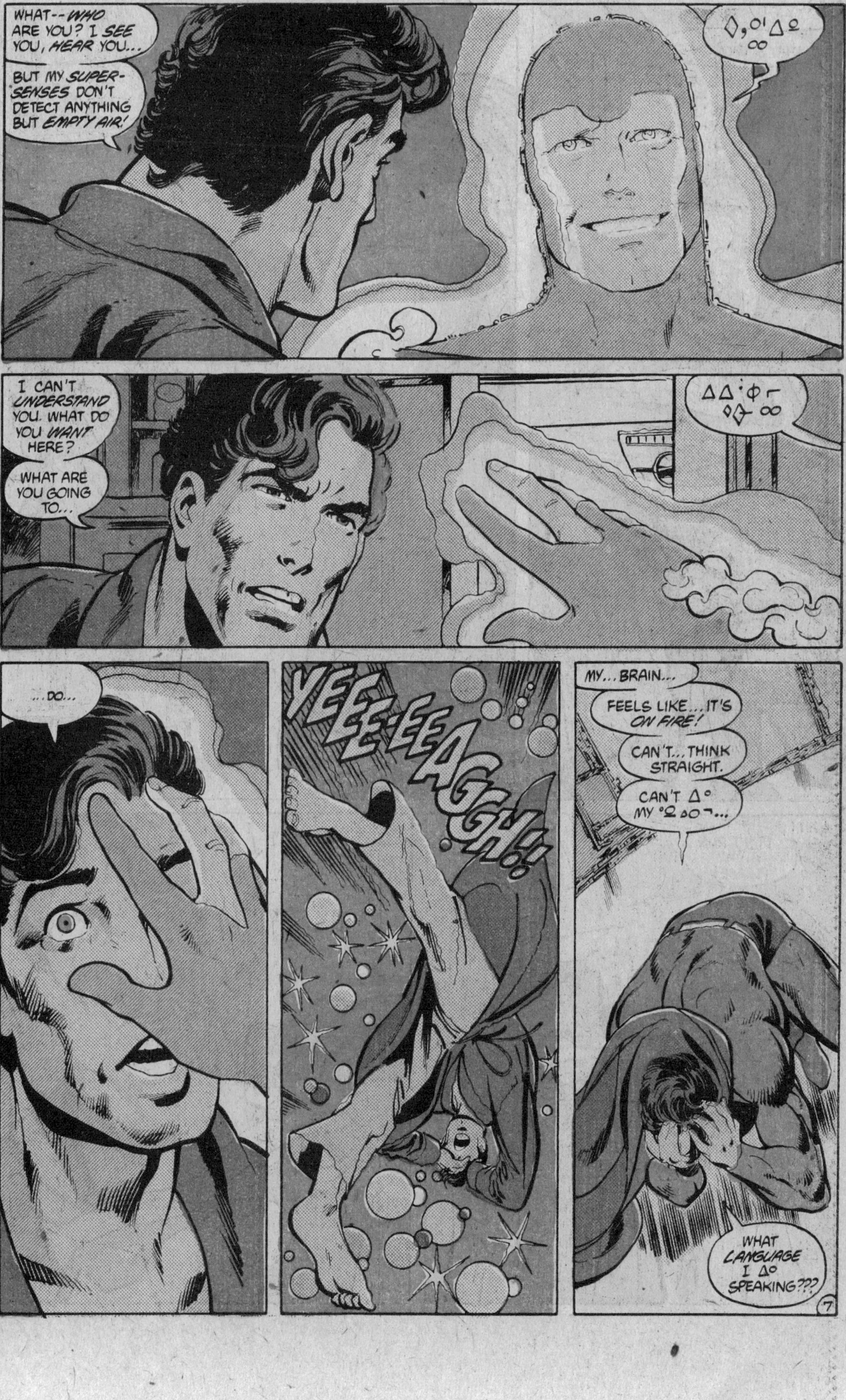
WHAT--WHO ARE YOU? I SEE YOU, HEAR YOU...
BUT MY SUPER-SENSES DON'T DETECT ANYTHING BUT EMPTY AIR!
I CAN'T UNDERSTAND YOU. WHAT DO YOU WANT HERE?
WHAT ARE YOU GOING TO...
...DO...
YEEE-EEAGGH!!!
MY... BRAIN...
FEELS LIKE... IT'S ON FIRE!
CAN'T... THINK STRAIGHT.
CAN'T Δ° MY °♀ ▵O¬...
WHAT LANGUAGE I Δ° SPEAKING???

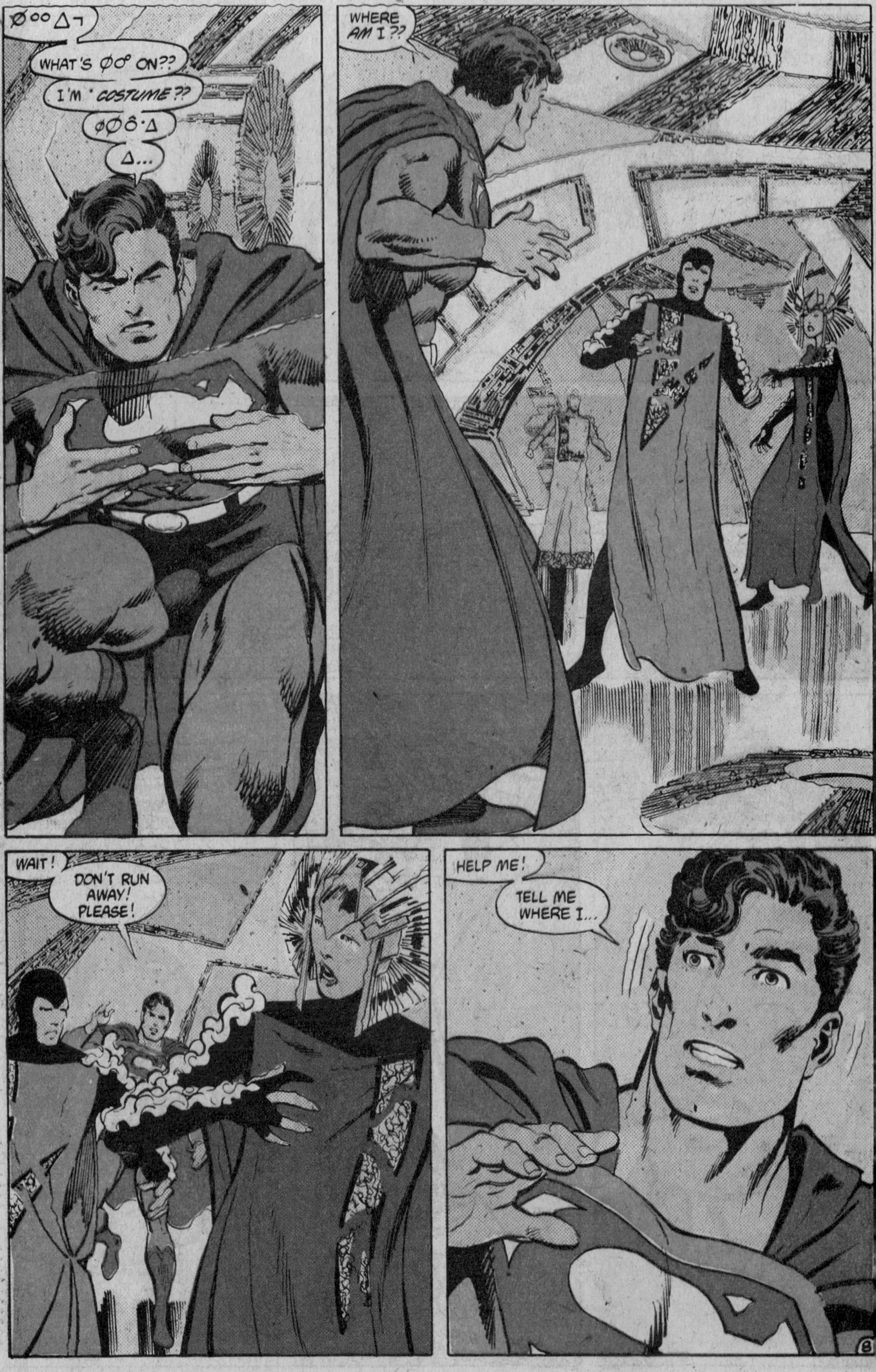
Øoo Δ¬
WHAT'S ØO° ON??
I'M ' COSTUME??
ØØÔ·Δ
Δ...
WHERE AM I??
WAIT!
DON'T RUN AWAY! PLEASE!
HELP ME!
TELL ME WHERE I...
8

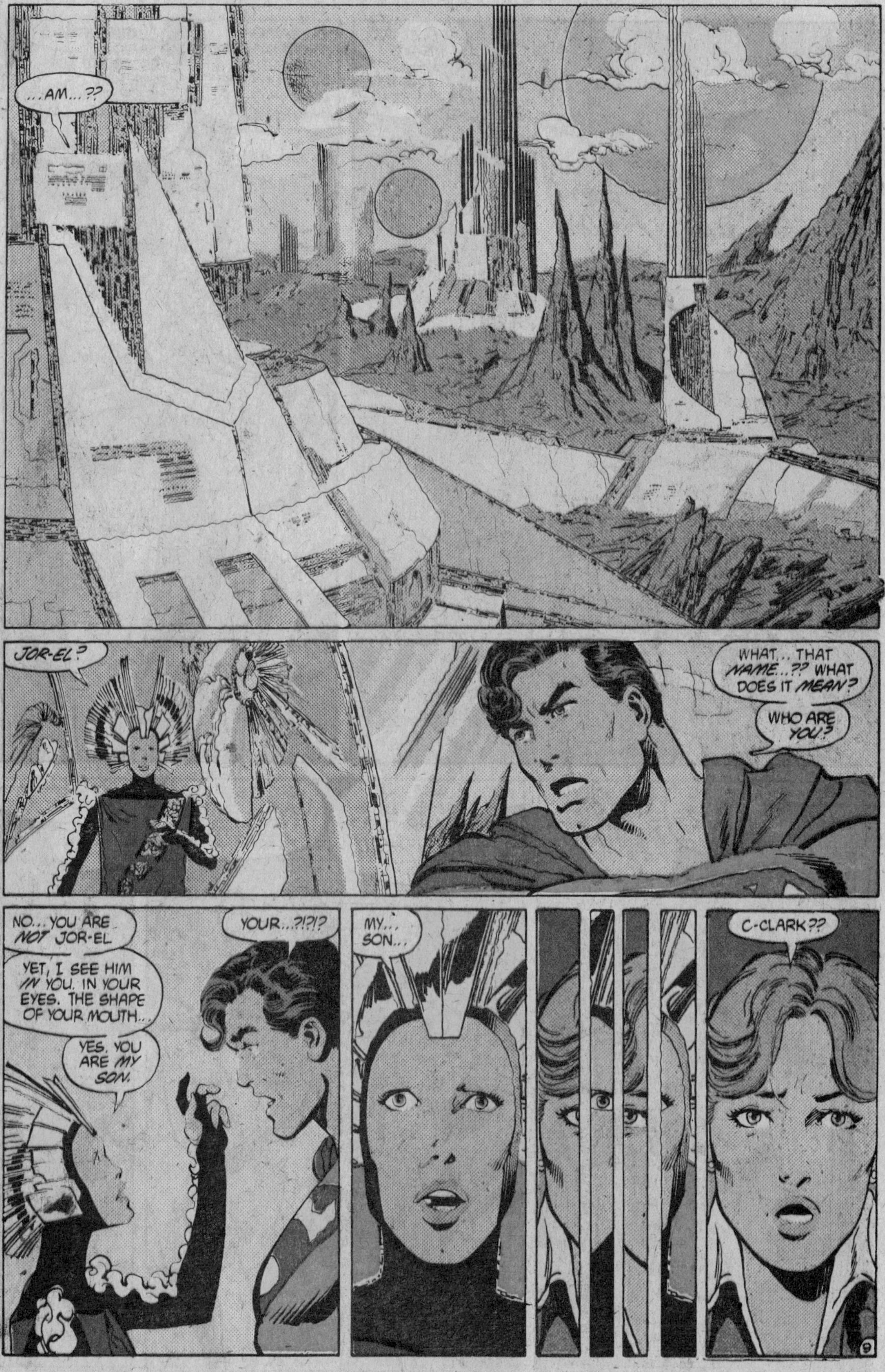
...AM...??
JOR-EL?
WHAT... THAT NAME...?? WHAT DOES IT MEAN?
WHO ARE YOU?
NO... YOU ARE NOT JOR-EL
YET, I SEE HIM IN YOU. IN YOUR EYES. THE SHAPE OF YOUR MOUTH...
YES, YOU ARE MY SON.
YOUR...?!?!?
MY... SON...
C-CLARK??
9

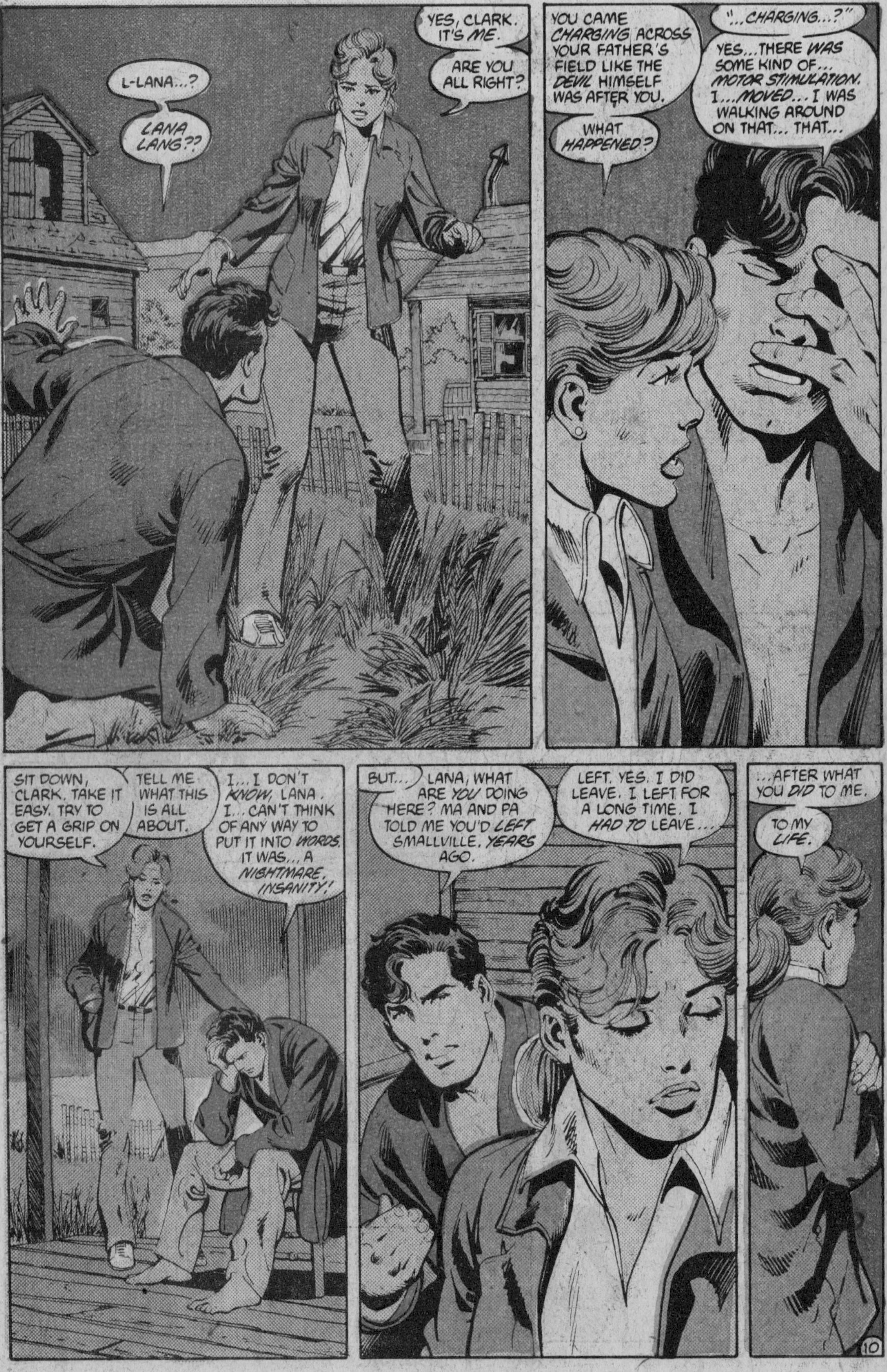
L-LANA...?
LANA LANG??
YES, CLARK. IT'S ME.
ARE YOU ALL RIGHT?
YOU CAME CHARGING ACROSS YOUR FATHER'S FIELD LIKE THE DEVIL HIMSELF WAS AFTER YOU.
WHAT HAPPENED?
"...CHARGING...?"
YES... THERE WAS SOME KIND OF... MOTOR STIMULATION. I... MOVED... I WAS WALKING AROUND ON THAT... THAT...
SIT DOWN, CLARK. TAKE IT EASY. TRY TO GET A GRIP ON YOURSELF.
TELL ME WHAT THIS IS ALL ABOUT.
I... I DON'T KNOW, LANA. I... CAN'T THINK OF ANY WAY TO PUT IT INTO WORDS. IT WAS... A NIGHTMARE. INSANITY!
BUT...
LANA, WHAT ARE YOU DOING HERE? MA AND PA TOLD ME YOU'D LEFT SMALLVILLE. YEARS AGO.
LEFT. YES. I DID LEAVE. I LEFT FOR A LONG TIME. I HAD TO LEAVE...
...AFTER WHAT YOU DID TO ME.
TO MY LIFE.

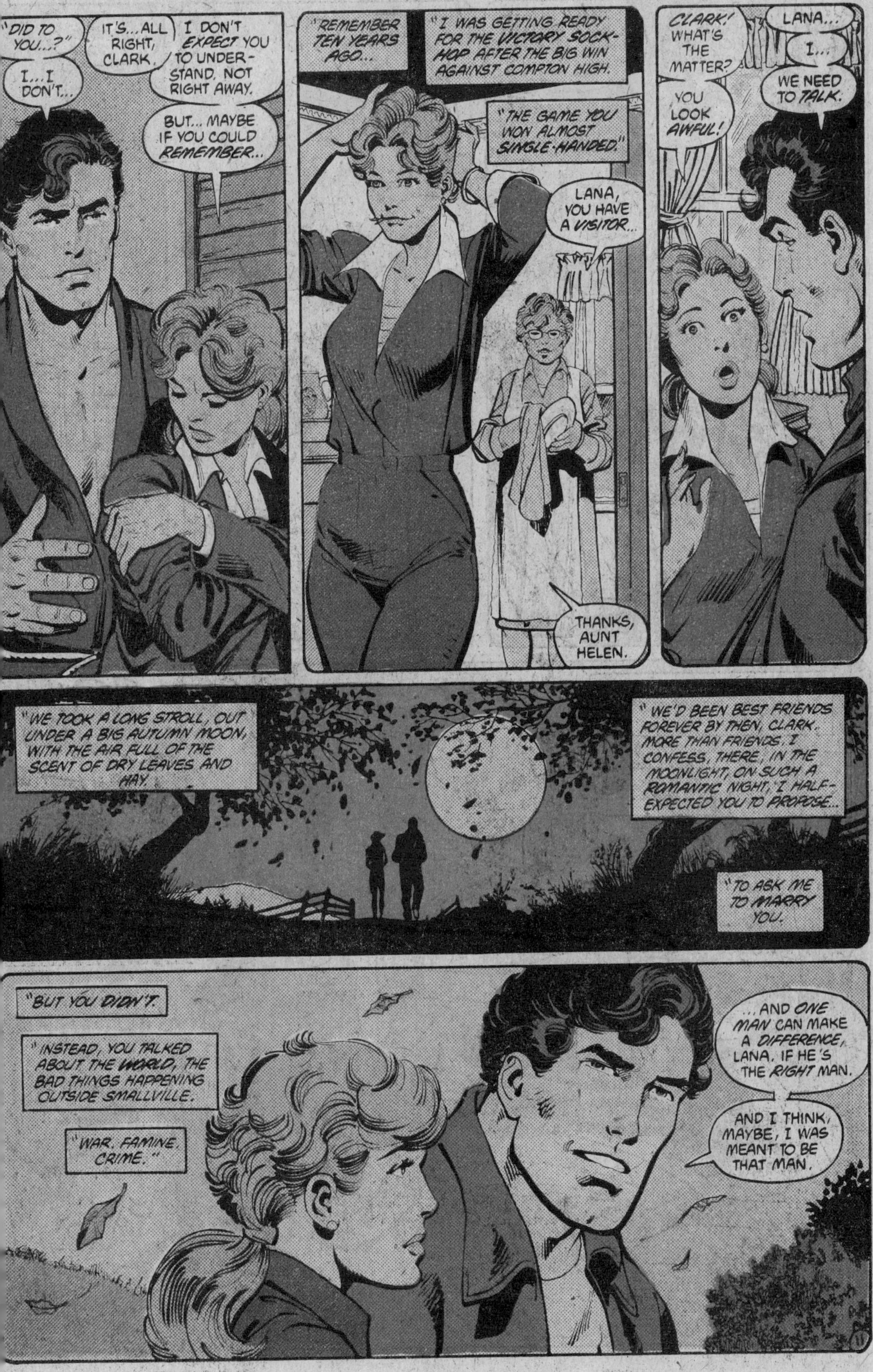
"DID TO YOU...?"
I...I DON'T...
IT'S...ALL RIGHT, CLARK.
I DON'T EXPECT YOU TO UNDERSTAND, NOT RIGHT AWAY.
BUT... MAYBE IF YOU COULD REMEMBER...
"REMEMBER TEN YEARS AGO...
"I WAS GETTING READY FOR THE VICTORY SOCK-HOP AFTER THE BIG WIN AGAINST COMPTON HIGH.
"THE GAME YOU WON ALMOST SINGLE-HANDED."
LANA, YOU HAVE A VISITOR...
THANKS, AUNT HELEN.
CLARK! WHAT'S THE MATTER?
YOU LOOK AWFUL!
LANA...
I...
WE NEED TO TALK.
"WE TOOK A LONG STROLL, OUT UNDER A BIG AUTUMN MOON, WITH THE AIR FULL OF THE SCENT OF DRY LEAVES AND HAY.
"WE'D BEEN BEST FRIENDS FOREVER BY THEN, CLARK. MORE THAN FRIENDS. I CONFESS, THERE, IN THE MOONLIGHT, ON SUCH A ROMANTIC NIGHT, I HALF-EXPECTED YOU TO PROPOSE...
"TO ASK ME TO MARRY YOU.
"BUT YOU DIDN'T.
"INSTEAD, YOU TALKED ABOUT THE WORLD, THE BAD THINGS HAPPENING OUTSIDE SMALLVILLE.
"WAR. FAMINE. CRIME."
...AND ONE MAN CAN MAKE A DIFFERENCE, LANA. IF HE'S THE RIGHT MAN.
AND I THINK, MAYBE, I WAS MEANT TO BE THAT MAN.
11

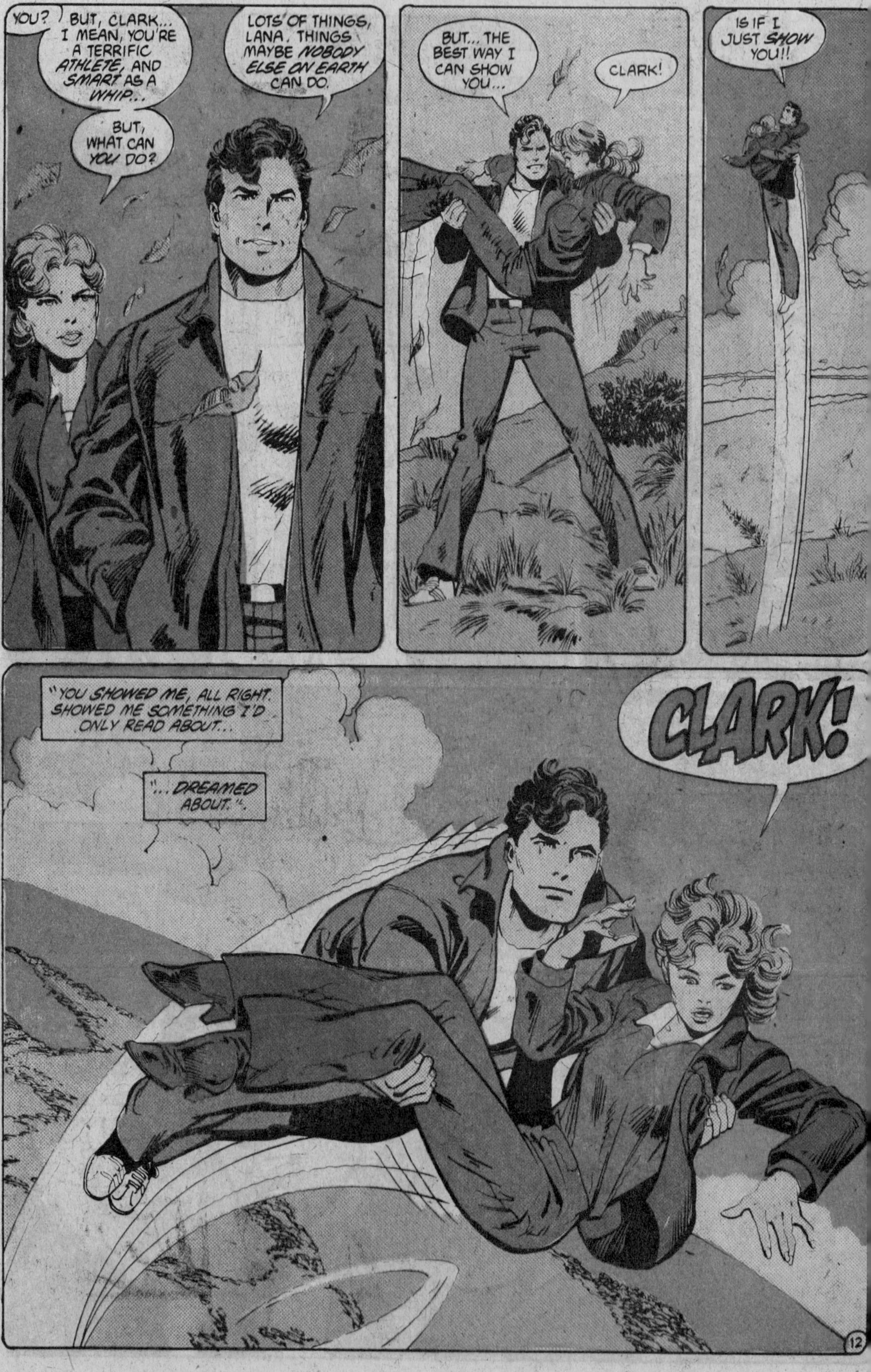

YOU?
BUT, CLARK... I MEAN, YOU'RE A TERRIFIC ATHLETE, AND SMART AS A WHIP...
BUT, WHAT CAN YOU DO?
LOTS OF THINGS, LANA. THINGS MAYBE NOBODY ELSE ON EARTH CAN DO.
BUT... THE BEST WAY I CAN SHOW YOU...
CLARK!
IS IF I JUST SHOW YOU!!
"YOU SHOWED ME, ALL RIGHT. SHOWED ME SOMETHING I'D ONLY READ ABOUT...
"...DREAMED ABOUT."
CLARK!

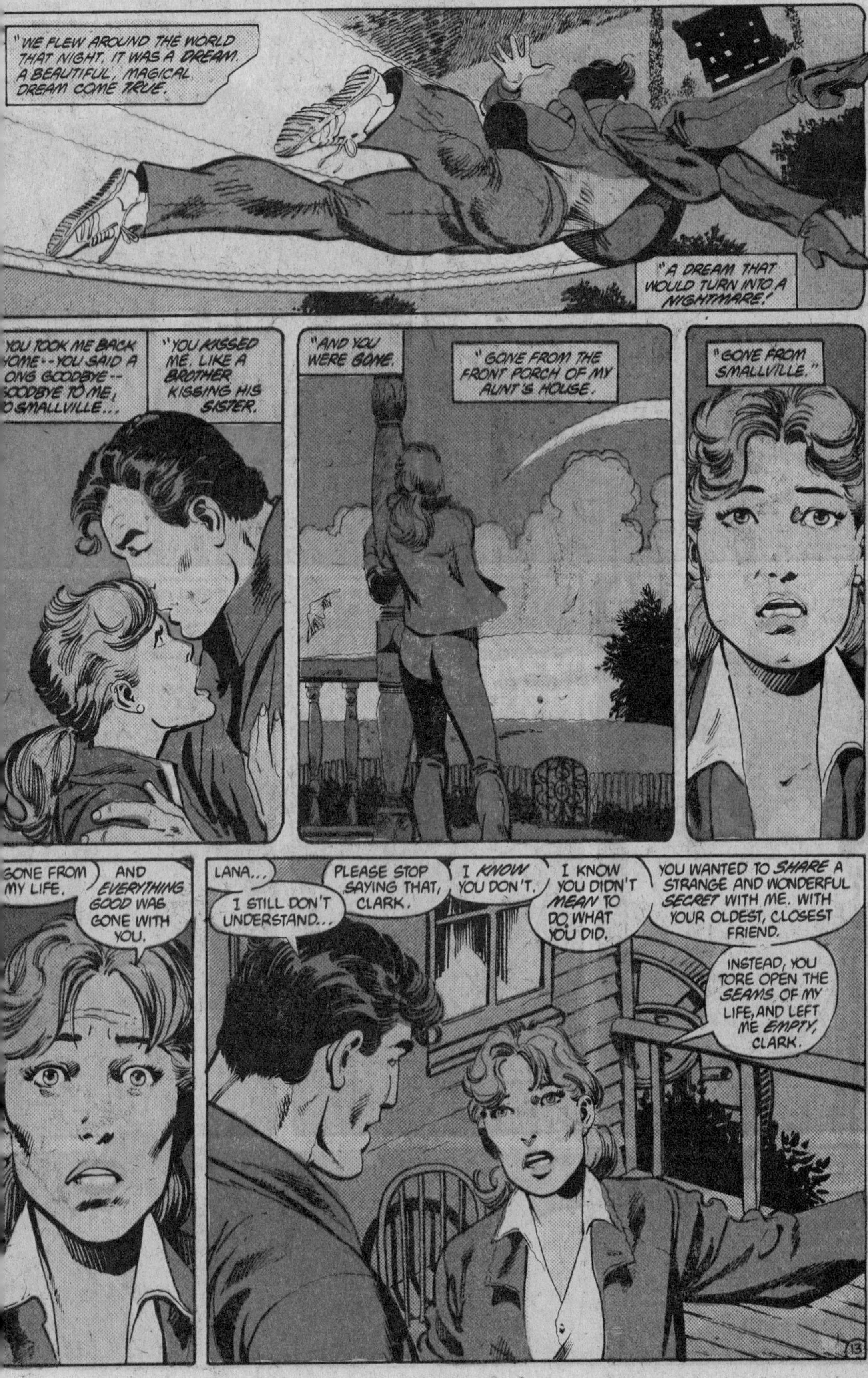
"WE FLEW AROUND THE WORLD THAT NIGHT. IT WAS A DREAM. A BEAUTIFUL, MAGICAL DREAM COME TRUE.
"A DREAM THAT WOULD TURN INTO A NIGHTMARE!
YOU TOOK ME BACK HOME--YOU SAID A ONG GOODBYE--GOODBYE TO ME, O SMALLVILLE...
"YOU KISSED ME. LIKE A BROTHER KISSING HIS SISTER.
"AND YOU WERE GONE.
"GONE FROM THE FRONT PORCH OF MY AUNT'S HOUSE.
"GONE FROM SMALLVILLE."
GONE FROM MY LIFE.
AND EVERYTHING GOOD WAS GONE WITH YOU.
LANA...
I STILL DON'T UNDERSTAND...
PLEASE STOP SAYING THAT, CLARK.
I KNOW YOU DON'T.
I KNOW YOU DIDN'T MEAN TO DO WHAT YOU DID.
YOU WANTED TO SHARE A STRANGE AND WONDERFUL SECRET WITH ME. WITH YOUR OLDEST, CLOSEST FRIEND.
INSTEAD, YOU TORE OPEN THE SEAMS OF MY LIFE, AND LEFT ME EMPTY, CLARK.
13

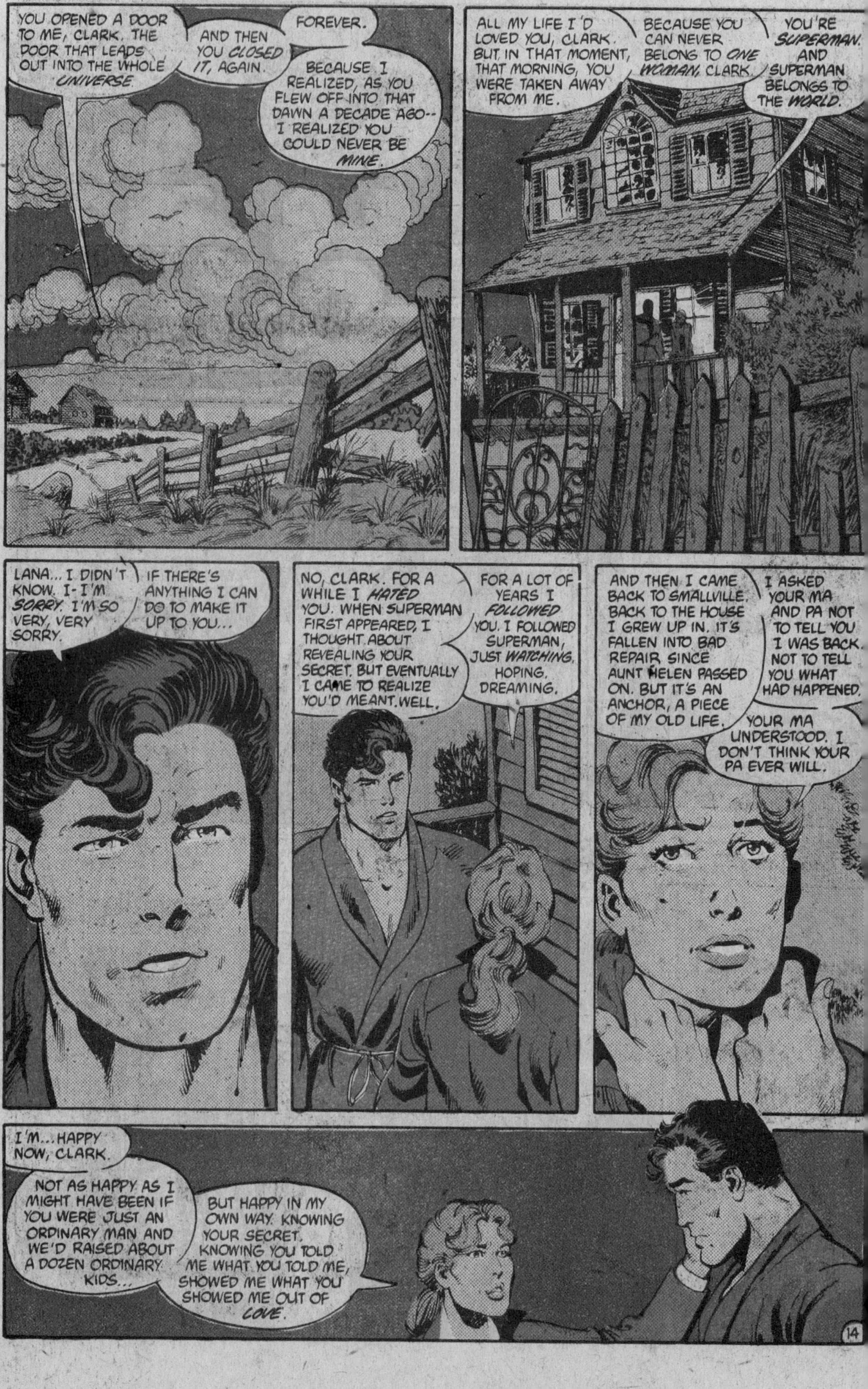
YOU OPENED A DOOR TO ME, CLARK. THE DOOR THAT LEADS OUT INTO THE WHOLE UNIVERSE.
AND THEN YOU CLOSED IT, AGAIN.
FOREVER.
BECAUSE I REALIZED, AS YOU FLEW OFF INTO THAT DAWN A DECADE AGO-- I REALIZED YOU COULD NEVER BE MINE.
ALL MY LIFE I'D LOVED YOU, CLARK. BUT IN THAT MOMENT, THAT MORNING, YOU WERE TAKEN AWAY FROM ME.
BECAUSE YOU CAN NEVER BELONG TO ONE WOMAN, CLARK.
YOU'RE SUPERMAN. AND SUPERMAN BELONGS TO THE WORLD.
LANA... I DIDN'T KNOW. I- I'M SORRY. I'M SO VERY, VERY SORRY.
IF THERE'S ANYTHING I CAN DO TO MAKE IT UP TO YOU...
NO, CLARK. FOR A WHILE I HATED YOU. WHEN SUPERMAN FIRST APPEARED, I THOUGHT ABOUT REVEALING YOUR SECRET. BUT EVENTUALLY I CAME TO REALIZE YOU'D MEANT WELL.
FOR A LOT OF YEARS I FOLLOWED YOU. I FOLLOWED SUPERMAN, JUST WATCHING. HOPING. DREAMING.
AND THEN I CAME BACK TO SMALLVILLE. BACK TO THE HOUSE I GREW UP IN. IT'S FALLEN INTO BAD REPAIR SINCE AUNT HELEN PASSED ON. BUT IT'S AN ANCHOR, A PIECE OF MY OLD LIFE.
I ASKED YOUR MA AND PA NOT TO TELL YOU I WAS BACK. NOT TO TELL YOU WHAT HAD HAPPENED.
YOUR MA UNDERSTOOD. I DON'T THINK YOUR PA EVER WILL.
I'M... HAPPY NOW, CLARK.
NOT AS HAPPY AS I MIGHT HAVE BEEN IF YOU WERE JUST AN ORDINARY MAN AND WE'D RAISED ABOUT A DOZEN ORDINARY KIDS...
BUT HAPPY IN MY OWN WAY. KNOWING YOUR SECRET. KNOWING YOU TOLD ME WHAT YOU TOLD ME, SHOWED ME WHAT YOU SHOWED ME OUT OF LOVE.
14

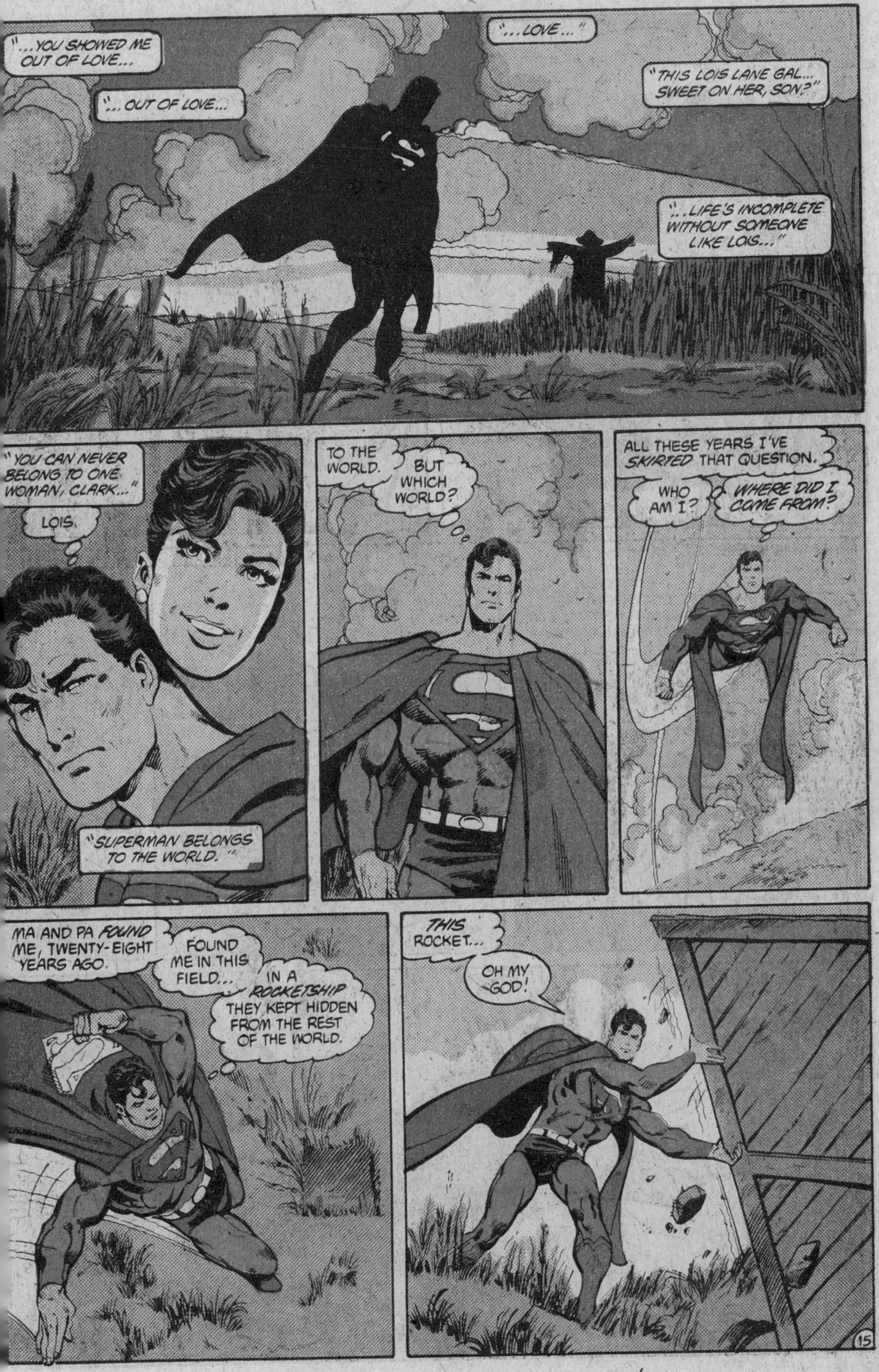
"...YOU SHOWED ME OUT OF LOVE...
"...OUT OF LOVE...
"...LOVE..."
"THIS LOIS LANE GAL... SWEET ON HER, SON?"
"...LIFE'S INCOMPLETE WITHOUT SOMEONE LIKE LOIS..."
"YOU CAN NEVER BELONG TO ONE WOMAN, CLARK..."
LOIS.
"SUPERMAN BELONGS TO THE WORLD."
TO THE WORLD.
BUT WHICH WORLD?
ALL THESE YEARS I'VE SKIRTED THAT QUESTION.
WHO AM I?
WHERE DID I COME FROM?
MA AND PA FOUND ME, TWENTY-EIGHT YEARS AGO.
FOUND ME IN THIS FIELD...
IN A ROCKETSHIP THEY KEPT HIDDEN FROM THE REST OF THE WORLD.
THIS ROCKET...
OH MY GOD!
15

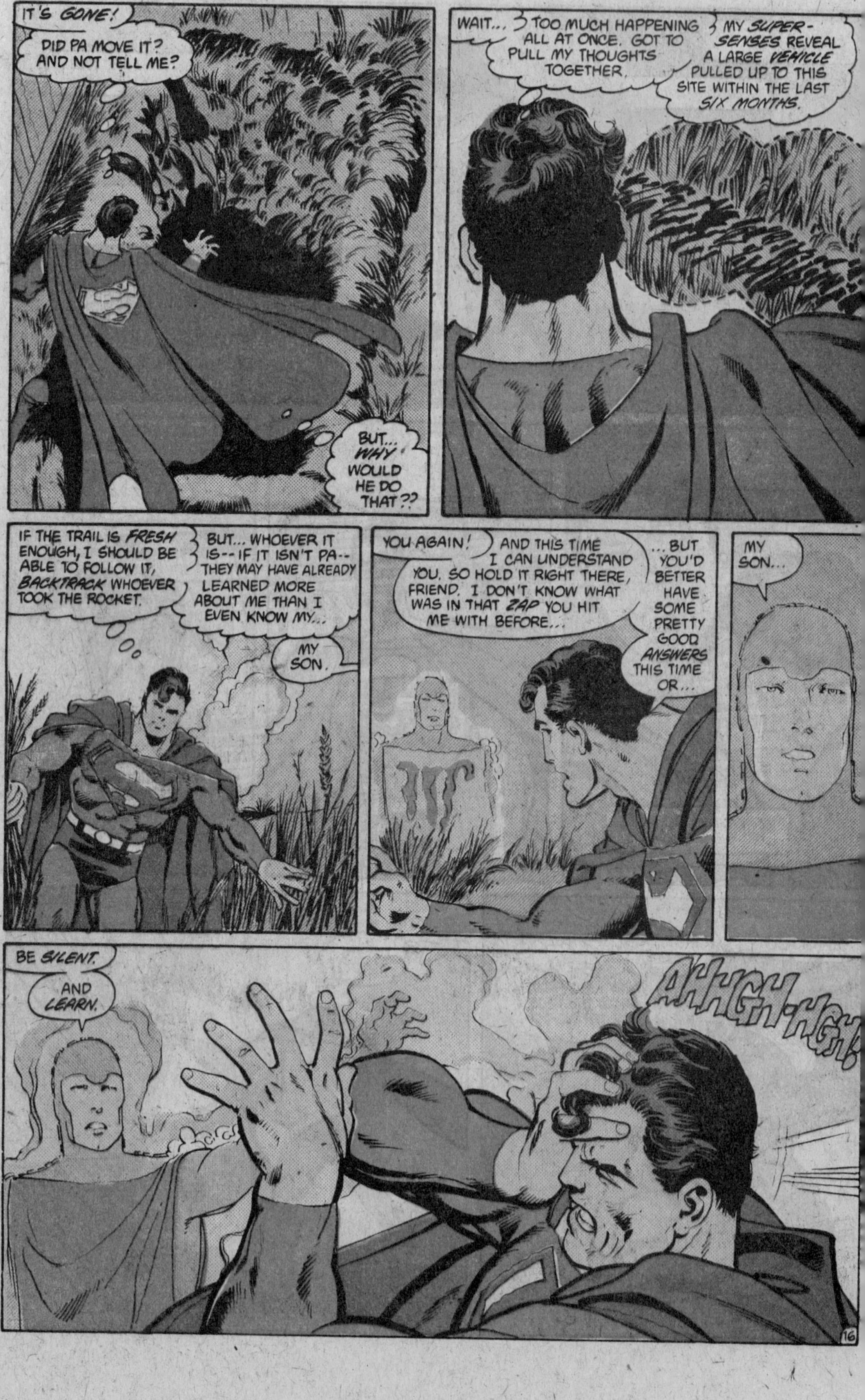
IT'S GONE!
DID PA MOVE IT? AND NOT TELL ME?
BUT... WHY WOULD HE DO THAT??
WAIT...
TOO MUCH HAPPENING ALL AT ONCE. GOT TO PULL MY THOUGHTS TOGETHER.
MY SUPER-SENSES REVEAL A LARGE VEHICLE PULLED UP TO THIS SITE WITHIN THE LAST SIX MONTHS.
IF THE TRAIL IS FRESH ENOUGH, I SHOULD BE ABLE TO FOLLOW IT, BACKTRACK WHOEVER TOOK THE ROCKET.
BUT... WHOEVER IT IS-- IF IT ISN'T PA-- THEY MAY HAVE ALREADY LEARNED MORE ABOUT ME THAN I EVEN KNOW MY...
MY SON.
YOU AGAIN!
AND THIS TIME I CAN UNDERSTAND YOU. SO HOLD IT RIGHT THERE, FRIEND. I DON'T KNOW WHAT WAS IN THAT ZAP YOU HIT ME WITH BEFORE...
...BUT YOU'D BETTER HAVE SOME PRETTY GOOD ANSWERS THIS TIME OR...
MY SON...
BE SILENT.
AND LEARN.
AHHGH-HGH!
16

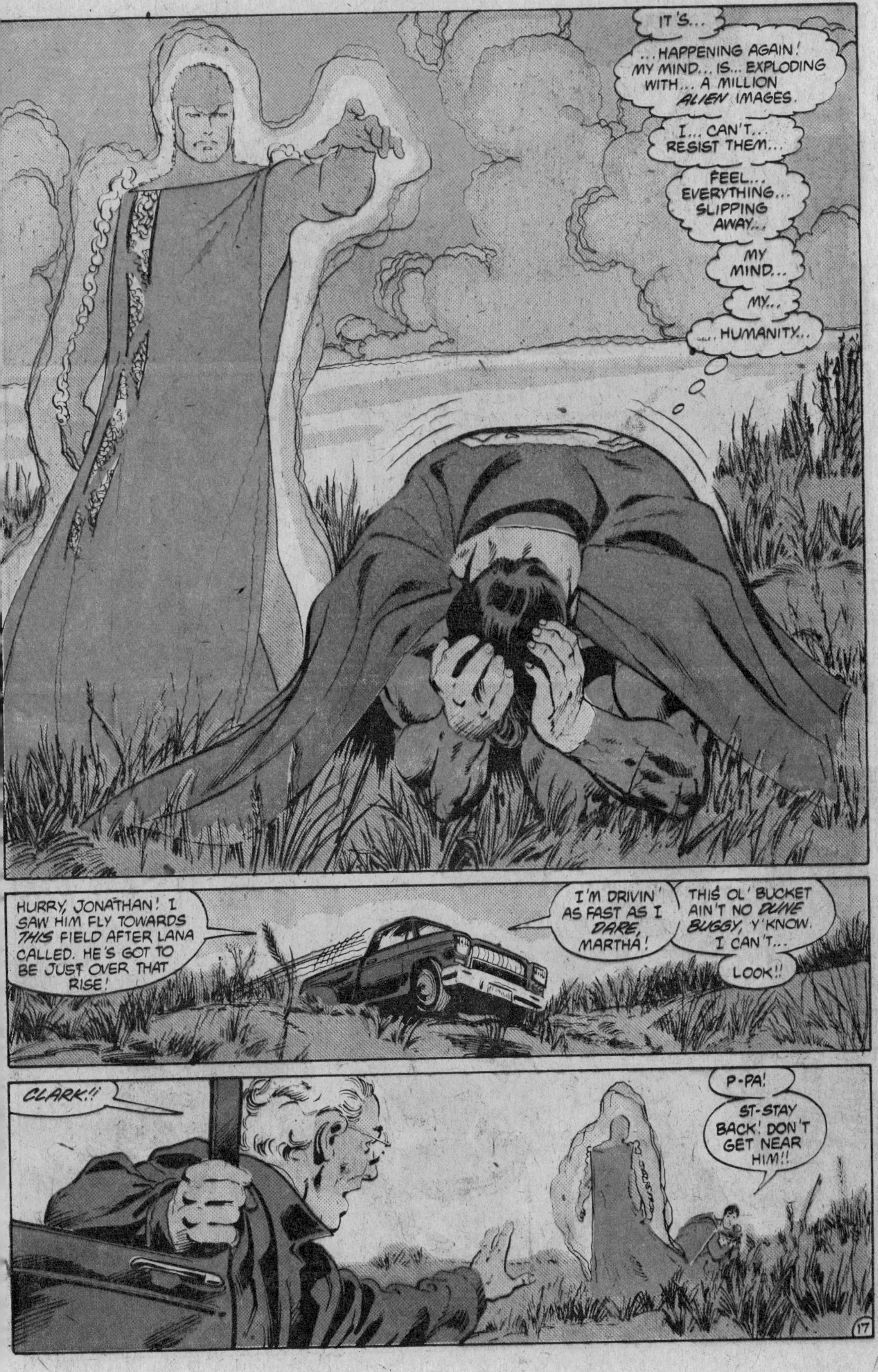
IT'S...
...HAPPENING AGAIN! MY MIND... IS... EXPLODING WITH... A MILLION ALIEN IMAGES.
I... CAN'T... RESIST THEM...
FEEL... EVERYTHING... SLIPPING AWAY...
MY MIND...
MY...
...HUMANITY...
HURRY, JONATHAN! I SAW HIM FLY TOWARDS THIS FIELD AFTER LANA CALLED. HE'S GOT TO BE JUST OVER THAT RISE!
I'M DRIVIN' AS FAST AS I DARE, MARTHA!
THIS OL' BUCKET AIN'T NO DUNE BUGGY, Y'KNOW. I CAN'T...
LOOK!!
CLARK!!
P-PA!
ST-STAY BACK! DON'T GET NEAR HIM!!

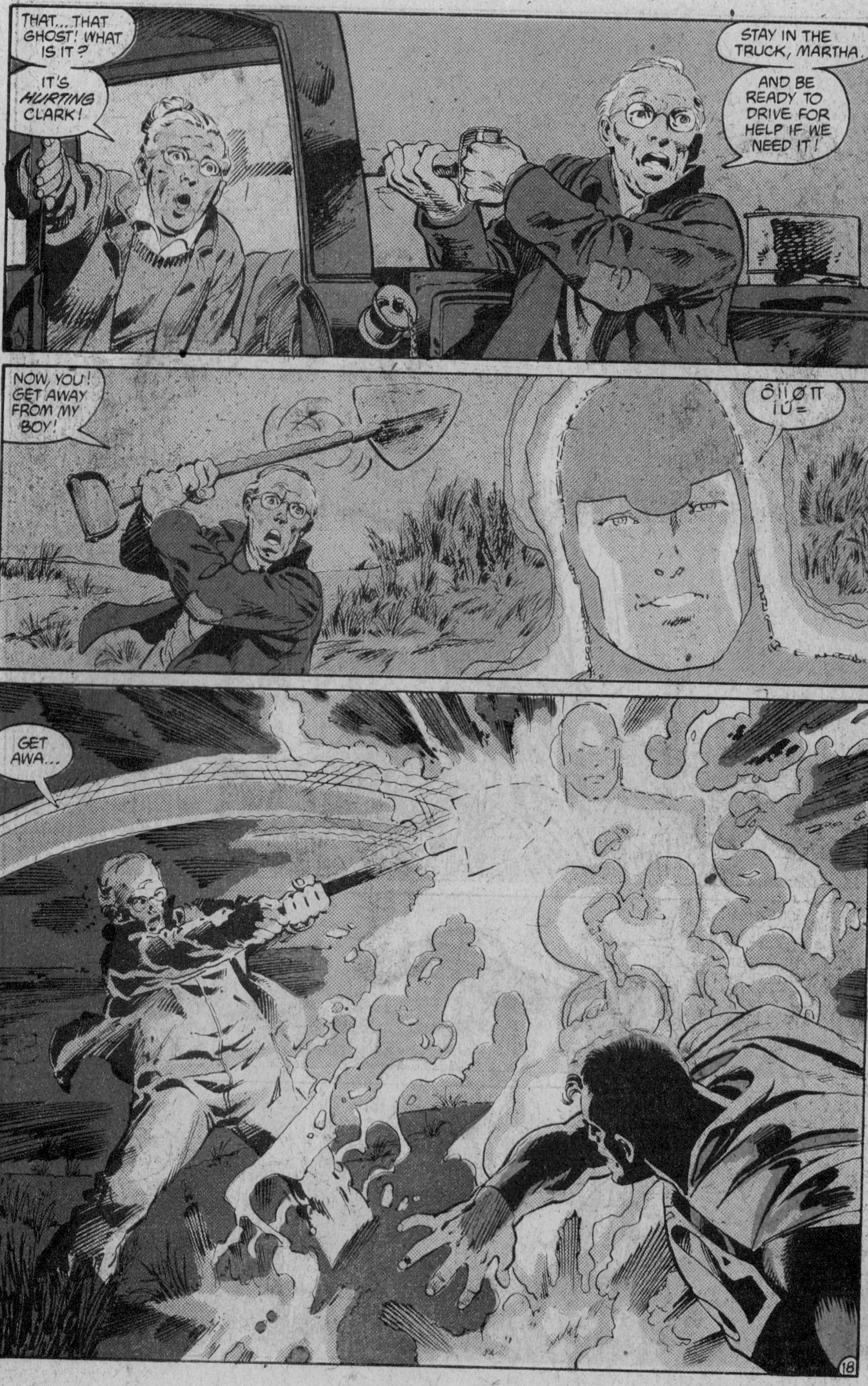
THAT... THAT GHOST! WHAT IS IT?
IT'S *HURTING* CLARK!
STAY IN THE TRUCK, MARTHA.
AND BE READY TO DRIVE FOR HELP IF WE NEED IT!
NOW, YOU! GET AWAY FROM MY BOY!
GET AWA...

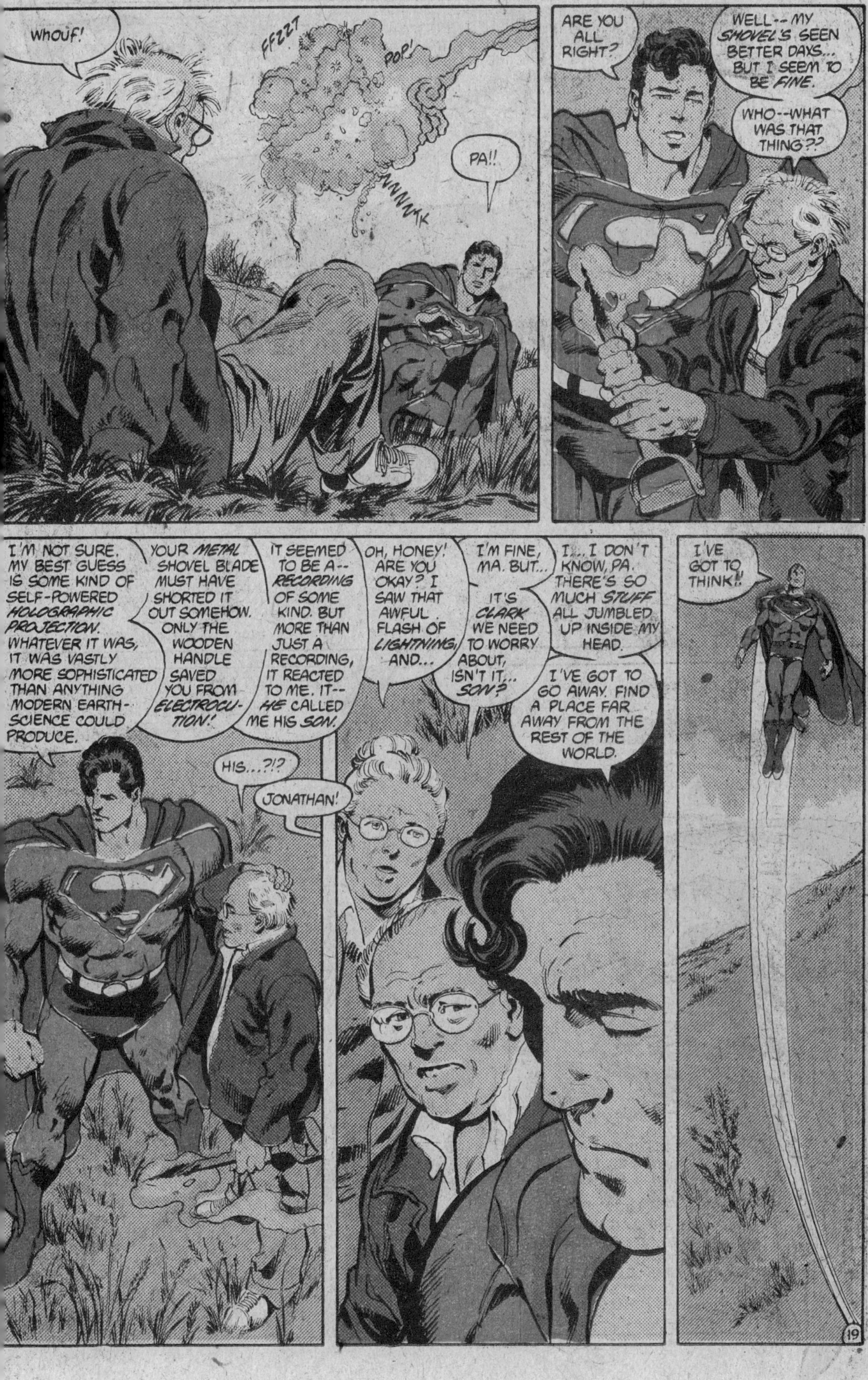

WHOUF!
FFZZZT
POP!
PA!!
NNNNNNK
ARE YOU ALL RIGHT?
WELL-- MY SHOVEL'S SEEN BETTER DAYS... BUT I SEEM TO BE FINE.
WHO--WHAT WAS THAT THING??
I'M NOT SURE. MY BEST GUESS IS SOME KIND OF SELF-POWERED HOLOGRAPHIC PROJECTION. WHATEVER IT WAS, IT WAS VASTLY MORE SOPHISTICATED THAN ANYTHING MODERN EARTH-SCIENCE COULD PRODUCE.
YOUR METAL SHOVEL BLADE MUST HAVE SHORTED IT OUT SOMEHOW. ONLY THE WOODEN HANDLE SAVED YOU FROM ELECTROCUTION!
IT SEEMED TO BE A--RECORDING OF SOME KIND. BUT MORE THAN JUST A RECORDING, IT REACTED TO ME. IT--HE CALLED ME HIS SON.
HIS...?!?
JONATHAN!
OH, HONEY! ARE YOU OKAY? I SAW THAT AWFUL FLASH OF LIGHTNING, AND...
I'M FINE, MA. BUT...
IT'S CLARK WE NEED TO WORRY ABOUT, ISN'T IT... SON?
I... I DON'T KNOW, PA. THERE'S SO MUCH STUFF ALL JUMBLED UP INSIDE MY HEAD.
I'VE GOT TO GO AWAY. FIND A PLACE FAR AWAY FROM THE REST OF THE WORLD.
I'VE GOT TO THINK!!

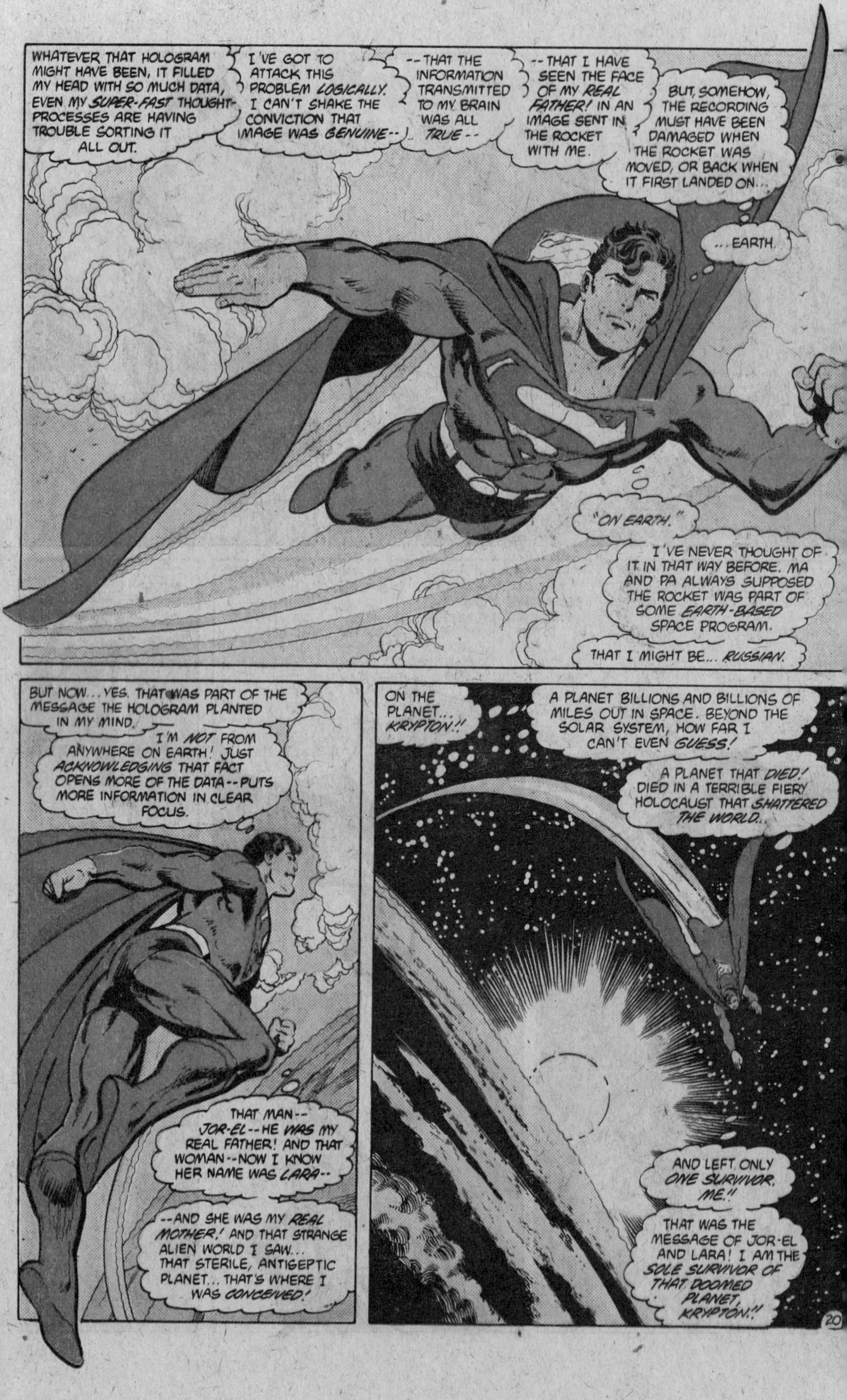
WHATEVER THAT HOLOGRAM MIGHT HAVE BEEN, IT FILLED MY HEAD WITH SO MUCH DATA, EVEN MY SUPER-FAST THOUGHT-PROCESSES ARE HAVING TROUBLE SORTING IT ALL OUT.
I'VE GOT TO ATTACK THIS PROBLEM LOGICALLY. I CAN'T SHAKE THE CONVICTION THAT IMAGE WAS GENUINE--
--THAT THE INFORMATION TRANSMITTED TO MY BRAIN WAS ALL TRUE--
--THAT I HAVE SEEN THE FACE OF MY REAL FATHER! IN AN IMAGE SENT IN THE ROCKET WITH ME.
BUT, SOMEHOW, THE RECORDING MUST HAVE BEEN DAMAGED WHEN THE ROCKET WAS MOVED, OR BACK WHEN IT FIRST LANDED ON...
...EARTH.
"ON EARTH."
I'VE NEVER THOUGHT OF IT IN THAT WAY BEFORE. MA AND PA ALWAYS SUPPOSED THE ROCKET WAS PART OF SOME EARTH-BASED SPACE PROGRAM.
THAT I MIGHT BE... RUSSIAN.
BUT NOW... YES. THAT WAS PART OF THE MESSAGE THE HOLOGRAM PLANTED IN MY MIND.
I'M NOT FROM ANYWHERE ON EARTH! JUST ACKNOWLEDGING THAT FACT OPENS MORE OF THE DATA--PUTS MORE INFORMATION IN CLEAR FOCUS.
THAT MAN--JOR-EL--HE WAS MY REAL FATHER! AND THAT WOMAN--NOW I KNOW HER NAME WAS LARA--
--AND SHE WAS MY REAL MOTHER! AND THAT STRANGE ALIEN WORLD I SAW... THAT STERILE, ANTISEPTIC PLANET... THAT'S WHERE I WAS CONCEIVED!
ON THE PLANET... KRYPTON!!
A PLANET BILLIONS AND BILLIONS OF MILES OUT IN SPACE. BEYOND THE SOLAR SYSTEM, HOW FAR I CAN'T EVEN GUESS!
A PLANET THAT DIED! DIED IN A TERRIBLE FIERY HOLOCAUST THAT SHATTERED THE WORLD...
AND LEFT ONLY ONE SURVIVOR. ME!!
THAT WAS THE MESSAGE OF JOR-EL AND LARA! I AM THE SOLE SURVIVOR OF THAT DOOMED PLANET, KRYPTON!!
20

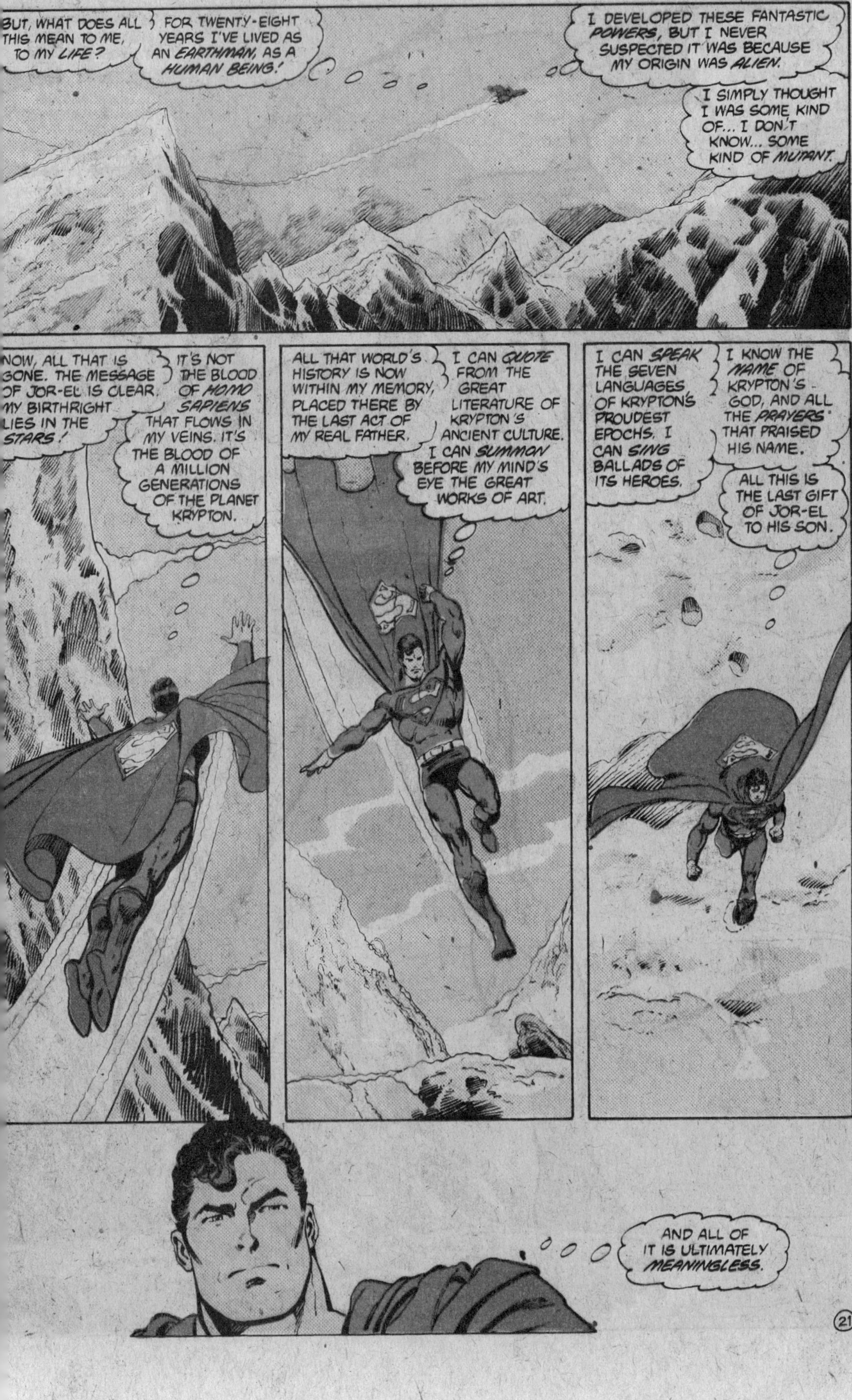
BUT, WHAT DOES ALL THIS MEAN TO ME, TO MY LIFE?
FOR TWENTY-EIGHT YEARS I'VE LIVED AS AN EARTHMAN, AS A HUMAN BEING!
I DEVELOPED THESE FANTASTIC POWERS, BUT I NEVER SUSPECTED IT WAS BECAUSE MY ORIGIN WAS ALIEN.
I SIMPLY THOUGHT I WAS SOME KIND OF... I DON'T KNOW... SOME KIND OF MUTANT.
NOW, ALL THAT IS GONE. THE MESSAGE OF JOR-EL IS CLEAR. MY BIRTHRIGHT LIES IN THE STARS!
IT'S NOT THE BLOOD OF HOMO SAPIENS THAT FLOWS IN MY VEINS. IT'S THE BLOOD OF A MILLION GENERATIONS OF THE PLANET KRYPTON.
ALL THAT WORLD'S HISTORY IS NOW WITHIN MY MEMORY, PLACED THERE BY THE LAST ACT OF MY REAL FATHER.
I CAN QUOTE FROM THE GREAT LITERATURE OF KRYPTON'S ANCIENT CULTURE.
I CAN SUMMON BEFORE MY MIND'S EYE THE GREAT WORKS OF ART.
I CAN SPEAK THE SEVEN LANGUAGES OF KRYPTON'S PROUDEST EPOCHS. I CAN SING BALLADS OF ITS HEROES.
I KNOW THE NAME OF KRYPTON'S GOD, AND ALL THE PRAYERS THAT PRAISED HIS NAME.
ALL THIS IS THE LAST GIFT OF JOR-EL TO HIS SON.
AND ALL OF IT IS ULTIMATELY MEANINGLESS.

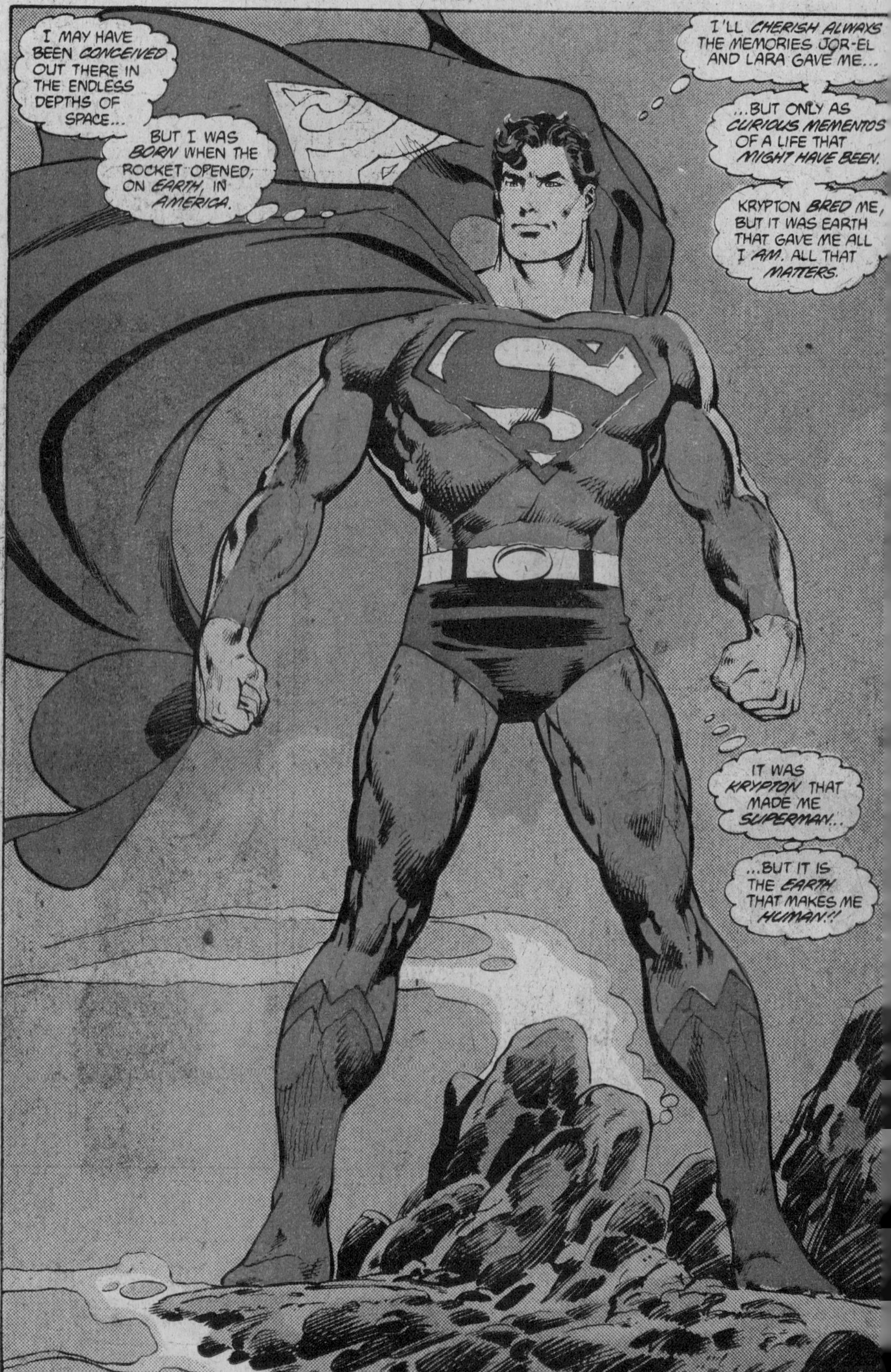
I MAY HAVE BEEN CONCEIVED OUT THERE IN THE ENDLESS DEPTHS OF SPACE...
BUT I WAS BORN WHEN THE ROCKET OPENED, ON EARTH, IN AMERICA.
I'LL CHERISH ALWAYS THE MEMORIES JOR-EL AND LARA GAVE ME...
...BUT ONLY AS CURIOUS MEMENTOS OF A LIFE THAT MIGHT HAVE BEEN.
KRYPTON BRED ME, BUT IT WAS EARTH THAT GAVE ME ALL I AM. ALL THAT MATTERS.
IT WAS KRYPTON THAT MADE ME SUPERMAN...
...BUT IT IS THE EARTH THAT MAKES ME HUMAN!!

THE SECRET ORIGIN OF GREEN LANTERN®

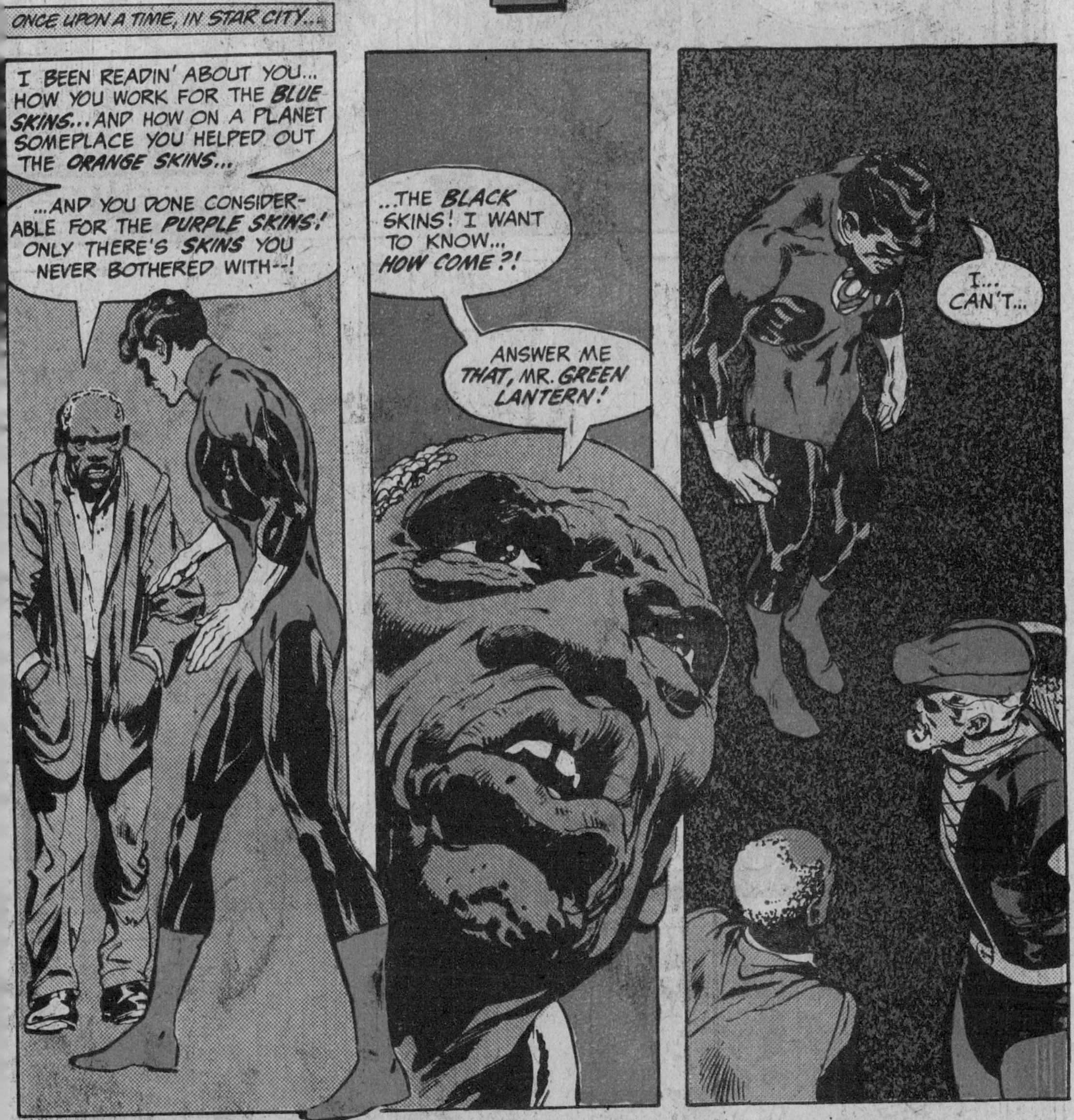
ONCE UPON A TIME, IN STAR CITY...
I BEEN READIN' ABOUT YOU... HOW YOU WORK FOR THE BLUE SKINS... AND HOW ON A PLANET SOMEPLACE YOU HELPED OUT THE ORANGE SKINS...
...AND YOU DONE CONSIDER-ABLE FOR THE PURPLE SKINS! ONLY THERE'S SKINS YOU NEVER BOTHERED WITH--!
...THE BLACK SKINS! I WANT TO KNOW... HOW COME?!
ANSWER ME THAT, MR. GREEN LANTERN!
I... CAN'T...

JAMES OWSLEY M.D. BRIGHT SCRIPT/PLOT/PENCILS · JOSÉ MARZAN JR. INKS · ROBERT GREENBERGER PLOT ASSIST · TIM HARKINS LETTERING · ANTHONY TOLLIN COLORING · MARK WAID EDITOR

PAGE ONE TAKEN FROM THE CLASSIC GREEN LANTERN/GREEN ARROW #76 BY DENNY O'NEIL AND NEAL ADAMS.

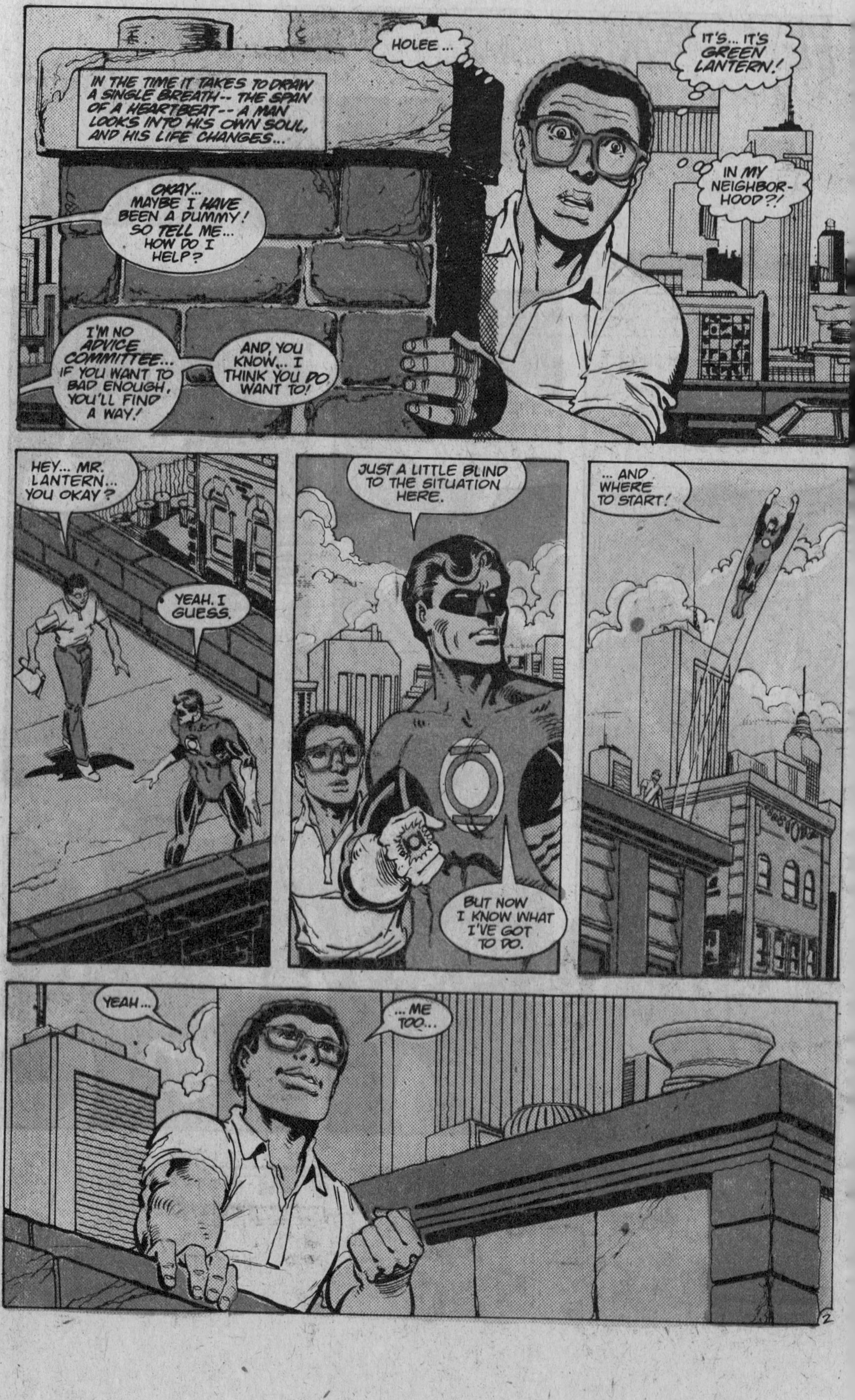
IN THE TIME IT TAKES TO DRAW A SINGLE BREATH-- THE SPAN OF A HEARTBEAT-- A MAN LOOKS INTO HIS OWN SOUL, AND HIS LIFE CHANGES...
HOLEE...
IT'S... IT'S GREEN LANTERN!
IN MY NEIGHBOR-HOOD?!
OKAY... MAYBE I HAVE BEEN A DUMMY! SO TELL ME... HOW DO I HELP?
I'M NO ADVICE COMMITTEE... IF YOU WANT TO BAD ENOUGH, YOU'LL FIND A WAY!
AND, YOU KNOW... I THINK YOU DO WANT TO!
HEY... MR. LANTERN... YOU OKAY?
YEAH. I GUESS.
JUST A LITTLE BLIND TO THE SITUATION HERE.
BUT NOW I KNOW WHAT I'VE GOT TO DO.
... AND WHERE TO START!
YEAH...
... ME TOO...
2

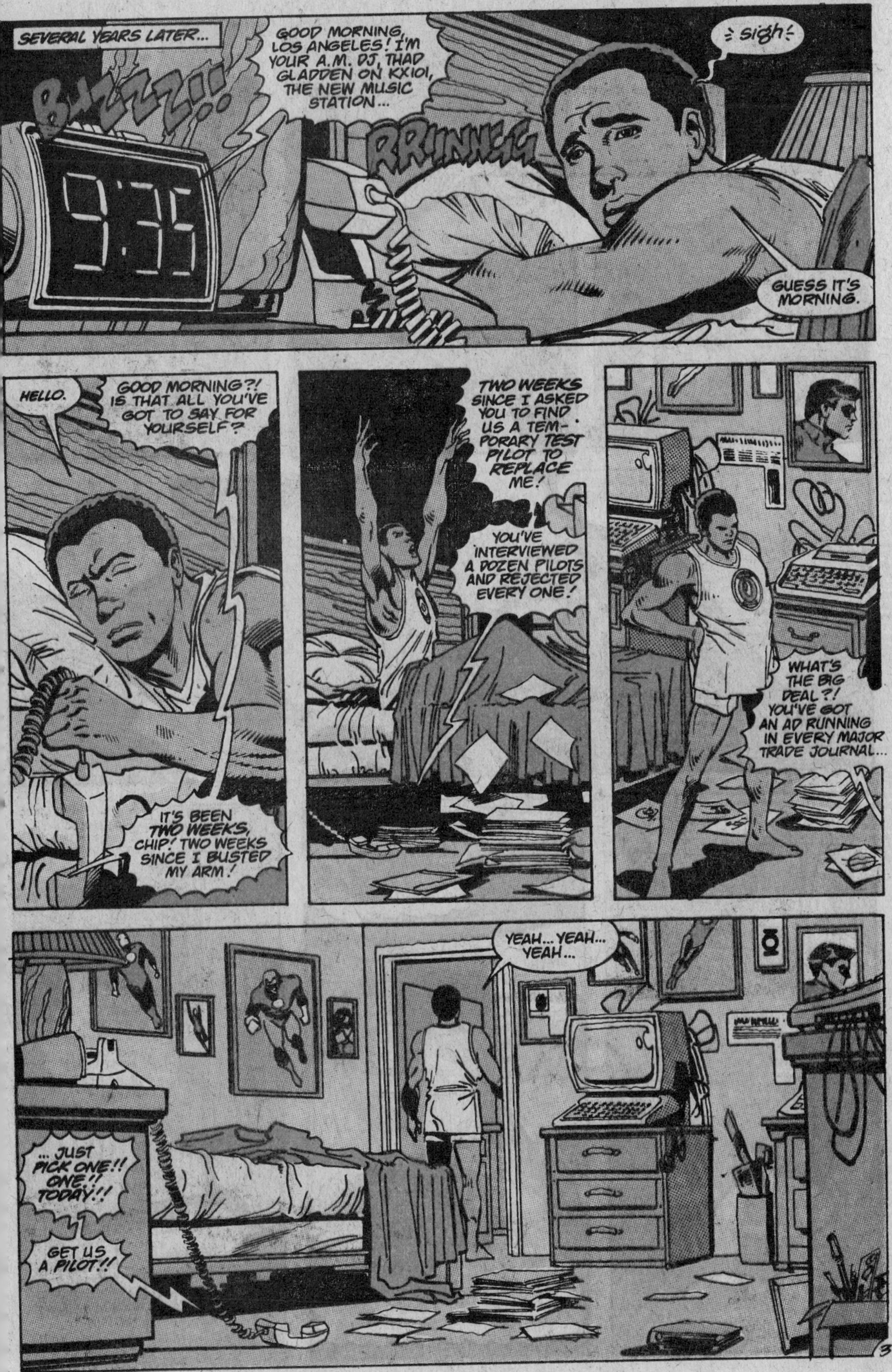
SEVERAL YEARS LATER...
GOOD MORNING, LOS ANGELES! I'M YOUR A.M. DJ, THAD GLADDEN ON KX101, THE NEW MUSIC STATION...
BZZZZ!!
sigh
9:35
RRINNGG
GUESS IT'S MORNING.
HELLO.
GOOD MORNING?! IS THAT ALL YOU'VE GOT TO SAY FOR YOURSELF?
IT'S BEEN TWO WEEKS, CHIP! TWO WEEKS SINCE I BUSTED MY ARM!
TWO WEEKS SINCE I ASKED YOU TO FIND US A TEMPORARY TEST PILOT TO REPLACE ME!
YOU'VE INTERVIEWED A DOZEN PILOTS AND REJECTED EVERY ONE!
WHAT'S THE BIG DEAL?! YOU'VE GOT AN AD RUNNING IN EVERY MAJOR TRADE JOURNAL...
YEAH... YEAH... YEAH...
... JUST PICK ONE!! ONE!! TODAY!!
GET US A PILOT!!

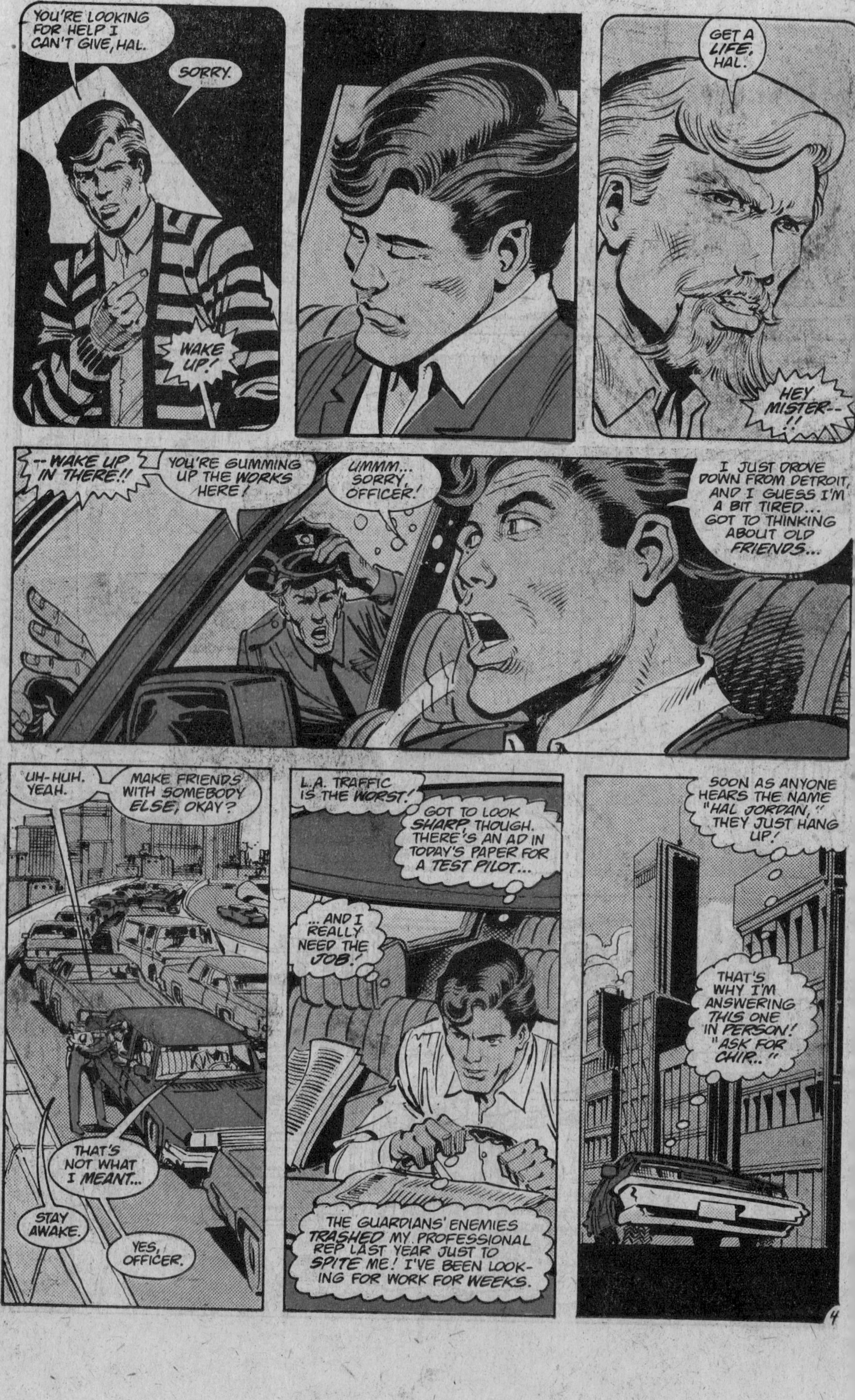
YOU'RE LOOKING FOR HELP I CAN'T GIVE, HAL.
SORRY.
WAKE UP!
GET A LIFE, HAL.
HEY MISTER--!!
--WAKE UP IN THERE!!
YOU'RE GUMMING UP THE WORKS HERE!
UMMM... SORRY, OFFICER!
I JUST DROVE DOWN FROM DETROIT, AND I GUESS I'M A BIT TIRED... GOT TO THINKING ABOUT OLD FRIENDS...
UH-HUH. YEAH.
MAKE FRIENDS WITH SOMEBODY ELSE, OKAY?
THAT'S NOT WHAT I MEANT...
STAY AWAKE.
YES, OFFICER.
L.A. TRAFFIC IS THE WORST!
GOT TO LOOK SHARP, THOUGH. THERE'S AN AD IN TODAY'S PAPER FOR A TEST PILOT...
...AND I REALLY NEED THE JOB!
THE GUARDIANS' ENEMIES TRASHED MY PROFESSIONAL REP LAST YEAR JUST TO SPITE ME! I'VE BEEN LOOKING FOR WORK FOR WEEKS.
SOON AS ANYONE HEARS THE NAME "HAL JORDAN," THEY JUST HANG UP!
THAT'S WHY I'M ANSWERING THIS ONE IN PERSON! "ASK FOR CHIP.."

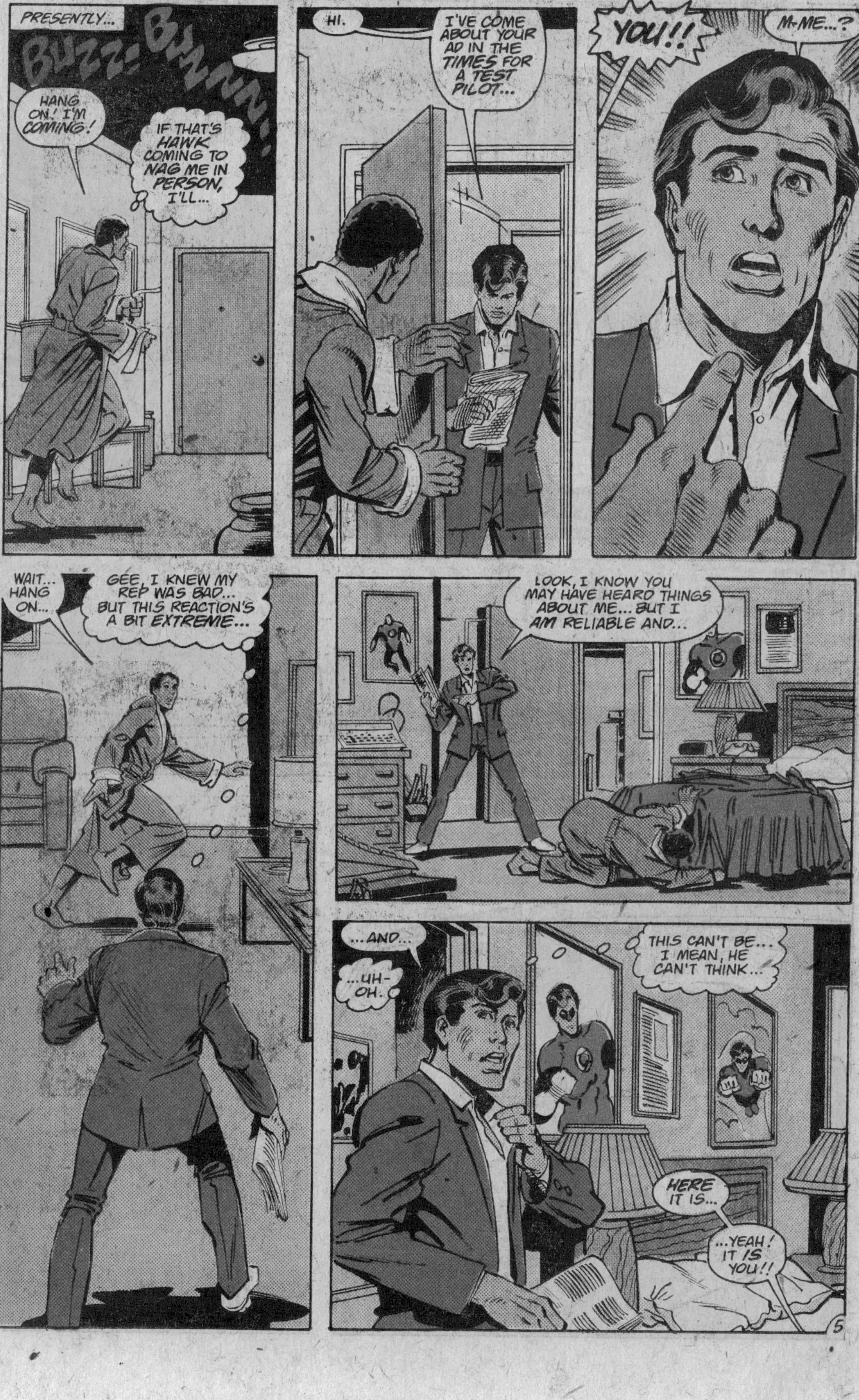
PRESENTLY...
BUZZ! BWANN!!
HANG ON! I'M COMING!
IF THAT'S HAWK COMING TO NAG ME IN PERSON, I'LL...
HI.
I'VE COME ABOUT YOUR AD IN THE TIMES FOR A TEST PILOT...
YOU!!
M-ME...?
WAIT... HANG ON...
GEE, I KNEW MY REP WAS BAD... BUT THIS REACTION'S A BIT EXTREME...
LOOK, I KNOW YOU MAY HAVE HEARD THINGS ABOUT ME... BUT I AM RELIABLE AND...
...AND...
...UH-OH.
THIS CAN'T BE... I MEAN, HE CAN'T THINK...
HERE IT IS...
...YEAH! IT IS YOU!!

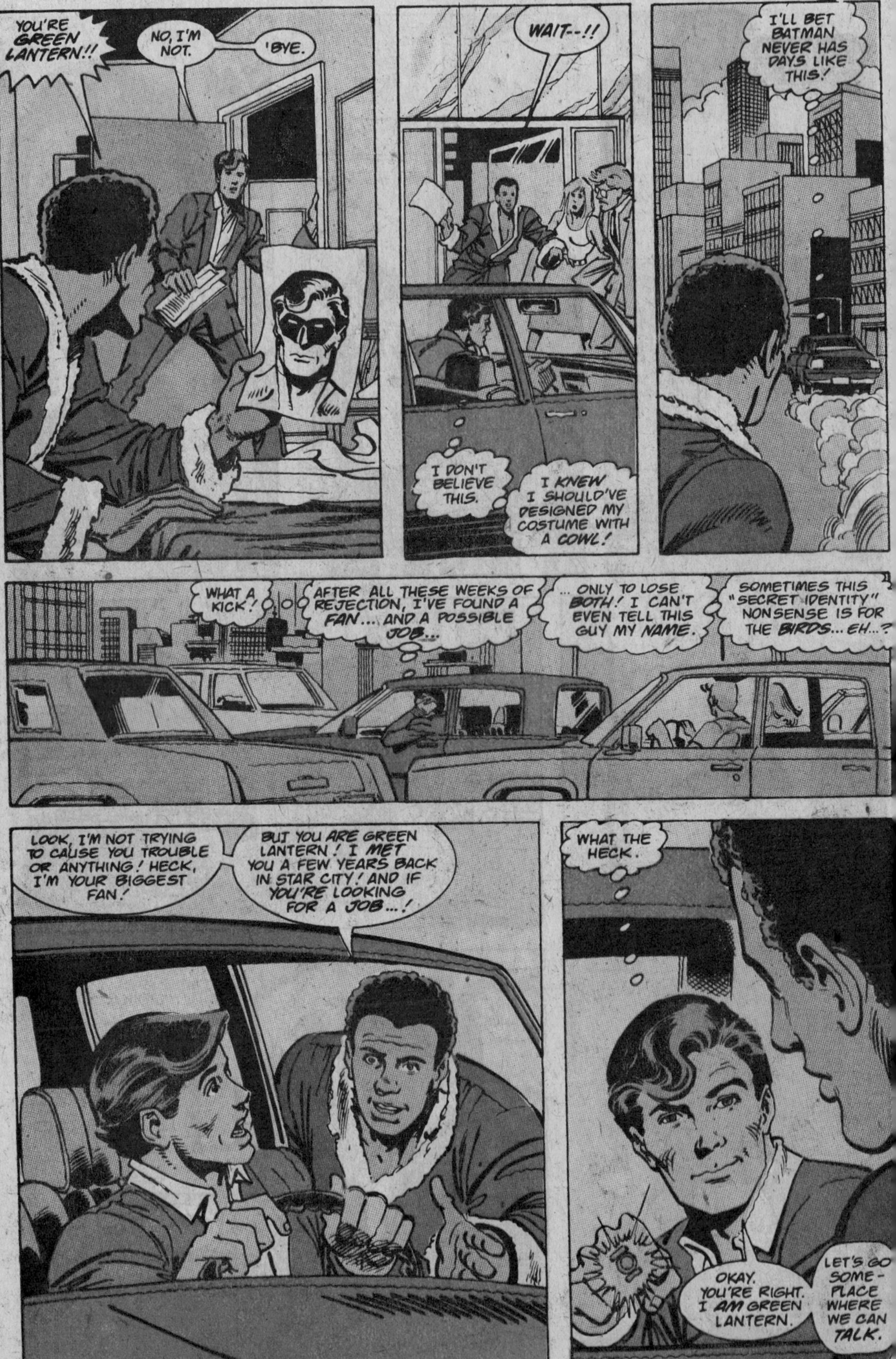
YOU'RE GREEN LANTERN!!
NO, I'M NOT.
'BYE.
WAIT--!!
I DON'T BELIEVE THIS.
I KNEW I SHOULD'VE DESIGNED MY COSTUME WITH A COWL!
I'LL BET BATMAN NEVER HAS DAYS LIKE THIS!
WHAT A KICK!
AFTER ALL THESE WEEKS OF REJECTION, I'VE FOUND A FAN... AND A POSSIBLE JOB...
...ONLY TO LOSE BOTH! I CAN'T EVEN TELL THIS GUY MY NAME.
SOMETIMES THIS "SECRET IDENTITY" NONSENSE IS FOR THE BIRDS... EH...?
LOOK, I'M NOT TRYING TO CAUSE YOU TROUBLE OR ANYTHING! HECK, I'M YOUR BIGGEST FAN!
BUT YOU ARE GREEN LANTERN! I MET YOU A FEW YEARS BACK IN STAR CITY! AND IF YOU'RE LOOKING FOR A JOB...!
WHAT THE HECK.
OKAY. YOU'RE RIGHT. I AM GREEN LANTERN.
LET'S GO SOME-PLACE WHERE WE CAN TALK.

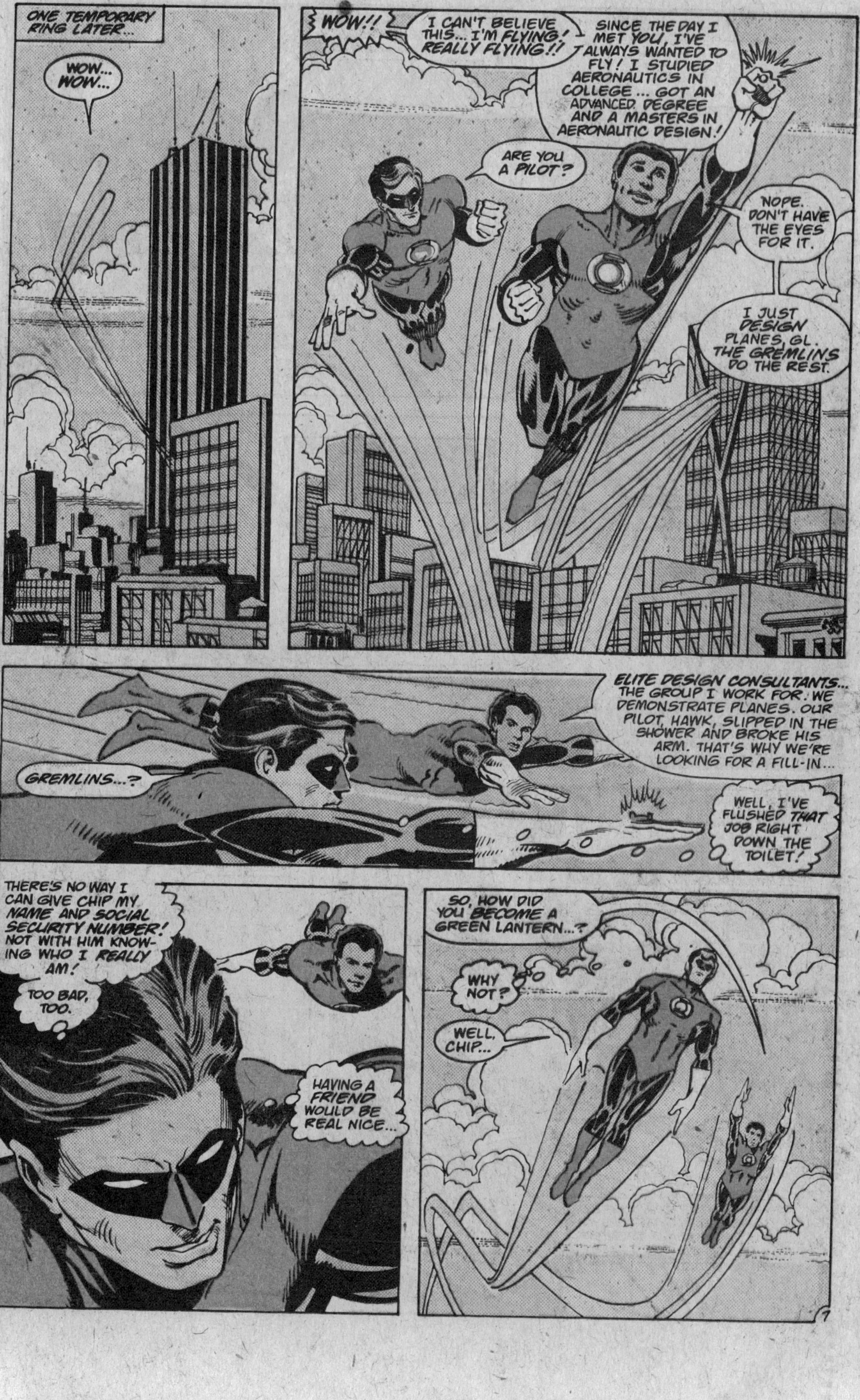
ONE TEMPORARY RING LATER...
WOW... WOW...
WOW!!
I CAN'T BELIEVE THIS... I'M FLYING! REALLY FLYING!!
SINCE THE DAY I MET YOU, I'VE ALWAYS WANTED TO FLY! I STUDIED AERONAUTICS IN COLLEGE... GOT AN ADVANCED DEGREE AND A MASTERS IN AERONAUTIC DESIGN!
ARE YOU A PILOT?
NOPE. DON'T HAVE THE EYES FOR IT.
I JUST DESIGN PLANES, GL. THE GREMLINS DO THE REST.
ELITE DESIGN CONSULTANTS... THE GROUP I WORK FOR. WE DEMONSTRATE PLANES. OUR PILOT, HAWK, SLIPPED IN THE SHOWER AND BROKE HIS ARM. THAT'S WHY WE'RE LOOKING FOR A FILL-IN...
GREMLINS...?
WELL, I'VE FLUSHED THAT JOB RIGHT DOWN THE TOILET!
THERE'S NO WAY I CAN GIVE CHIP MY NAME AND SOCIAL SECURITY NUMBER! NOT WITH HIM KNOWING WHO I REALLY AM!
TOO BAD, TOO.
HAVING A FRIEND WOULD BE REAL NICE...
SO, HOW DID YOU BECOME A GREEN LANTERN...?
WHY NOT?
WELL, CHIP...

"IT ALL BEGAN WHEN AN ALIEN SPACECRAFT LOST POWER AND FELL INTO THE EARTH'S GRAVITATIONAL FIELD.

"THE ALIEN ON BOARD WAS NAMED ABIN SUR.

"HE WAS THE GREEN LANTERN OF SPACE SECTOR 2814. THE SECTOR EARTH IS IN.

"ABIN COULDN'T HOLD THE SHIP TOGETHER. HE CRASH-LANDED OUT IN THE DESERT.

"SUR WAS DYING... NOT FROM THE CRASH, BUT FROM A DISEASE RIDDLING HIS BODY.

"WITH TIME RUNNING OUT, ABIN COMMANDED HIS POWER RING TO SEEK OUT A SUCCESSOR!

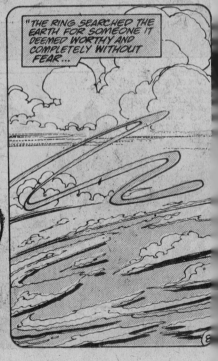

"THE RING SEARCHED THE EARTH FOR SOMEONE IT DEEMED WORTHY AND COMPLETELY WITHOUT FEAR...

8

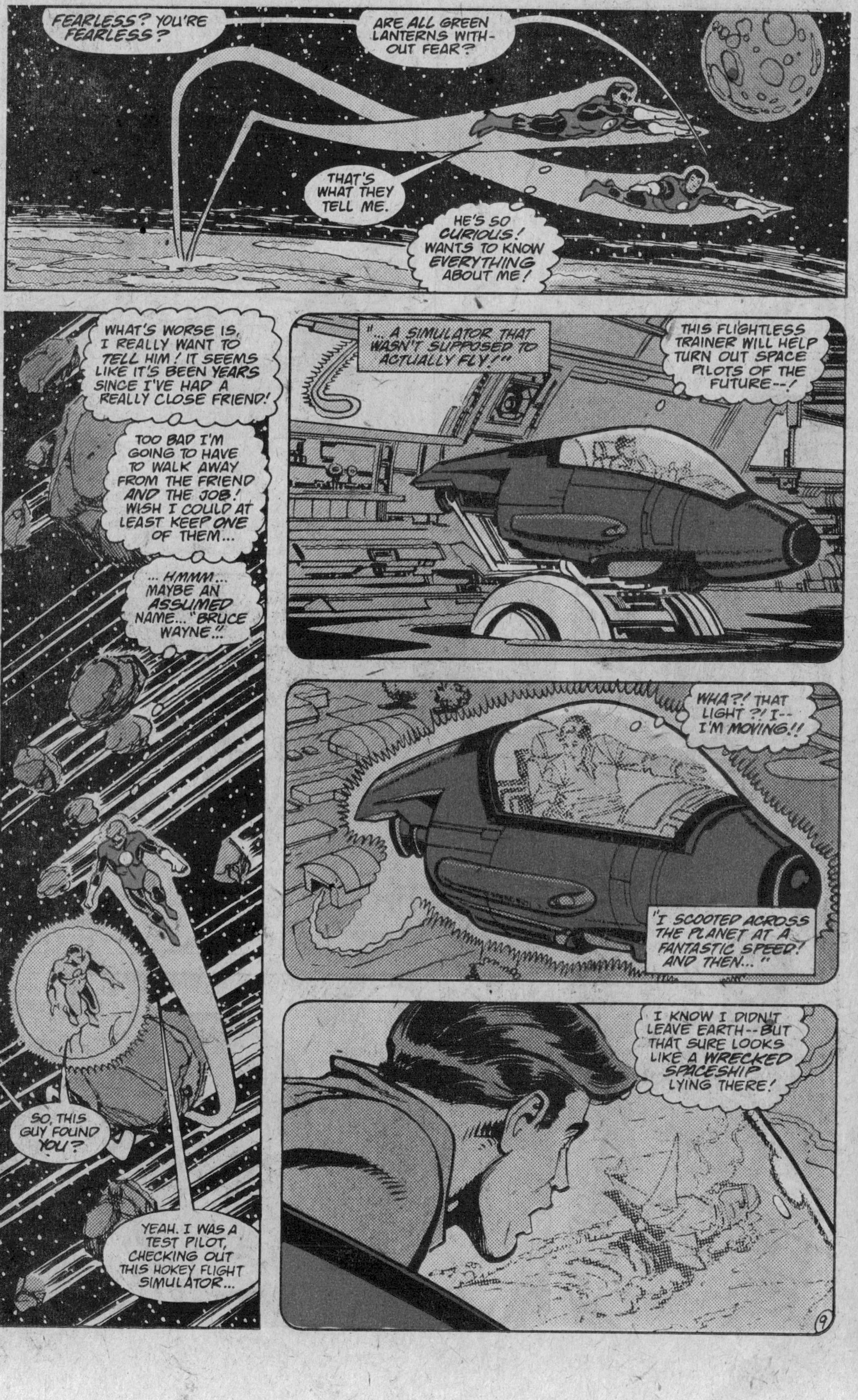
FEARLESS? YOU'RE FEARLESS?
ARE ALL GREEN LANTERNS WITH-OUT FEAR?
THAT'S WHAT THEY TELL ME.
HE'S SO CURIOUS! WANTS TO KNOW EVERYTHING ABOUT ME!
WHAT'S WORSE IS, I REALLY WANT TO TELL HIM! IT SEEMS LIKE IT'S BEEN YEARS SINCE I'VE HAD A REALLY CLOSE FRIEND!
TOO BAD I'M GOING TO HAVE TO WALK AWAY FROM THE FRIEND AND THE JOB! WISH I COULD AT LEAST KEEP ONE OF THEM...
... HMMM... MAYBE AN ASSUMED NAME... "BRUCE WAYNE."
SO, THIS GUY FOUND YOU?
YEAH. I WAS A TEST PILOT, CHECKING OUT THIS HOKEY FLIGHT SIMULATOR...
"...A SIMULATOR THAT WASN'T SUPPOSED TO ACTUALLY FLY!"
THIS FLIGHTLESS TRAINER WILL HELP TURN OUT SPACE PILOTS OF THE FUTURE--!
WHA?! THAT LIGHT?! I-- I'M MOVING!!
"I SCOOTED ACROSS THE PLANET AT A FANTASTIC SPEED! AND THEN..."
I KNOW I DIDN'T LEAVE EARTH--BUT THAT SURE LOOKS LIKE A WRECKED SPACESHIP LYING THERE!
9

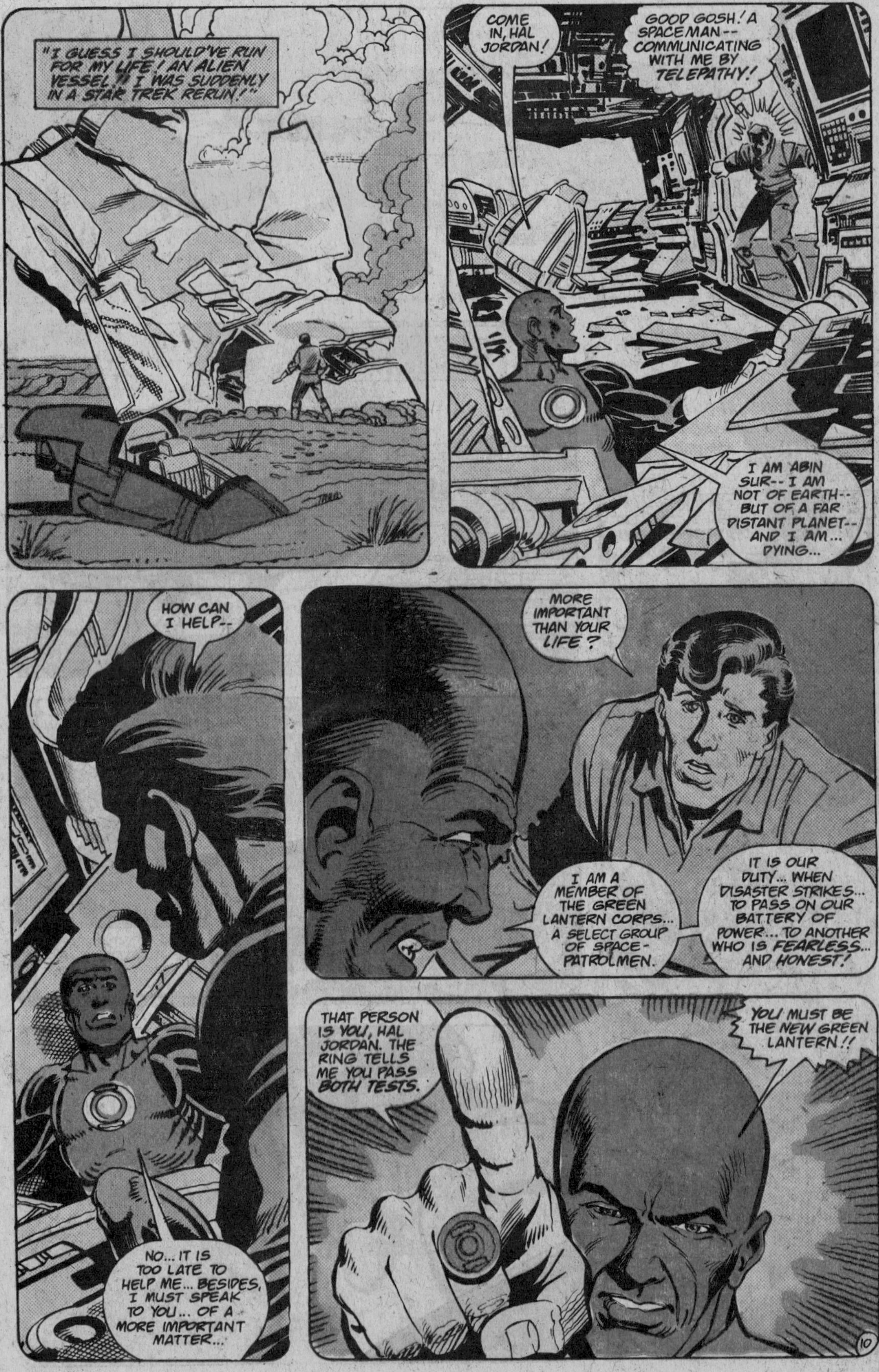
"I GUESS I SHOULD'VE RUN FOR MY LIFE! AN ALIEN VESSEL?! I WAS SUDDENLY IN A STAR TREK RERUN!"
COME IN, HAL JORDAN!
GOOD GOSH! A SPACEMAN-- COMMUNICATING WITH ME BY TELEPATHY!
I AM ABIN SUR-- I AM NOT OF EARTH-- BUT OF A FAR DISTANT PLANET-- AND I AM... DYING...
HOW CAN I HELP--
NO... IT IS TOO LATE TO HELP ME... BESIDES, I MUST SPEAK TO YOU... OF A MORE IMPORTANT MATTER...
MORE IMPORTANT THAN YOUR LIFE?
I AM A MEMBER OF THE GREEN LANTERN CORPS... A SELECT GROUP OF SPACE-PATROLMEN.
IT IS OUR DUTY... WHEN DISASTER STRIKES... TO PASS ON OUR BATTERY OF POWER... TO ANOTHER WHO IS FEARLESS... AND HONEST!
THAT PERSON IS YOU, HAL JORDAN. THE RING TELLS ME YOU PASS BOTH TESTS.
YOU MUST BE THE NEW GREEN LANTERN!!
10

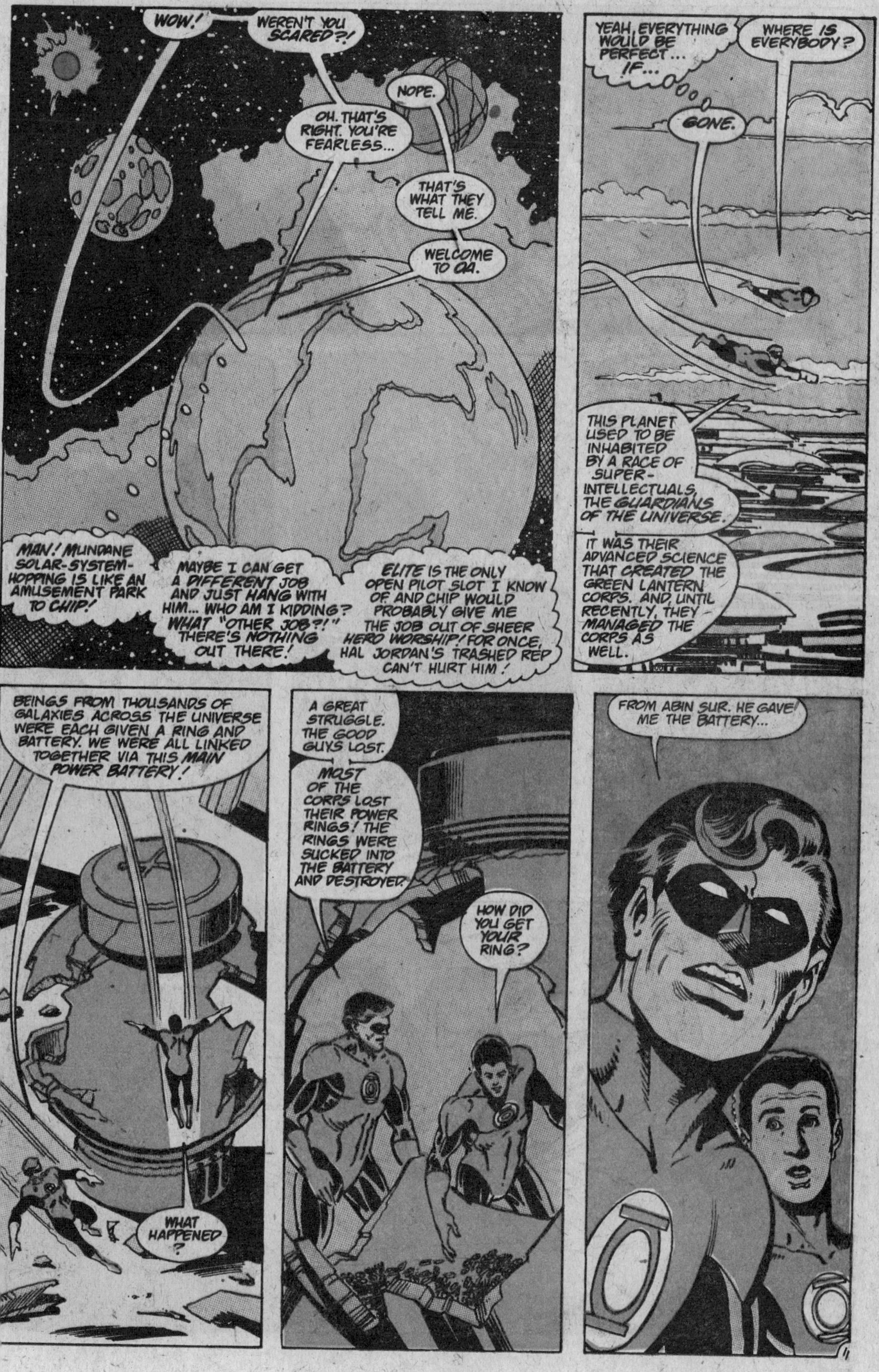
WOW!
WEREN'T YOU SCARED?!
NOPE.
OH. THAT'S RIGHT. YOU'RE FEARLESS...
THAT'S WHAT THEY TELL ME.
WELCOME TO OA.
MAN! MUNDANE SOLAR-SYSTEM-HOPPING IS LIKE AN AMUSEMENT PARK TO CHIP!
MAYBE I CAN GET A DIFFERENT JOB AND JUST HANG WITH HIM... WHO AM I KIDDING? WHAT "OTHER JOB?!" THERE'S NOTHING OUT THERE!
ELITE IS THE ONLY OPEN PILOT SLOT I KNOW OF AND CHIP WOULD PROBABLY GIVE ME THE JOB OUT OF SHEER HERO WORSHIP! FOR ONCE, HAL JORDAN'S TRASHED REP CAN'T HURT HIM!
YEAH, EVERYTHING WOULD BE PERFECT... IF...
WHERE IS EVERYBODY?
GONE.
THIS PLANET USED TO BE INHABITED BY A RACE OF SUPER-INTELLECTUALS, THE GUARDIANS OF THE UNIVERSE.
IT WAS THEIR ADVANCED SCIENCE THAT CREATED THE GREEN LANTERN CORPS. AND, UNTIL RECENTLY, THEY MANAGED THE CORPS AS WELL.
BEINGS FROM THOUSANDS OF GALAXIES ACROSS THE UNIVERSE WERE EACH GIVEN A RING AND BATTERY. WE WERE ALL LINKED TOGETHER VIA THIS MAIN POWER BATTERY!
WHAT HAPPENED?
A GREAT STRUGGLE. THE GOOD GUYS LOST.
MOST OF THE CORPS LOST THEIR POWER RINGS! THE RINGS WERE SUCKED INTO THE BATTERY AND DESTROYED.
HOW DID YOU GET YOUR RING?
FROM ABIN SUR. HE GAVE ME THE BATTERY...
11

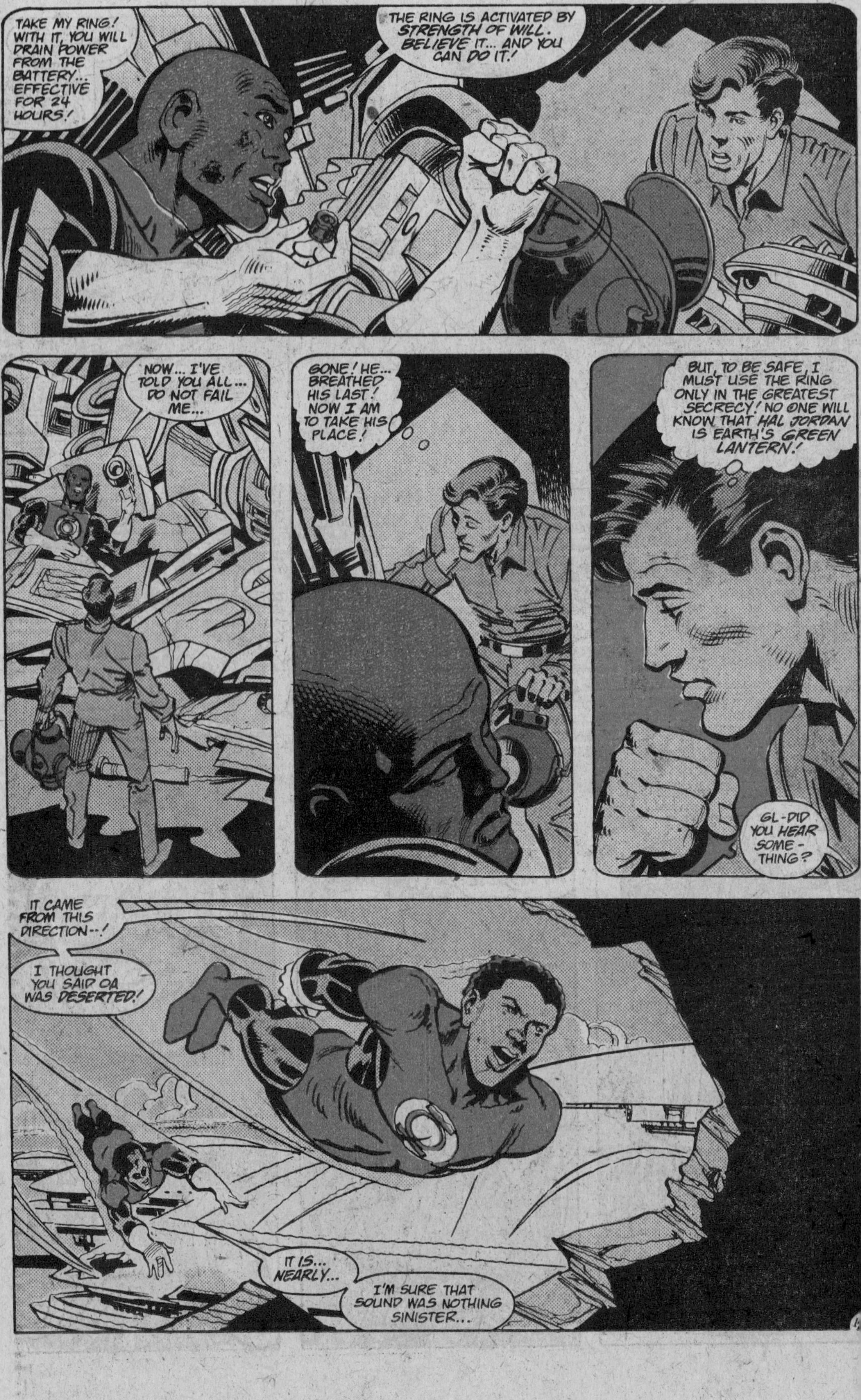
TAKE MY RING! WITH IT, YOU WILL DRAIN POWER FROM THE BATTERY... EFFECTIVE FOR 24 HOURS!
THE RING IS ACTIVATED BY STRENGTH OF WILL. BELIEVE IT... AND YOU CAN DO IT!
NOW... I'VE TOLD YOU ALL... DO NOT FAIL ME...
GONE! HE... BREATHED HIS LAST! NOW I AM TO TAKE HIS PLACE!
BUT, TO BE SAFE, I MUST USE THE RING ONLY IN THE GREATEST SECRECY! NO ONE WILL KNOW THAT HAL JORDAN IS EARTH'S GREEN LANTERN!
GL-DID YOU HEAR SOME-THING?
IT CAME FROM THIS DIRECTION--!
I THOUGHT YOU SAID OA WAS DESERTED!
IT IS... NEARLY...
I'M SURE THAT SOUND WAS NOTHING SINISTER...

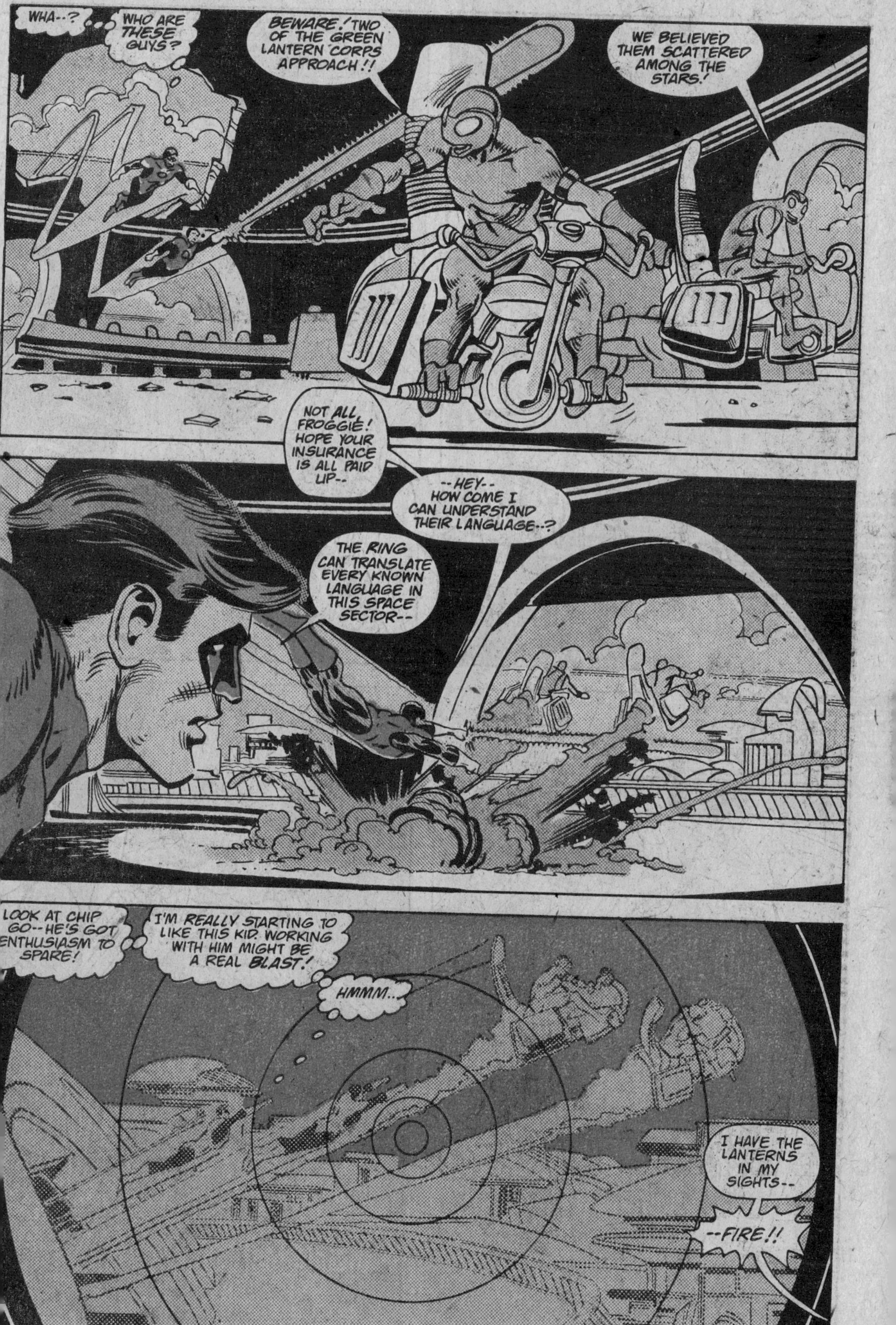
WHA--?
WHO ARE THESE GUYS?
BEWARE! TWO OF THE GREEN LANTERN CORPS APPROACH!!
WE BELIEVED THEM SCATTERED AMONG THE STARS!
NOT ALL, FROGGIE! HOPE YOUR INSURANCE IS ALL PAID UP--
--HEY-- HOW COME I CAN UNDERSTAND THEIR LANGUAGE--?
THE RING CAN TRANSLATE EVERY KNOWN LANGUAGE IN THIS SPACE SECTOR--
LOOK AT CHIP GO--HE'S GOT ENTHUSIASM TO SPARE!
I'M REALLY STARTING TO LIKE THIS KID. WORKING WITH HIM MIGHT BE A REAL BLAST!
HMMM...
I HAVE THE LANTERNS IN MY SIGHTS--
--FIRE!!

YEEEAARRGGHH!!

D-RANSOWW!!

WHERE DID-- HOW DID--

MORE RAIDERS-- BEHIND ME!

THESE GUYS MUST BE SCAVENGERS... HERE TO PICK THROUGH THE REMNANTS OF THE OAN CIVILIZATION!

I SUPPOSE THEY REALIZE ESCAPING FROM ME IS IMPOSSIBLE...

...SO THEY'VE DECIDED TO GO ON THE OFFENSIVE!

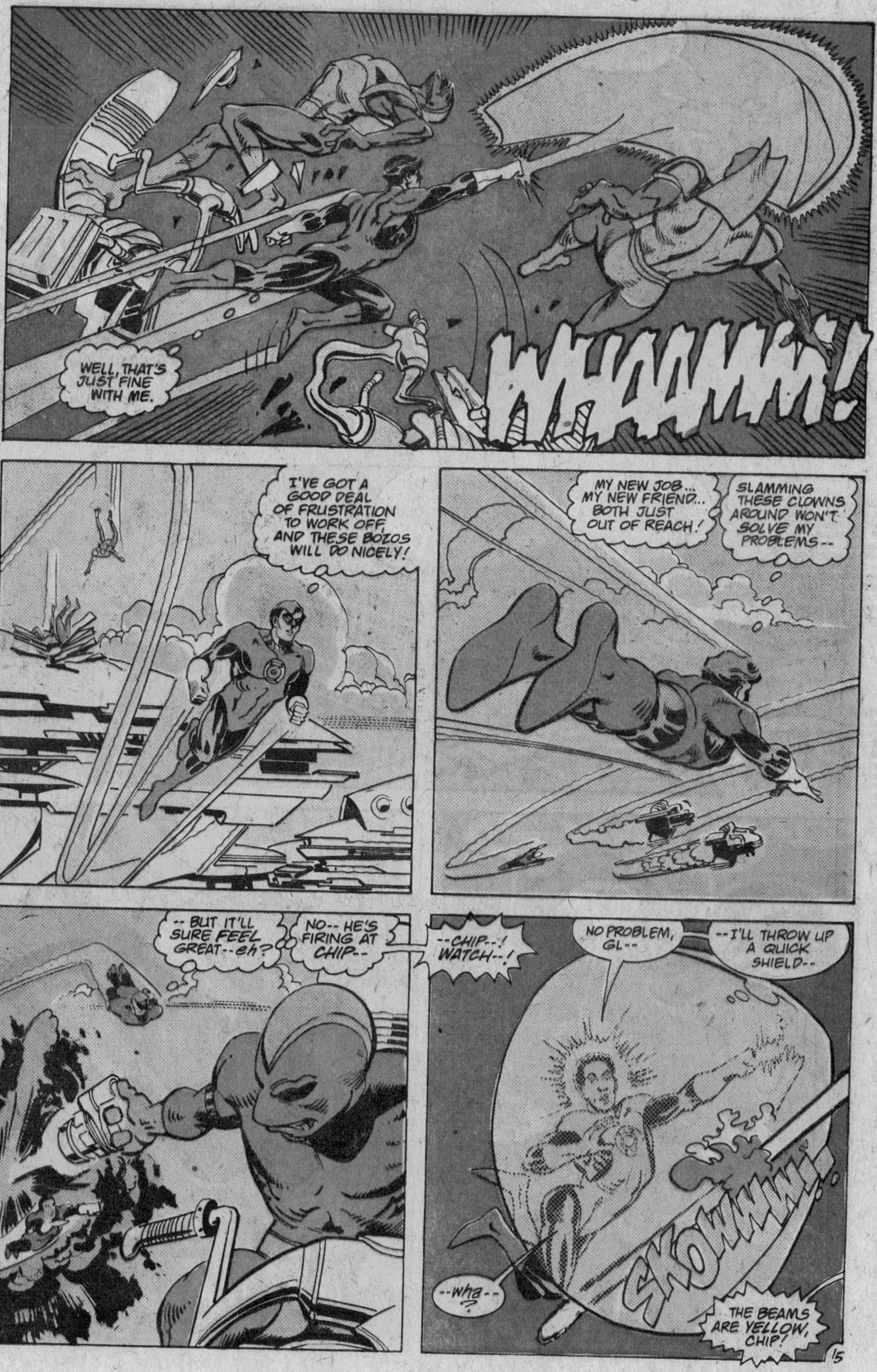
WELL, THAT'S JUST FINE WITH ME.
WHAMM!
I'VE GOT A GOOD DEAL OF FRUSTRATION TO WORK OFF, AND THESE BOZOS WILL DO NICELY!
MY NEW JOB... MY NEW FRIEND... BOTH JUST OUT OF REACH!
SLAMMING THESE CLOWNS AROUND WON'T SOLVE MY PROBLEMS--
-- BUT IT'LL SURE FEEL GREAT--eh?
NO-- HE'S FIRING AT CHIP--
--CHIP--! WATCH--!
NO PROBLEM, GL--
--I'LL THROW UP A QUICK SHIELD--
SKOWWW!
--wha--?
THE BEAMS ARE YELLOW, CHIP!
15

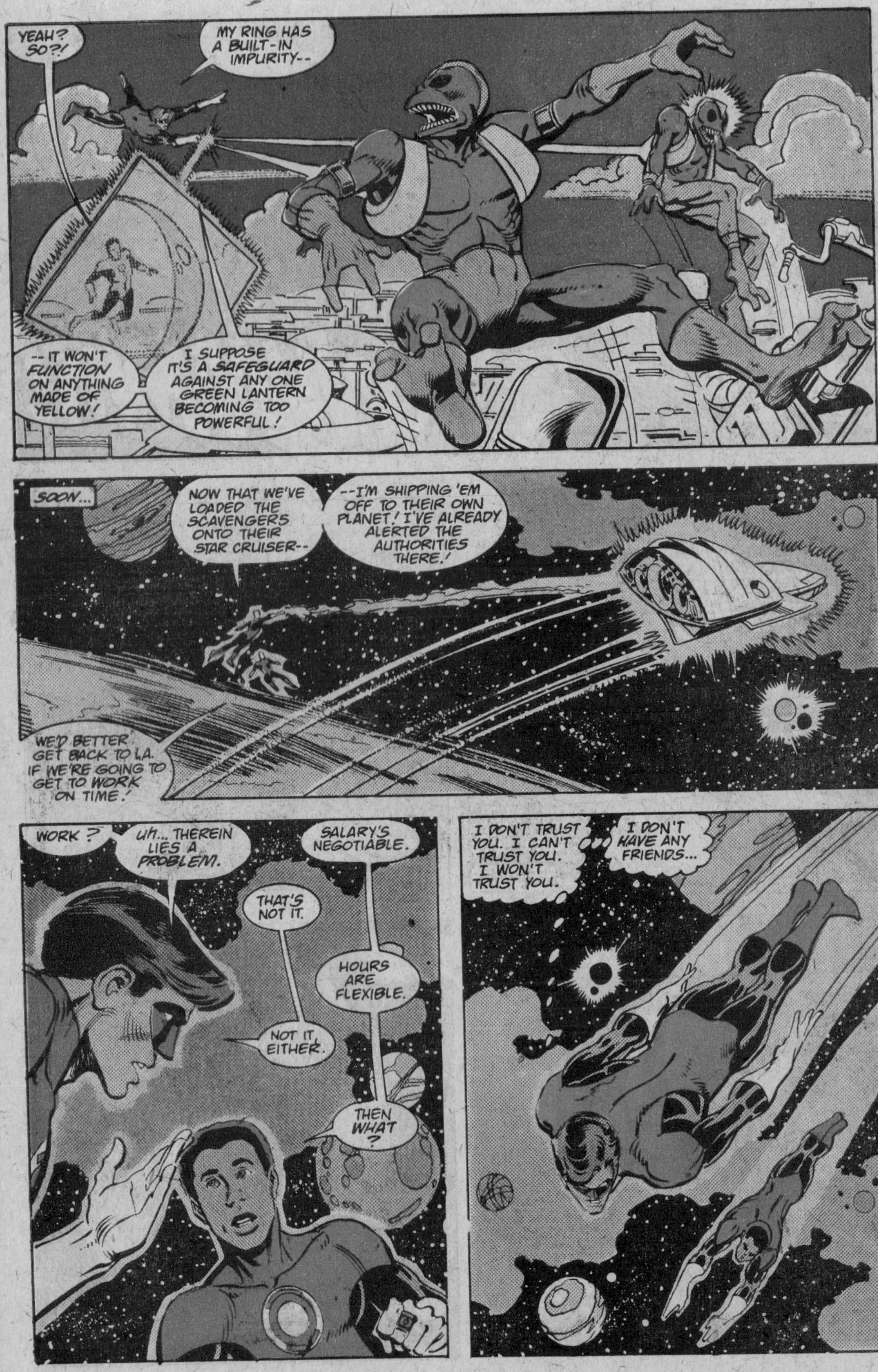
YEAH? SO?!
MY RING HAS A BUILT-IN IMPURITY--
--IT WON'T FUNCTION ON ANYTHING MADE OF YELLOW!
I SUPPOSE IT'S A SAFEGUARD AGAINST ANY ONE GREEN LANTERN BECOMING TOO POWERFUL!
SOON...
NOW THAT WE'VE LOADED THE SCAVENGERS ONTO THEIR STAR CRUISER--
--I'M SHIPPING 'EM OFF TO THEIR OWN PLANET! I'VE ALREADY ALERTED THE AUTHORITIES THERE!
WE'D BETTER GET BACK TO L.A. IF WE'RE GOING TO GET TO WORK ON TIME!
WORK?
UH... THEREIN LIES A PROBLEM.
SALARY'S NEGOTIABLE.
THAT'S NOT IT.
HOURS ARE FLEXIBLE.
NOT IT, EITHER.
THEN WHAT?
I DON'T TRUST YOU. I CAN'T TRUST YOU. I WON'T TRUST YOU.
I DON'T HAVE ANY FRIENDS...

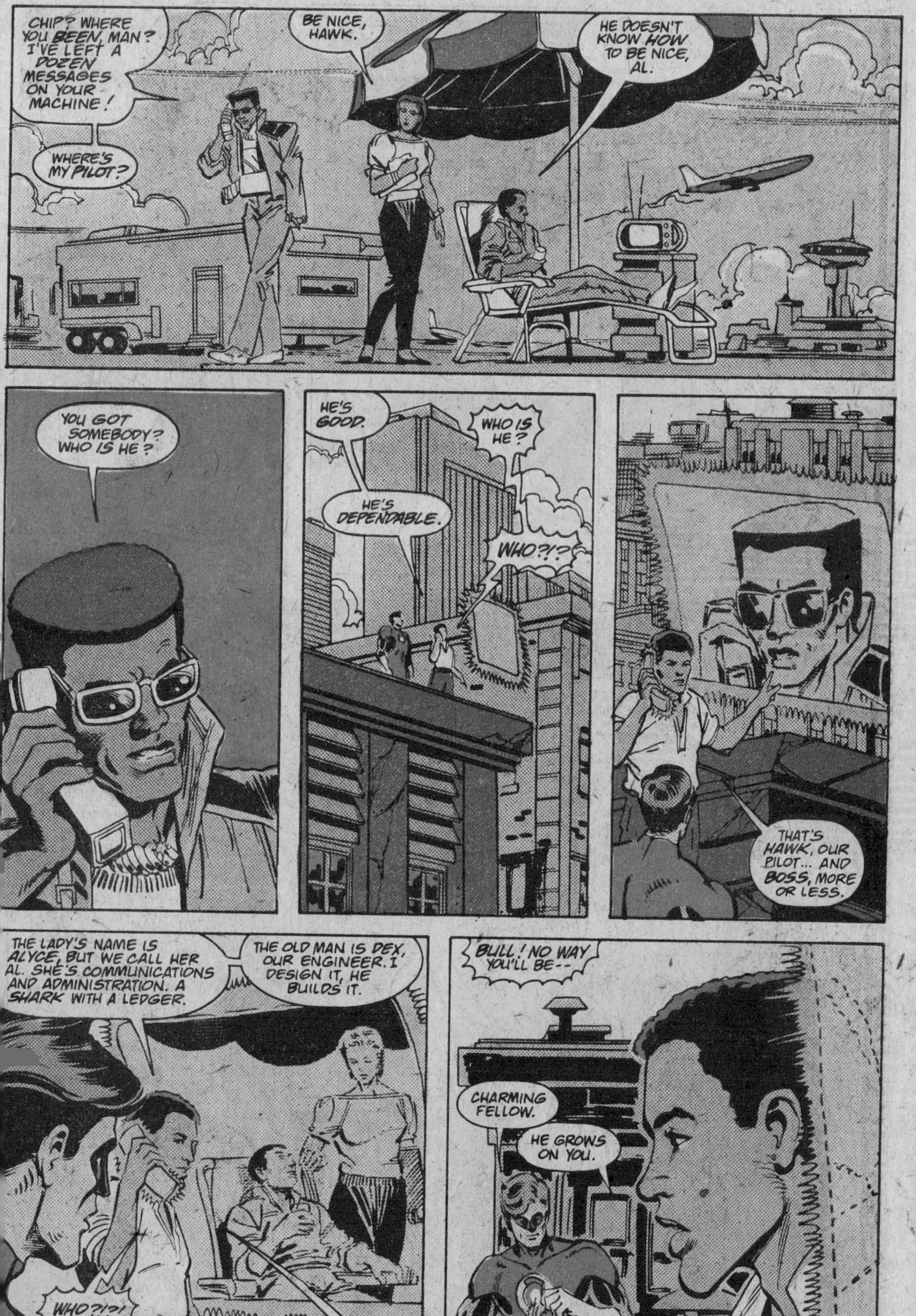
CHIP? WHERE YOU BEEN, MAN? I'VE LEFT A DOZEN MESSAGES ON YOUR MACHINE!
WHERE'S MY PILOT?
BE NICE, HAWK.
HE DOESN'T KNOW HOW TO BE NICE, AL.
YOU GOT SOMEBODY? WHO IS HE?
HE'S GOOD.
WHO IS HE?
HE'S DEPENDABLE.
WHO?!?
THAT'S HAWK, OUR PILOT... AND BOSS, MORE OR LESS.
THE LADY'S NAME IS ALYCE, BUT WE CALL HER AL. SHE'S COMMUNICATIONS AND ADMINISTRATION. A SHARK WITH A LEDGER.
THE OLD MAN IS DEX, OUR ENGINEER. I DESIGN IT, HE BUILDS IT.
WHO?!?!
WE'LL BE THERE IN TEN MINUTES, HAWK.
BULL! NO WAY YOU'LL BE--
CHARMING FELLOW.
HE GROWS ON YOU.
SO-- IF WE'RE GOING SOMEWHERE...

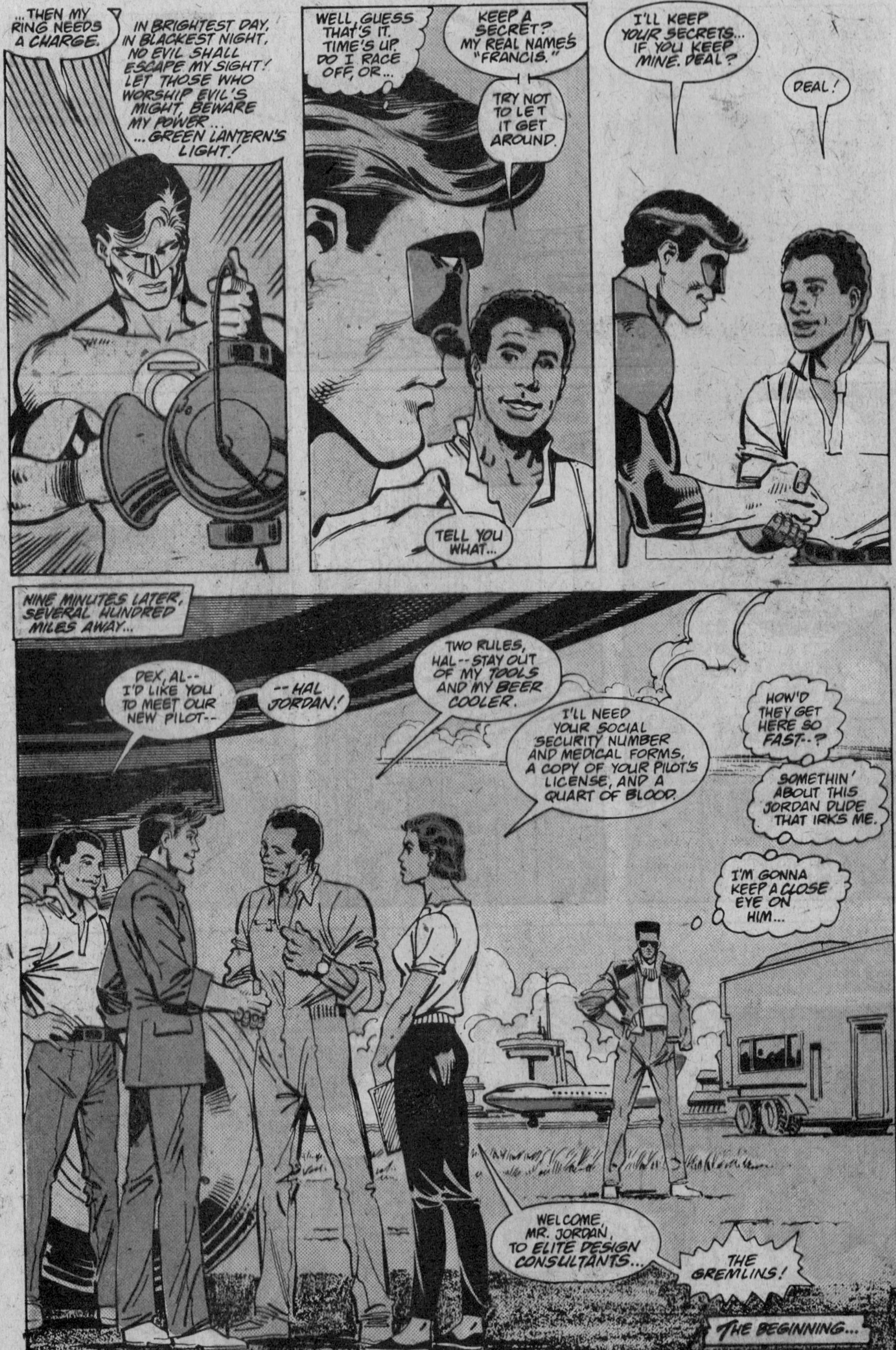
...THEN MY RING NEEDS A CHARGE.
IN BRIGHTEST DAY, IN BLACKEST NIGHT, NO EVIL SHALL ESCAPE MY SIGHT! LET THOSE WHO WORSHIP EVIL'S MIGHT, BEWARE MY POWER... ...GREEN LANTERN'S LIGHT!
WELL, GUESS THAT'S IT. TIME'S UP. DO I RACE OFF, OR...
KEEP A SECRET? MY REAL NAME'S "FRANCIS."
TRY NOT TO LET IT GET AROUND.
TELL YOU WHAT...
I'LL KEEP YOUR SECRETS... IF YOU KEEP MINE. DEAL?
DEAL!
NINE MINUTES LATER, SEVERAL HUNDRED MILES AWAY...
DEX, AL-- I'D LIKE YOU TO MEET OUR NEW PILOT--
--HAL JORDAN!
TWO RULES, HAL--STAY OUT OF MY TOOLS AND MY BEER COOLER.
I'LL NEED YOUR SOCIAL SECURITY NUMBER AND MEDICAL FORMS, A COPY OF YOUR PILOT'S LICENSE, AND A QUART OF BLOOD.
HOW'D THEY GET HERE SO FAST--?
SOMETHIN' ABOUT THIS JORDAN DUDE THAT IRKS ME.
I'M GONNA KEEP A CLOSE EYE ON HIM...
WELCOME, MR. JORDAN, TO ELITE DESIGN CONSULTANTS...
THE GREMLINS!
THE BEGINNING...

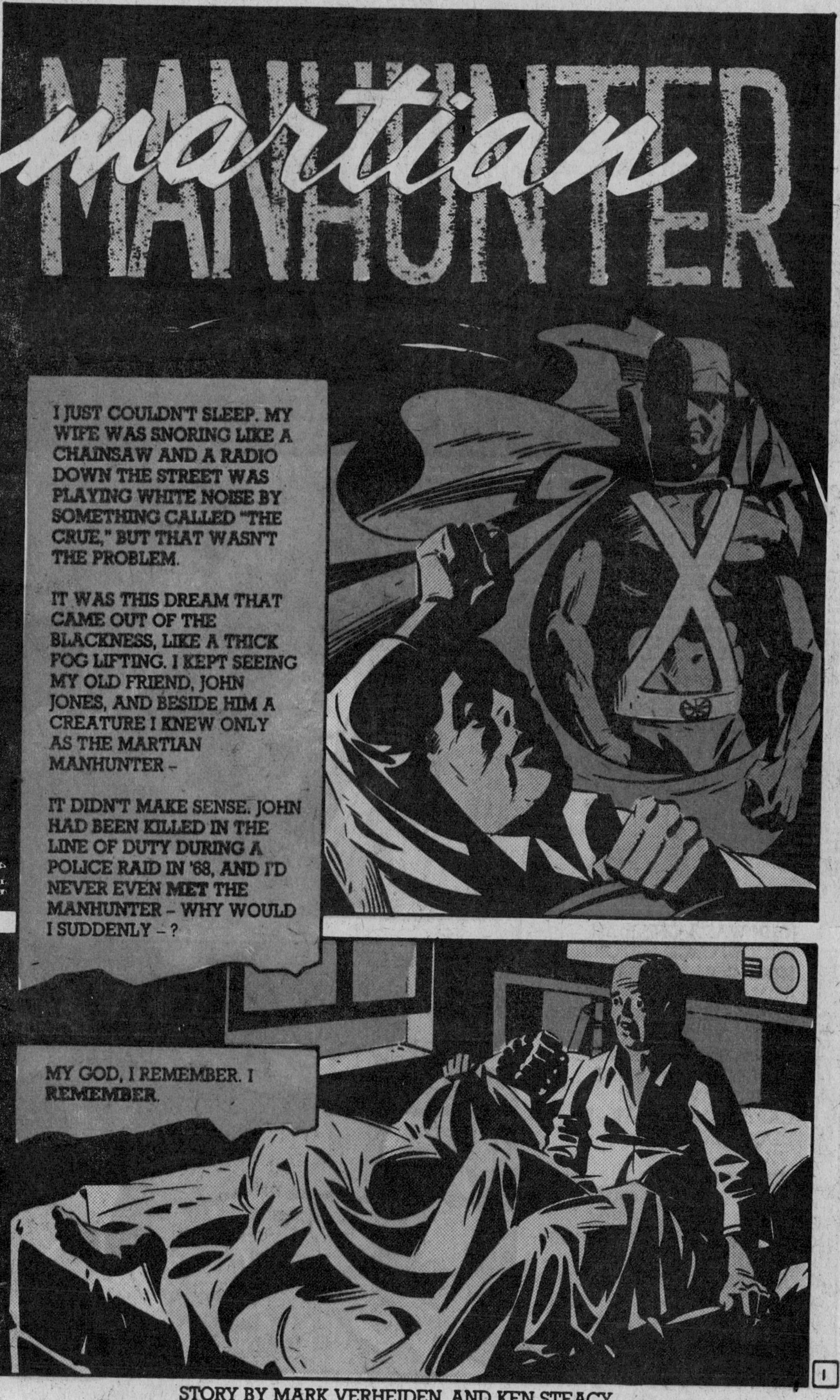
martian MANHUNTER
I JUST COULDN'T SLEEP. MY WIFE WAS SNORING LIKE A CHAINSAW AND A RADIO DOWN THE STREET WAS PLAYING WHITE NOISE BY SOMETHING CALLED "THE CRUE," BUT THAT WASN'T THE PROBLEM.
IT WAS THIS DREAM THAT CAME OUT OF THE BLACKNESS, LIKE A THICK FOG LIFTING. I KEPT SEEING MY OLD FRIEND, JOHN JONES, AND BESIDE HIM A CREATURE I KNEW ONLY AS THE MARTIAN MANHUNTER –
IT DIDN'T MAKE SENSE. JOHN HAD BEEN KILLED IN THE LINE OF DUTY DURING A POLICE RAID IN '68, AND I'D NEVER EVEN MET THE MANHUNTER – WHY WOULD I SUDDENLY – ?
MY GOD, I REMEMBER. I REMEMBER.
1

STORY BY MARK VERHEIDEN AND KEN STEACY
MARTIAN MANHUNTER CREATED BY JOE SAMACHSON AND JOE CERTA

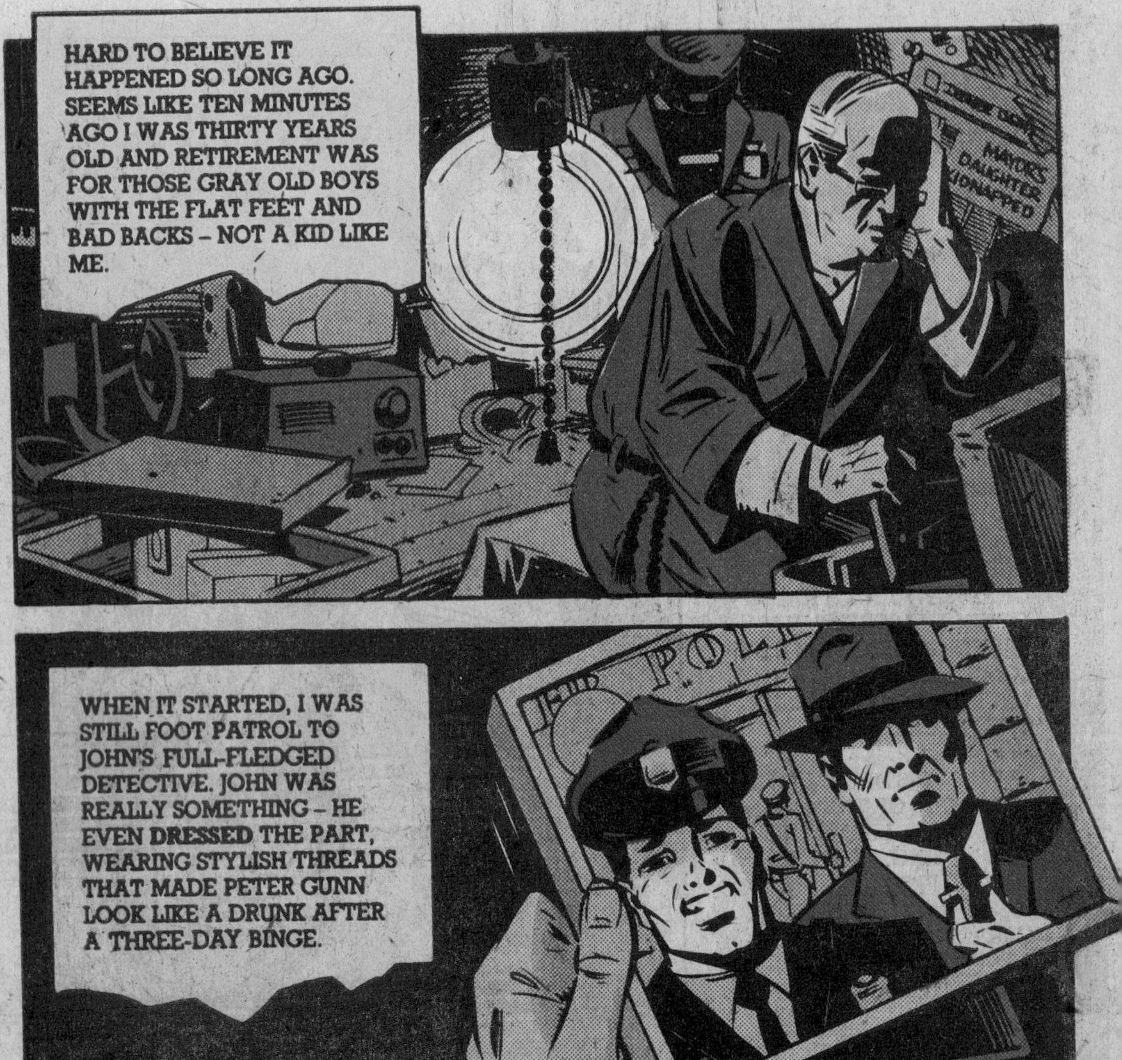
HARD TO BELIEVE IT HAPPENED SO LONG AGO. SEEMS LIKE TEN MINUTES AGO I WAS THIRTY YEARS OLD AND RETIREMENT WAS FOR THOSE GRAY OLD BOYS WITH THE FLAT FEET AND BAD BACKS – NOT A KID LIKE ME.
MAYOR'S DAUGHTER KIDNAPPED
WHEN IT STARTED, I WAS STILL FOOT PATROL TO JOHN'S FULL-FLEDGED DETECTIVE. JOHN WAS REALLY SOMETHING – HE EVEN **DRESSED** THE PART, WEARING STYLISH THREADS THAT MADE PETER GUNN LOOK LIKE A DRUNK AFTER A THREE-DAY BINGE.
JOHN WAS A ONE-MAN POLICE FORCE, NOTCHING MORE COLLARS THAN THE REST OF US COMBINED – AND MAKING IT LOOK **EASY**. HE COLLECTED COMMENDATIONS LIKE POSTAGE STAMPS AND COULD HAVE MADE CAPTAIN NO SWEAT – **IF** HE'D WANTED IT.
STRANGE, THOUGH – LOOKING BACK, I CAN NEVER REMEMBER HIM SMILING. HE ACCEPTED THE ACCOLADES AND THE AWARDS, BUT JOHN WASN'T IN IT FOR THE GLORY. THERE WAS SOMETHING ELSE –

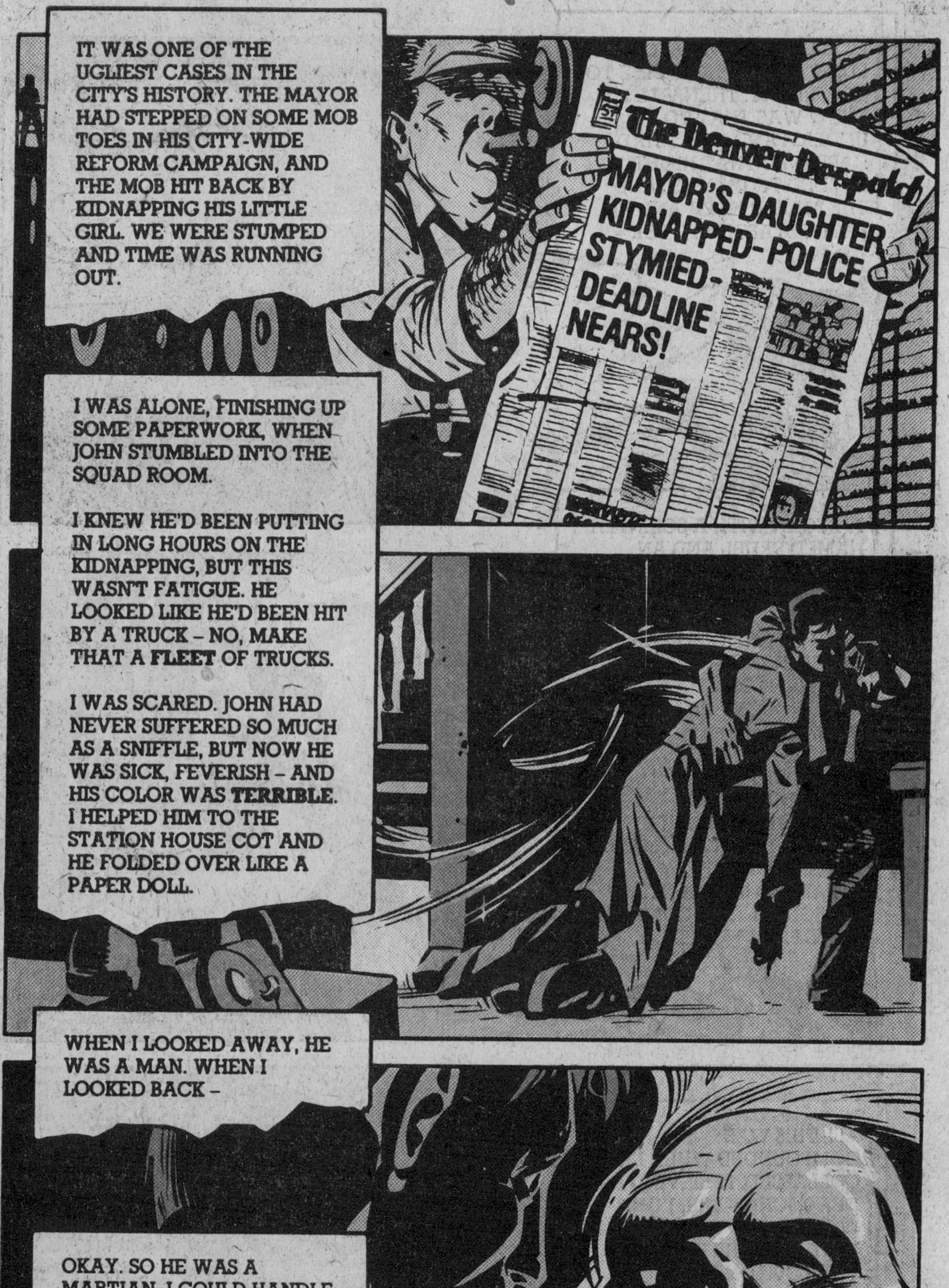
IT WAS ONE OF THE UGLIEST CASES IN THE CITY'S HISTORY. THE MAYOR HAD STEPPED ON SOME MOB TOES IN HIS CITY-WIDE REFORM CAMPAIGN, AND THE MOB HIT BACK BY KIDNAPPING HIS LITTLE GIRL. WE WERE STUMPED AND TIME WAS RUNNING OUT.
The Denver Despatch
MAYOR'S DAUGHTER KIDNAPPED-POLICE STYMIED-DEADLINE NEARS!
I WAS ALONE, FINISHING UP SOME PAPERWORK, WHEN JOHN STUMBLED INTO THE SQUAD ROOM.
I KNEW HE'D BEEN PUTTING IN LONG HOURS ON THE KIDNAPPING, BUT THIS WASN'T FATIGUE. HE LOOKED LIKE HE'D BEEN HIT BY A TRUCK – NO, MAKE THAT A **FLEET** OF TRUCKS.
I WAS SCARED. JOHN HAD NEVER SUFFERED SO MUCH AS A SNIFFLE, BUT NOW HE WAS SICK, FEVERISH – AND HIS COLOR WAS **TERRIBLE**. I HELPED HIM TO THE STATION HOUSE COT AND HE FOLDED OVER LIKE A PAPER DOLL.
WHEN I LOOKED AWAY, HE WAS A MAN. WHEN I LOOKED BACK –
OKAY. SO HE WAS A MARTIAN. I COULD HANDLE THAT. MY HEART WAS POUNDING LIKE A GENE KRUPA SOLO AND YOU COULD HAVE MISTAKEN MY EYES FOR PING-PONG BALLS, BUT A COP IS, UH, **TRAINED** TO HANDLE THE UNEXPECTED.
IT WAS ABOUT THEN THE MOVIE STARTED.
3

I CALL IT A MOVIE BECAUSE I DON'T KNOW HOW ELSE TO DESCRIBE IT. THEN, ALL I KNEW WAS THAT TO UNDERSTAND WHAT HAD HAPPENED THAT NIGHT, I NEEDED TO UNDERSTAND THE **MANHUNTER** AND HIS PAST. I STARTED TO **SEE** –

IT BEGAN WITH A SCIENTIST NAMED ERDEL AND AN EXPERIMENT GONE WILD. SEEKING TO COLLECT SPECIMENS OF NEW LIFE WITH A PARTICLE BEAM, ERDEL INSTEAD FOUND MARTIAN J'ONN J'ONZZ – AND BROUGHT HIM TO EARTH.

DR. ERDEL HADN'T EXPECTED TO FIND SENTIENT LIFE WITH HIS BEAM, WHICH WAS SMALL COMFORT TO THE STRANDED MANHUNTER. PERSONALLY, I WOULD HAVE BEEN TICKED.

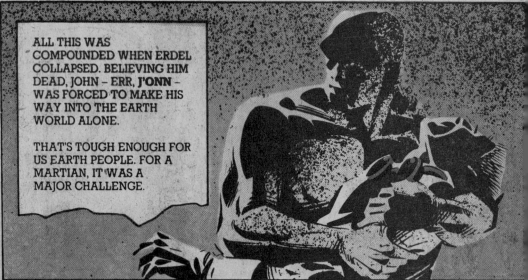

ALL THIS WAS COMPOUNDED WHEN ERDEL COLLAPSED. BELIEVING HIM DEAD, JOHN – ERR, **J'ONN** – WAS FORCED TO MAKE HIS WAY INTO THE EARTH WORLD ALONE.

THAT'S TOUGH ENOUGH FOR US EARTH PEOPLE. FOR A MARTIAN, IT WAS A MAJOR CHALLENGE.

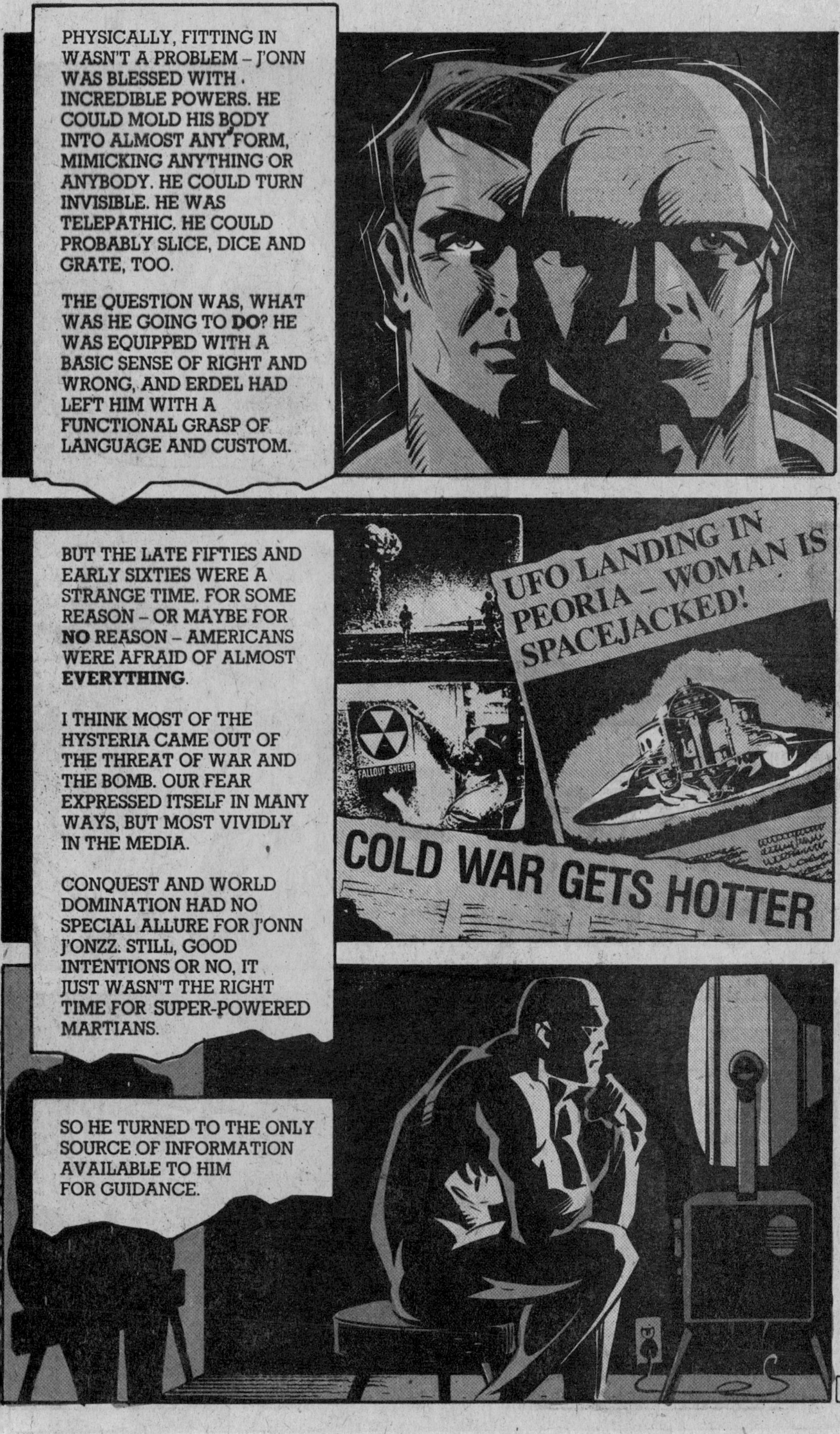
PHYSICALLY, FITTING IN WASN'T A PROBLEM – J'ONN WAS BLESSED WITH INCREDIBLE POWERS. HE COULD MOLD HIS BODY INTO ALMOST ANY FORM, MIMICKING ANYTHING OR ANYBODY. HE COULD TURN INVISIBLE. HE WAS TELEPATHIC. HE COULD PROBABLY SLICE, DICE AND GRATE, TOO.
THE QUESTION WAS, WHAT WAS HE GOING TO **DO**? HE WAS EQUIPPED WITH A BASIC SENSE OF RIGHT AND WRONG, AND ERDEL HAD LEFT HIM WITH A FUNCTIONAL GRASP OF LANGUAGE AND CUSTOM.
BUT THE LATE FIFTIES AND EARLY SIXTIES WERE A STRANGE TIME. FOR SOME REASON – OR MAYBE FOR **NO** REASON – AMERICANS WERE AFRAID OF ALMOST **EVERYTHING**.
I THINK MOST OF THE HYSTERIA CAME OUT OF THE THREAT OF WAR AND THE BOMB. OUR FEAR EXPRESSED ITSELF IN MANY WAYS, BUT MOST VIVIDLY IN THE MEDIA.
UFO LANDING IN PEORIA – WOMAN IS SPACEJACKED!
FALLOUT SHELTER
COLD WAR GETS HOTTER
CONQUEST AND WORLD DOMINATION HAD NO SPECIAL ALLURE FOR J'ONN J'ONZZ. STILL, GOOD INTENTIONS OR NO, IT JUST WASN'T THE RIGHT TIME FOR SUPER-POWERED MARTIANS.
SO HE TURNED TO THE ONLY SOURCE OF INFORMATION AVAILABLE TO HIM FOR GUIDANCE.

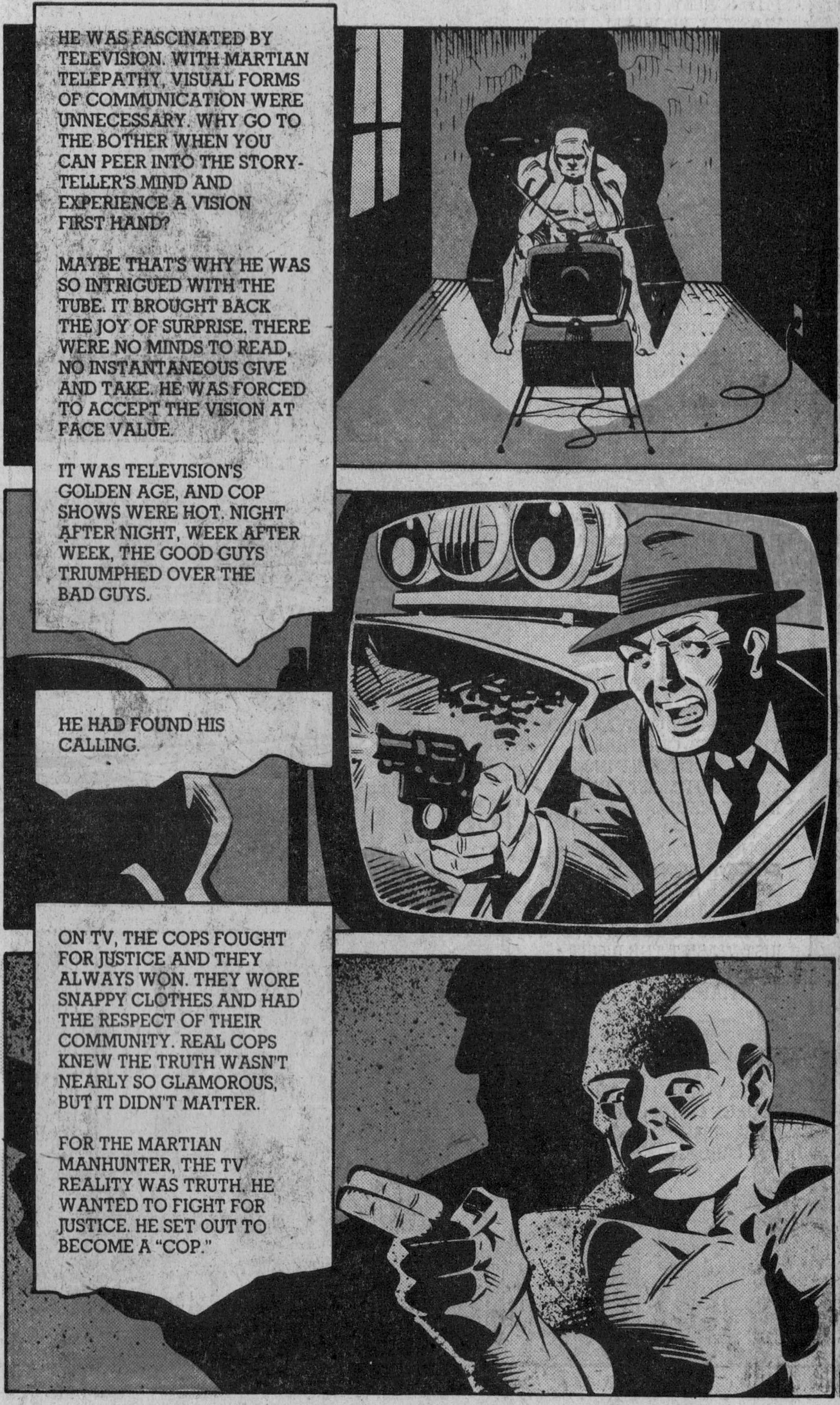
HE WAS FASCINATED BY TELEVISION. WITH MARTIAN TELEPATHY, VISUAL FORMS OF COMMUNICATION WERE UNNECESSARY. WHY GO TO THE BOTHER WHEN YOU CAN PEER INTO THE STORY-TELLER'S MIND AND EXPERIENCE A VISION FIRST HAND?
MAYBE THAT'S WHY HE WAS SO INTRIGUED WITH THE TUBE. IT BROUGHT BACK THE JOY OF SURPRISE. THERE WERE NO MINDS TO READ, NO INSTANTANEOUS GIVE AND TAKE. HE WAS FORCED TO ACCEPT THE VISION AT FACE VALUE.
IT WAS TELEVISION'S GOLDEN AGE, AND COP SHOWS WERE HOT. NIGHT AFTER NIGHT, WEEK AFTER WEEK, THE GOOD GUYS TRIUMPHED OVER THE BAD GUYS.
HE HAD FOUND HIS CALLING.
ON TV, THE COPS FOUGHT FOR JUSTICE AND THEY ALWAYS WON. THEY WORE SNAPPY CLOTHES AND HAD THE RESPECT OF THEIR COMMUNITY. REAL COPS KNEW THE TRUTH WASN'T NEARLY SO GLAMOROUS, BUT IT DIDN'T MATTER.
FOR THE MARTIAN MANHUNTER, THE TV REALITY WAS TRUTH. HE WANTED TO FIGHT FOR JUSTICE. HE SET OUT TO BECOME A "COP."

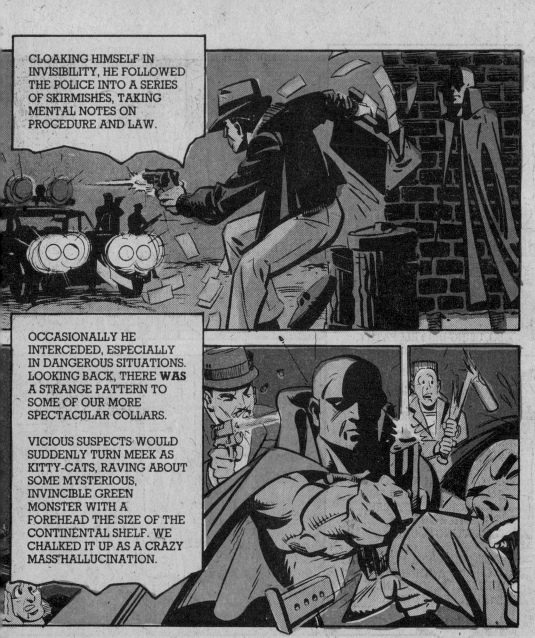

CLOAKING HIMSELF IN INVISIBILITY, HE FOLLOWED THE POLICE INTO A SERIES OF SKIRMISHES, TAKING MENTAL NOTES ON PROCEDURE AND LAW.

OCCASIONALLY HE INTERCEDED, ESPECIALLY IN DANGEROUS SITUATIONS. LOOKING BACK, THERE **WAS** A STRANGE PATTERN TO SOME OF OUR MORE SPECTACULAR COLLARS.

VICIOUS SUSPECTS WOULD SUDDENLY TURN MEEK AS KITTY-CATS, RAVING ABOUT SOME MYSTERIOUS, INVINCIBLE GREEN MONSTER WITH A FOREHEAD THE SIZE OF THE CONTINENTAL SHELF. WE CHALKED IT UP AS A CRAZY MASS HALLUCINATION.

ONE DAY, HE WAS READY.

7

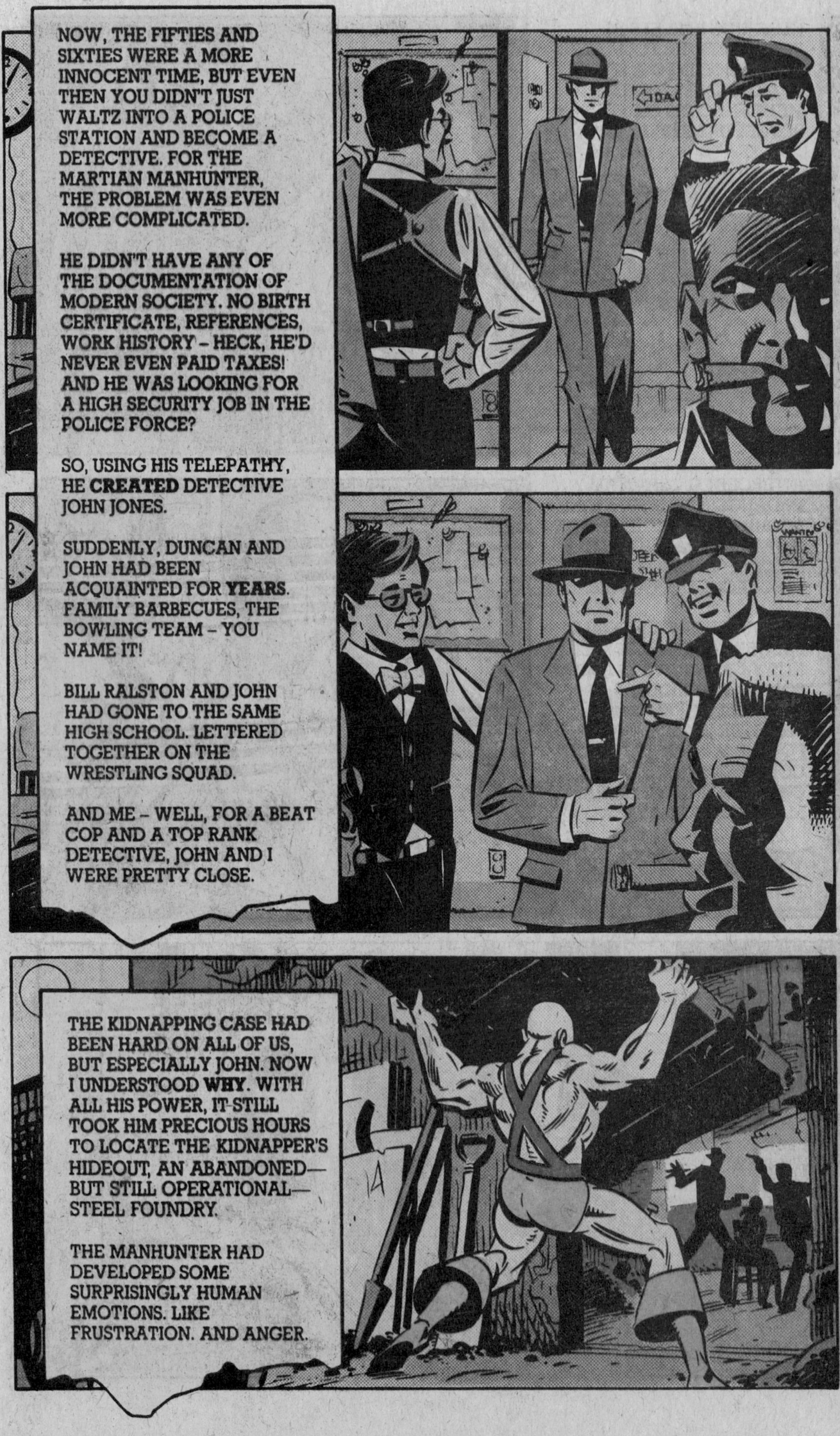
NOW, THE FIFTIES AND SIXTIES WERE A MORE INNOCENT TIME, BUT EVEN THEN YOU DIDN'T JUST WALTZ INTO A POLICE STATION AND BECOME A DETECTIVE. FOR THE MARTIAN MANHUNTER, THE PROBLEM WAS EVEN MORE COMPLICATED.
HE DIDN'T HAVE ANY OF THE DOCUMENTATION OF MODERN SOCIETY. NO BIRTH CERTIFICATE, REFERENCES, WORK HISTORY – HECK, HE'D NEVER EVEN PAID TAXES! AND HE WAS LOOKING FOR A HIGH SECURITY JOB IN THE POLICE FORCE?
SO, USING HIS TELEPATHY, HE **CREATED** DETECTIVE JOHN JONES.
SUDDENLY, DUNCAN AND JOHN HAD BEEN ACQUAINTED FOR **YEARS**. FAMILY BARBECUES, THE BOWLING TEAM – YOU NAME IT!
BILL RALSTON AND JOHN HAD GONE TO THE SAME HIGH SCHOOL. LETTERED TOGETHER ON THE WRESTLING SQUAD.
AND ME – WELL, FOR A BEAT COP AND A TOP RANK DETECTIVE, JOHN AND I WERE PRETTY CLOSE.
THE KIDNAPPING CASE HAD BEEN HARD ON ALL OF US, BUT ESPECIALLY JOHN. NOW I UNDERSTOOD **WHY**. WITH ALL HIS POWER, IT STILL TOOK HIM PRECIOUS HOURS TO LOCATE THE KIDNAPPER'S HIDEOUT, AN ABANDONED— BUT STILL OPERATIONAL— STEEL FOUNDRY.
THE MANHUNTER HAD DEVELOPED SOME SURPRISINGLY HUMAN EMOTIONS. LIKE FRUSTRATION. AND ANGER.

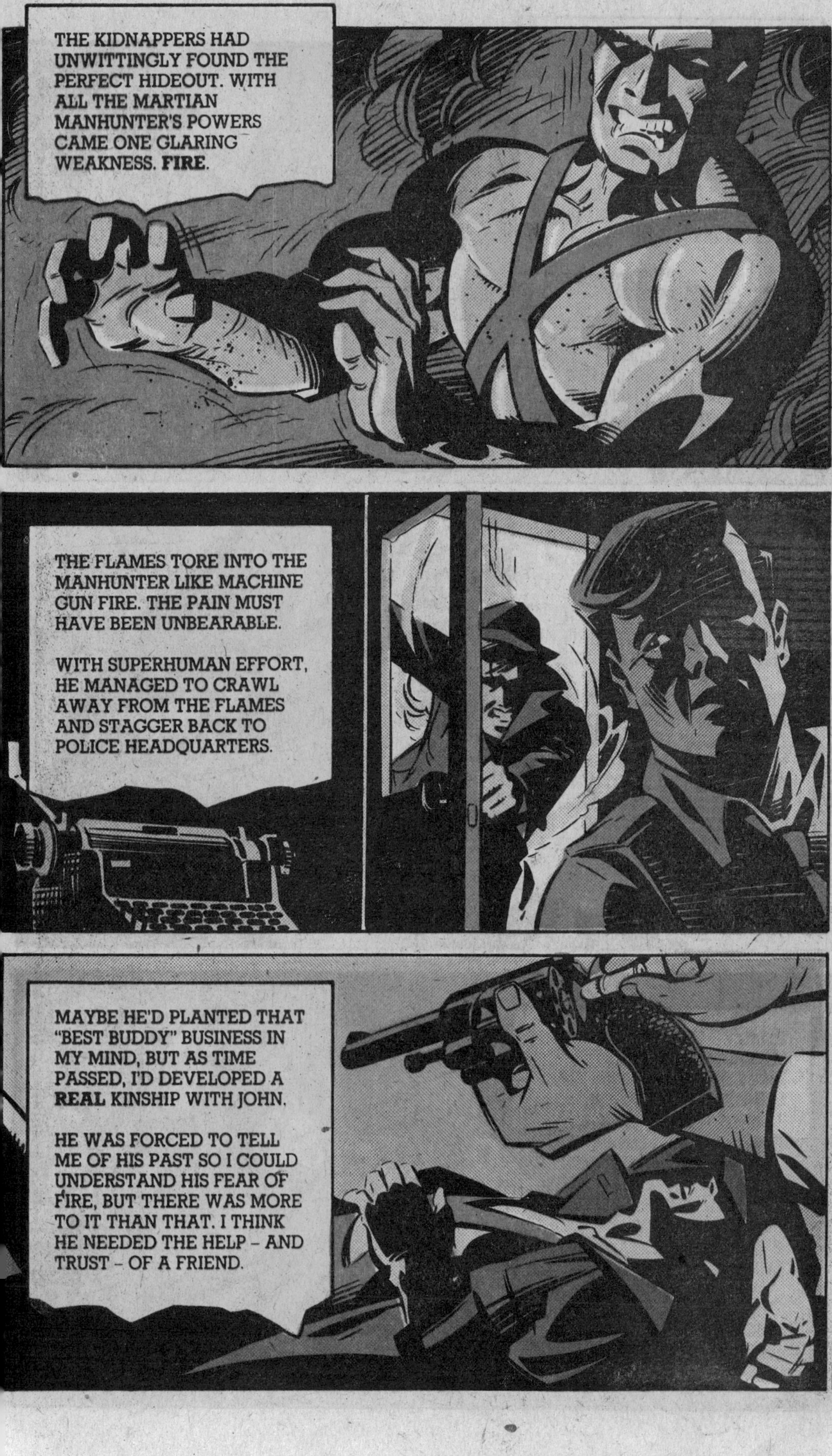
THE KIDNAPPERS HAD UNWITTINGLY FOUND THE PERFECT HIDEOUT. WITH ALL THE MARTIAN MANHUNTER'S POWERS CAME ONE GLARING WEAKNESS. FIRE.
THE FLAMES TORE INTO THE MANHUNTER LIKE MACHINE GUN FIRE. THE PAIN MUST HAVE BEEN UNBEARABLE.
WITH SUPERHUMAN EFFORT, HE MANAGED TO CRAWL AWAY FROM THE FLAMES AND STAGGER BACK TO POLICE HEADQUARTERS.
MAYBE HE'D PLANTED THAT "BEST BUDDY" BUSINESS IN MY MIND, BUT AS TIME PASSED, I'D DEVELOPED A REAL KINSHIP WITH JOHN.
HE WAS FORCED TO TELL ME OF HIS PAST SO I COULD UNDERSTAND HIS FEAR OF FIRE, BUT THERE WAS MORE TO IT THAN THAT. I THINK HE NEEDED THE HELP – AND TRUST – OF A FRIEND.

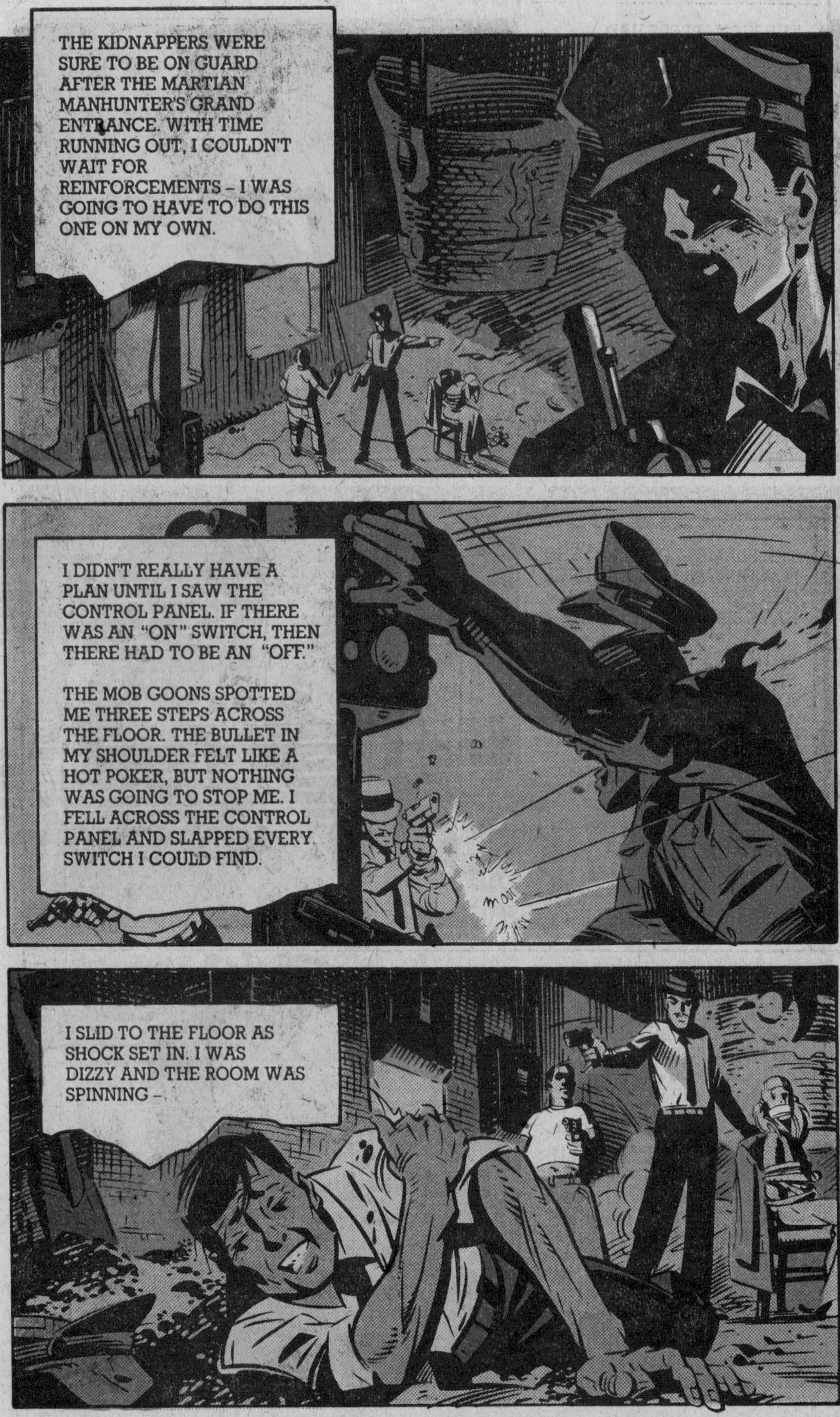
THE KIDNAPPERS WERE SURE TO BE ON GUARD AFTER THE MARTIAN MANHUNTER'S GRAND ENTRANCE. WITH TIME RUNNING OUT, I COULDN'T WAIT FOR REINFORCEMENTS – I WAS GOING TO HAVE TO DO THIS ONE ON MY OWN.
I DIDN'T REALLY HAVE A PLAN UNTIL I SAW THE CONTROL PANEL. IF THERE WAS AN "ON" SWITCH, THEN THERE HAD TO BE AN "OFF."
THE MOB GOONS SPOTTED ME THREE STEPS ACROSS THE FLOOR. THE BULLET IN MY SHOULDER FELT LIKE A HOT POKER, BUT NOTHING WAS GOING TO STOP ME. I FELL ACROSS THE CONTROL PANEL AND SLAPPED EVERY SWITCH I COULD FIND.
I SLID TO THE FLOOR AS SHOCK SET IN. I WAS DIZZY AND THE ROOM WAS SPINNING –

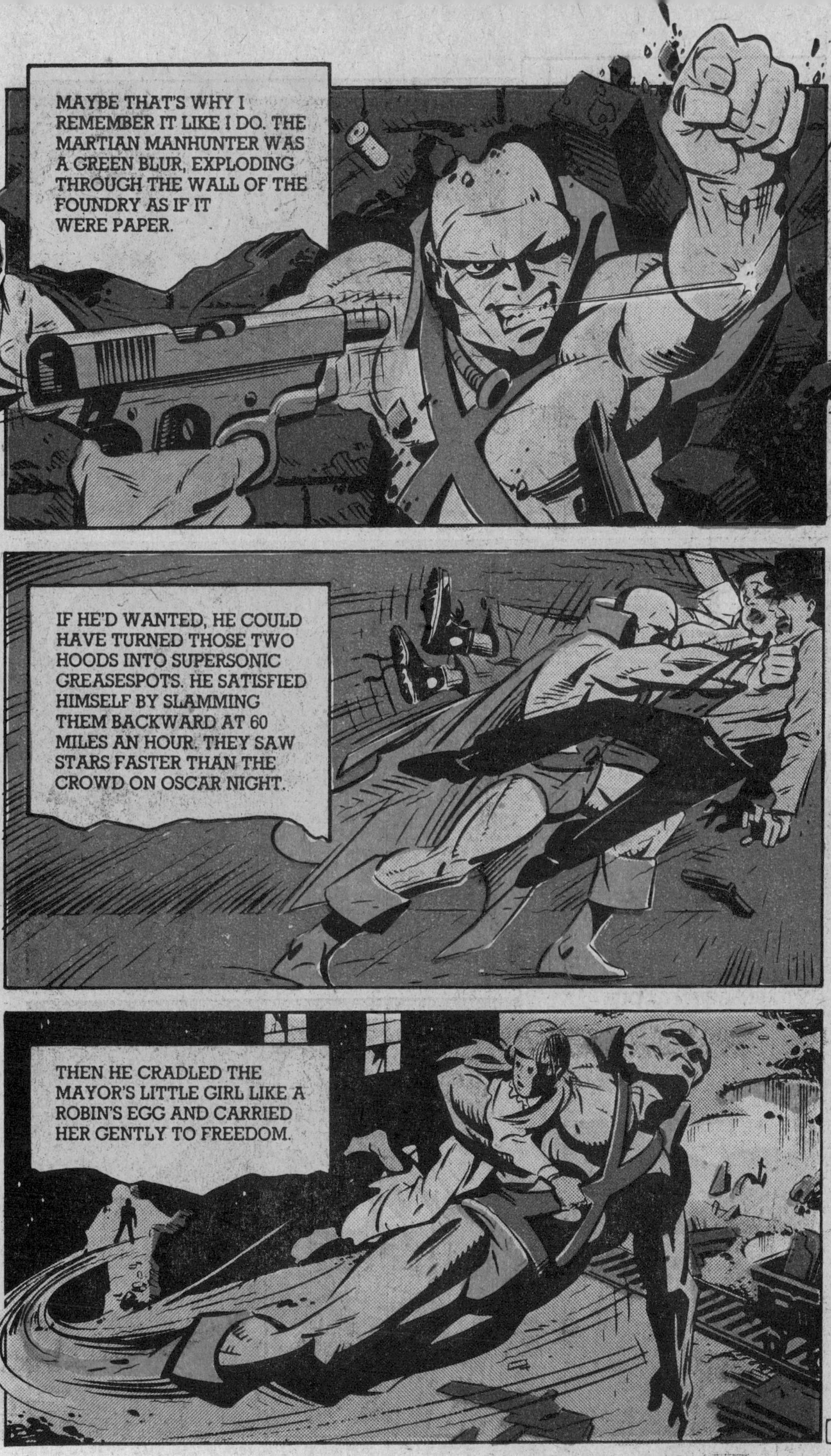
MAYBE THAT'S WHY I REMEMBER IT LIKE I DO. THE MARTIAN MANHUNTER WAS A GREEN BLUR, EXPLODING THROUGH THE WALL OF THE FOUNDRY AS IF IT WERE PAPER.
IF HE'D WANTED, HE COULD HAVE TURNED THOSE TWO HOODS INTO SUPERSONIC GREASESPOTS. HE SATISFIED HIMSELF BY SLAMMING THEM BACKWARD AT 60 MILES AN HOUR. THEY SAW STARS FASTER THAN THE CROWD ON OSCAR NIGHT.
THEN HE CRADLED THE MAYOR'S LITTLE GIRL LIKE A ROBIN'S EGG AND CARRIED HER GENTLY TO FREEDOM.

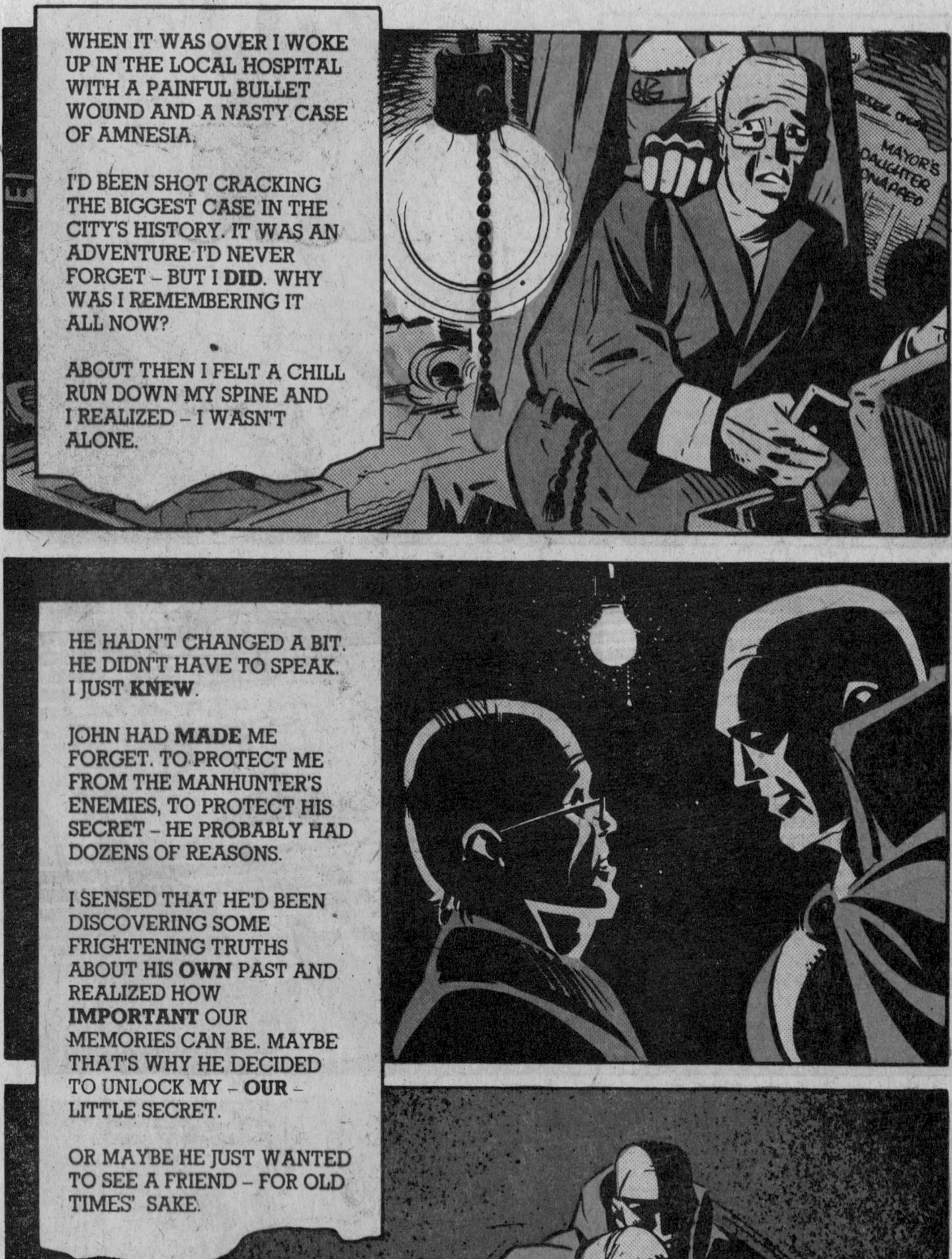
WHEN IT WAS OVER I WOKE UP IN THE LOCAL HOSPITAL WITH A PAINFUL BULLET WOUND AND A NASTY CASE OF AMNESIA.
I'D BEEN SHOT CRACKING THE BIGGEST CASE IN THE CITY'S HISTORY. IT WAS AN ADVENTURE I'D NEVER FORGET – BUT I **DID**. WHY WAS I REMEMBERING IT ALL NOW?
ABOUT THEN I FELT A CHILL RUN DOWN MY SPINE AND I REALIZED – I WASN'T ALONE.
HE HADN'T CHANGED A BIT. HE DIDN'T HAVE TO SPEAK. I JUST **KNEW**.
JOHN HAD **MADE** ME FORGET. TO PROTECT ME FROM THE MANHUNTER'S ENEMIES, TO PROTECT HIS SECRET – HE PROBABLY HAD DOZENS OF REASONS.
I SENSED THAT HE'D BEEN DISCOVERING SOME FRIGHTENING TRUTHS ABOUT HIS **OWN** PAST AND REALIZED HOW **IMPORTANT** OUR MEMORIES CAN BE. MAYBE THAT'S WHY HE DECIDED TO UNLOCK MY – **OUR** – LITTLE SECRET.
OR MAYBE HE JUST WANTED TO SEE A FRIEND – FOR OLD TIMES' SAKE.
MY GOD, I **REMEMBER**. AND SO DOES **HE**.

FLASH FACTS

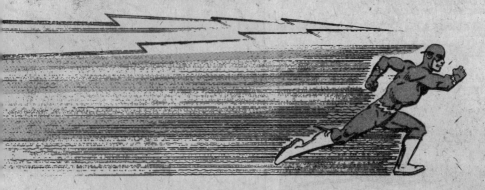

THE FASTER AN OBJECT TRAVELS, THE MORE ITS MASS INCREASES -- UNTIL AT THE SPEED OF LIGHT (186,000 MILES A SECOND) ITS MASS BECOMES INFINITE AND THE OBJECT CAN'T MOVE AT ALL...

HOWEVER, SCIENTISTS HAVE SPECULATED ABOUT THE POSSIBLE EXISTENCE OF A SUBATOMIC PARTICLE THEY CALL THE TACHYON. JUST AS AN ORDINARY PARTICLE SUCH AS AN ELECTRON CAN EXIST ONLY AT SPEEDS LESS THAN THAT OF LIGHT, SO A TACHYON COULD EXIST ONLY AT SPEEDS MORE THAN THAT OF LIGHT...

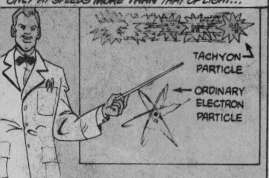

TACHYON PARTICLE

ORDINARY ELECTRON PARTICLE

ONE THEORY HAS IT THAT TACHYONS MOVE SO QUICKLY THAT THEY ARE ACTUALLY PASSING BACKWARD THROUGH TIME!

Flash Comics

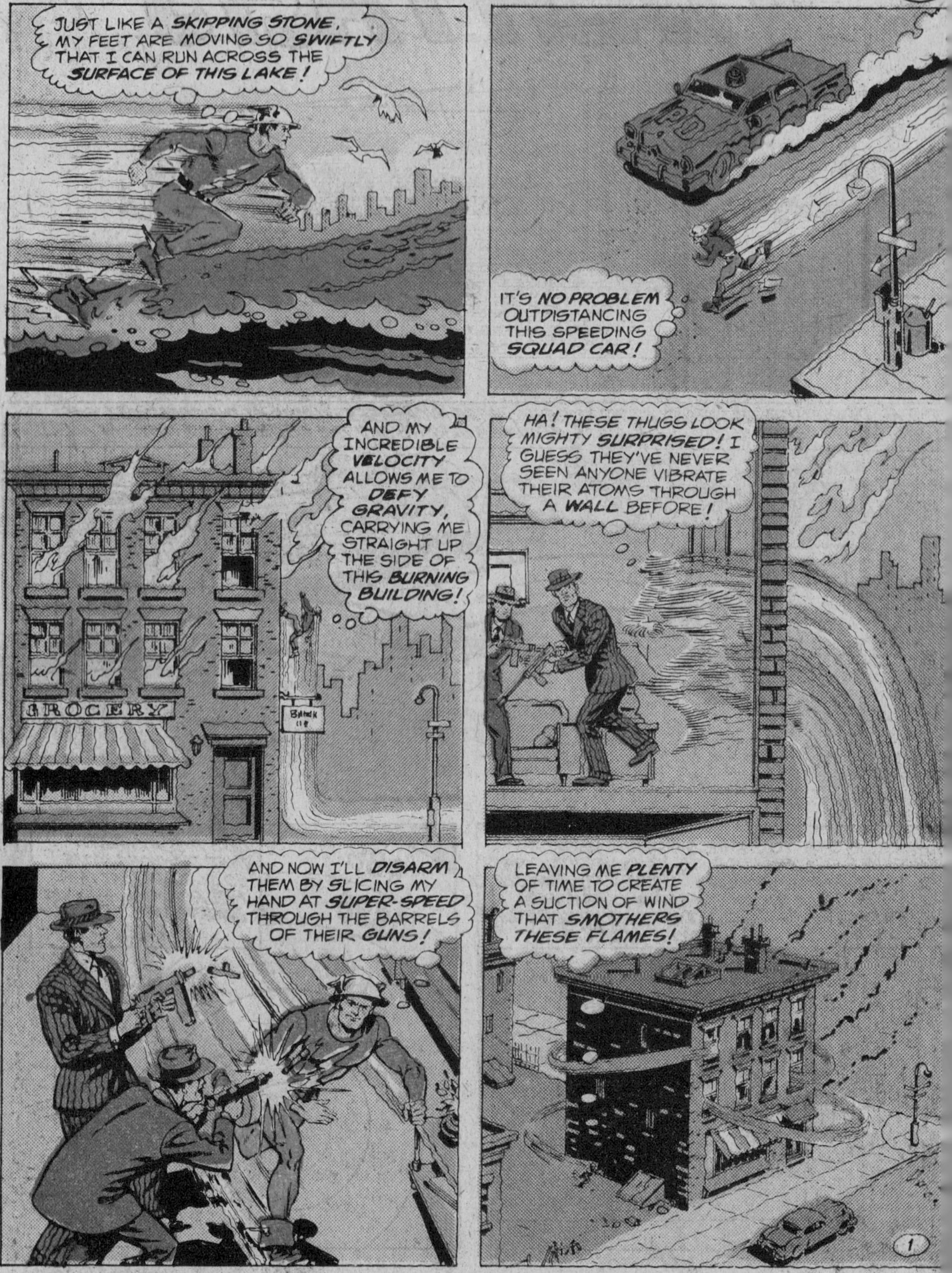
JUST LIKE A SKIPPING STONE, MY FEET ARE MOVING SO SWIFTLY THAT I CAN RUN ACROSS THE SURFACE OF THIS LAKE!
IT'S NO PROBLEM OUTDISTANCING THIS SPEEDING SQUAD CAR!
PD
AND MY INCREDIBLE VELOCITY ALLOWS ME TO DEFY GRAVITY, CARRYING ME STRAIGHT UP THE SIDE OF THIS BURNING BUILDING!
GROCERY
HA! THESE THUGS LOOK MIGHTY SURPRISED! I GUESS THEY'VE NEVER SEEN ANYONE VIBRATE THEIR ATOMS THROUGH A WALL BEFORE!
AND NOW I'LL DISARM THEM BY SLICING MY HAND AT SUPER-SPEED THROUGH THE BARRELS OF THEIR GUNS!
LEAVING ME PLENTY OF TIME TO CREATE A SUCTION OF WIND THAT SMOTHERS THESE FLAMES!
1

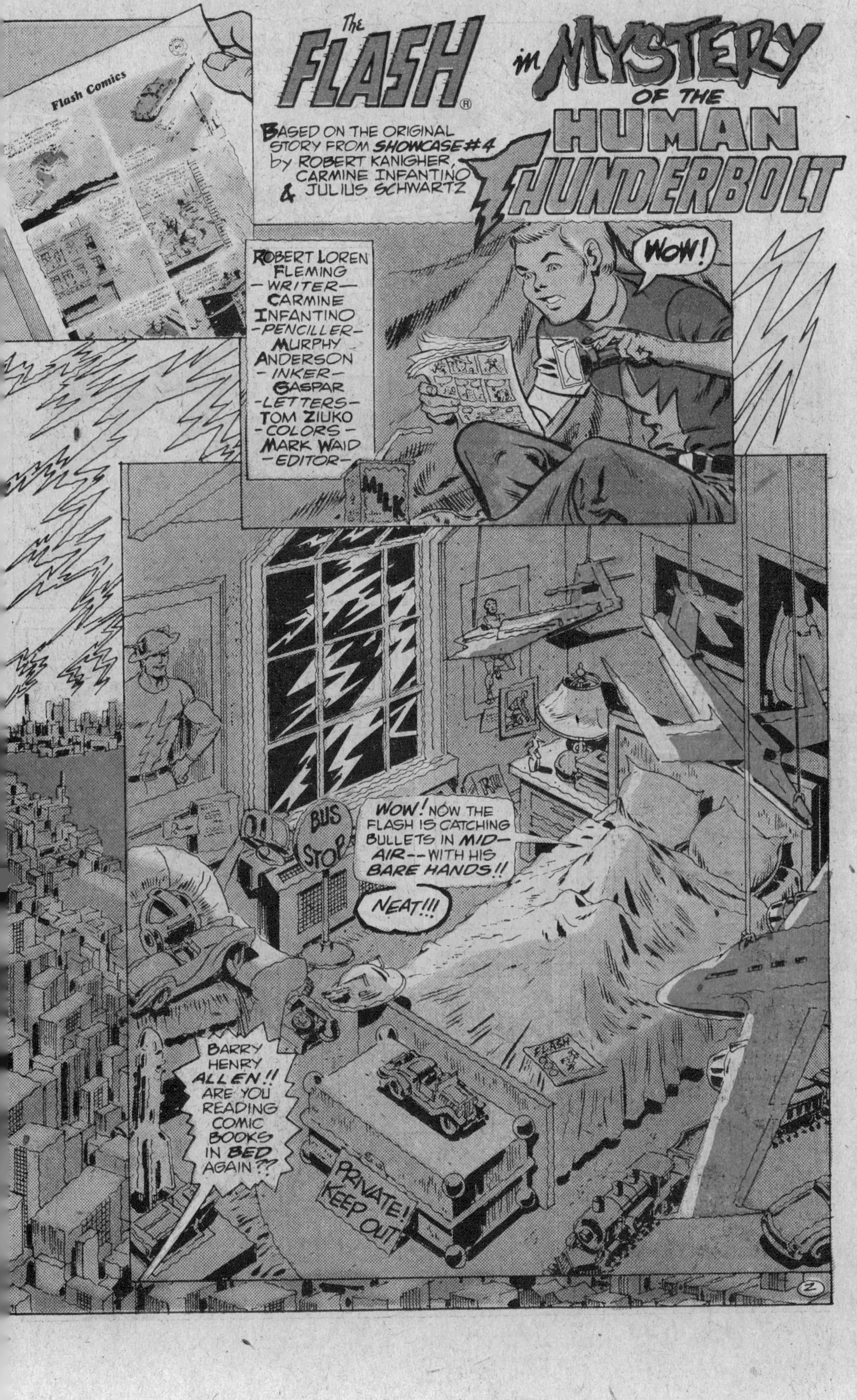
Flash Comics
The FLASH® in MYSTERY OF THE HUMAN THUNDERBOLT
BASED ON THE ORIGINAL STORY FROM SHOWCASE #4 by ROBERT KANIGHER, CARMINE INFANTINO & JULIUS SCHWARTZ
ROBERT LOREN FLEMING -WRITER- CARMINE INFANTINO -PENCILLER- MURPHY ANDERSON -INKER- GASPAR -LETTERS- TOM ZIUKO -COLORS- MARK WAID -EDITOR-
WOW!
MILK
WOW! NOW THE FLASH IS CATCHING BULLETS IN MID-AIR--WITH HIS BARE HANDS!!
NEAT!!!
BUS STOP
BARRY HENRY ALLEN!! ARE YOU READING COMIC BOOKS IN BED AGAIN??
PRIVATE! KEEP OUT
FLASH
2

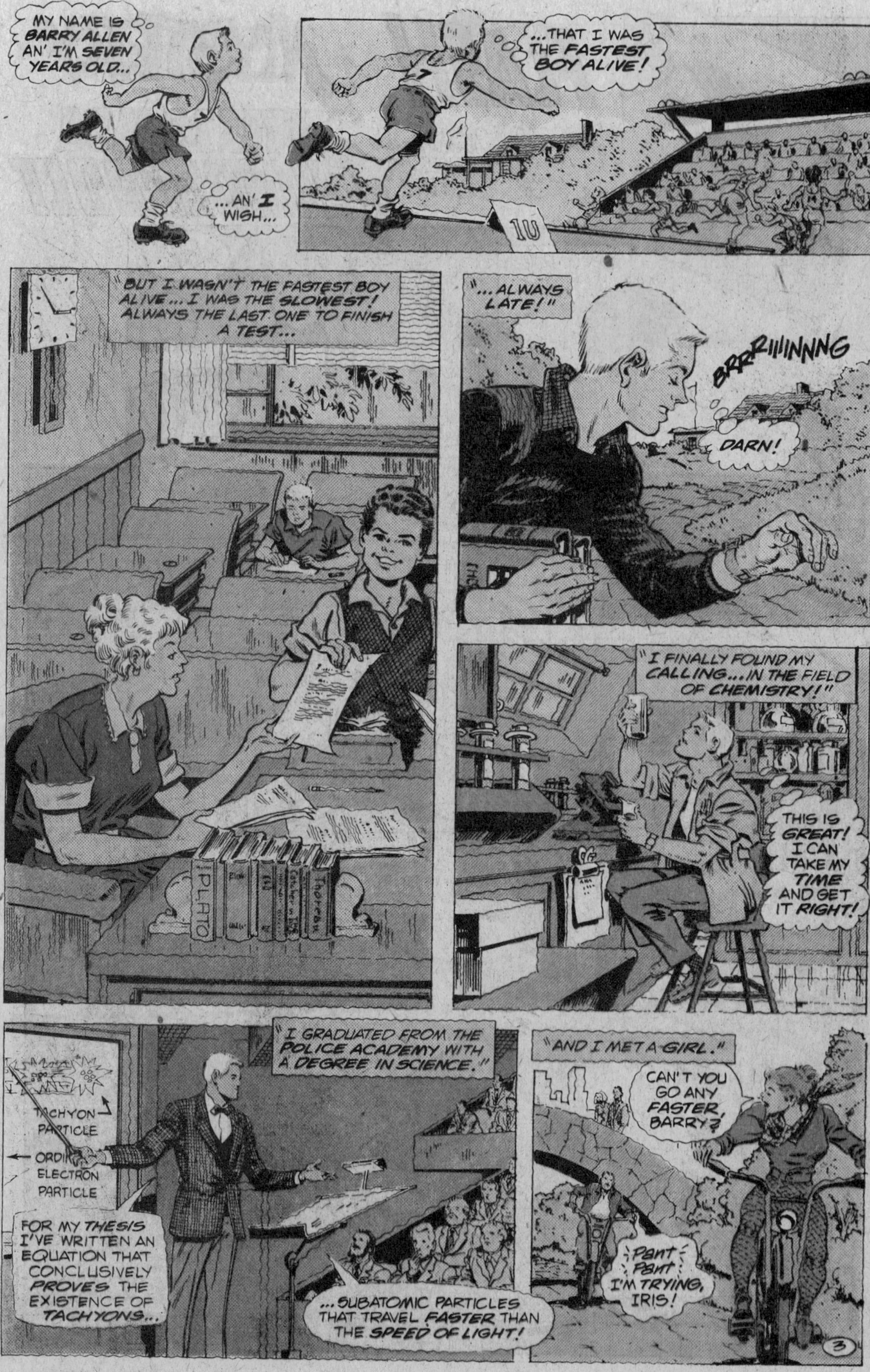
MY NAME IS BARRY ALLEN AN' I'M SEVEN YEARS OLD...
...AN' I WISH...
...THAT I WAS THE FASTEST BOY ALIVE!
1U
"BUT I WASN'T THE FASTEST BOY ALIVE... I WAS THE SLOWEST! ALWAYS THE LAST ONE TO FINISH A TEST...
PLATO
"...ALWAYS LATE!"
BRRRIIIINNNG
DARN!
"I FINALLY FOUND MY CALLING... IN THE FIELD OF CHEMISTRY!"
THIS IS GREAT! I CAN TAKE MY TIME AND GET IT RIGHT!
"I GRADUATED FROM THE POLICE ACADEMY WITH A DEGREE IN SCIENCE."
TACHYON PARTICLE
ORDIN
ELECTRON PARTICLE
FOR MY THESIS I'VE WRITTEN AN EQUATION THAT CONCLUSIVELY PROVES THE EXISTENCE OF TACHYONS...
...SUBATOMIC PARTICLES THAT TRAVEL FASTER THAN THE SPEED OF LIGHT!
"AND I MET A GIRL."
CAN'T YOU GO ANY FASTER, BARRY?
Pant Pant I'M TRYING, IRIS!

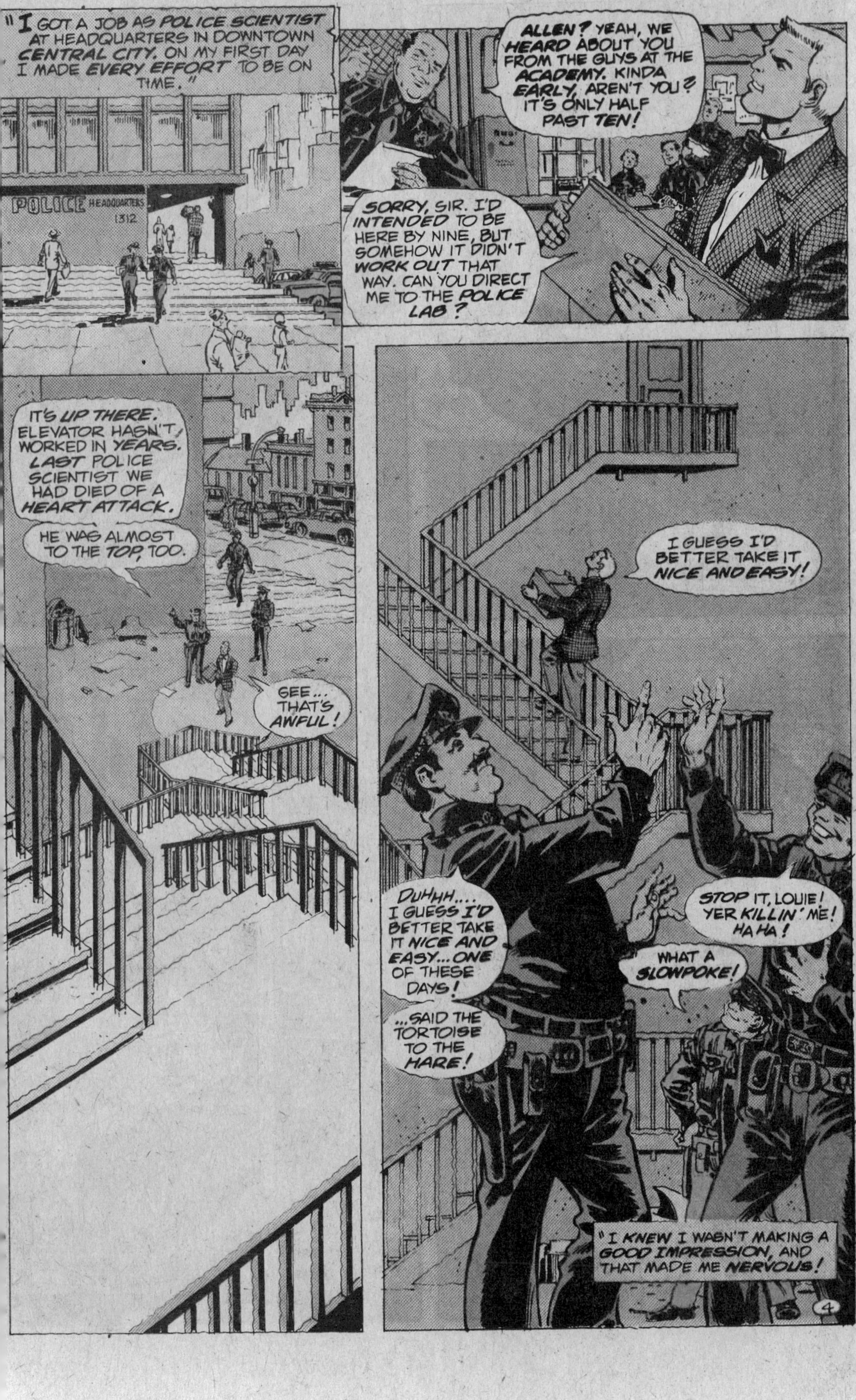
"I GOT A JOB AS POLICE SCIENTIST AT HEADQUARTERS IN DOWNTOWN CENTRAL CITY. ON MY FIRST DAY I MADE EVERY EFFORT TO BE ON TIME."
POLICE HEADQUARTERS
1312
ALLEN? YEAH, WE HEARD ABOUT YOU FROM THE GUYS AT THE ACADEMY. KINDA EARLY, AREN'T YOU? IT'S ONLY HALF PAST TEN!
SORRY, SIR. I'D INTENDED TO BE HERE BY NINE, BUT SOMEHOW IT DIDN'T WORK OUT THAT WAY. CAN YOU DIRECT ME TO THE POLICE LAB?
IT'S UP THERE. ELEVATOR HASN'T WORKED IN YEARS. LAST POLICE SCIENTIST WE HAD DIED OF A HEART ATTACK.
HE WAS ALMOST TO THE TOP, TOO.
GEE... THAT'S AWFUL!
I GUESS I'D BETTER TAKE IT NICE AND EASY!
DUHHH.... I GUESS I'D BETTER TAKE IT NICE AND EASY... ONE OF THESE DAYS!
...SAID THE TORTOISE TO THE HARE!
STOP IT, LOUIE! YER KILLIN' ME! HA HA!
WHAT A SLOWPOKE!
"I KNEW I WASN'T MAKING A GOOD IMPRESSION, AND THAT MADE ME NERVOUS!"

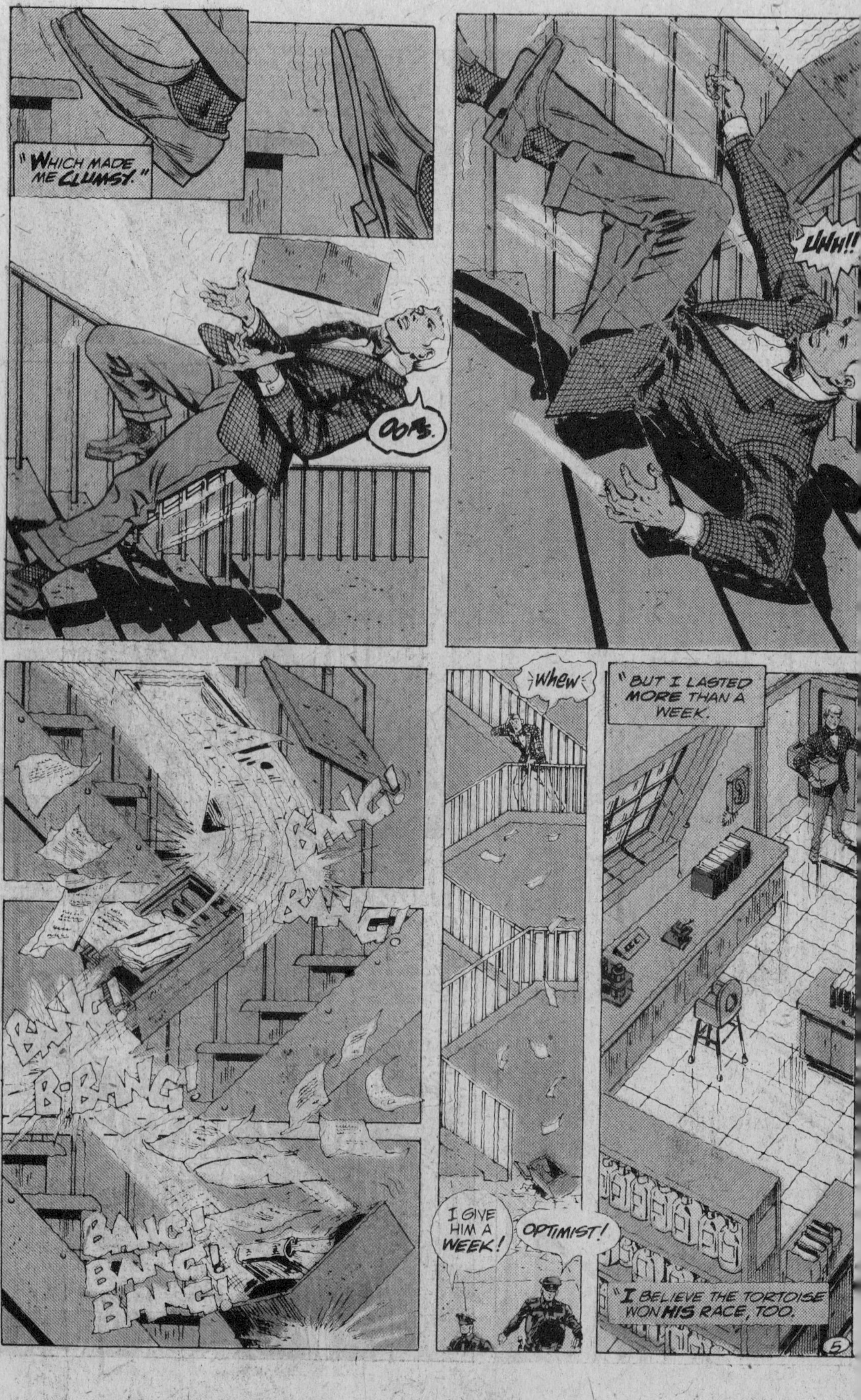
"WHICH MADE ME CLUMSY."
OOPS.
UWH!!
BANG!
BANG!
B-B-BANG!
BANG! BANG! BANG!
whew
I GIVE HIM A WEEK!
OPTIMIST!
"BUT I LASTED MORE THAN A WEEK.
"I BELIEVE THE TORTOISE WON HIS RACE, TOO.
5

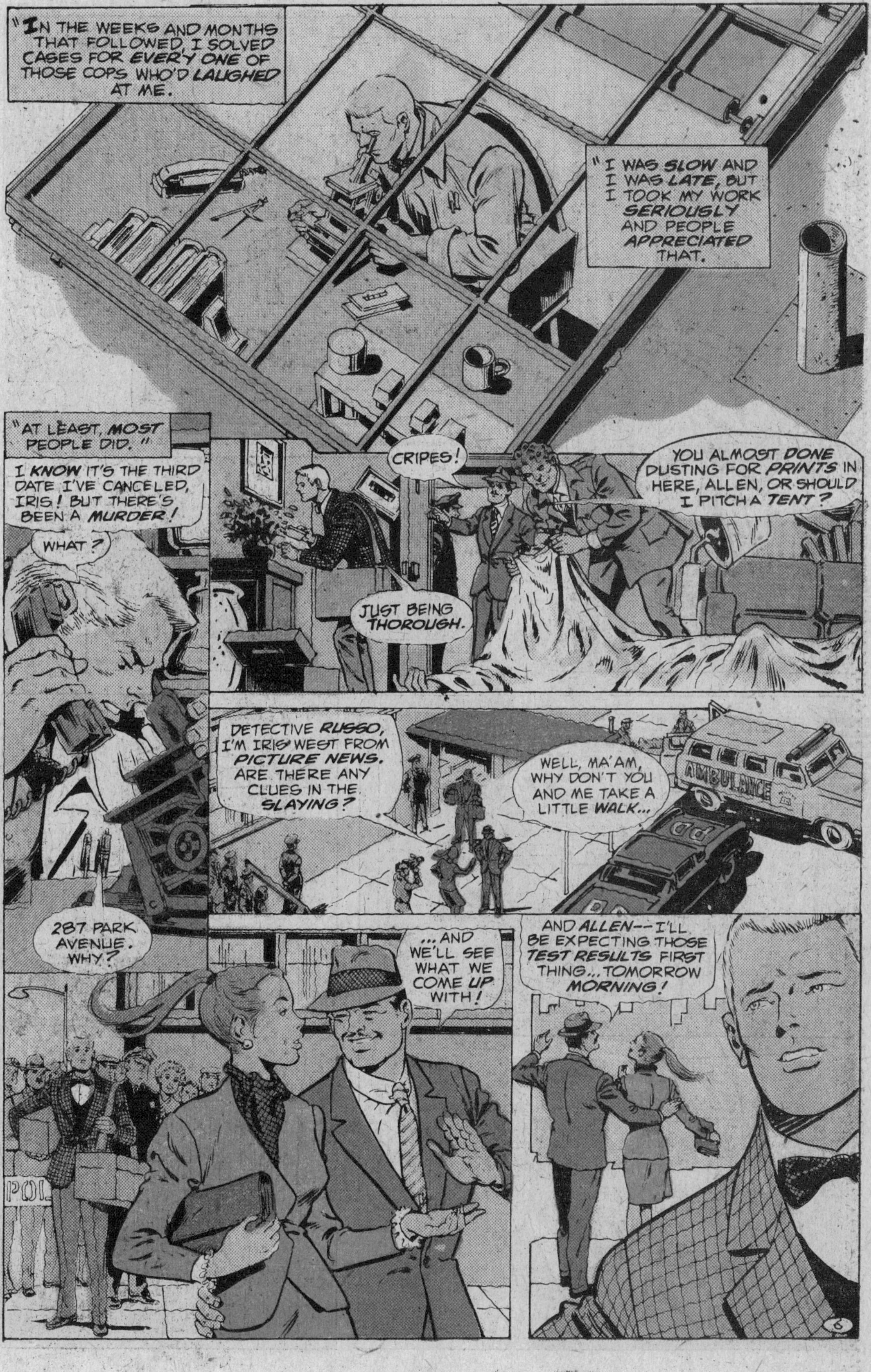
"IN THE WEEKS AND MONTHS THAT FOLLOWED, I SOLVED CASES FOR EVERY ONE OF THOSE COPS WHO'D LAUGHED AT ME.
"I WAS SLOW AND I WAS LATE, BUT I TOOK MY WORK SERIOUSLY AND PEOPLE APPRECIATED THAT.
"AT LEAST, MOST PEOPLE DID."
I KNOW IT'S THE THIRD DATE I'VE CANCELED, IRIS! BUT THERE'S BEEN A MURDER!
WHAT?
CRIPES!
YOU ALMOST DONE DUSTING FOR PRINTS IN HERE, ALLEN, OR SHOULD I PITCH A TENT?
JUST BEING THOROUGH.
DETECTIVE RUSSO, I'M IRIS WEST FROM PICTURE NEWS. ARE THERE ANY CLUES IN THE SLAYING?
WELL, MA'AM, WHY DON'T YOU AND ME TAKE A LITTLE WALK...
AMBULANCE
PD
287 PARK AVENUE. WHY?
...AND WE'LL SEE WHAT WE COME UP WITH!
POL
AND ALLEN--I'LL BE EXPECTING THOSE TEST RESULTS FIRST THING... TOMORROW MORNING!

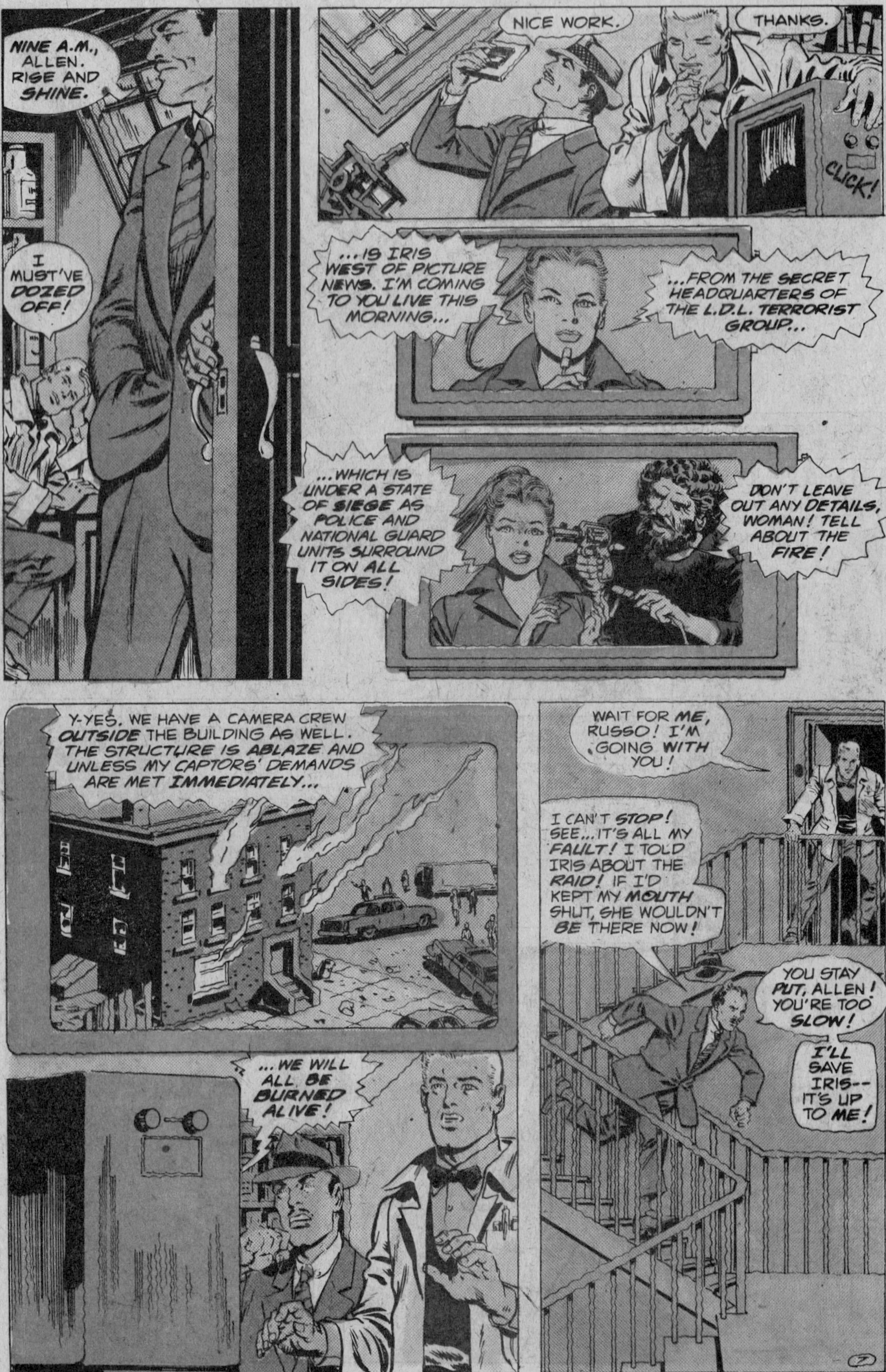
NINE A.M., ALLEN. RISE AND SHINE.
I MUST'VE DOZED OFF!
NICE WORK.
THANKS.
CLICK!
...IS IRIS WEST OF PICTURE NEWS. I'M COMING TO YOU LIVE THIS MORNING...
...FROM THE SECRET HEADQUARTERS OF THE L.D.L. TERRORIST GROUP...
...WHICH IS UNDER A STATE OF SIEGE AS POLICE AND NATIONAL GUARD UNITS SURROUND IT ON ALL SIDES!
DON'T LEAVE OUT ANY DETAILS, WOMAN! TELL ABOUT THE FIRE!
Y-YES. WE HAVE A CAMERA CREW OUTSIDE THE BUILDING AS WELL. THE STRUCTURE IS ABLAZE AND UNLESS MY CAPTORS' DEMANDS ARE MET IMMEDIATELY...
...WE WILL ALL BE BURNED ALIVE!
WAIT FOR ME, RUSSO! I'M GOING WITH YOU!
I CAN'T STOP! SEE...IT'S ALL MY FAULT! I TOLD IRIS ABOUT THE RAID! IF I'D KEPT MY MOUTH SHUT, SHE WOULDN'T BE THERE NOW!
YOU STAY PUT, ALLEN! YOU'RE TOO SLOW!
I'LL SAVE IRIS-- IT'S UP TO ME!
7

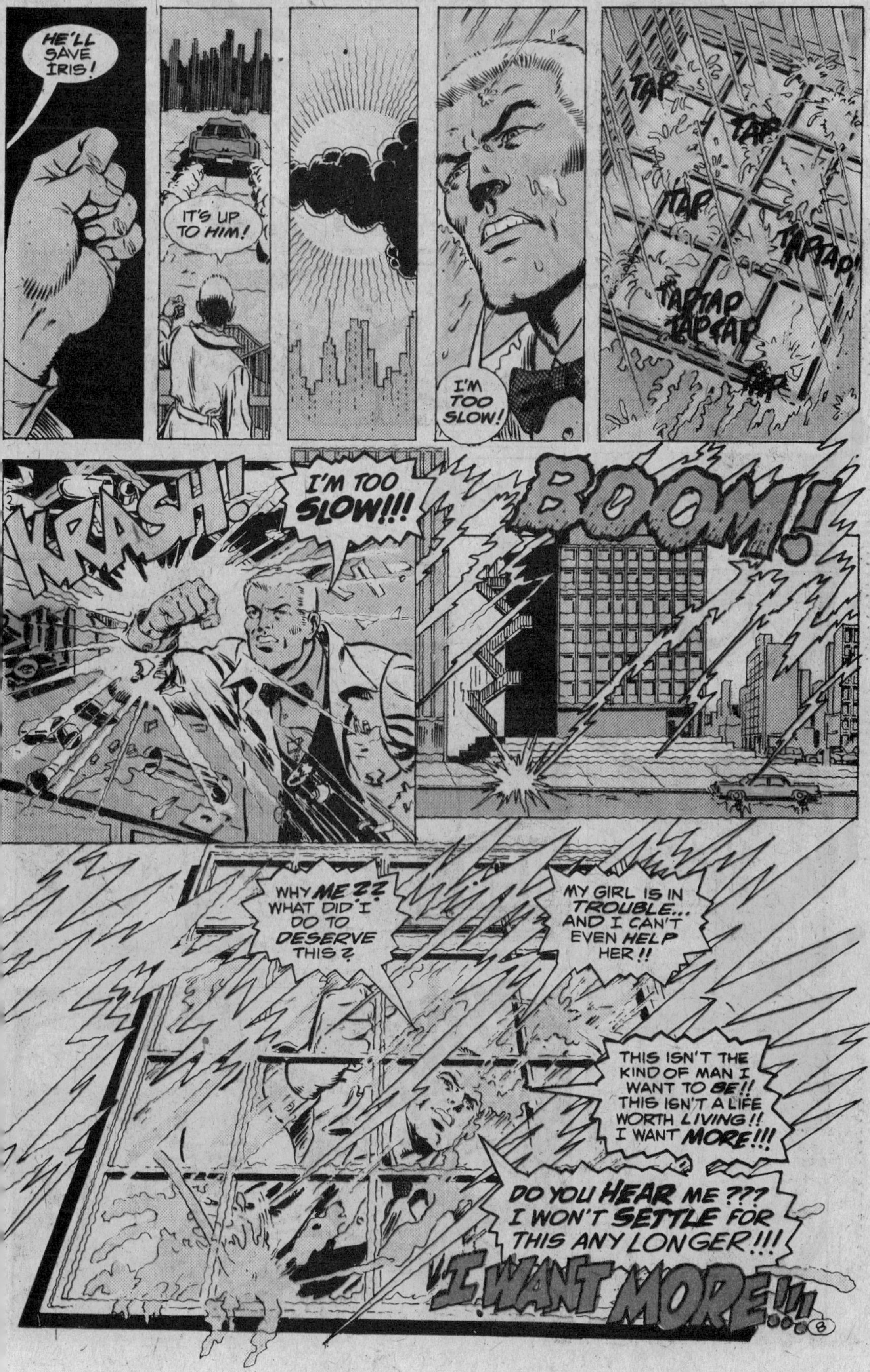
HE'LL SAVE IRIS!
IT'S UP TO HIM!
I'M TOO SLOW!
TAP
TAP
TAP
TAPTAP!
TAPTAP TAPTAP
TAP
KRASH!
I'M TOO SLOW!!!
BOOM!
WHY ME?? WHAT DID I DO TO DESERVE THIS?
MY GIRL IS IN TROUBLE... AND I CAN'T EVEN HELP HER!!
THIS ISN'T THE KIND OF MAN I WANT TO BE!! THIS ISN'T A LIFE WORTH LIVING!! I WANT MORE!!!
DO YOU HEAR ME??? I WON'T SETTLE FOR THIS ANY LONGER!!!
I WANT MORE!!!
8

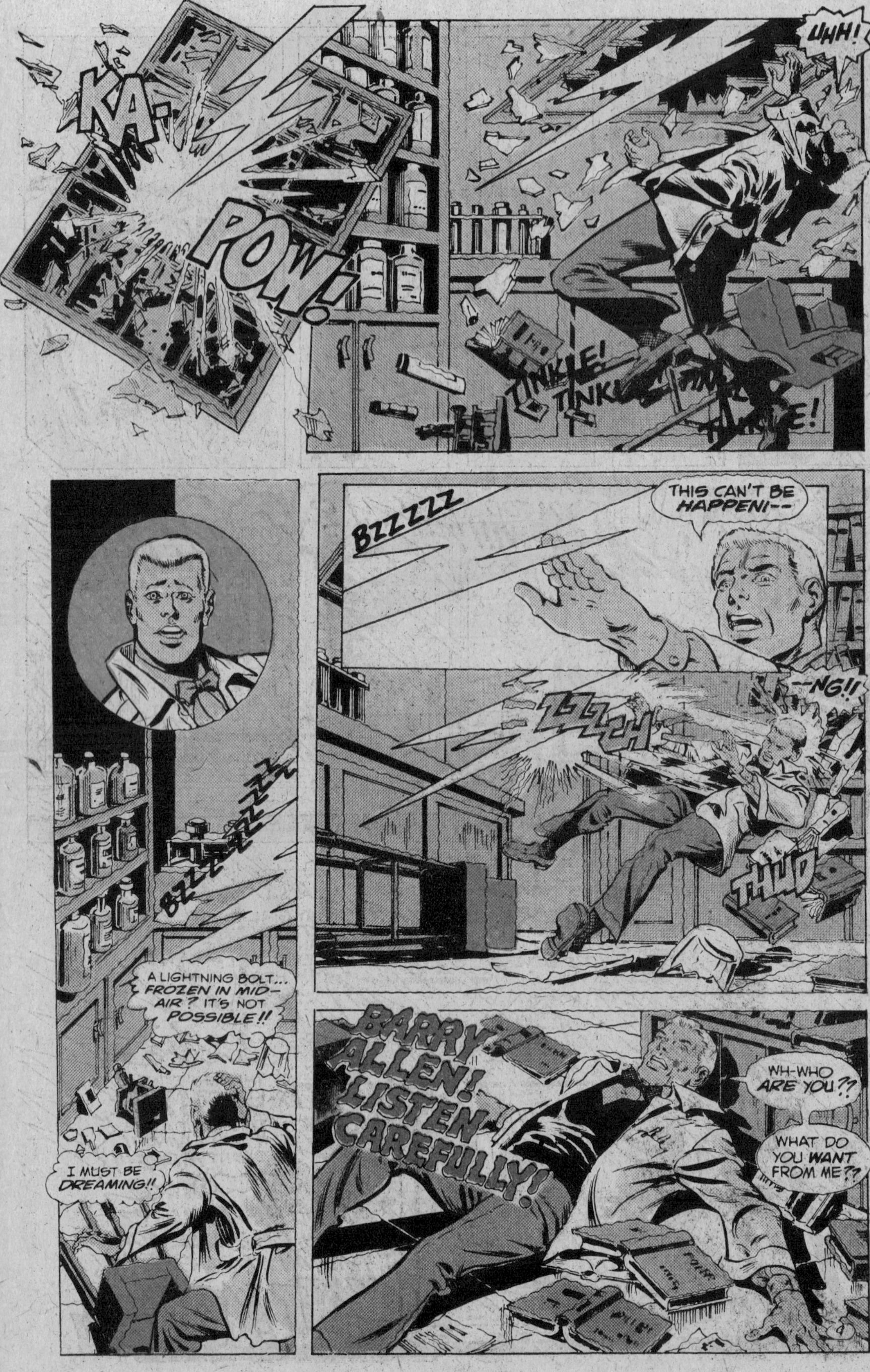

KA-
POW!
UHH!
TINKLE! TINKLE! TINKLE!
BZZZZZ
THIS CAN'T BE HAPPENI--
A LIGHTNING BOLT... FROZEN IN MID-AIR? IT'S NOT POSSIBLE!!
I MUST BE DREAMING!!
--NG!!
THUD
BARRY ALLEN! LISTEN CAREFULLY!
WH-WHO ARE YOU??
WHAT DO YOU WANT FROM ME??

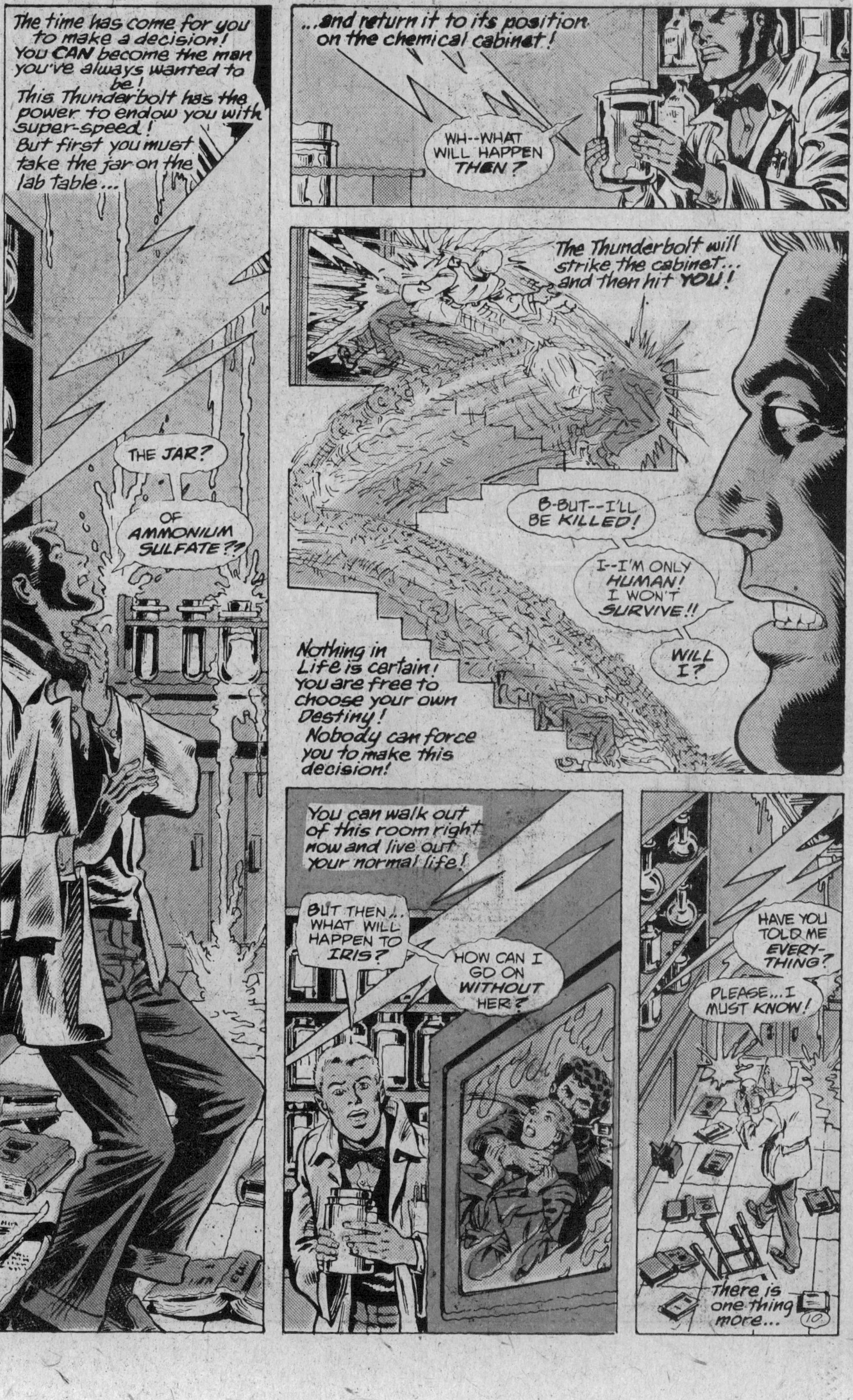
The time has come for you to make a decision! You CAN become the man you've always wanted to be! This Thunderbolt has the power to endow you with super-speed! But first you must take the jar on the lab table...
THE JAR?
OF AMMONIUM SULFATE??
...and return it to its position on the chemical cabinet!
WH--WHAT WILL HAPPEN THEN?
The Thunderbolt will strike the cabinet... and then hit YOU!
B-BUT--I'LL BE KILLED!
I--I'M ONLY HUMAN! I WON'T SURVIVE!!
WILL I?
Nothing in Life is certain! You are free to choose your own Destiny! Nobody can force you to make this decision!
You can walk out of this room right now and live out your normal life!
BUT THEN... WHAT WILL HAPPEN TO IRIS?
HOW CAN I GO ON WITHOUT HER?
HAVE YOU TOLD ME EVERY-THING?
PLEASE... I MUST KNOW!
There is one thing more...
10

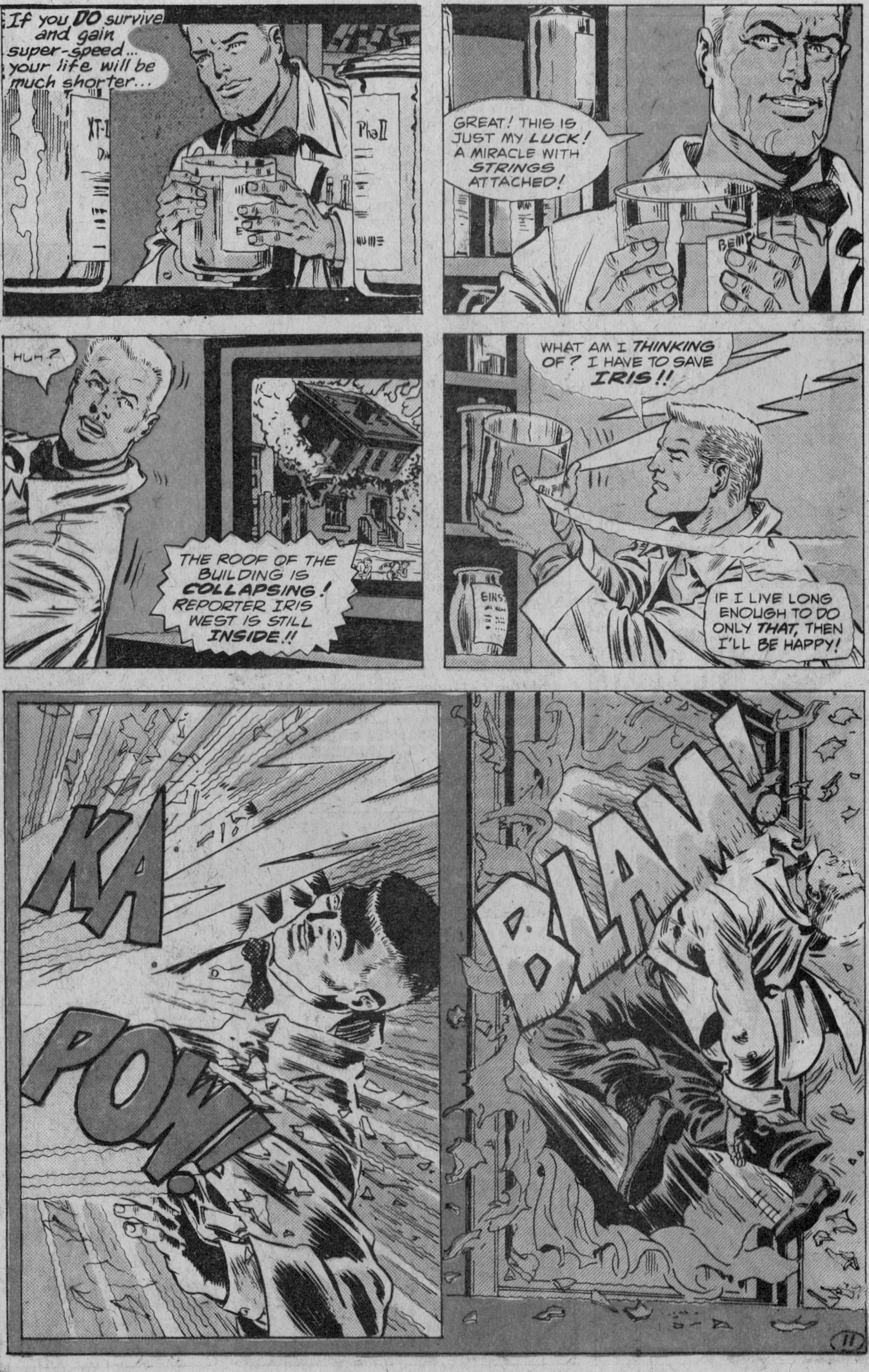

If you DO survive and gain super-speed... your life will be much shorter...
GREAT! THIS IS JUST MY LUCK! A MIRACLE WITH STRINGS ATTACHED!
HUH?
THE ROOF OF THE BUILDING IS COLLAPSING! REPORTER IRIS WEST IS STILL INSIDE!!
WHAT AM I THINKING OF? I HAVE TO SAVE IRIS!!
IF I LIVE LONG ENOUGH TO DO ONLY THAT, THEN I'LL BE HAPPY!
KA
POW
BLAM!

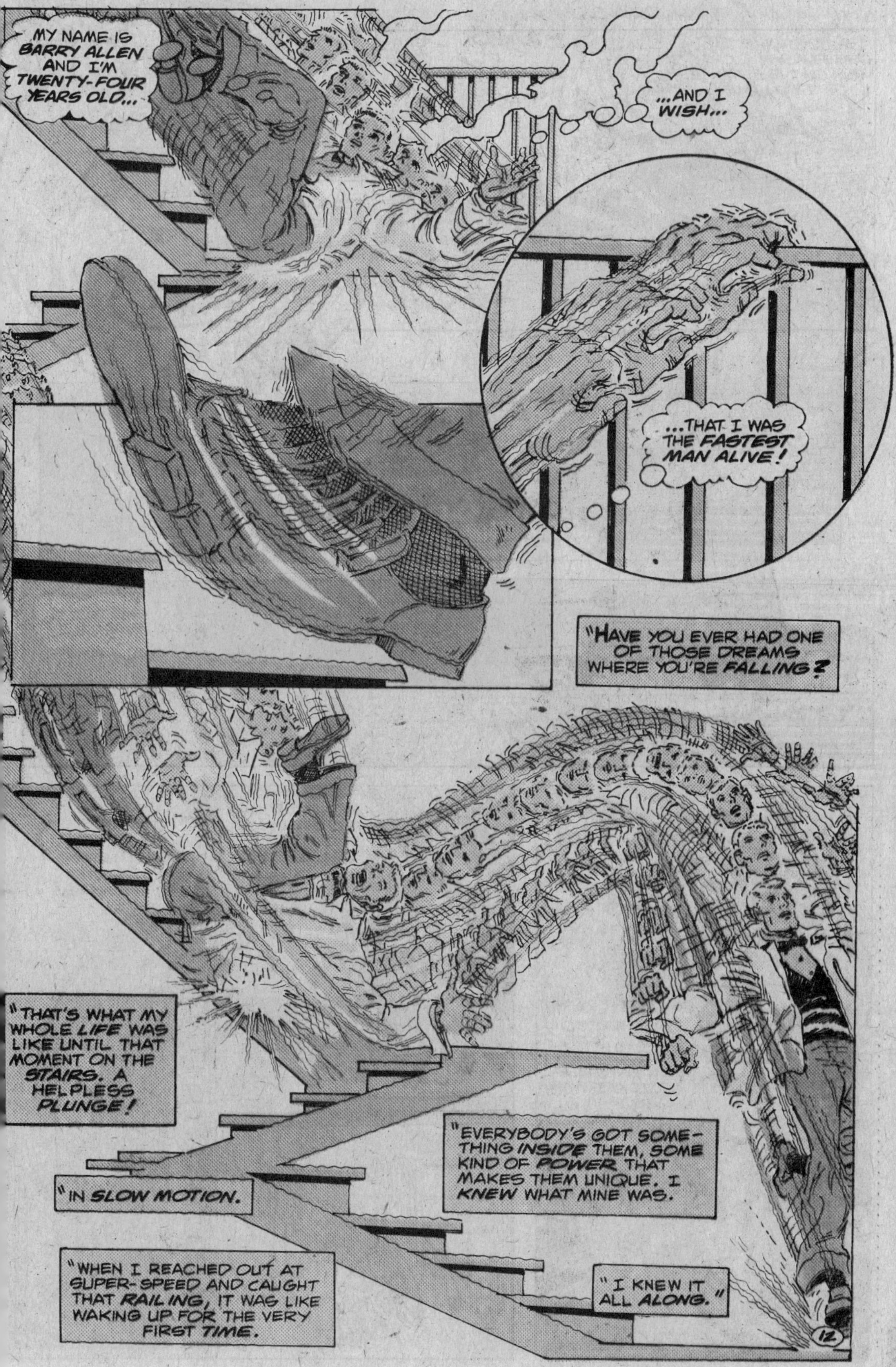
MY NAME IS BARRY ALLEN AND I'M TWENTY-FOUR YEARS OLD...
...AND I WISH...
...THAT I WAS THE FASTEST MAN ALIVE!
"HAVE YOU EVER HAD ONE OF THOSE DREAMS WHERE YOU'RE FALLING?
"THAT'S WHAT MY WHOLE LIFE WAS LIKE UNTIL THAT MOMENT ON THE STAIRS. A HELPLESS PLUNGE!
"IN SLOW MOTION.
"EVERYBODY'S GOT SOME-THING INSIDE THEM, SOME KIND OF POWER THAT MAKES THEM UNIQUE. I KNEW WHAT MINE WAS.
"WHEN I REACHED OUT AT SUPER-SPEED AND CAUGHT THAT RAILING, IT WAS LIKE WAKING UP FOR THE VERY FIRST TIME.
"I KNEW IT ALL ALONG."
12

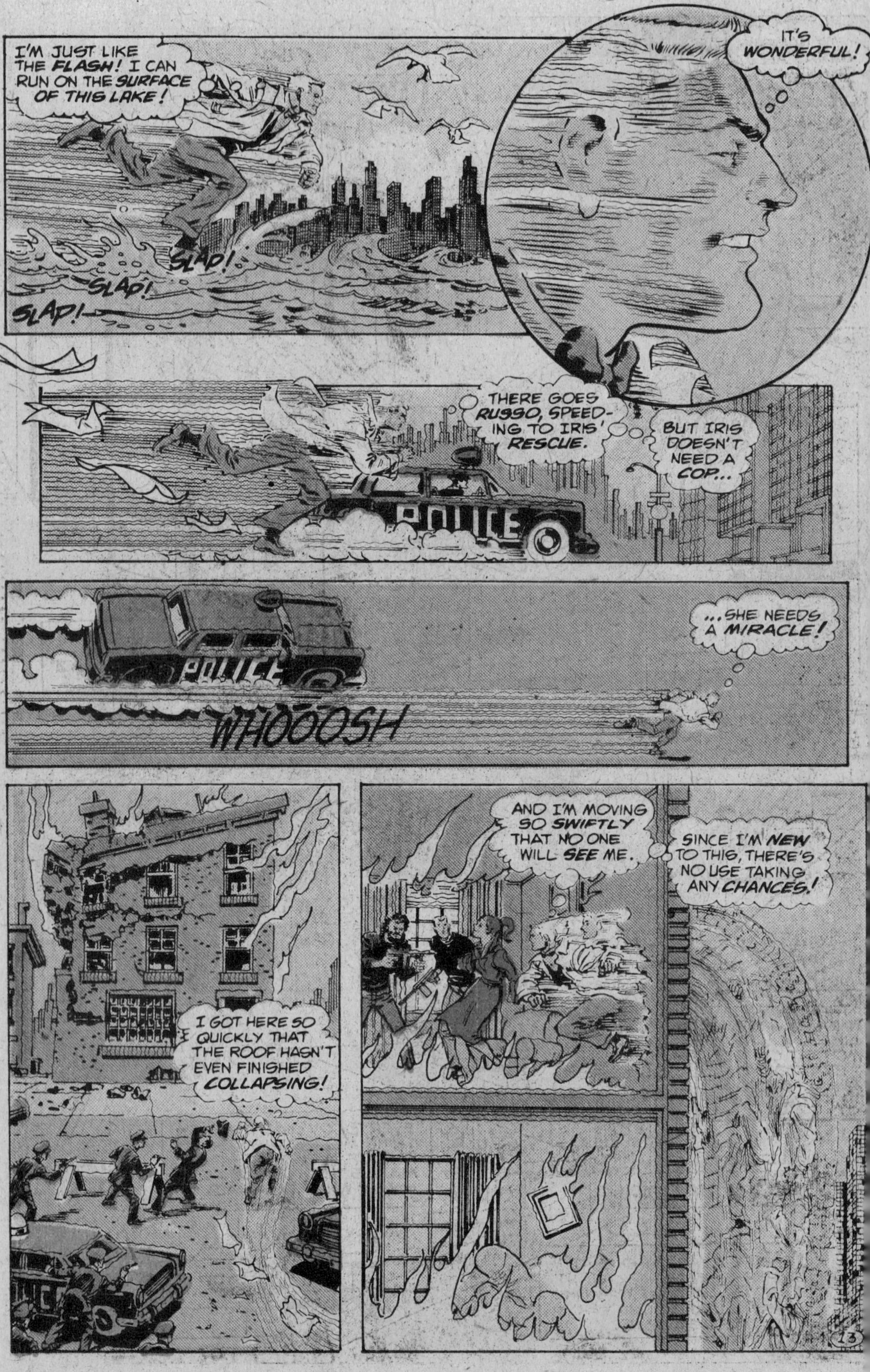
I'M JUST LIKE THE FLASH! I CAN RUN ON THE SURFACE OF THIS LAKE!
SLAP!
SLAP!
SLAP!
IT'S WONDERFUL!
THERE GOES RUSSO, SPEEDING TO IRIS' RESCUE.
BUT IRIS DOESN'T NEED A COP...
POLICE
...SHE NEEDS A MIRACLE!
POLICE
WHOOOSH
I GOT HERE SO QUICKLY THAT THE ROOF HASN'T EVEN FINISHED COLLAPSING!
AND I'M MOVING SO SWIFTLY THAT NO ONE WILL SEE ME.
SINCE I'M NEW TO THIS, THERE'S NO USE TAKING ANY CHANCES!
13

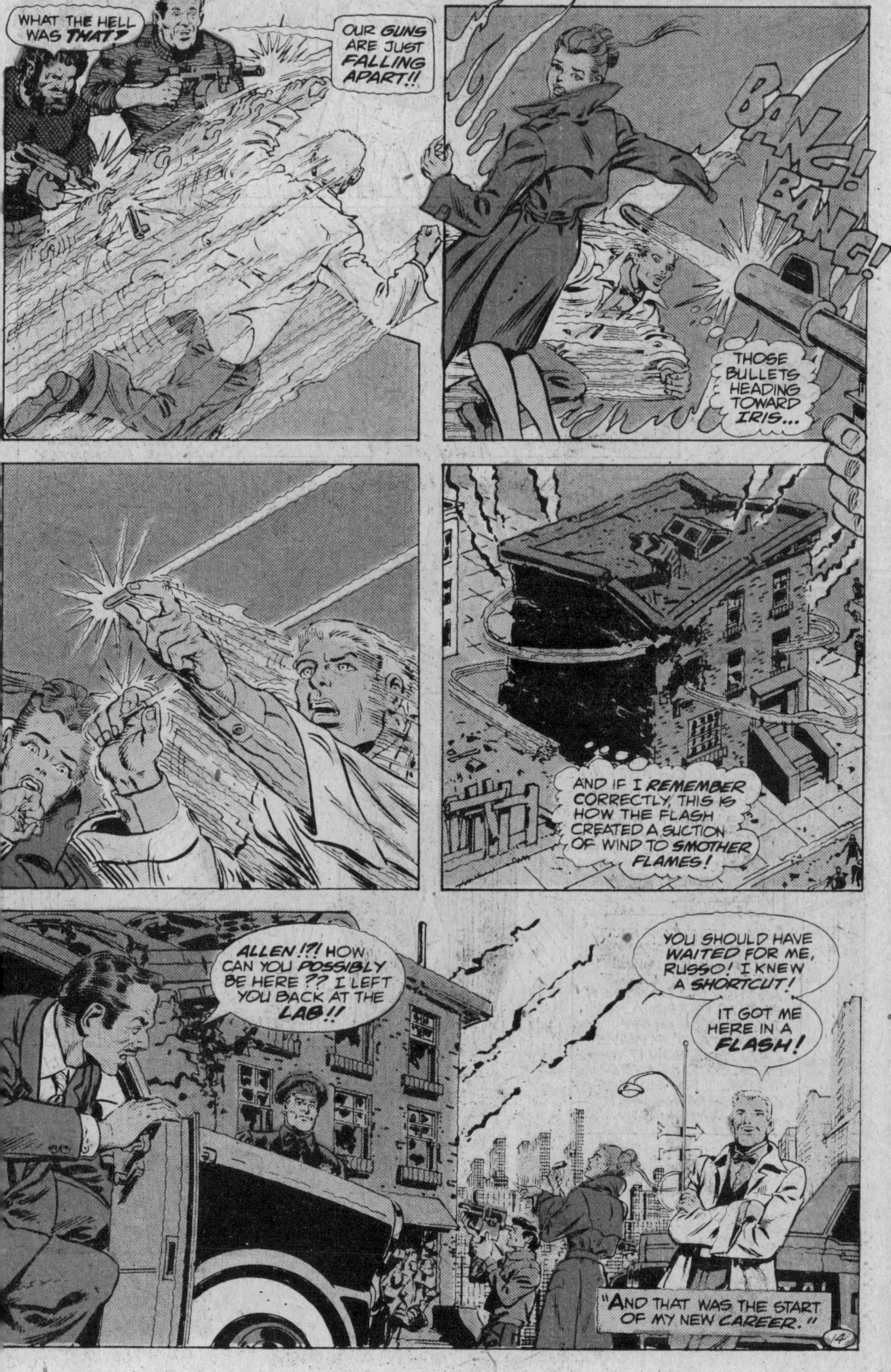
WHAT THE HELL WAS THAT?
OUR GUNS ARE JUST FALLING APART!!
BANG! BANG! BANG!
THOSE BULLETS HEADING TOWARD IRIS...
AND IF I REMEMBER CORRECTLY, THIS IS HOW THE FLASH CREATED A SUCTION OF WIND TO SMOTHER FLAMES!
ALLEN!?! HOW CAN YOU POSSIBLY BE HERE?? I LEFT YOU BACK AT THE LAB!!
YOU SHOULD HAVE WAITED FOR ME, RUSSO! I KNEW A SHORTCUT!
IT GOT ME HERE IN A FLASH!
"AND THAT WAS THE START OF MY NEW CAREER."
14

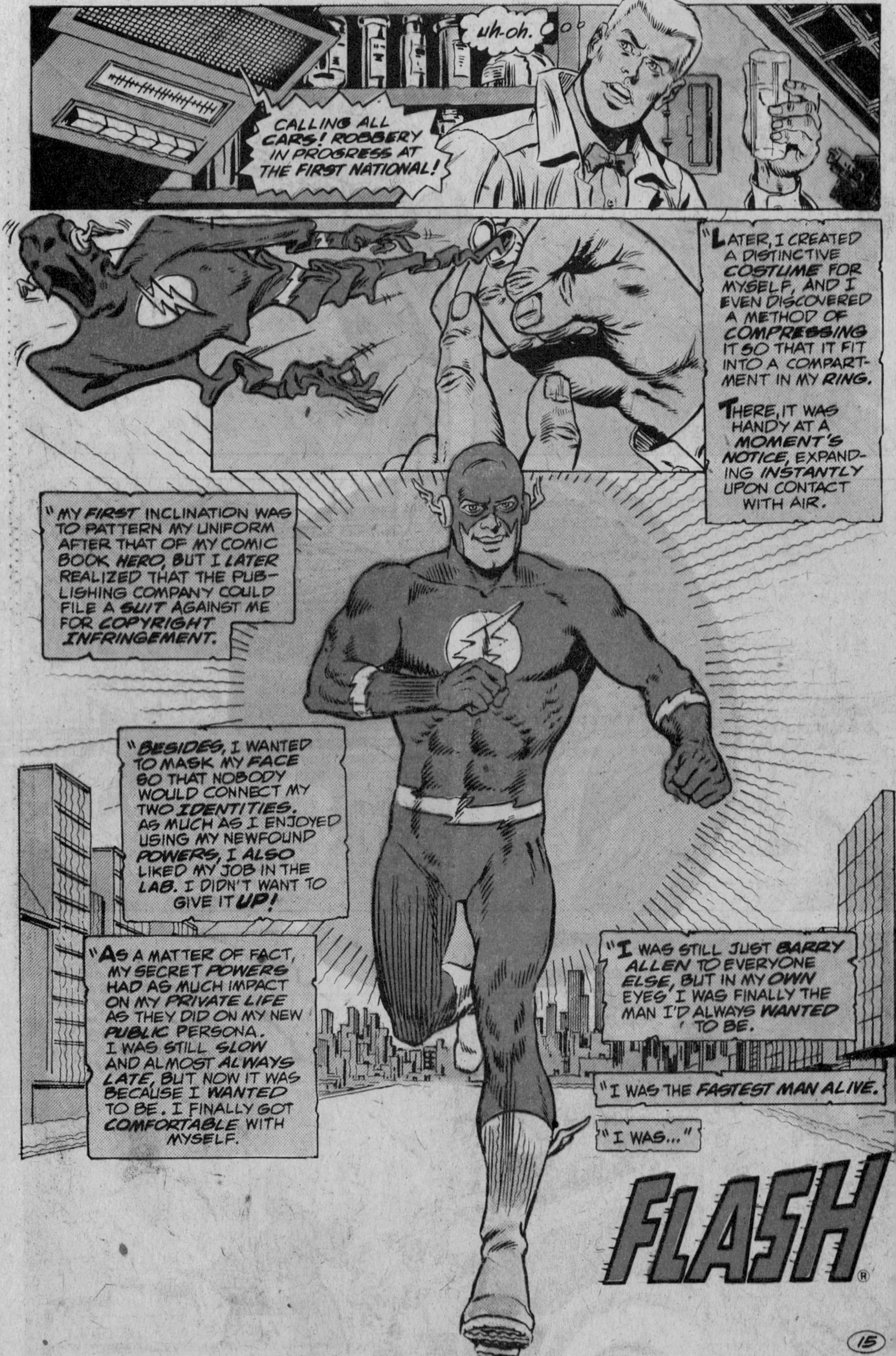
uh-oh.
CALLING ALL CARS! ROBBERY IN PROGRESS AT THE FIRST NATIONAL!
"LATER, I CREATED A DISTINCTIVE COSTUME FOR MYSELF, AND I EVEN DISCOVERED A METHOD OF COMPRESSING IT SO THAT IT FIT INTO A COMPARTMENT IN MY RING.
THERE, IT WAS HANDY AT A MOMENT'S NOTICE, EXPANDING INSTANTLY UPON CONTACT WITH AIR.
"MY FIRST INCLINATION WAS TO PATTERN MY UNIFORM AFTER THAT OF MY COMIC BOOK HERO, BUT I LATER REALIZED THAT THE PUBLISHING COMPANY COULD FILE A SUIT AGAINST ME FOR COPYRIGHT INFRINGEMENT.
"BESIDES, I WANTED TO MASK MY FACE SO THAT NOBODY WOULD CONNECT MY TWO IDENTITIES. AS MUCH AS I ENJOYED USING MY NEWFOUND POWERS, I ALSO LIKED MY JOB IN THE LAB. I DIDN'T WANT TO GIVE IT UP!
"AS A MATTER OF FACT, MY SECRET POWERS HAD AS MUCH IMPACT ON MY PRIVATE LIFE AS THEY DID ON MY NEW PUBLIC PERSONA. I WAS STILL SLOW AND ALMOST ALWAYS LATE, BUT NOW IT WAS BECAUSE I WANTED TO BE. I FINALLY GOT COMFORTABLE WITH MYSELF.
"I WAS STILL JUST BARRY ALLEN TO EVERYONE ELSE, BUT IN MY OWN EYES I WAS FINALLY THE MAN I'D ALWAYS WANTED TO BE.
"I WAS THE FASTEST MAN ALIVE.
"I WAS..."
FLASH®

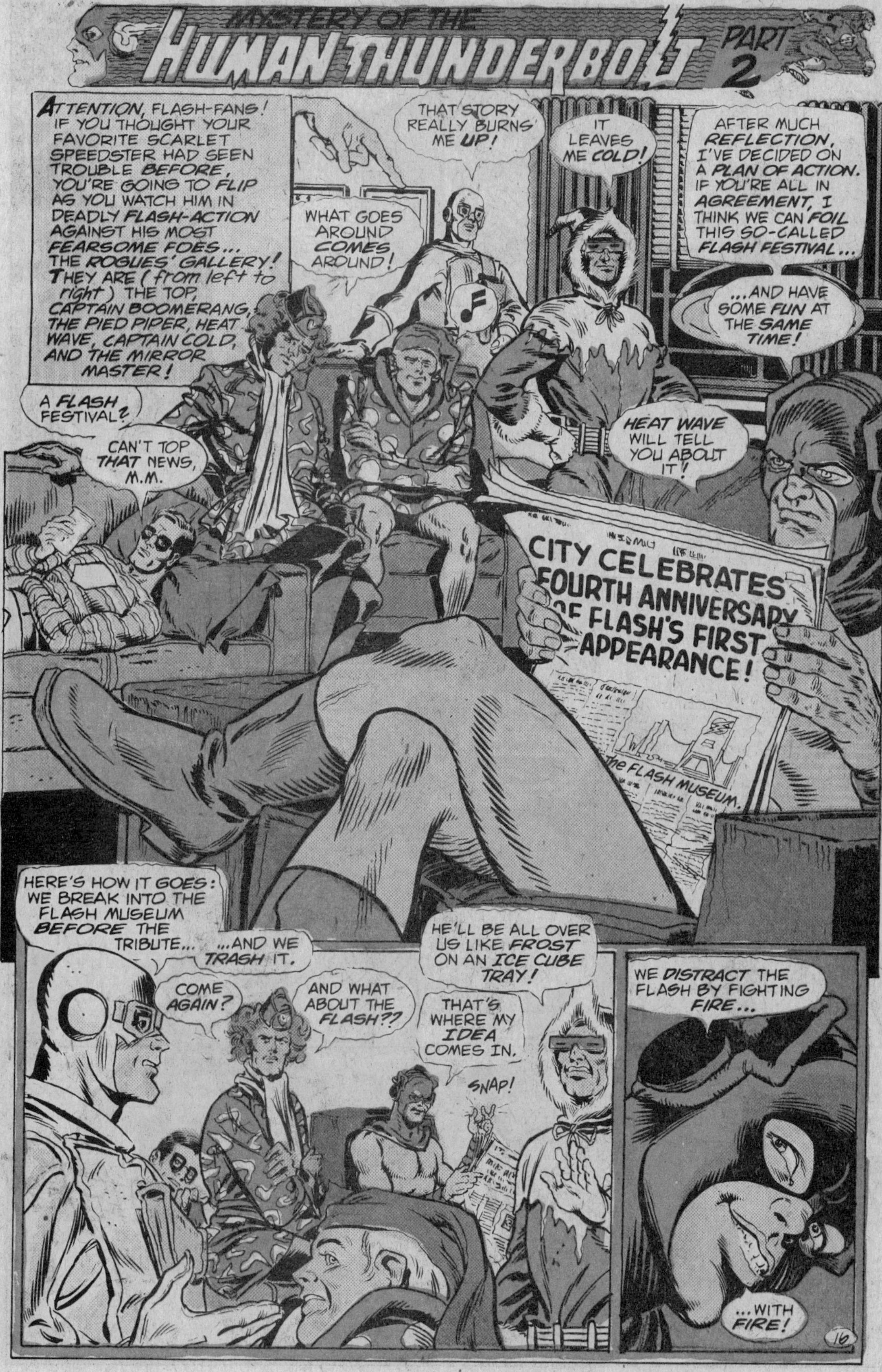
MYSTERY OF THE
HUMAN THUNDERBOLT
PART 2
ATTENTION, FLASH-FANS! IF YOU THOUGHT YOUR FAVORITE SCARLET SPEEDSTER HAD SEEN TROUBLE BEFORE, YOU'RE GOING TO FLIP AS YOU WATCH HIM IN DEADLY FLASH-ACTION AGAINST HIS MOST FEARSOME FOES... THE ROGUES' GALLERY! THEY ARE (from left to right) THE TOP, CAPTAIN BOOMERANG, THE PIED PIPER, HEAT WAVE, CAPTAIN COLD, AND THE MIRROR MASTER!
THAT STORY REALLY BURNS ME UP!
IT LEAVES ME COLD!
AFTER MUCH REFLECTION, I'VE DECIDED ON A PLAN OF ACTION. IF YOU'RE ALL IN AGREEMENT, I THINK WE CAN FOIL THIS SO-CALLED FLASH FESTIVAL...
WHAT GOES AROUND COMES AROUND!
...AND HAVE SOME FUN AT THE SAME TIME!
A FLASH FESTIVAL?
CAN'T TOP THAT NEWS, M.M.
HEAT WAVE WILL TELL YOU ABOUT IT!
CITY CELEBRATES FOURTH ANNIVERSARY OF FLASH'S FIRST APPEARANCE!
the FLASH MUSEUM.
HERE'S HOW IT GOES: WE BREAK INTO THE FLASH MUSEUM BEFORE THE TRIBUTE...
...AND WE TRASH IT.
COME AGAIN?
AND WHAT ABOUT THE FLASH??
HE'LL BE ALL OVER US LIKE FROST ON AN ICE CUBE TRAY!
THAT'S WHERE MY IDEA COMES IN.
SNAP!
WE DISTRACT THE FLASH BY FIGHTING FIRE...
...WITH FIRE!
16

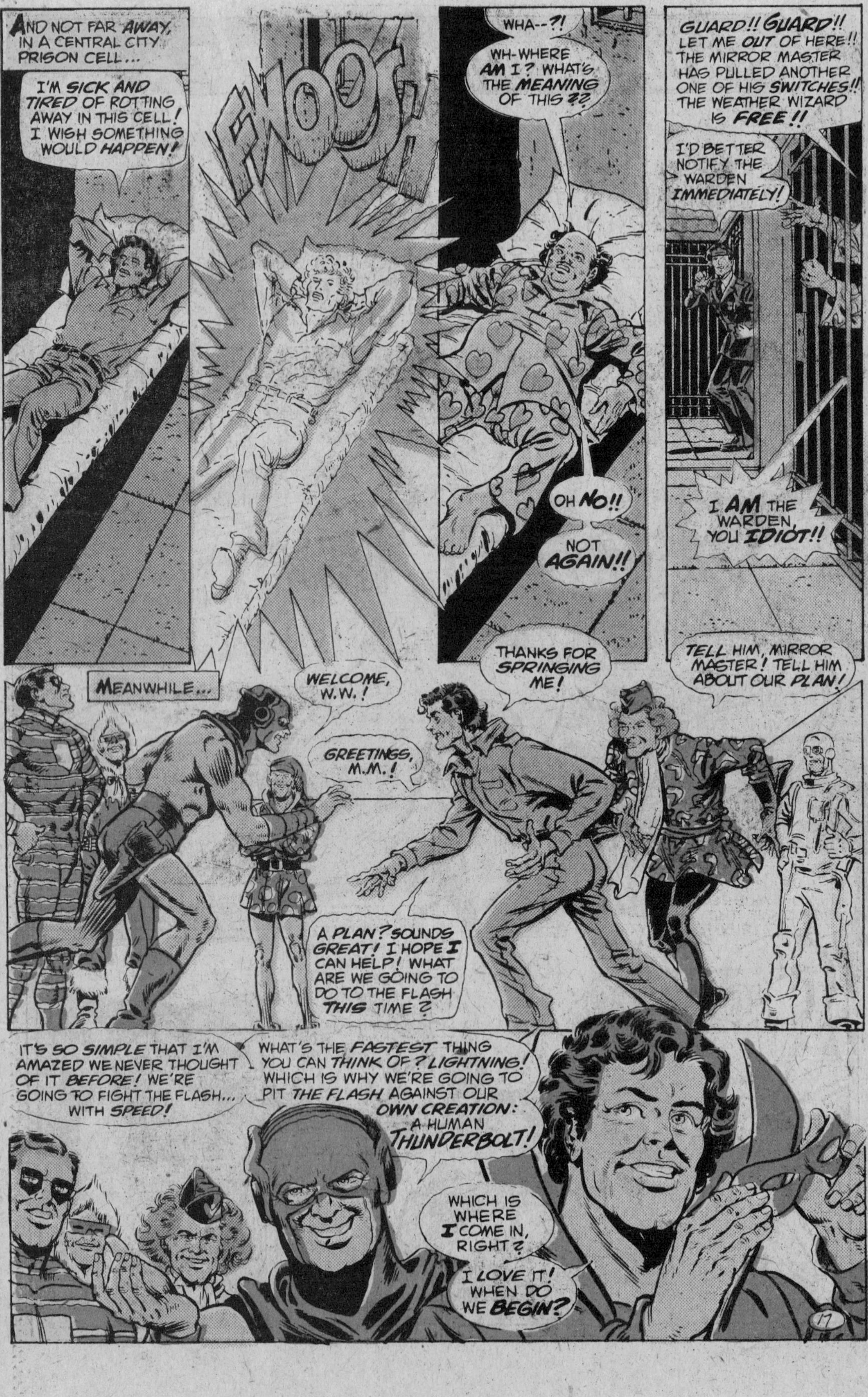
AND NOT FAR AWAY, IN A CENTRAL CITY PRISON CELL...
I'M SICK AND TIRED OF ROTTING AWAY IN THIS CELL! I WISH SOMETHING WOULD HAPPEN!
FWOOSH
WHA--?!
WH-WHERE AM I? WHAT'S THE MEANING OF THIS ??
OH NO!!
NOT AGAIN!!
GUARD!! GUARD!! LET ME OUT OF HERE!! THE MIRROR MASTER HAS PULLED ANOTHER ONE OF HIS SWITCHES!! THE WEATHER WIZARD IS FREE!!
I'D BETTER NOTIFY THE WARDEN IMMEDIATELY!
I AM THE WARDEN, YOU IDIOT!!
MEANWHILE...
WELCOME, W.W.!
THANKS FOR SPRINGING ME!
GREETINGS, M.M.!
TELL HIM, MIRROR MASTER! TELL HIM ABOUT OUR PLAN!
A PLAN? SOUNDS GREAT! I HOPE I CAN HELP! WHAT ARE WE GOING TO DO TO THE FLASH THIS TIME?
IT'S SO SIMPLE THAT I'M AMAZED WE NEVER THOUGHT OF IT BEFORE! WE'RE GOING TO FIGHT THE FLASH... WITH SPEED!
WHAT'S THE FASTEST THING YOU CAN THINK OF? LIGHTNING! WHICH IS WHY WE'RE GOING TO PIT THE FLASH AGAINST OUR OWN CREATION: A HUMAN THUNDERBOLT!
WHICH IS WHERE I COME IN, RIGHT?
I LOVE IT! WHEN DO WE BEGIN?
17

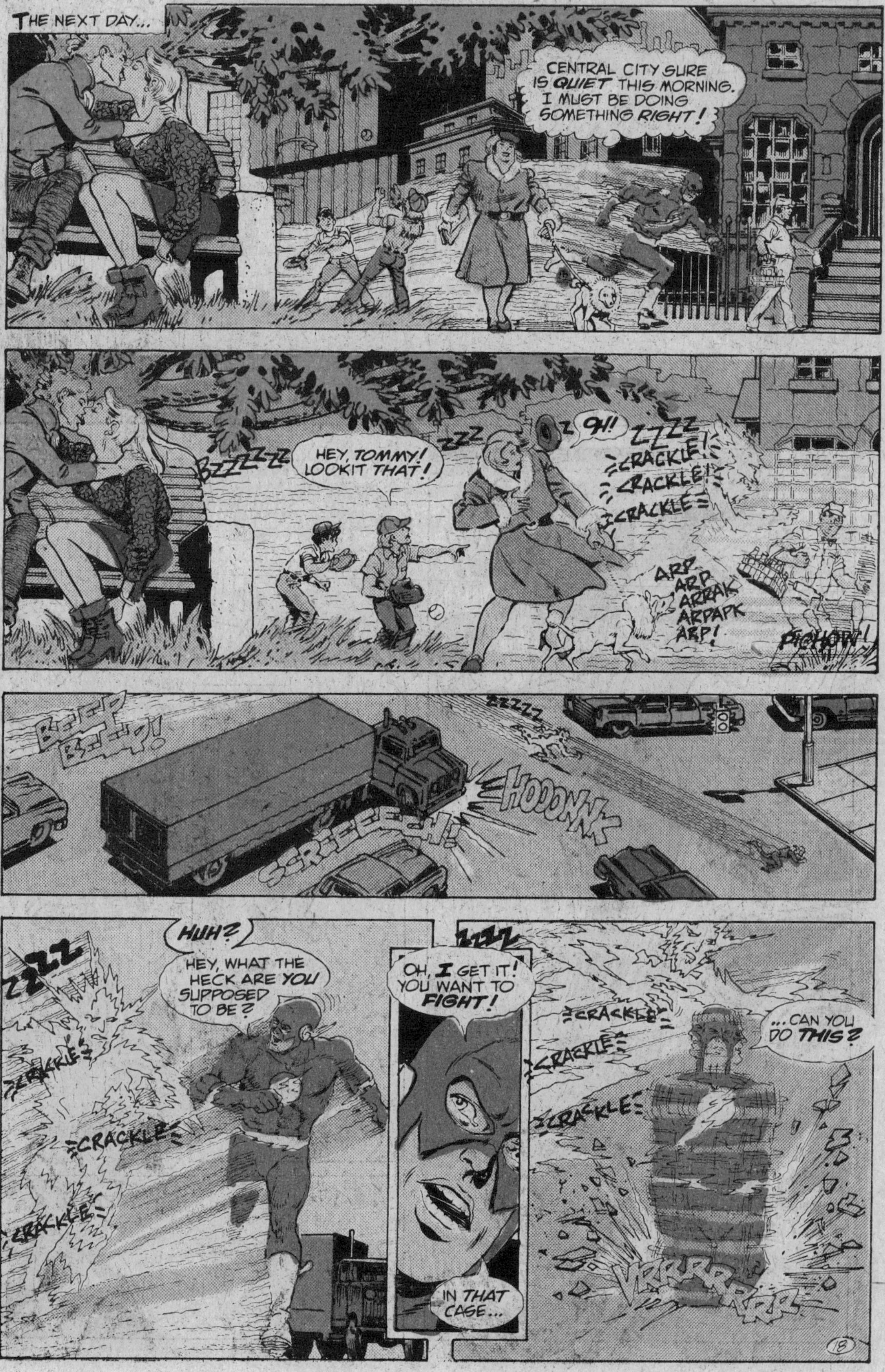
THE NEXT DAY...
CENTRAL CITY SURE IS QUIET THIS MORNING. I MUST BE DOING SOMETHING RIGHT!
BZZZZZZ
HEY, TOMMY! LOOKIT THAT!
ZZZ
OH!
ZZZZ
CRACKLE!
CRACKLE!
CRACKLE
ARP ARP ARRAK ARPAPK ARP!
PICHOW!
BEEEP BEEEP!
ZZZZZ
HOOONNK
SCREEECH!
HUH?
HEY, WHAT THE HECK ARE YOU SUPPOSED TO BE?
ZZZZ
CRACKLE
CRACKLE
CRACKLE
OH, I GET IT! YOU WANT TO FIGHT!
IN THAT CASE...
ZZZZ
CRACKLE
CRACKLE
CRACKLE
...CAN YOU DO THIS?
VRRRRRR

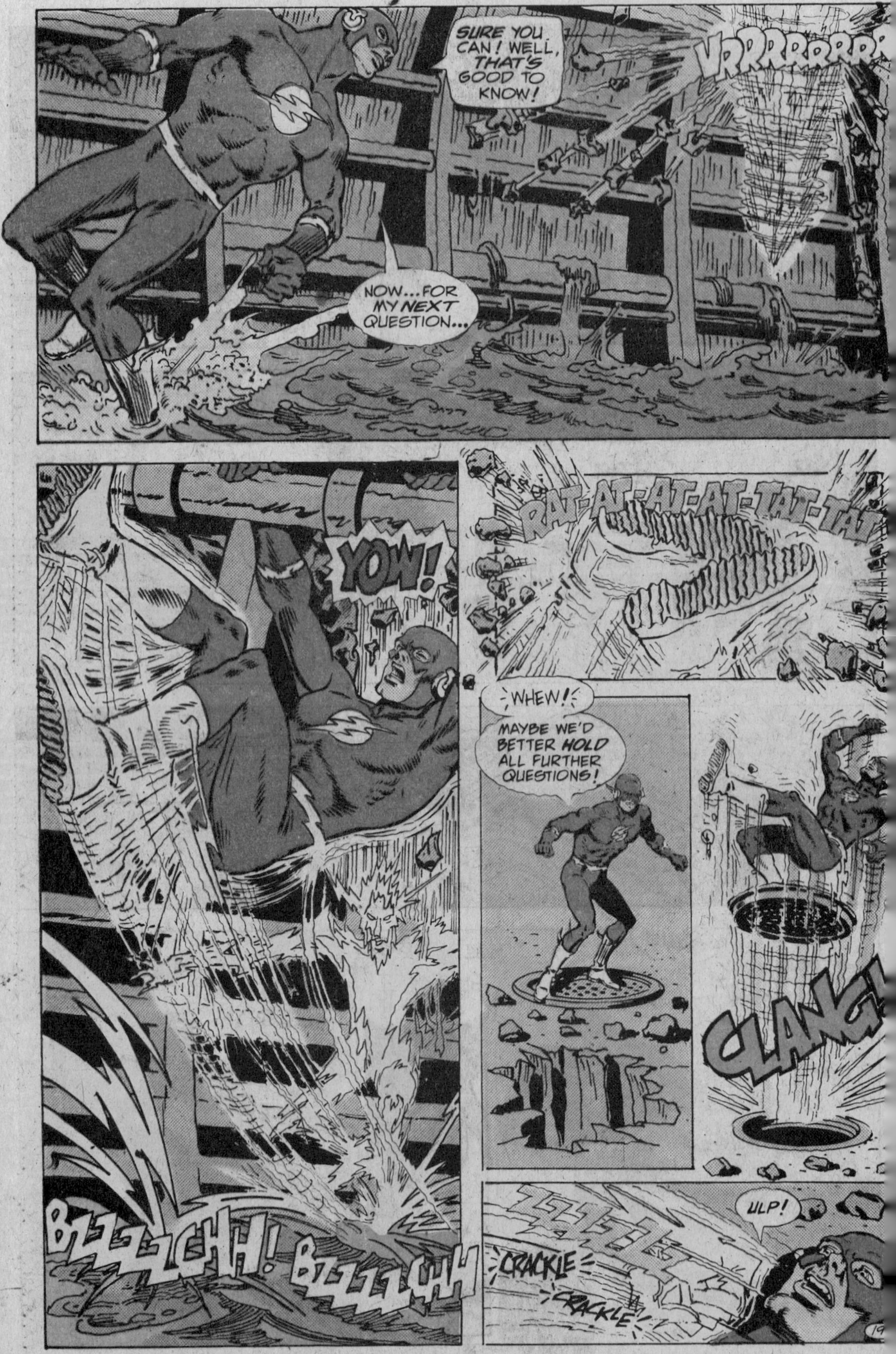
SURE YOU CAN! WELL, THAT'S GOOD TO KNOW!
VRRRRRRR
NOW...FOR MY NEXT QUESTION...
YOW!
BZZZCHH! BZZZCHH
RAT-AT-AT-AT-TAT-TAT
WHEW!
MAYBE WE'D BETTER HOLD ALL FURTHER QUESTIONS!
CLANG
CRACKLE
CRACKLE
ULP!

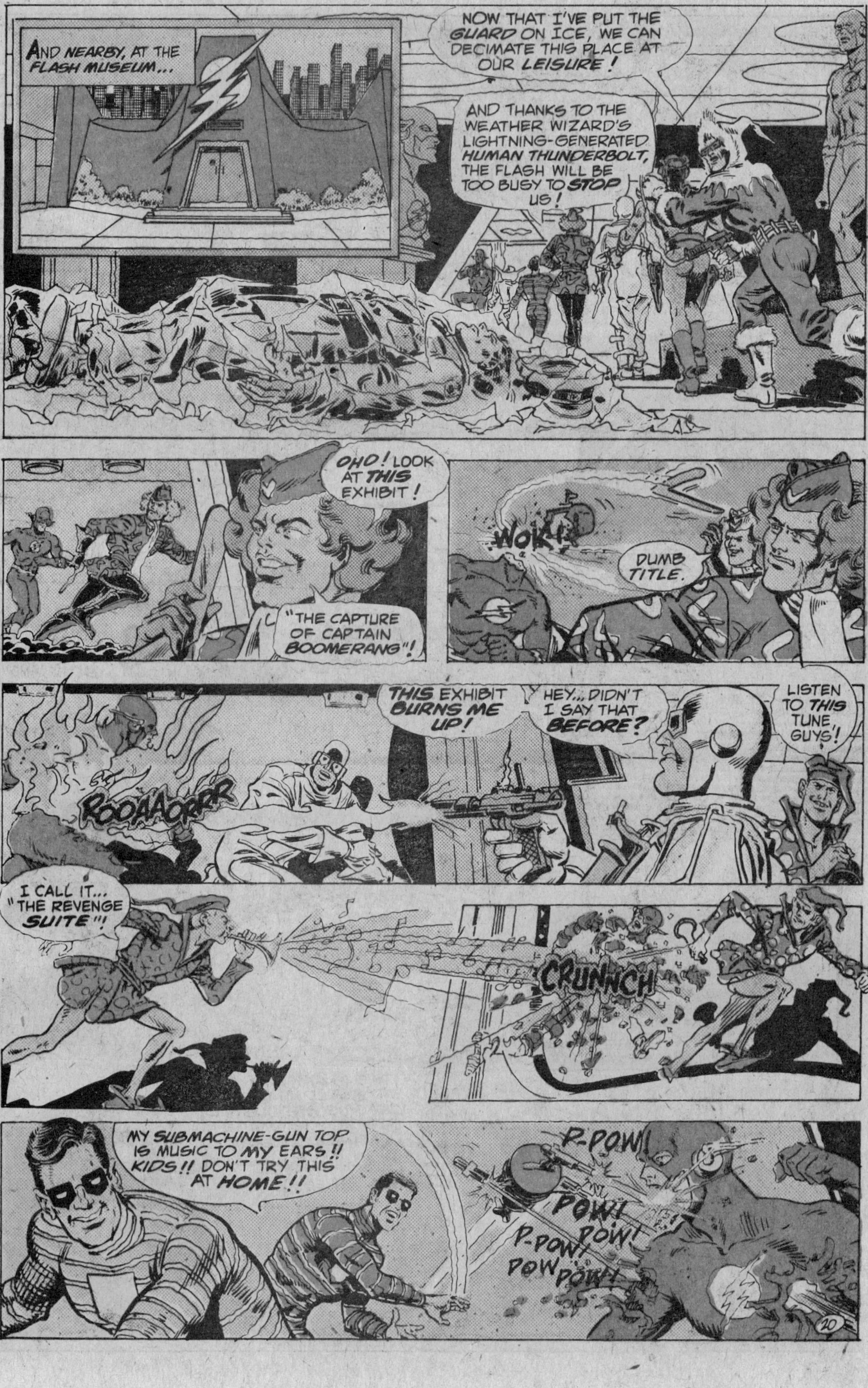

AND NEARBY, AT THE FLASH MUSEUM...
NOW THAT I'VE PUT THE GUARD ON ICE, WE CAN DECIMATE THIS PLACE AT OUR LEISURE!
AND THANKS TO THE WEATHER WIZARD'S LIGHTNING-GENERATED HUMAN THUNDERBOLT, THE FLASH WILL BE TOO BUSY TO STOP US!
OHO! LOOK AT THIS EXHIBIT!
"THE CAPTURE OF CAPTAIN BOOMERANG"!
WOK!
DUMB TITLE.
ROOAAORRR
THIS EXHIBIT BURNS ME UP!
HEY... DIDN'T I SAY THAT BEFORE?
LISTEN TO THIS TUNE, GUYS!
I CALL IT... "THE REVENGE SUITE"!
CRUNNCH
MY SUBMACHINE-GUN TOP IS MUSIC TO MY EARS!! KIDS!! DON'T TRY THIS AT HOME!!
P-POW!
POW!
POW!
P-POW!
POW
POW!

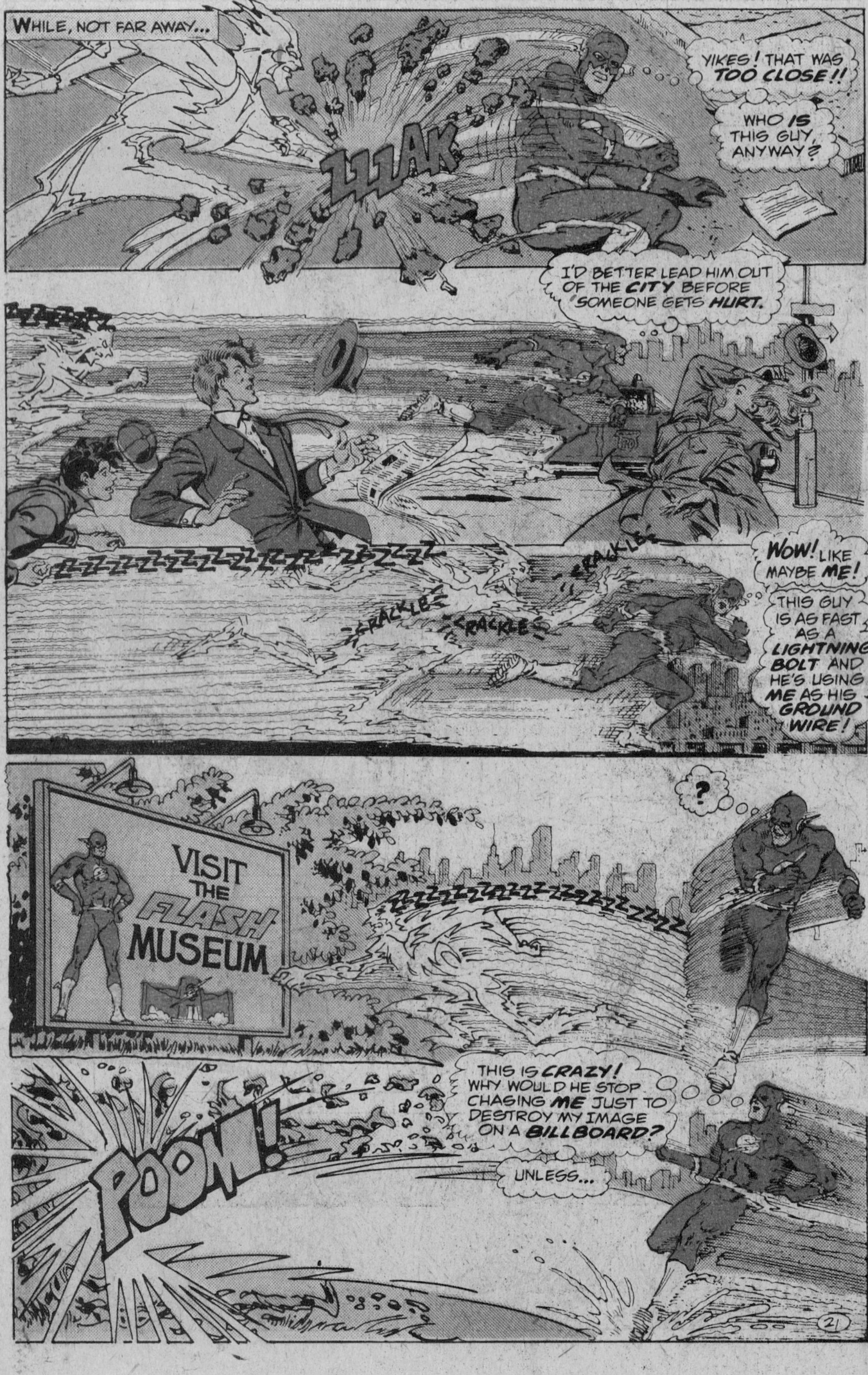

WHILE, NOT FAR AWAY...
ZZZAK
YIKES! THAT WAS TOO CLOSE!!
WHO IS THIS GUY, ANYWAY?
I'D BETTER LEAD HIM OUT OF THE CITY BEFORE SOMEONE GETS HURT.
CRACKLE
CRACKLE
CRACKLE
WOW! LIKE MAYBE ME!
THIS GUY IS AS FAST AS A LIGHTNING BOLT AND HE'S USING ME AS HIS GROUND WIRE!
VISIT THE FLASH MUSEUM
?
THIS IS CRAZY! WHY WOULD HE STOP CHASING ME JUST TO DESTROY MY IMAGE ON A BILLBOARD?
UNLESS...
POOM!
21

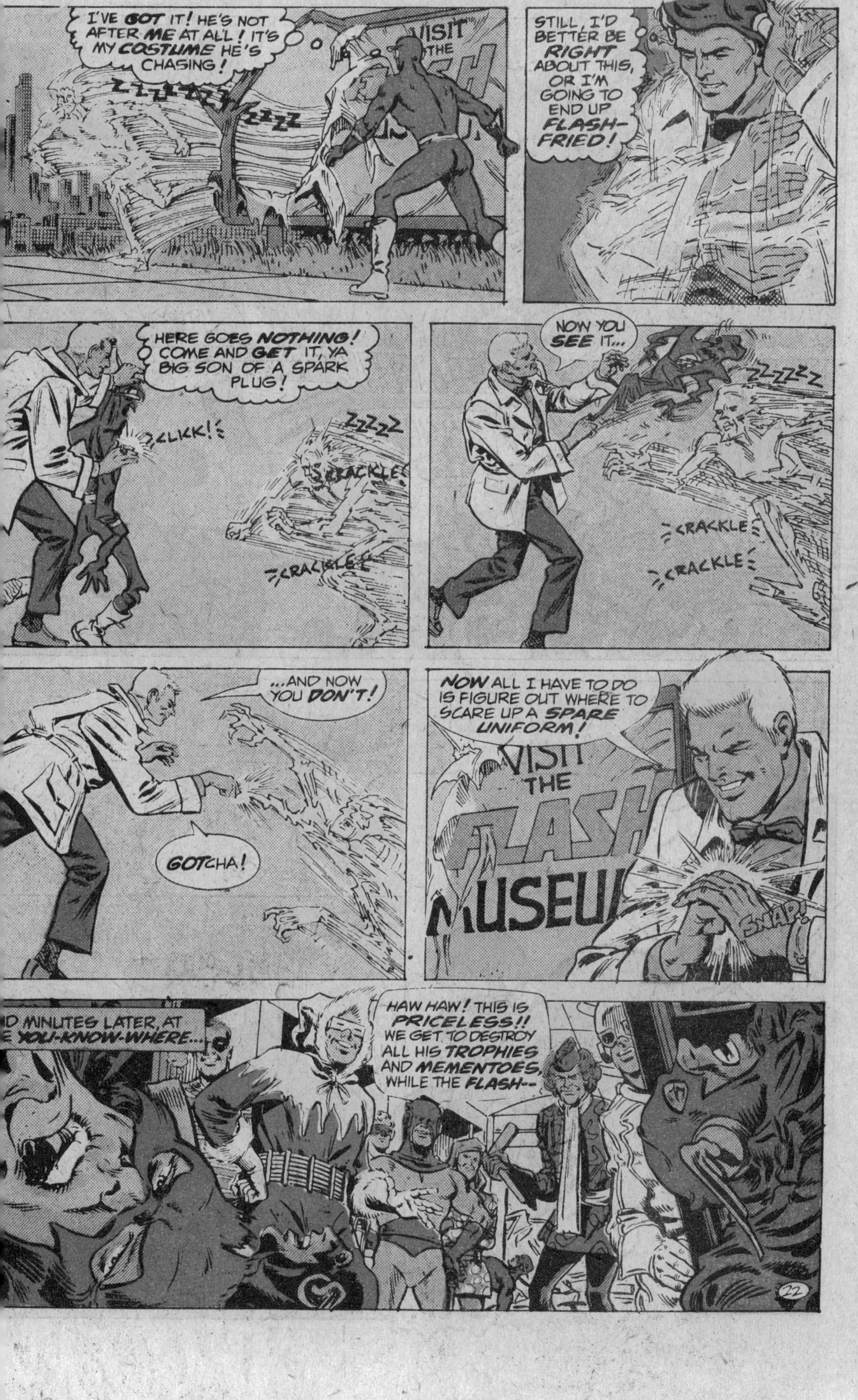

I'VE GOT IT! HE'S NOT AFTER ME AT ALL! IT'S MY COSTUME HE'S CHASING!
ZZZZZZZ
ZZZZ
STILL, I'D BETTER BE RIGHT ABOUT THIS, OR I'M GOING TO END UP FLASH-FRIED!
HERE GOES NOTHING! COME AND GET IT, YA BIG SON OF A SPARK PLUG!
CLIKK!
ZZZZZ
CRACKLE
CRACKLE
NOW YOU SEE IT...
ZZZZZZ
CRACKLE
CRACKLE
...AND NOW YOU DON'T!
GOTCHA!
NOW ALL I HAVE TO DO IS FIGURE OUT WHERE TO SCARE UP A SPARE UNIFORM!
VISIT THE FLASH MUSEU
SNAP!
D MINUTES LATER, AT E YOU-KNOW-WHERE...
HAW HAW! THIS IS PRICELESS!! WE GET TO DESTROY ALL HIS TROPHIES AND MEMENTOES, WHILE THE FLASH--
22

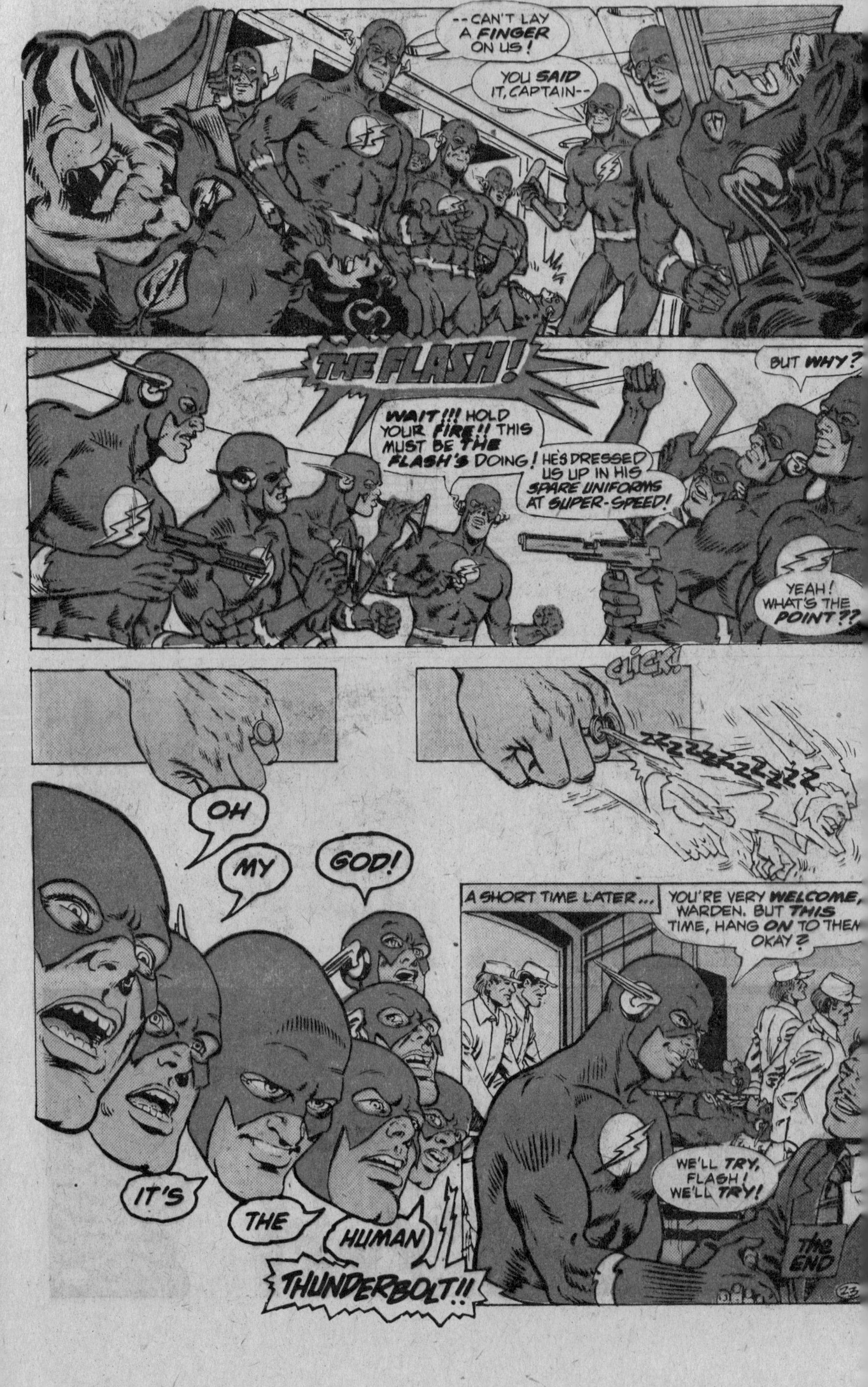
--CAN'T LAY A FINGER ON US!
YOU SAID IT, CAPTAIN--
THE FLASH!
BUT WHY?
WAIT!!! HOLD YOUR FIRE!! THIS MUST BE THE FLASH'S DOING!
HE'S DRESSED US UP IN HIS SPARE UNIFORMS AT SUPER-SPEED!
YEAH! WHAT'S THE POINT??
CLICK!
ZZZZZZZZZZZZZ
OH
MY
GOD!
IT'S
THE
HUMAN
THUNDERBOLT!!
A SHORT TIME LATER...
YOU'RE VERY WELCOME, WARDEN. BUT THIS TIME, HANG ON TO THEM OKAY?
WE'LL TRY, FLASH! WE'LL TRY!
THE END
23

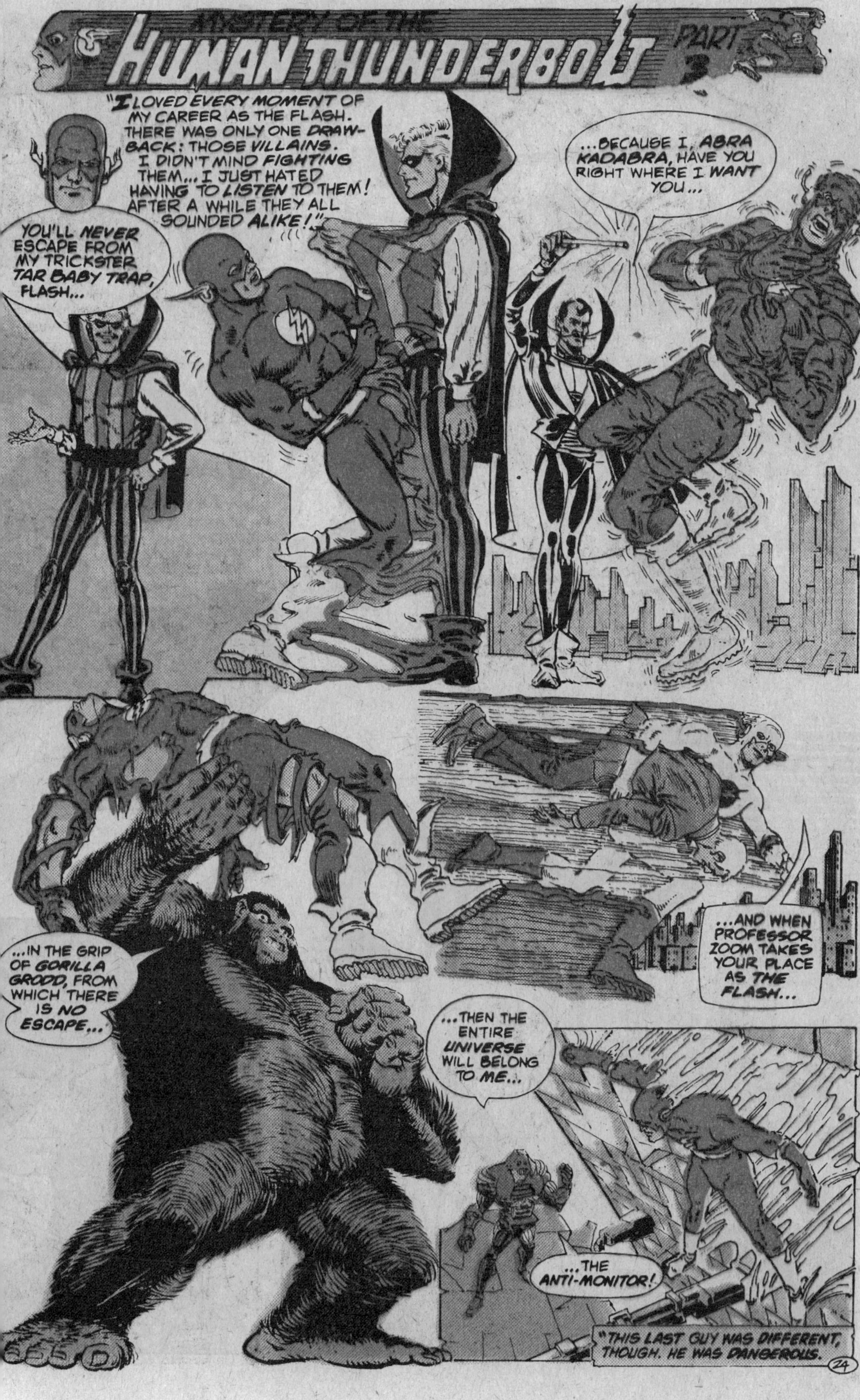
MYSTERY OF THE HUMAN THUNDERBOLT PART 3
"I LOVED EVERY MOMENT OF MY CAREER AS THE FLASH. THERE WAS ONLY ONE DRAW-BACK: THOSE VILLAINS. I DIDN'T MIND FIGHTING THEM... I JUST HATED HAVING TO LISTEN TO THEM! AFTER A WHILE THEY ALL SOUNDED ALIKE!"
YOU'LL NEVER ESCAPE FROM MY TRICKSTER TAR BABY TRAP, FLASH...
...BECAUSE I, ABRA KADABRA, HAVE YOU RIGHT WHERE I WANT YOU...
...IN THE GRIP OF GORILLA GRODD, FROM WHICH THERE IS NO ESCAPE...
...AND WHEN PROFESSOR ZOOM TAKES YOUR PLACE AS THE FLASH...
...THEN THE ENTIRE UNIVERSE WILL BELONG TO ME...
...THE ANTI-MONITOR!
"THIS LAST GUY WAS DIFFERENT, THOUGH. HE WAS DANGEROUS.
24

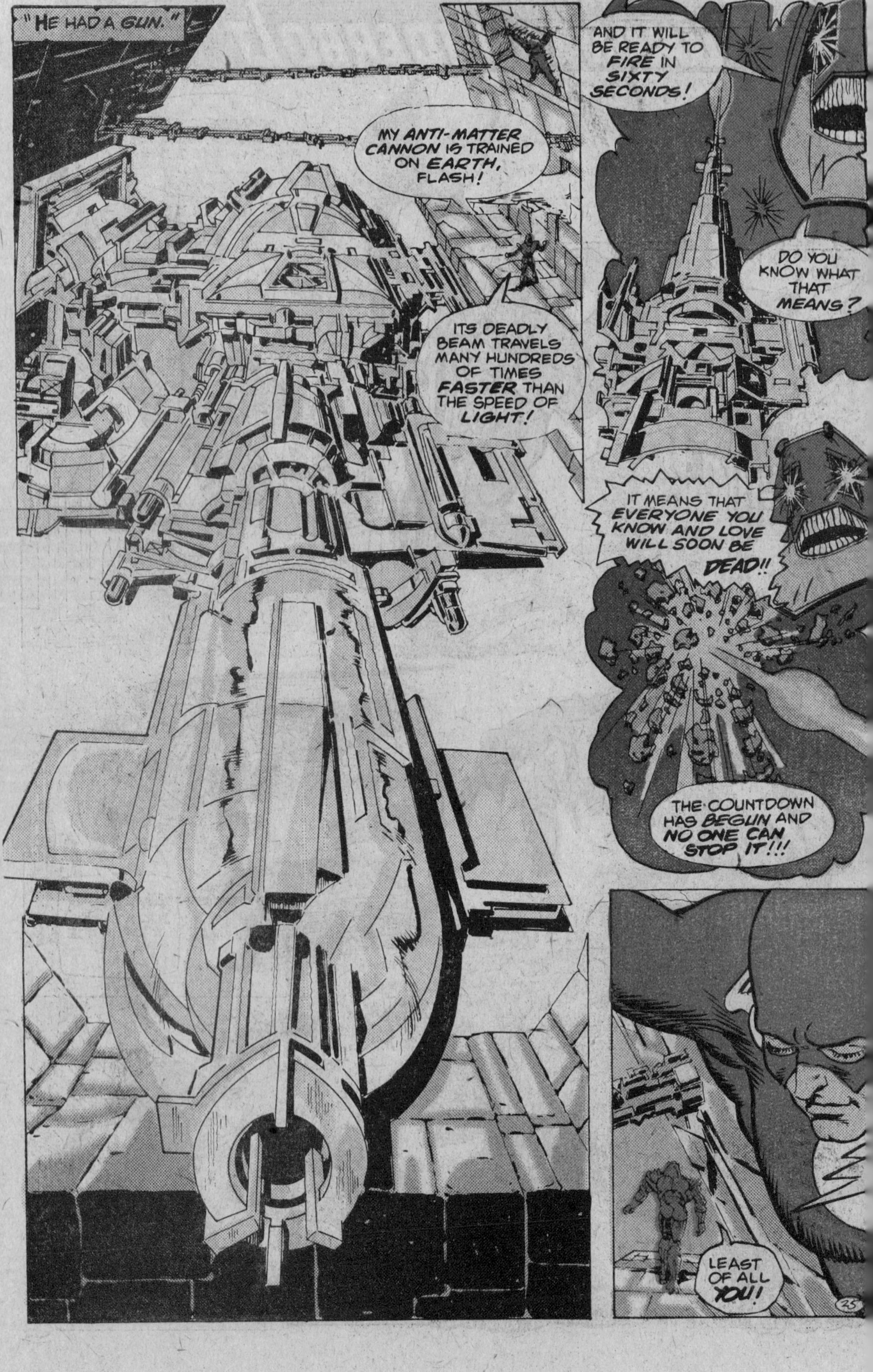
"HE HAD A GUN."
MY ANTI-MATTER CANNON IS TRAINED ON EARTH, FLASH!
ITS DEADLY BEAM TRAVELS MANY HUNDREDS OF TIMES FASTER THAN THE SPEED OF LIGHT!
AND IT WILL BE READY TO FIRE IN SIXTY SECONDS!
DO YOU KNOW WHAT THAT MEANS?
IT MEANS THAT EVERYONE YOU KNOW AND LOVE WILL SOON BE DEAD!!
THE COUNTDOWN HAS BEGUN AND NO ONE CAN STOP IT!!!
LEAST OF ALL YOU!

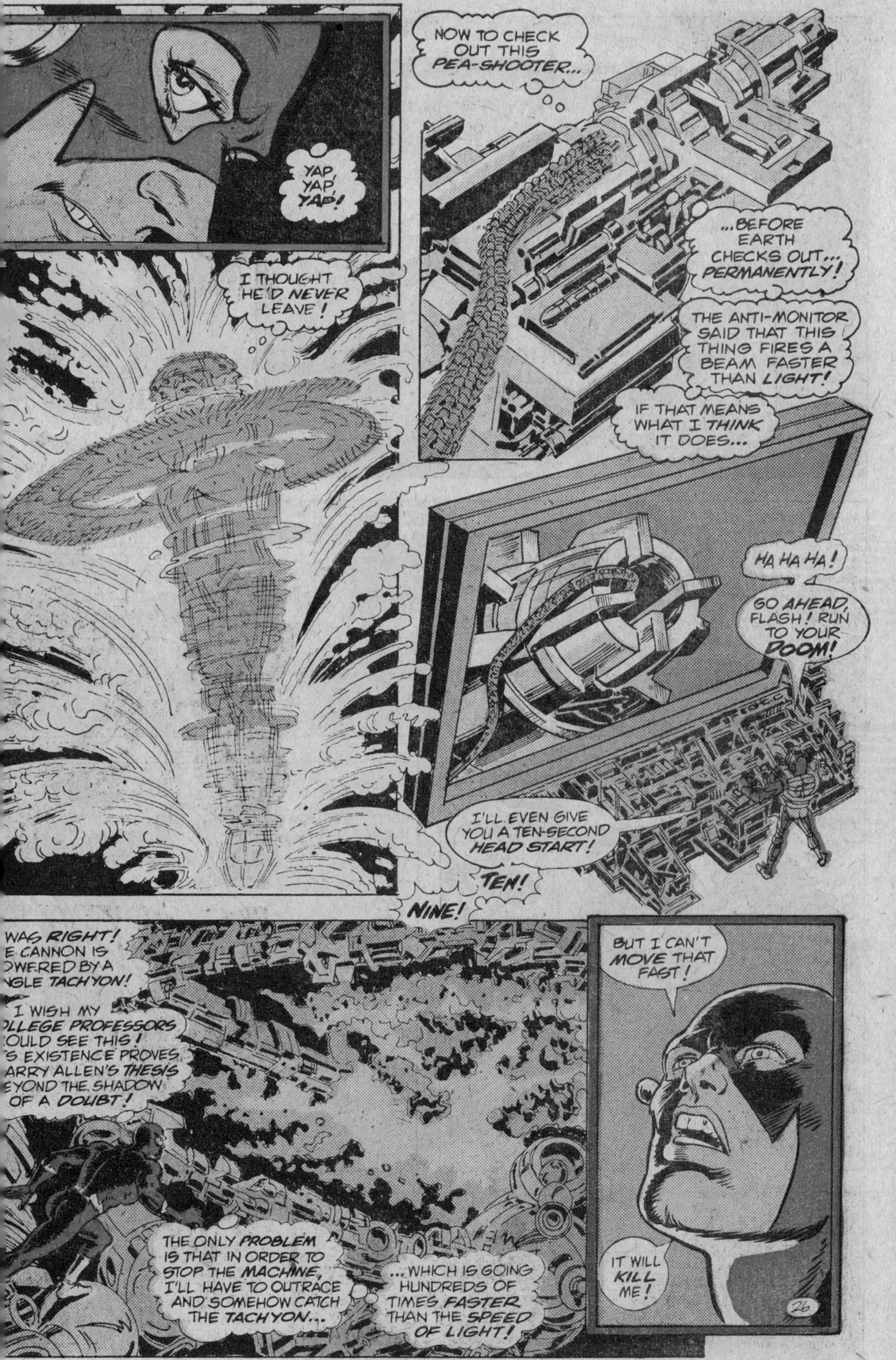

YAP, YAP, YAP!
I THOUGHT HE'D NEVER LEAVE!
NOW TO CHECK OUT THIS PEA-SHOOTER...
...BEFORE EARTH CHECKS OUT... PERMANENTLY!
THE ANTI-MONITOR SAID THAT THIS THING FIRES A BEAM FASTER THAN LIGHT!
IF THAT MEANS WHAT I THINK IT DOES...
HA HA HA!
GO AHEAD, FLASH! RUN TO YOUR DOOM!
I'LL EVEN GIVE YOU A TEN-SECOND HEAD START!
TEN!
NINE!
WAS RIGHT! E CANNON IS OWERED BY A NGLE TACHYON!
I WISH MY OLLEGE PROFESSORS OULD SEE THIS! 'S EXISTENCE PROVES ARRY ALLEN'S THESIS EYOND THE SHADOW OF A DOUBT!
THE ONLY PROBLEM IS THAT IN ORDER TO STOP THE MACHINE, I'LL HAVE TO OUTRACE AND SOMEHOW CATCH THE TACHYON...
...WHICH IS GOING HUNDREDS OF TIMES FASTER THAN THE SPEED OF LIGHT!
BUT I CAN'T MOVE THAT FAST!
IT WILL KILL ME!
26

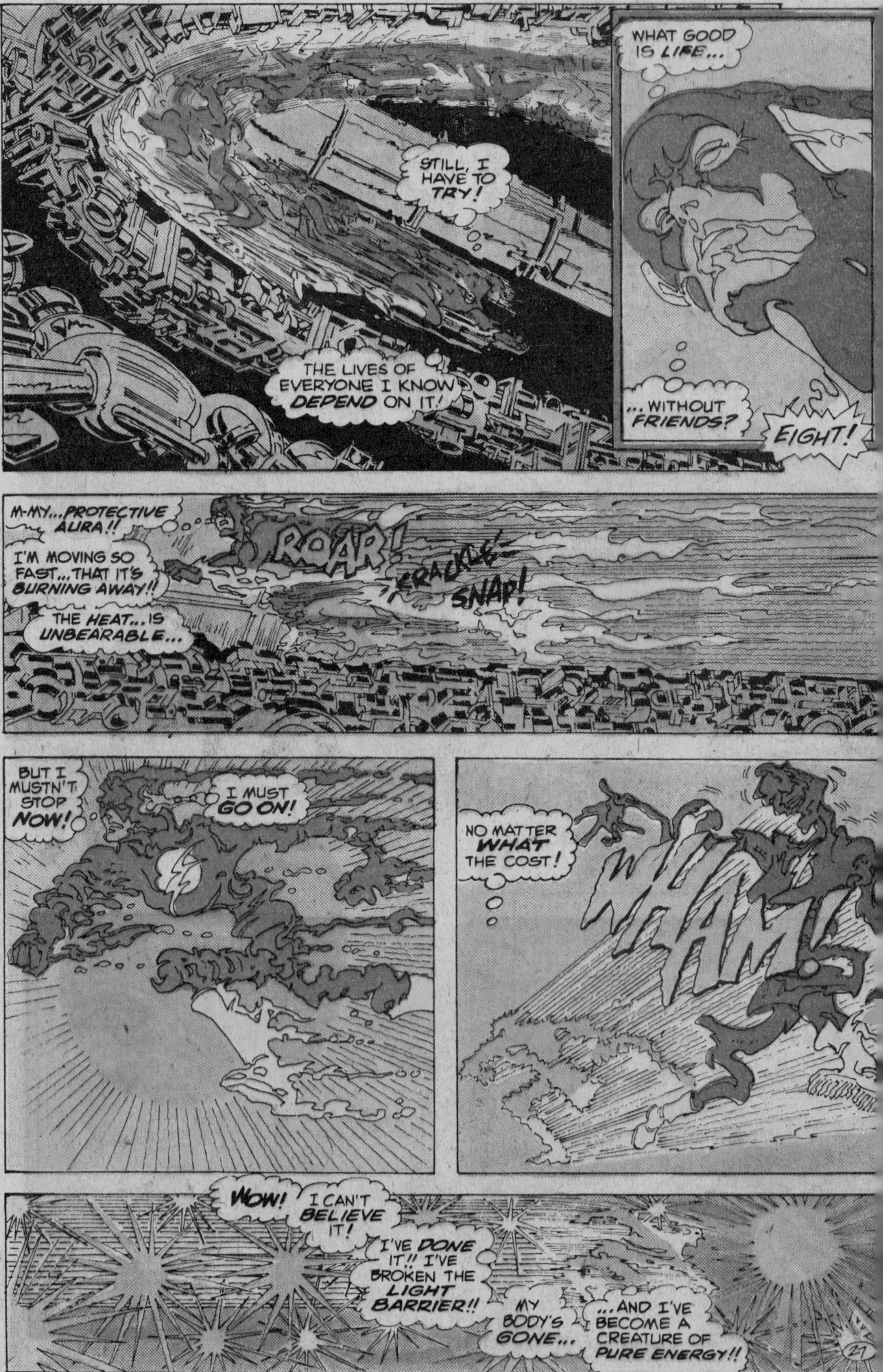
STILL, I HAVE TO TRY!
THE LIVES OF EVERYONE I KNOW DEPEND ON IT!
WHAT GOOD IS LIFE...
...WITHOUT FRIENDS?
EIGHT!
M-MY... PROTECTIVE AURA!!
I'M MOVING SO FAST... THAT IT'S BURNING AWAY!!
THE HEAT... IS UNBEARABLE...
ROAR!
KRACKLE
SNAP!
BUT I MUSTN'T STOP NOW!
I MUST GO ON!
NO MATTER WHAT THE COST!
WHAM!
WOW! I CAN'T BELIEVE IT!
I'VE DONE IT!! I'VE BROKEN THE LIGHT BARRIER!!
MY BODY'S GONE...
...AND I'VE BECOME A CREATURE OF PURE ENERGY!!

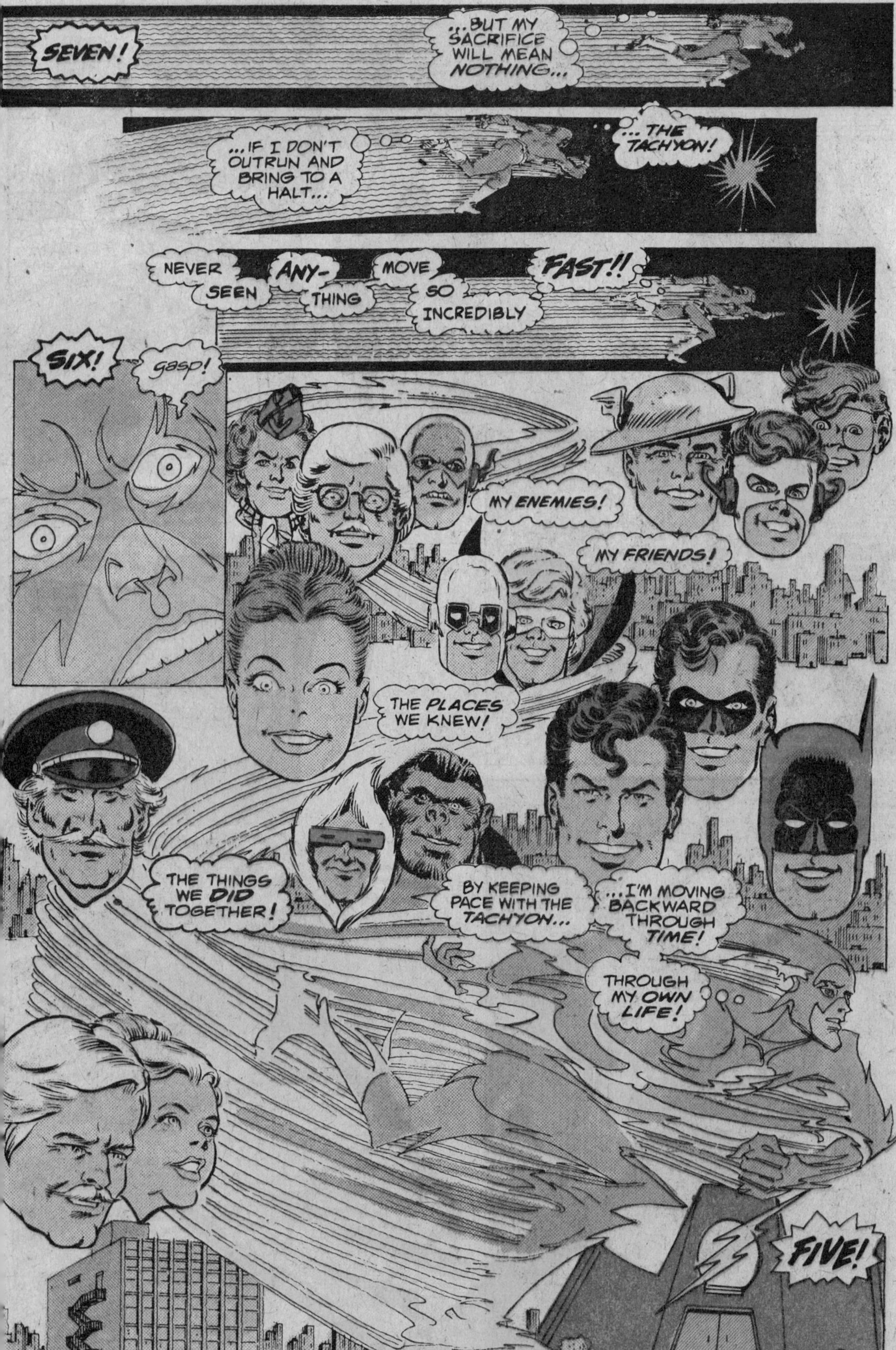
SEVEN!
...BUT MY SACRIFICE WILL MEAN NOTHING...
...IF I DON'T OUTRUN AND BRING TO A HALT...
...THE TACHYON!
NEVER SEEN ANY-THING MOVE SO INCREDIBLY FAST!!
SIX!
gasp!
MY ENEMIES!
MY FRIENDS!
THE PLACES WE KNEW!
THE THINGS WE DID TOGETHER!
BY KEEPING PACE WITH THE TACHYON...
...I'M MOVING BACKWARD THROUGH TIME!
THROUGH MY OWN LIFE!
FIVE!
28

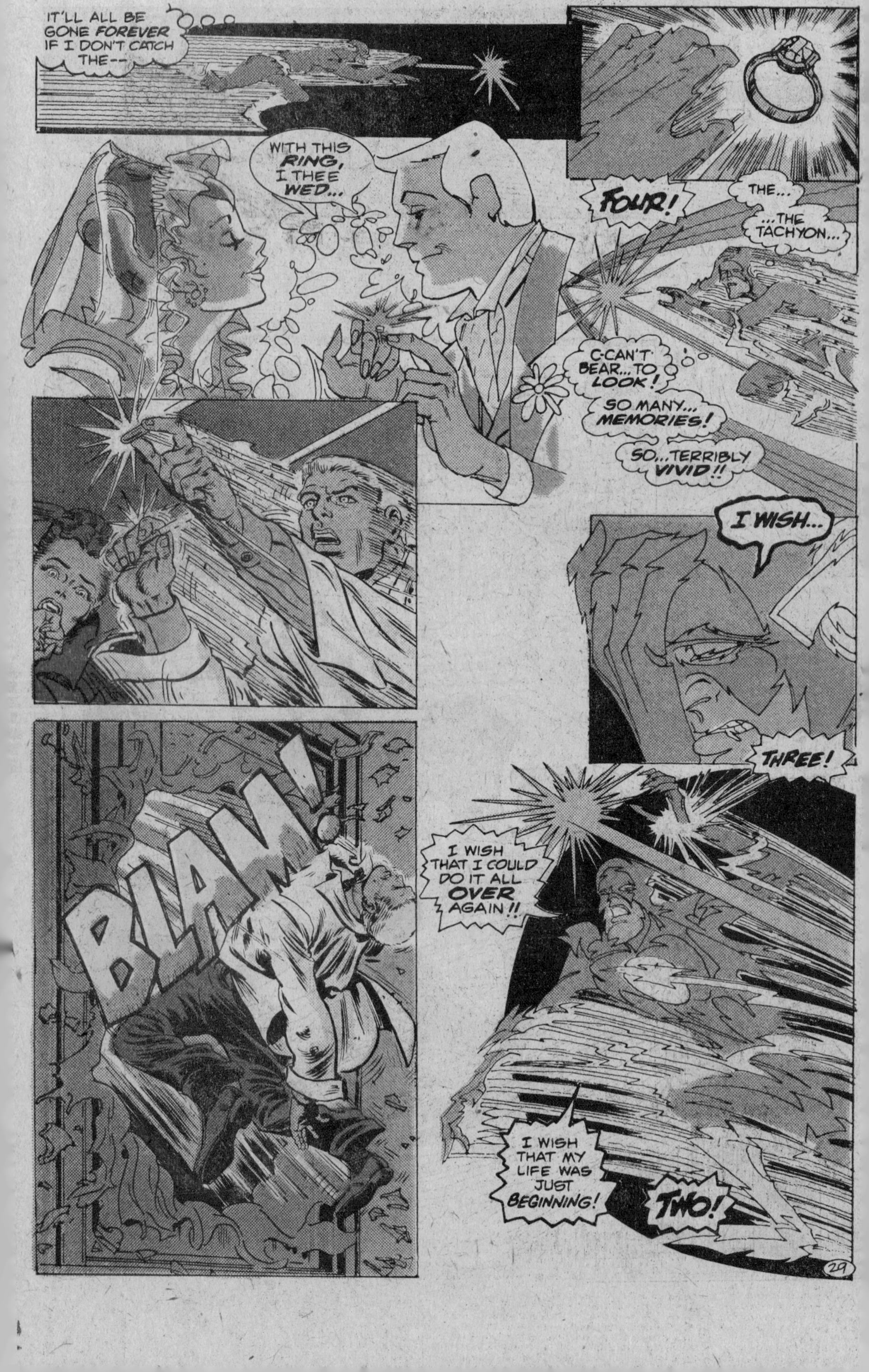

IT'LL ALL BE GONE FOREVER IF I DON'T CATCH THE--
WITH THIS RING, I THEE WED...
FOUR!
THE...
...THE TACHYON...
C-CAN'T BEAR... TO LOOK!
SO MANY... MEMORIES!
SO... TERRIBLY VIVID!!
I WISH...
THREE!
BLAM!
I WISH THAT I COULD DO IT ALL OVER AGAIN!!
I WISH THAT MY LIFE WAS JUST BEGINNING!
TWO!

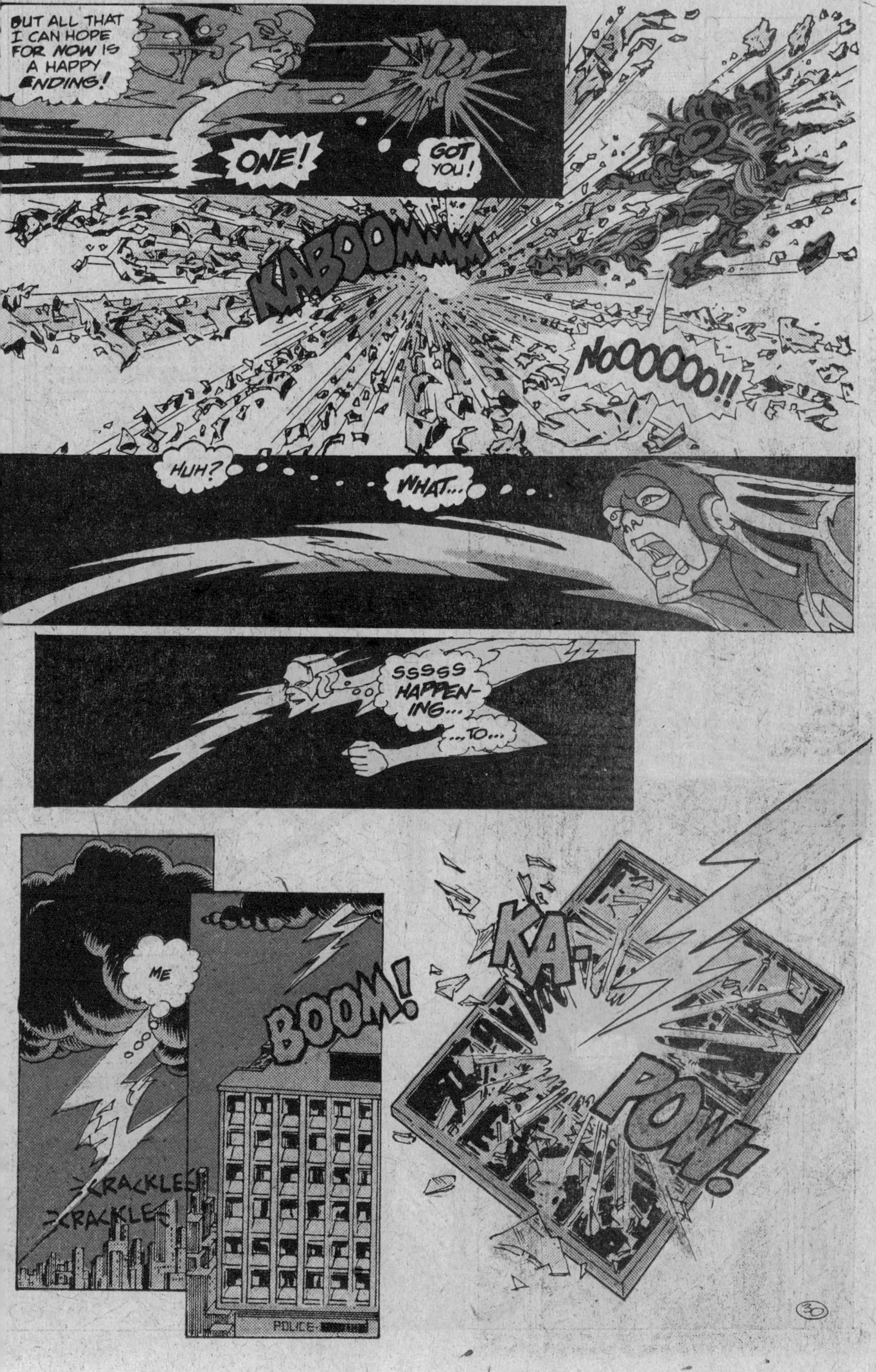
BUT ALL THAT I CAN HOPE FOR NOW IS A HAPPY ENDING!
ONE!
GOT YOU!
KABOOMMMM
NOOOOOO!!
HUH?
WHAT...
SSSSS HAPPENING...
...TO...
ME
BOOM!
KRACKLE
KRACKLE
POLICE
KA-POW!

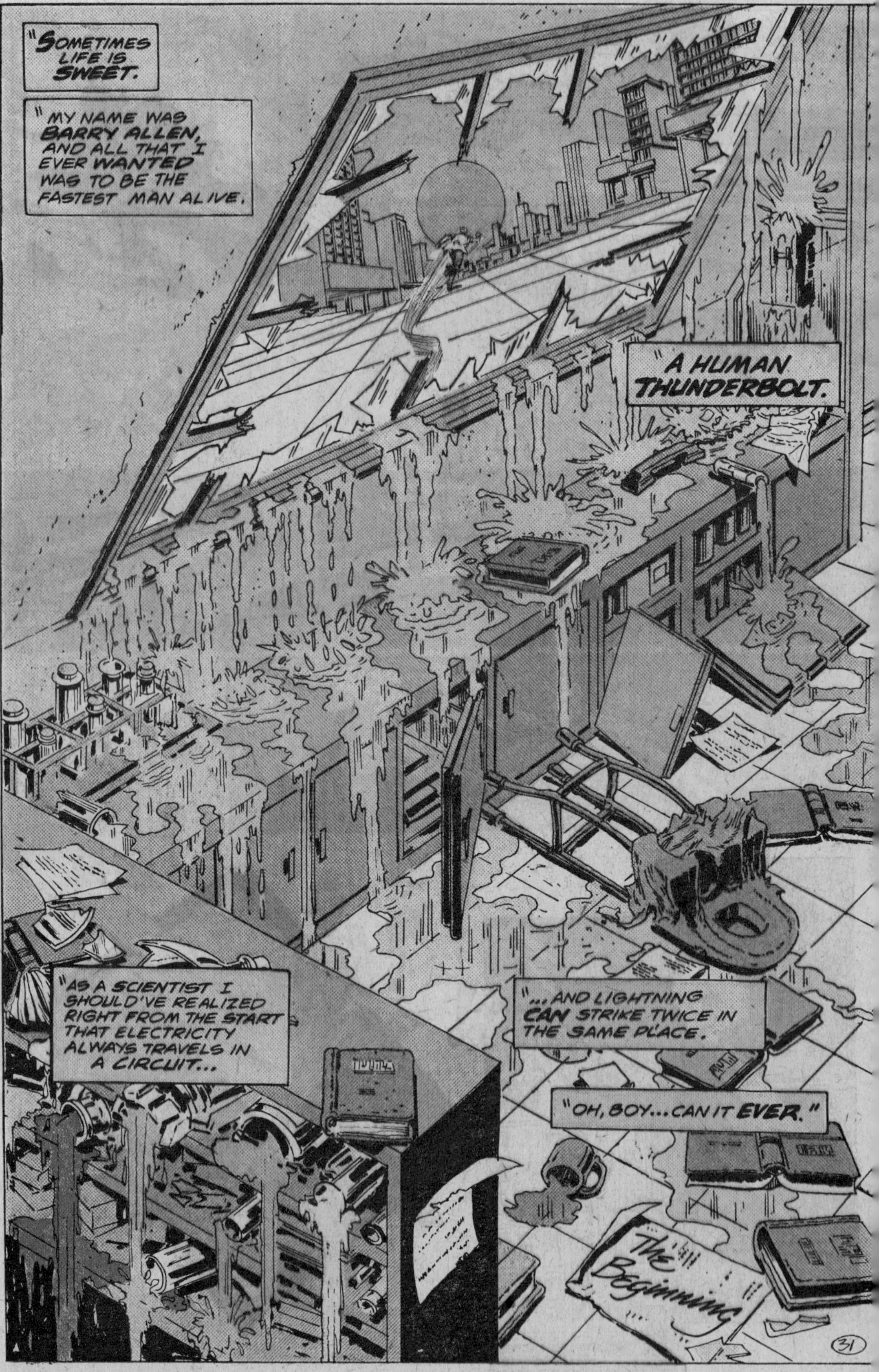
"SOMETIMES LIFE IS SWEET.
"MY NAME WAS BARRY ALLEN, AND ALL THAT I EVER WANTED WAS TO BE THE FASTEST MAN ALIVE.
"A HUMAN THUNDERBOLT.
"AS A SCIENTIST I SHOULD'VE REALIZED RIGHT FROM THE START THAT ELECTRICITY ALWAYS TRAVELS IN A CIRCUIT...
"...AND LIGHTNING CAN STRIKE TWICE IN THE SAME PLACE.
"OH, BOY...CAN IT EVER."
The Beginning

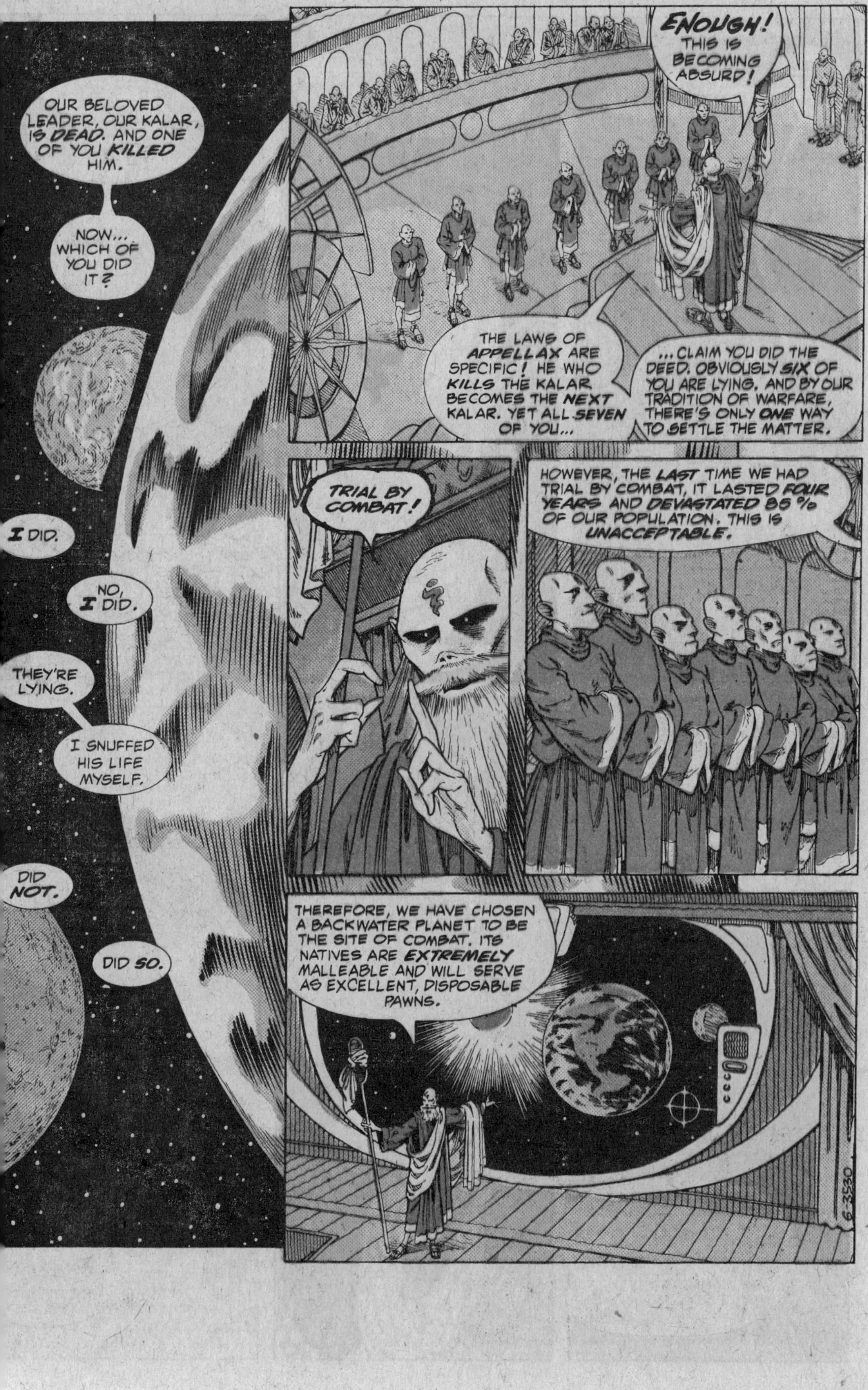

OUR BELOVED LEADER, OUR KALAR, IS **DEAD**. AND ONE OF YOU **KILLED** HIM.
NOW... WHICH OF YOU DID IT?
I DID.
NO, **I** DID.
THEY'RE LYING.
I SNUFFED HIS LIFE MYSELF.
DID **NOT**.
DID **SO**.
ENOUGH! THIS IS BECOMING ABSURD!
THE LAWS OF **APPELLAX** ARE SPECIFIC! HE WHO **KILLS** THE KALAR BECOMES THE **NEXT** KALAR. YET ALL **SEVEN** OF YOU...
...CLAIM YOU DID THE DEED. OBVIOUSLY **SIX** OF YOU ARE LYING. AND BY OUR TRADITION OF WARFARE, THERE'S ONLY **ONE** WAY TO SETTLE THE MATTER.
TRIAL BY COMBAT!
HOWEVER, THE **LAST** TIME WE HAD TRIAL BY COMBAT, IT LASTED **FOUR YEARS** AND **DEVASTATED** 85 % OF OUR POPULATION. THIS IS **UNACCEPTABLE.**
THEREFORE, WE HAVE CHOSEN A BACKWATER PLANET TO BE THE SITE OF COMBAT. ITS NATIVES ARE **EXTREMELY** MALLEABLE AND WILL SERVE AS EXCELLENT, DISPOSABLE PAWNS.

ITS NATIVES CALL IT...

...EARTH!

"BATTLE FORMS" HAVE BEEN RANDOMLY SELECTED FOR YOU. YOUR MINDS WILL BE IMPLANTED IN THEM, AND YOU WILL BE SENT TO YOUR BATTLE-GROUND!

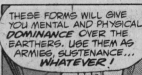

THESE FORMS WILL GIVE YOU MENTAL AND PHYSICAL DOMINANCE OVER THE EARTHERS. USE THEM AS ARMIES, SUSTENANCE... WHATEVER!

WE WILL MONITOR YOU CLOSELY. YOU WILL BE AUTOMATICALLY DIS-QUALIFIED IF YOU ARE PHYSICALLY OVERCOME. IN THAT EVENT, YOUR MIND WILL RICOCHET BACK HERE TO YOUR REAL BODY AND YOU WILL BE EXILED, AS BEFITS A LOSER.

NOW HURRY. YOUR INDIVIDUAL TRAVEL PODS AWAIT. HAVE YOURSELVES IMPLANTED INTO YOUR BATTLEFORMS. THEN GO TO EARTH. WHOEVER WAGES THE MOST SUCCESSFUL CAMPAIGN WILL BE KALAR!

A QUESTION, JUDGE. WHAT IF WE ARE OVERCOME-- DEFEATED-- BY SOMEONE OTHER THAN ONE OF THE COMPETITORS?

YOU MEAN, BY AN EARTHER? ABSURD.

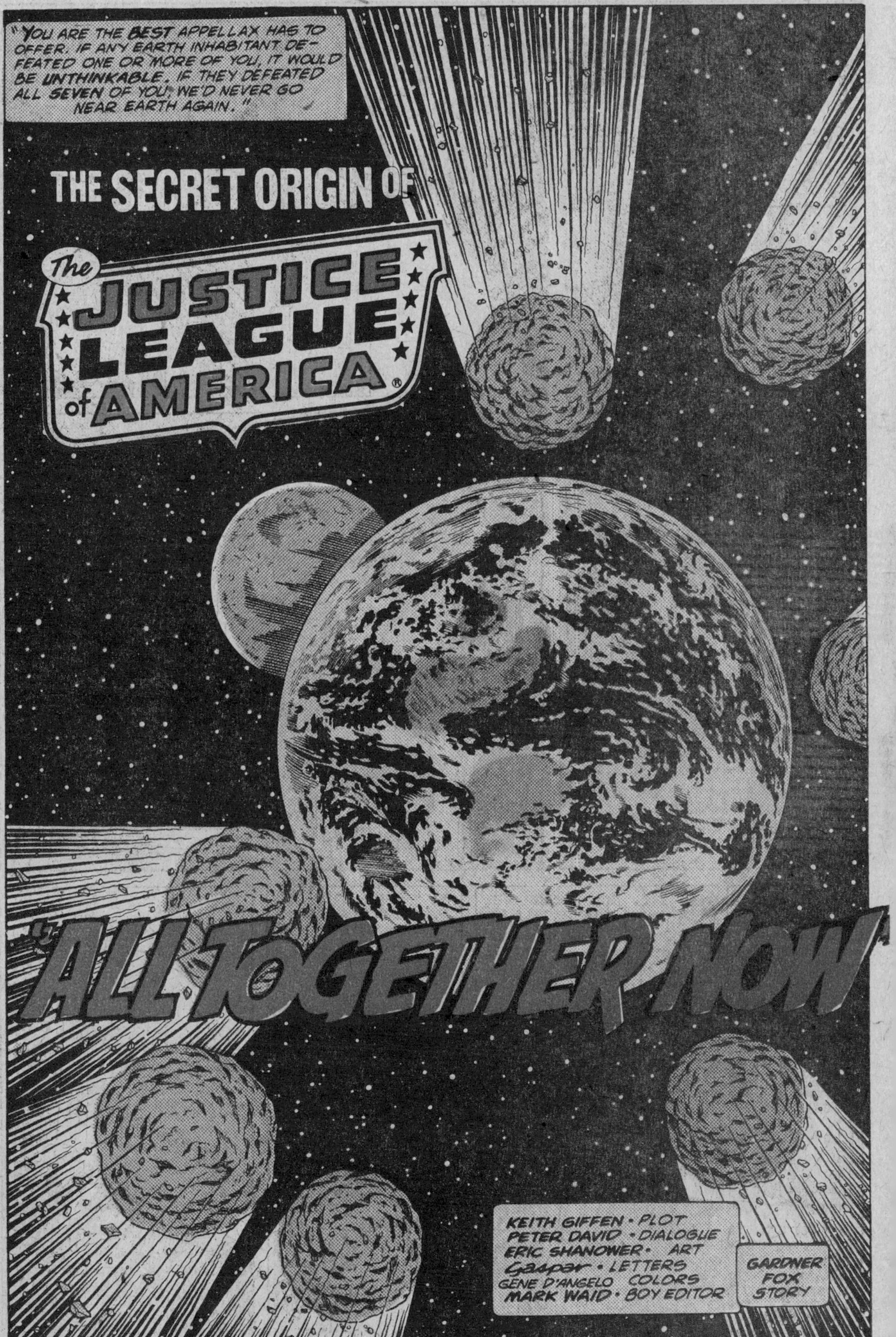

"YOU ARE THE BEST APPELLAX HAS TO OFFER. IF ANY EARTH INHABITANT DEFEATED ONE OR MORE OF YOU, IT WOULD BE UNTHINKABLE. IF THEY DEFEATED ALL SEVEN OF YOU, WE'D NEVER GO NEAR EARTH AGAIN."
THE SECRET ORIGIN OF
The JUSTICE LEAGUE of AMERICA®
"ALL TOGETHER NOW"
KEITH GIFFEN • PLOT
PETER DAVID • DIALOGUE
ERIC SHANOWER • ART
Gaspar • LETTERS
GENE D'ANGELO COLORS
MARK WAID • BOY EDITOR
GARDNER FOX STORY

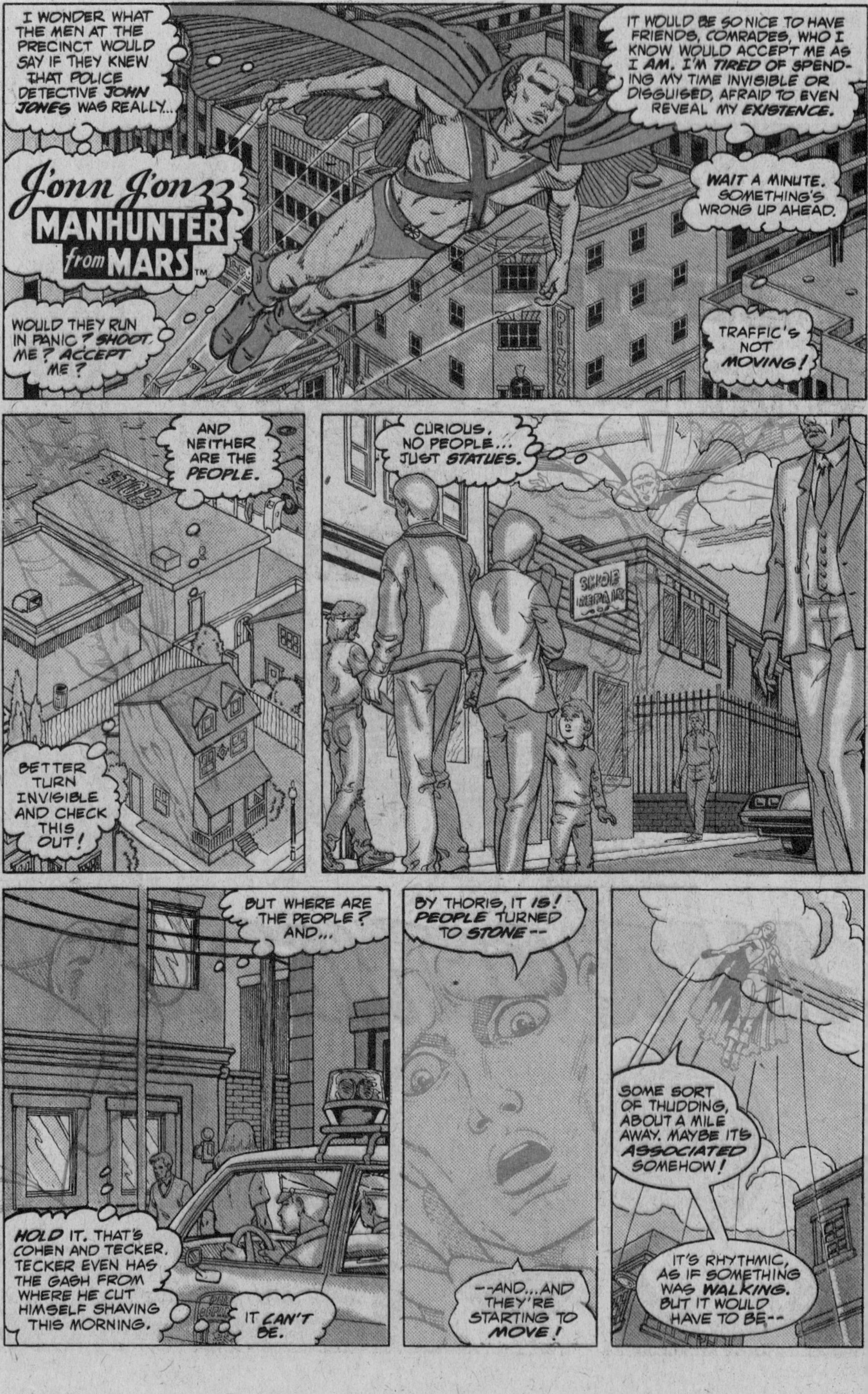
I WONDER WHAT THE MEN AT THE PRECINCT WOULD SAY IF THEY KNEW THAT POLICE DETECTIVE JOHN JONES WAS REALLY...
J'onn J'onzz
MANHUNTER from MARS
WOULD THEY RUN IN PANIC? SHOOT ME? ACCEPT ME?
IT WOULD BE SO NICE TO HAVE FRIENDS, COMRADES, WHO I KNOW WOULD ACCEPT ME AS I AM. I'M TIRED OF SPENDING MY TIME INVISIBLE OR DISGUISED, AFRAID TO EVEN REVEAL MY EXISTENCE.
WAIT A MINUTE. SOMETHING'S WRONG UP AHEAD.
TRAFFIC'S NOT MOVING!
AND NEITHER ARE THE PEOPLE.
BETTER TURN INVISIBLE AND CHECK THIS OUT!
CURIOUS, NO PEOPLE... JUST STATUES.
SHOE REPAIR
BUT WHERE ARE THE PEOPLE? AND...
HOLD IT. THAT'S COHEN AND TECKER. TECKER EVEN HAS THE GASH FROM WHERE HE CUT HIMSELF SHAVING THIS MORNING.
IT CAN'T BE.
BY THORIS, IT IS! PEOPLE TURNED TO STONE--
--AND... AND THEY'RE STARTING TO MOVE!
SOME SORT OF THUDDING, ABOUT A MILE AWAY. MAYBE IT'S ASSOCIATED SOMEHOW!
IT'S RHYTHMIC, AS IF SOMETHING WAS WALKING. BUT IT WOULD HAVE TO BE--

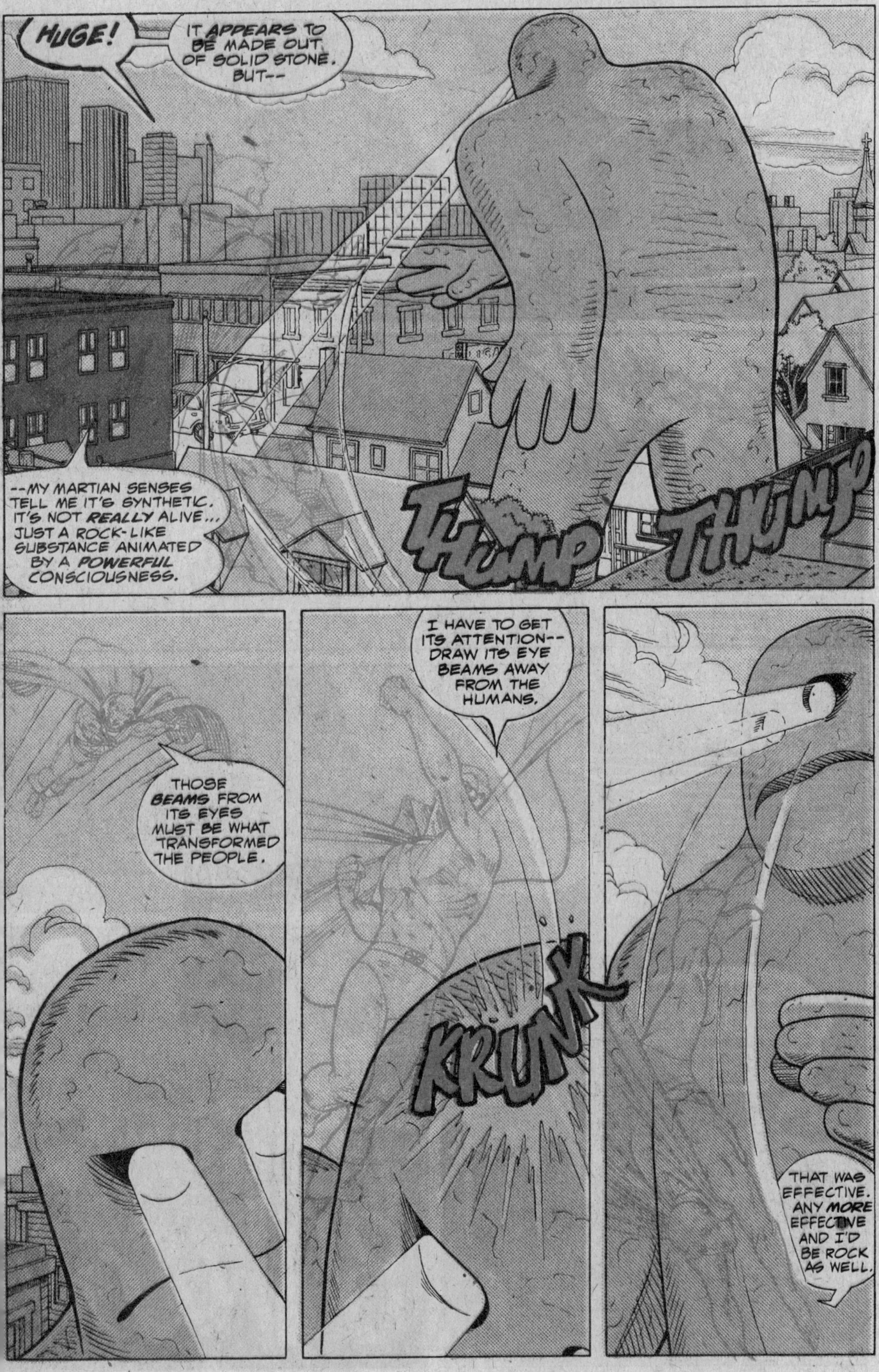
HUGE!
IT APPEARS TO BE MADE OUT OF SOLID STONE. BUT--
--MY MARTIAN SENSES TELL ME IT'S SYNTHETIC. IT'S NOT REALLY ALIVE... JUST A ROCK-LIKE SUBSTANCE ANIMATED BY A POWERFUL CONSCIOUSNESS.
THUMP THUMP
THOSE BEAMS FROM ITS EYES MUST BE WHAT TRANSFORMED THE PEOPLE.
I HAVE TO GET ITS ATTENTION-- DRAW ITS EYE BEAMS AWAY FROM THE HUMANS.
KRUNK
THAT WAS EFFECTIVE. ANY MORE EFFECTIVE AND I'D BE ROCK AS WELL.

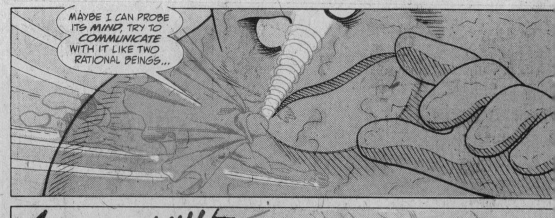

MAYBE I CAN PROBE ITS *MIND*, TRY TO *COMMUNICATE* WITH IT LIKE TWO RATIONAL BEINGS...

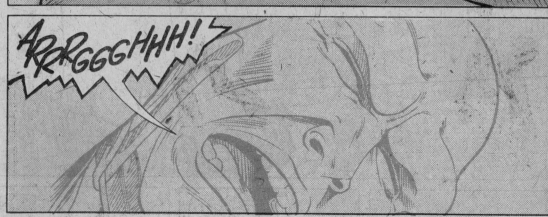

ARRRGGGHHH!

ARE YOU CAUSED PAIN BY MY *OVERWHELMING SUPERIORITY*, MARTIAN?

NO. YOUR *OVERWHELMING EVIL!*

WAIT...YOU CAN *SEE* ME? AND YOU KNOW I'M *MARTIAN!*

YOUR PUNY PROBE *BACKFIRED!* I KNOW ALL ABOUT YOU, J'ONZZ... INCLUDING YOUR *WEAKNESS* FOR *FIRE!*

THE GAS STOP

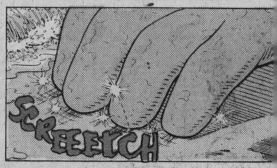

SCREEECH

SPARKS FROM HIS FINGERS *IGNITED* THE GAS. IF I FALL *INTO* IT, I'M *THROUGH!*

BUWOOM!

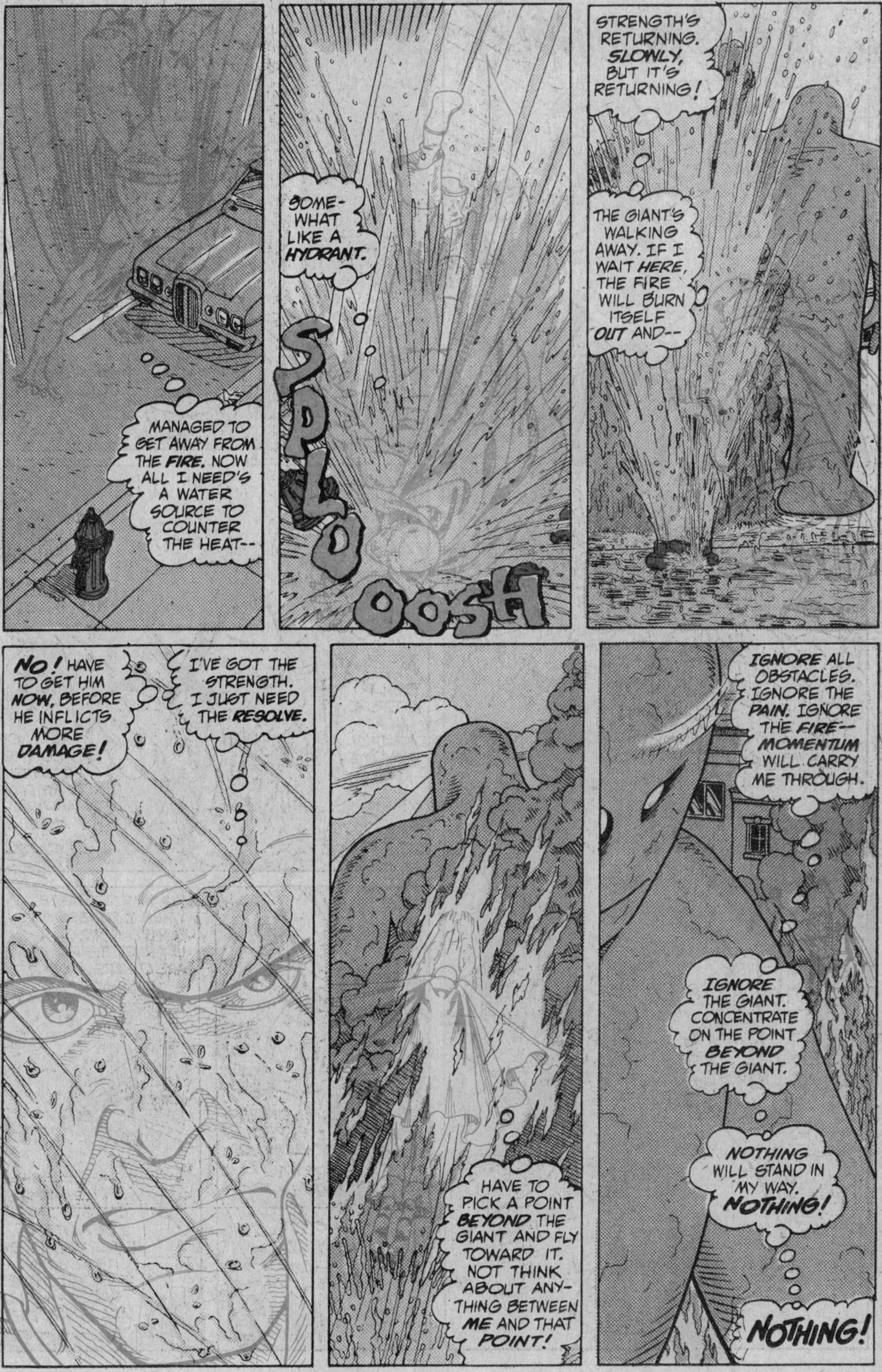
MANAGED TO GET AWAY FROM THE FIRE. NOW ALL I NEED'S A WATER SOURCE TO COUNTER THE HEAT--
SOME-WHAT LIKE A HYDRANT.
SPLOOOSH
STRENGTH'S RETURNING. SLOWLY, BUT IT'S RETURNING!
THE GIANT'S WALKING AWAY. IF I WAIT HERE, THE FIRE WILL BURN ITSELF OUT AND--
NO! HAVE TO GET HIM NOW, BEFORE HE INFLICTS MORE DAMAGE!
I'VE GOT THE STRENGTH. I JUST NEED THE RESOLVE.
HAVE TO PICK A POINT BEYOND THE GIANT AND FLY TOWARD IT. NOT THINK ABOUT ANY-THING BETWEEN ME AND THAT POINT!
IGNORE ALL OBSTACLES. IGNORE THE PAIN. IGNORE THE FIRE-- MOMENTUM WILL CARRY ME THROUGH.
IGNORE THE GIANT. CONCENTRATE ON THE POINT BEYOND THE GIANT.
NOTHING WILL STAND IN MY WAY. NOTHING!
NOTHING!

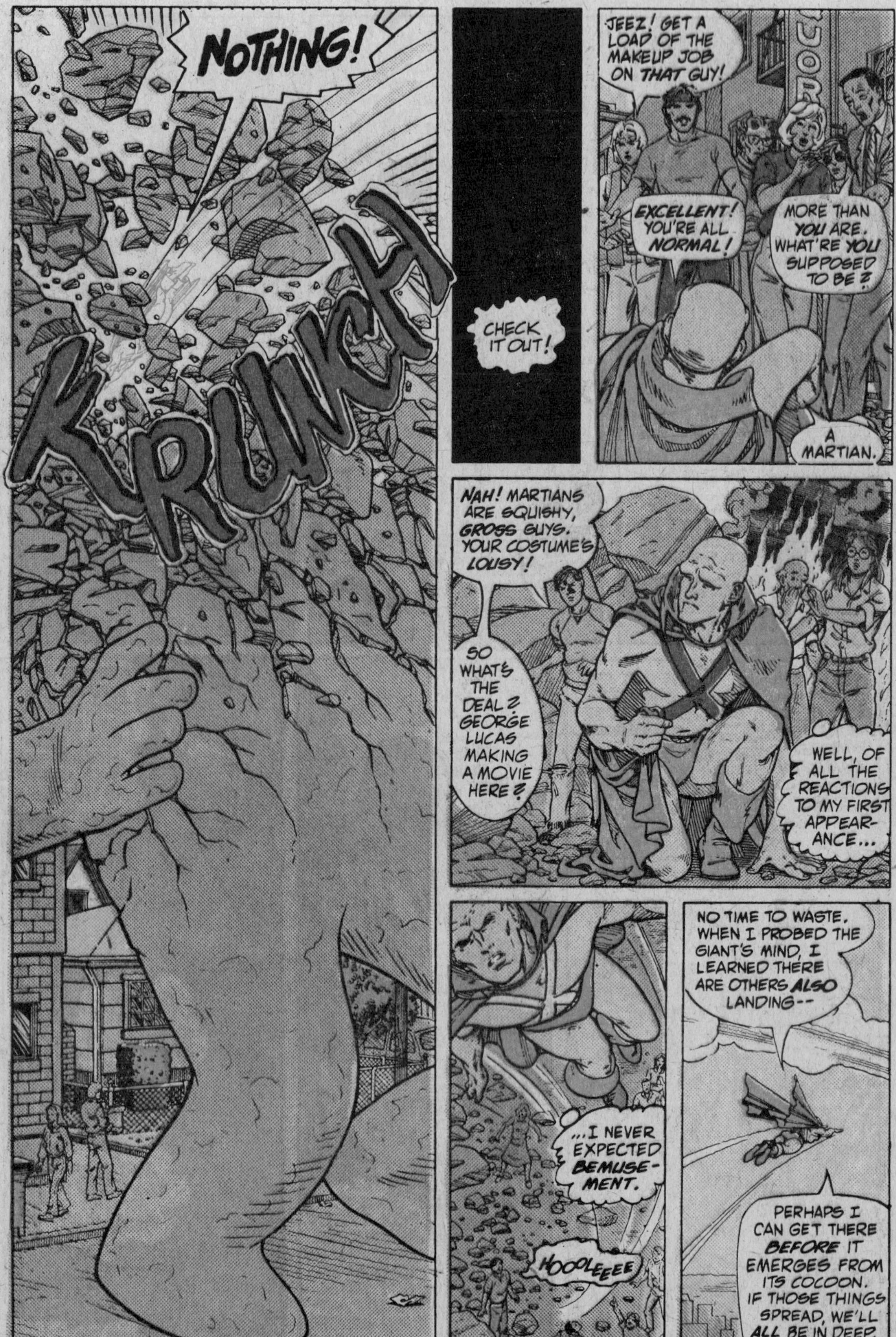
NOTHING!
KRUNCH
CHECK IT OUT!
JEEZ! GET A LOAD OF THE MAKEUP JOB ON THAT GUY!
EXCELLENT! YOU'RE ALL NORMAL!
MORE THAN YOU ARE. WHAT'RE YOU SUPPOSED TO BE?
A MARTIAN.
NAH! MARTIANS ARE SQUISHY, GROSS GUYS. YOUR COSTUME'S LOUSY!
SO WHAT'S THE DEAL? GEORGE LUCAS MAKING A MOVIE HERE?
WELL, OF ALL THE REACTIONS TO MY FIRST APPEARANCE...
...I NEVER EXPECTED BEMUSEMENT.
HOOOLEEEE
NO TIME TO WASTE. WHEN I PROBED THE GIANT'S MIND, I LEARNED THERE ARE OTHERS ALSO LANDING--
PERHAPS I CAN GET THERE BEFORE IT EMERGES FROM ITS COCOON. IF THOSE THINGS SPREAD, WE'LL ALL BE IN DEEP.

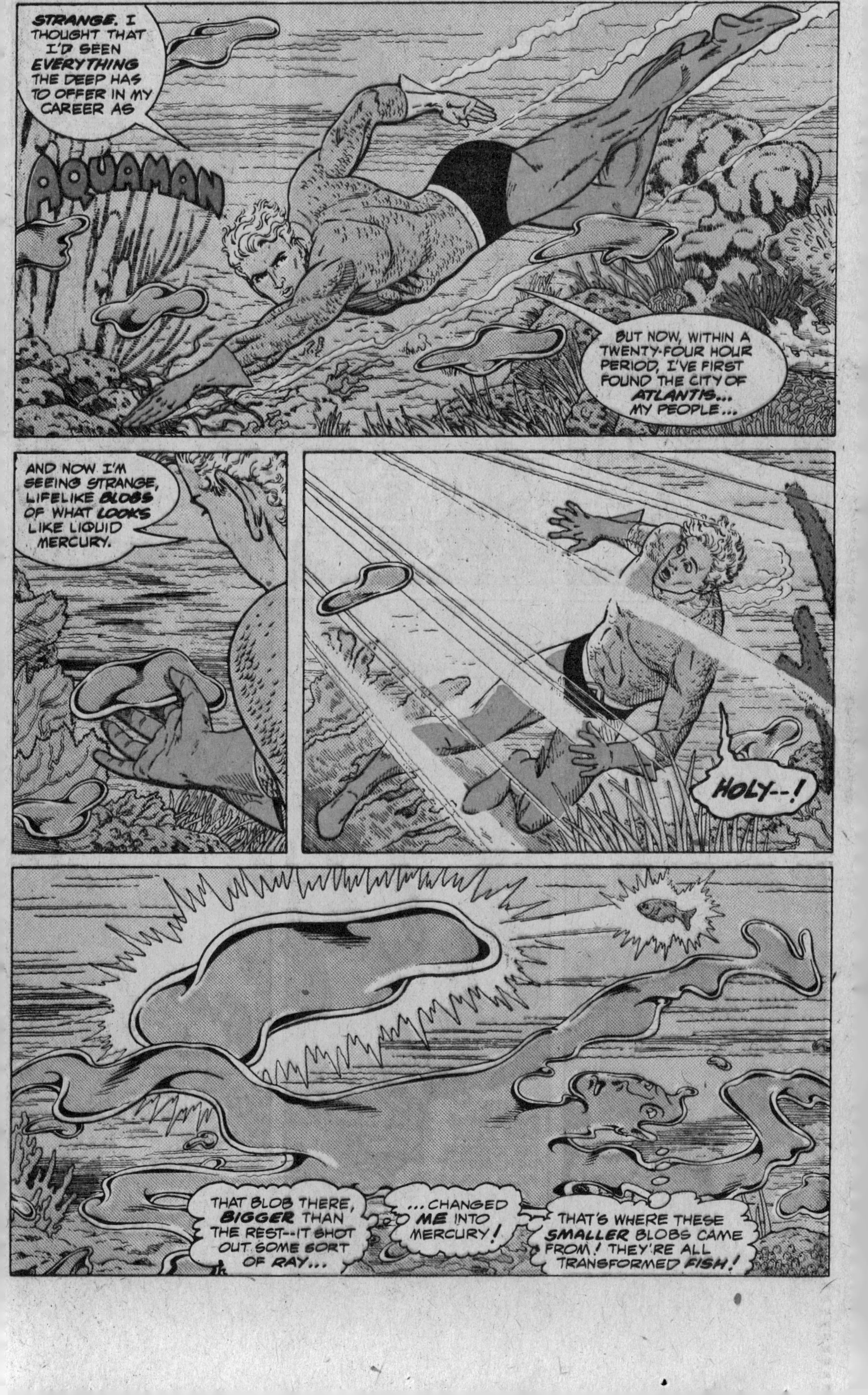
STRANGE. I THOUGHT THAT I'D SEEN EVERYTHING THE DEEP HAS TO OFFER IN MY CAREER AS
AQUAMAN
BUT NOW, WITHIN A TWENTY-FOUR HOUR PERIOD, I'VE FIRST FOUND THE CITY OF ATLANTIS... MY PEOPLE...
AND NOW I'M SEEING STRANGE, LIFELIKE BLOBS OF WHAT LOOKS LIKE LIQUID MERCURY.
HOLY--!
THAT BLOB THERE, BIGGER THAN THE REST--IT SHOT OUT SOME SORT OF RAY...
...CHANGED ME INTO MERCURY!
THAT'S WHERE THESE SMALLER BLOBS CAME FROM! THEY'RE ALL TRANSFORMED FISH!

ALL RIGHT. NOW THAT I'VE FIGURED THAT OUT, WHAT'S MY NEXT MOVE?
I'VE NO CONTROL OVER MY BODY AT ALL... I'M AT THE MERCY OF THE CURRENTS AND THAT CREATURE.
STILL, MAYBE I CAN USE THE CURRENTS TO MY ADVANTAGE... RIDE THEM TO ATTACK THAT THING!
OF COURSE, ONCE I GET THERE, WHAT AM I GOING TO DO? I'VE ALWAYS FELT THAT MY POWERS, COMPARED TO OTHER SUPER-HUMANS, WERE FAIRLY UNIMPRESSIVE. BUT I NEVER FELT SO HELPLESS!
IT SENSED ME COMING AND JUST GOT OUT OF MY WAY.
OH NO! I CAN FEEL MY BODY STARTING TO COME APART!
IT'S EVERYTHING THAT I CAN DO TO STOP THE CURRENT FROM DRAGGING ME APART! AND THAT THING'S STRONGER THAN EVER!
SOME KING OF THE SEA I AM, UNABLE TO SAVE ANY OF MY SUBJECTS, OR EVEN MYSELF. I'M RE-DEFINING THE WORD "USELESS."

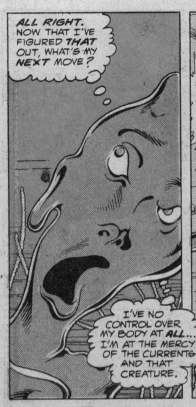

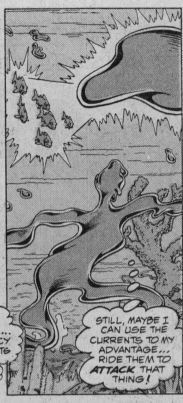

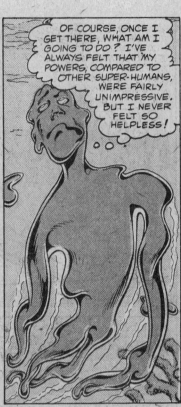

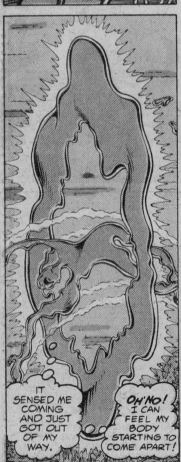

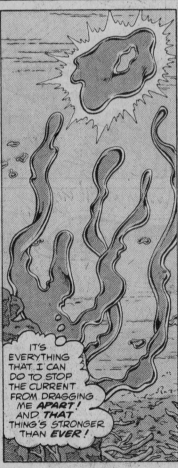

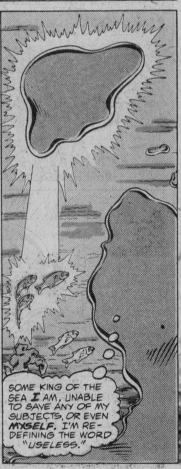

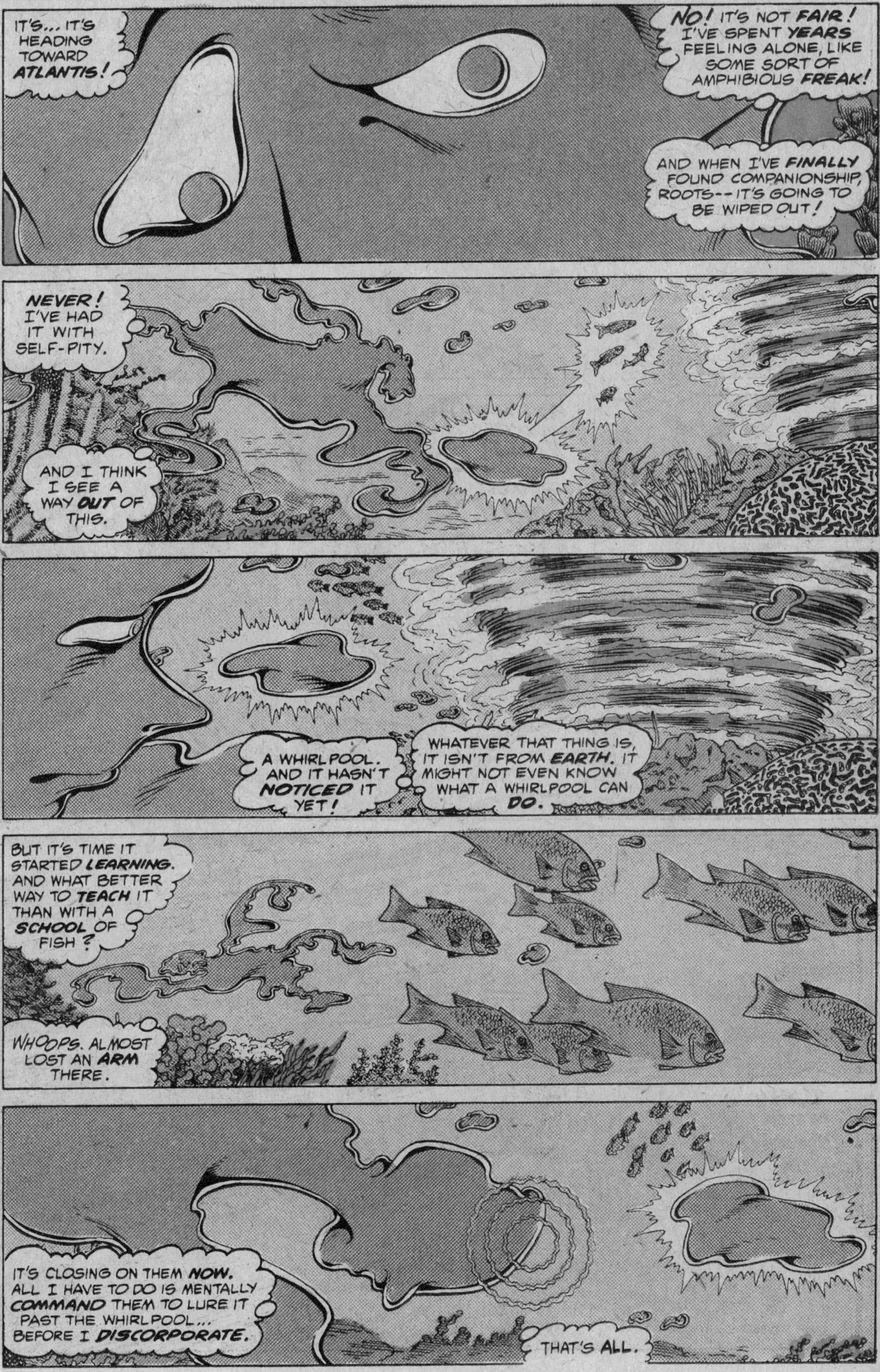
IT'S... IT'S HEADING TOWARD ATLANTIS!
NO! IT'S NOT FAIR! I'VE SPENT YEARS FEELING ALONE, LIKE SOME SORT OF AMPHIBIOUS FREAK!
AND WHEN I'VE FINALLY FOUND COMPANIONSHIP, ROOTS-- IT'S GOING TO BE WIPED OUT!
NEVER! I'VE HAD IT WITH SELF-PITY.
AND I THINK I SEE A WAY OUT OF THIS.
A WHIRLPOOL. AND IT HASN'T NOTICED IT YET!
WHATEVER THAT THING IS, IT ISN'T FROM EARTH. IT MIGHT NOT EVEN KNOW WHAT A WHIRLPOOL CAN DO.
BUT IT'S TIME IT STARTED LEARNING. AND WHAT BETTER WAY TO TEACH IT THAN WITH A SCHOOL OF FISH?
WHOOPS. ALMOST LOST AN ARM THERE.
IT'S CLOSING ON THEM NOW. ALL I HAVE TO DO IS MENTALLY COMMAND THEM TO LURE IT PAST THE WHIRLPOOL... BEFORE I DISCORPORATE.
THAT'S ALL.

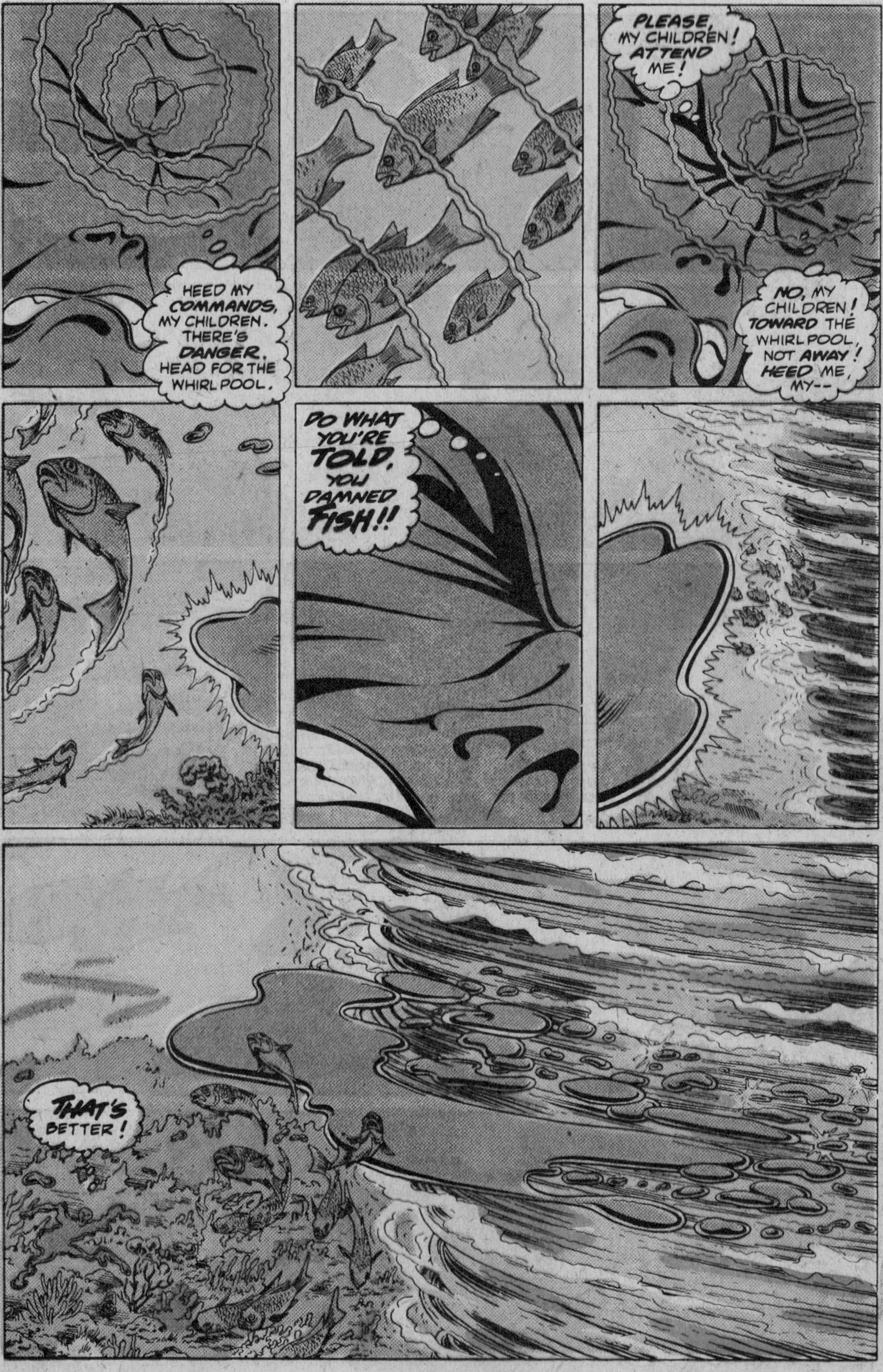
HEED MY COMMANDS, MY CHILDREN. THERE'S DANGER. HEAD FOR THE WHIRLPOOL.
PLEASE, MY CHILDREN! ATTEND ME!
NO, MY CHILDREN! TOWARD THE WHIRLPOOL, NOT AWAY! HEED ME, MY--
DO WHAT YOU'RE TOLD, YOU DAMNED FISH!!
THAT'S BETTER!

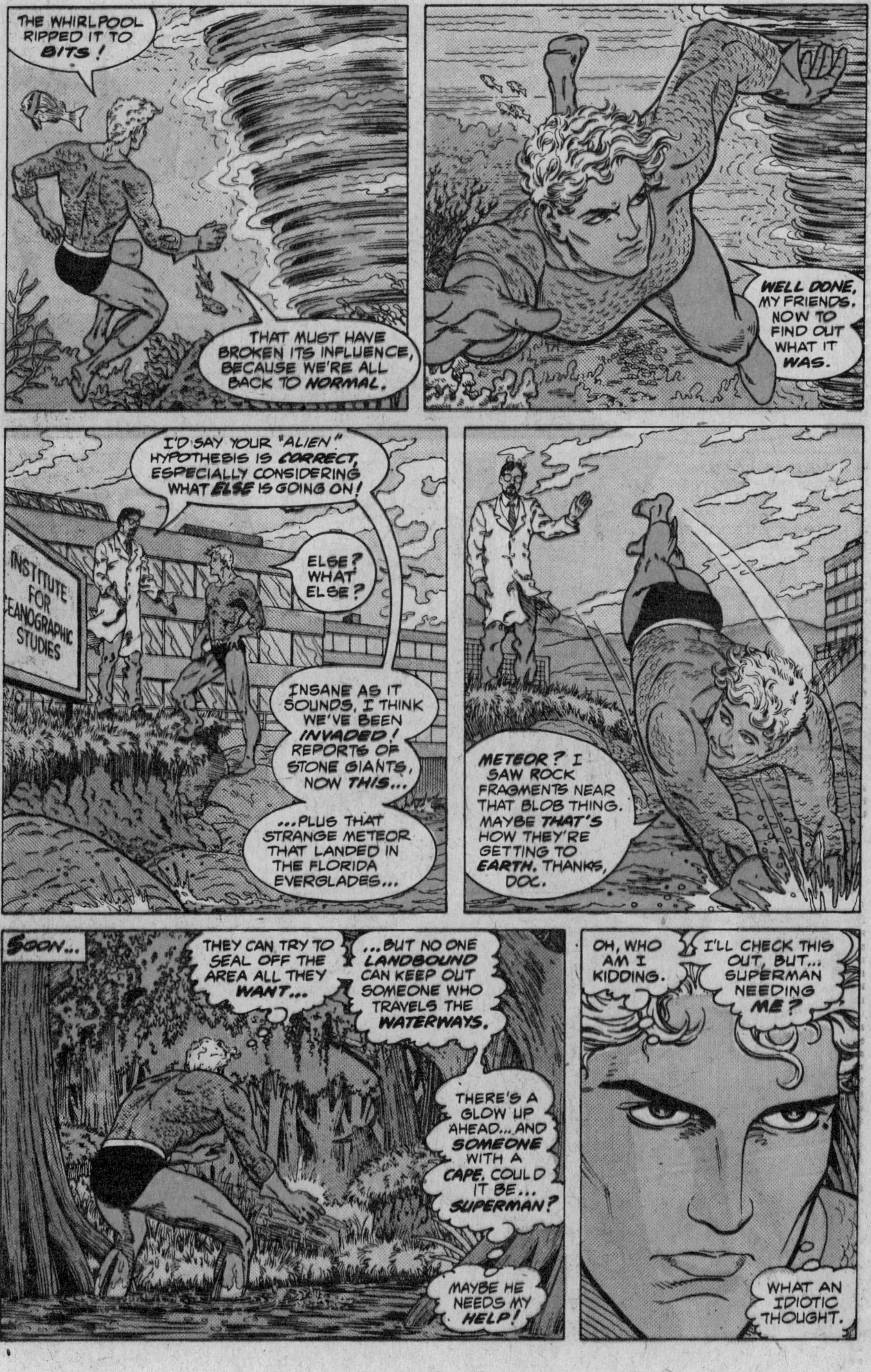
THE WHIRLPOOL RIPPED IT TO BITS!
THAT MUST HAVE BROKEN ITS INFLUENCE, BECAUSE WE'RE ALL BACK TO NORMAL.
WELL DONE, MY FRIENDS. NOW TO FIND OUT WHAT IT WAS.
I'D SAY YOUR "ALIEN" HYPOTHESIS IS CORRECT, ESPECIALLY CONSIDERING WHAT ELSE IS GOING ON!
INSTITUTE FOR OCEANOGRAPHIC STUDIES
ELSE? WHAT ELSE?
INSANE AS IT SOUNDS, I THINK WE'VE BEEN INVADED! REPORTS OF STONE GIANTS, NOW THIS...
...PLUS THAT STRANGE METEOR THAT LANDED IN THE FLORIDA EVERGLADES...
METEOR? I SAW ROCK FRAGMENTS NEAR THAT BLOB THING. MAYBE THAT'S HOW THEY'RE GETTING TO EARTH. THANKS, DOC.
SOON...
THEY CAN TRY TO SEAL OFF THE AREA ALL THEY WANT...
...BUT NO ONE LANDBOUND CAN KEEP OUT SOMEONE WHO TRAVELS THE WATERWAYS.
THERE'S A GLOW UP AHEAD... AND SOMEONE WITH A CAPE. COULD IT BE... SUPERMAN?
MAYBE HE NEEDS MY HELP!
OH, WHO AM I KIDDING.
I'LL CHECK THIS OUT, BUT... SUPERMAN NEEDING ME?
WHAT AN IDIOTIC THOUGHT.

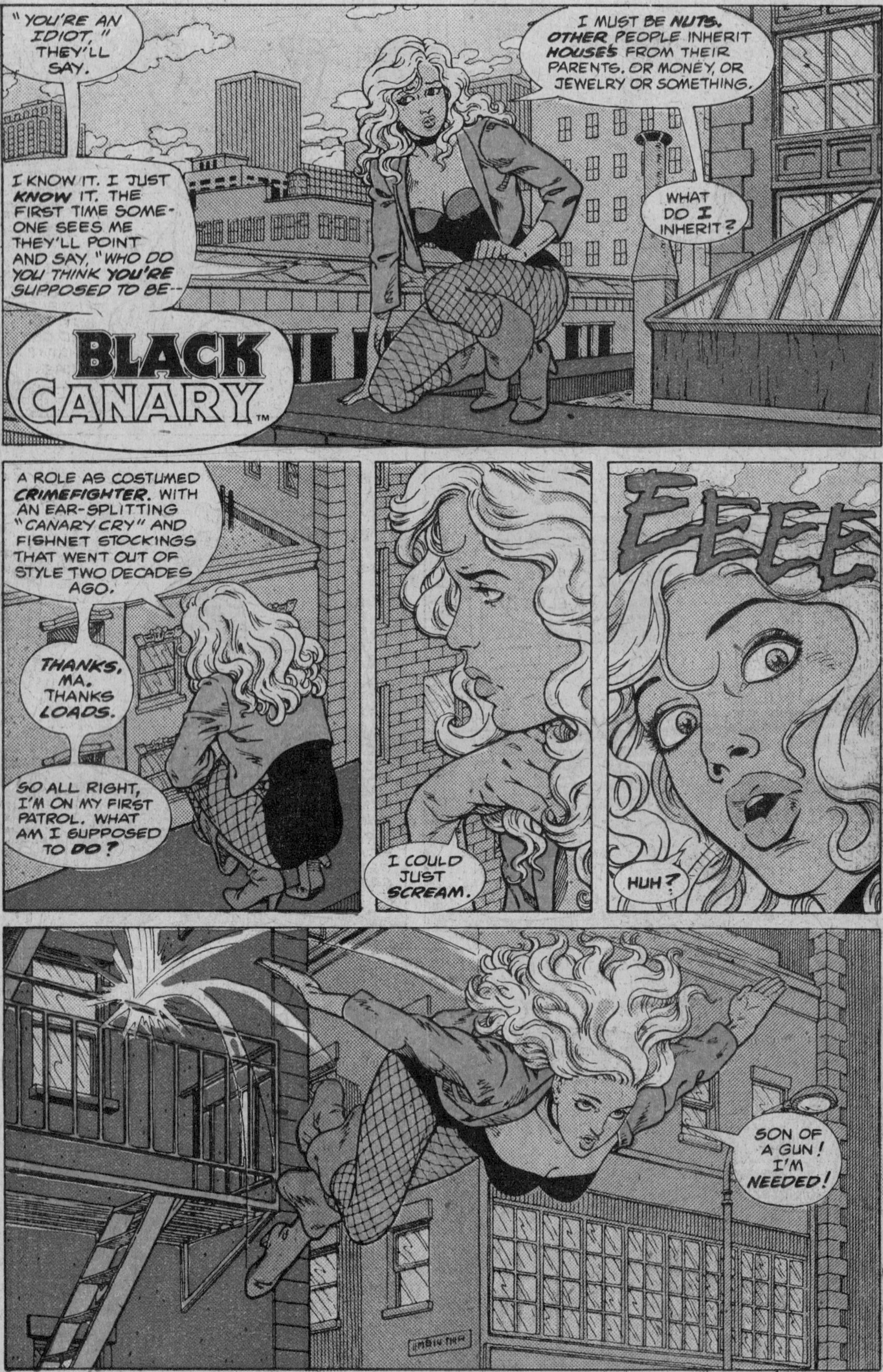
"YOU'RE AN IDIOT," THEY'LL SAY.
I KNOW IT. I JUST KNOW IT. THE FIRST TIME SOMEONE SEES ME THEY'LL POINT AND SAY, "WHO DO YOU THINK YOU'RE SUPPOSED TO BE--
BLACK CANARY™
I MUST BE NUTS. OTHER PEOPLE INHERIT HOUSES FROM THEIR PARENTS. OR MONEY, OR JEWELRY OR SOMETHING.
WHAT DO I INHERIT?
A ROLE AS COSTUMED CRIMEFIGHTER. WITH AN EAR-SPLITTING "CANARY CRY" AND FISHNET STOCKINGS THAT WENT OUT OF STYLE TWO DECADES AGO.
THANKS, MA. THANKS LOADS.
SO ALL RIGHT, I'M ON MY FIRST PATROL. WHAT AM I SUPPOSED TO DO?
I COULD JUST SCREAM.
EEEE
HUH?
SON OF A GUN! I'M NEEDED!

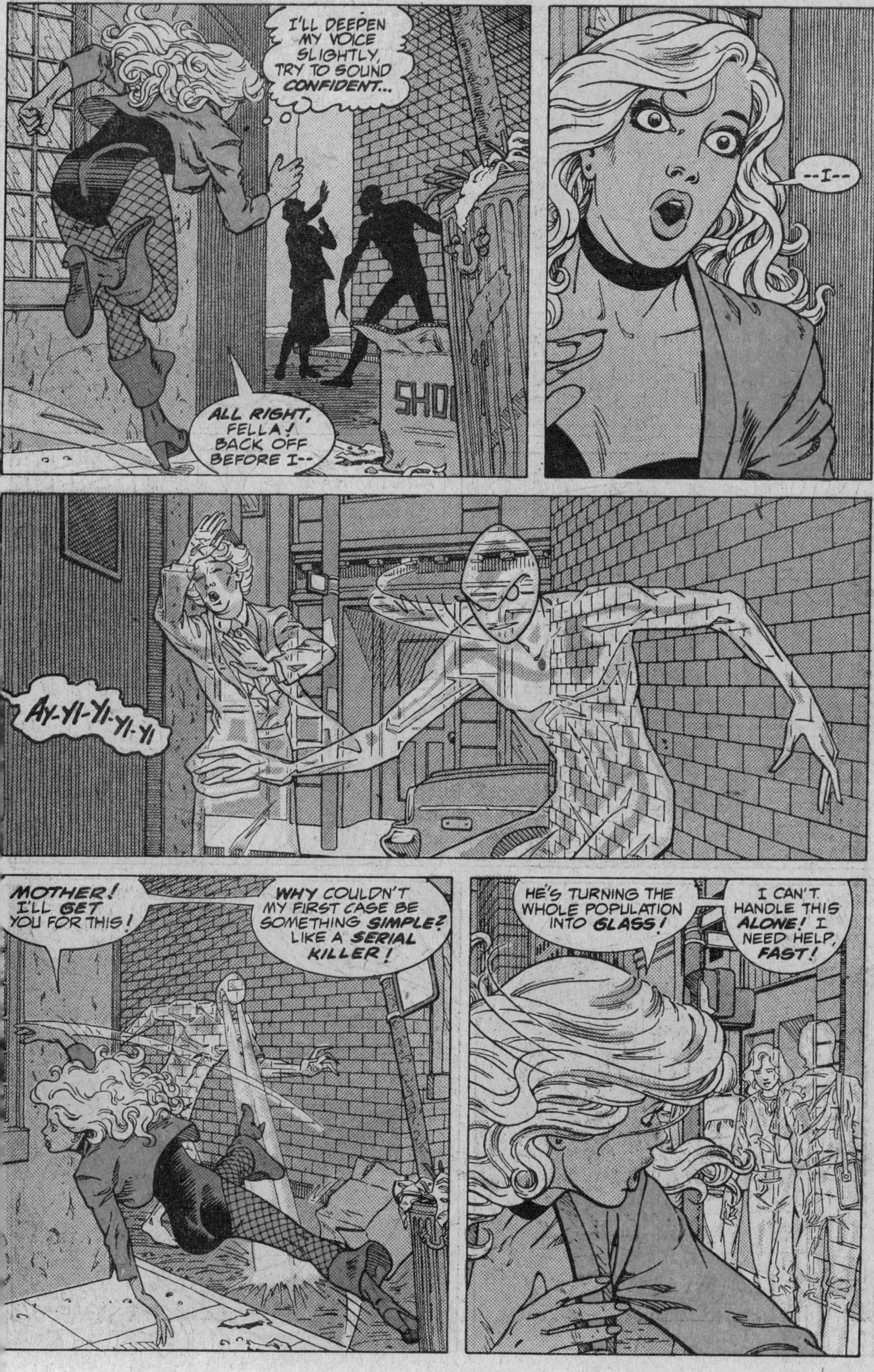
I'LL DEEPEN MY VOICE SLIGHTLY, TRY TO SOUND CONFIDENT...
ALL RIGHT, FELLA! BACK OFF BEFORE I--
SHO
--I--
AY-YI-YI-YI-YI
MOTHER! I'LL GET YOU FOR THIS!
WHY COULDN'T MY FIRST CASE BE SOMETHING SIMPLE? LIKE A SERIAL KILLER!
HE'S TURNING THE WHOLE POPULATION INTO GLASS!
I CAN'T HANDLE THIS ALONE! I NEED HELP, FAST!

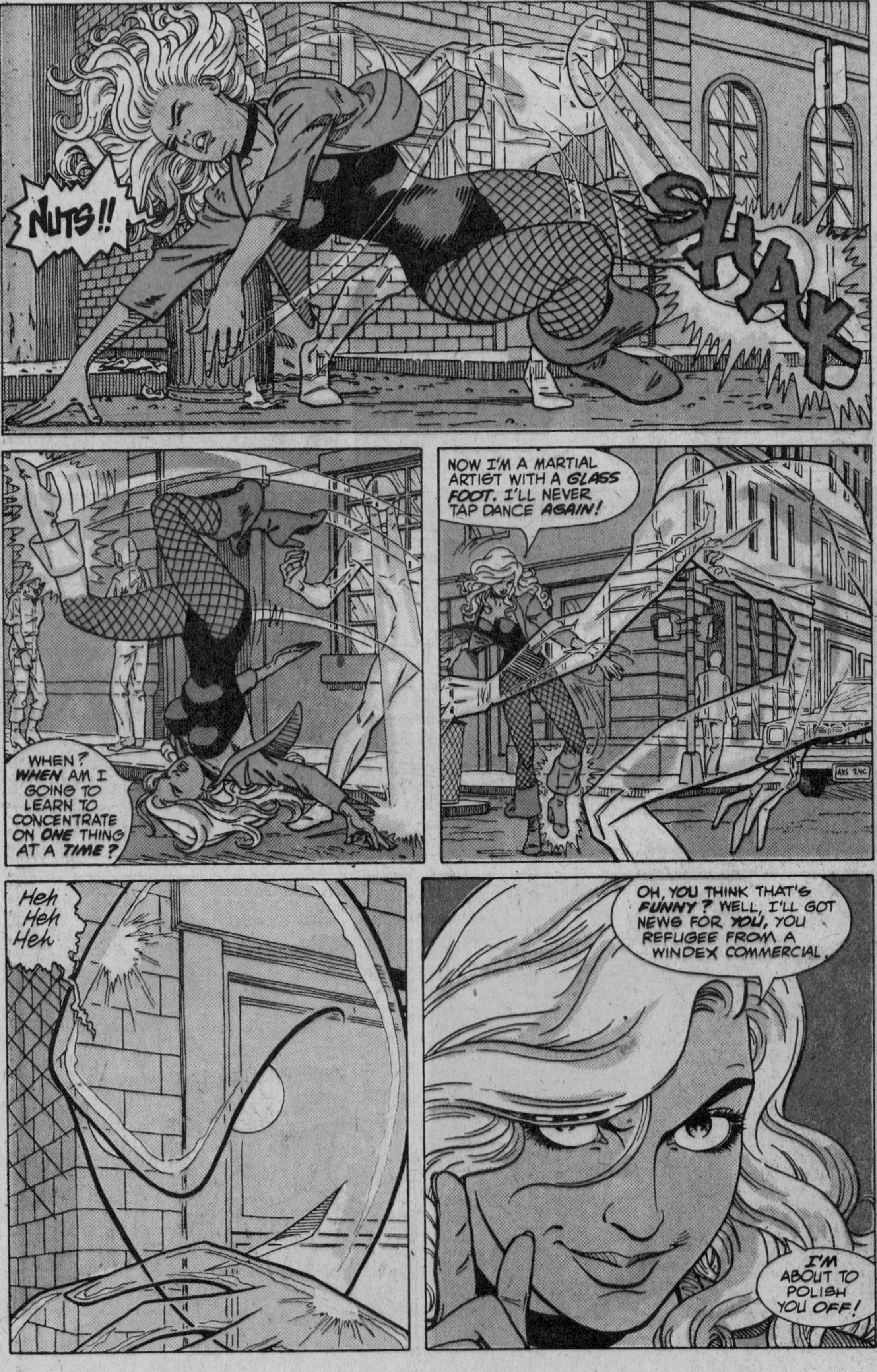
NUTS!!
SHAK
WHEN? WHEN AM I GOING TO LEARN TO CONCENTRATE ON ONE THING AT A TIME?
NOW I'M A MARTIAL ARTIST WITH A GLASS FOOT. I'LL NEVER TAP DANCE AGAIN!
Heh Heh Heh
OH, YOU THINK THAT'S FUNNY? WELL, I'LL GOT NEWS FOR YOU, YOU REFUGEE FROM A WINDEX COMMERCIAL,
I'M ABOUT TO POLISH YOU OFF!

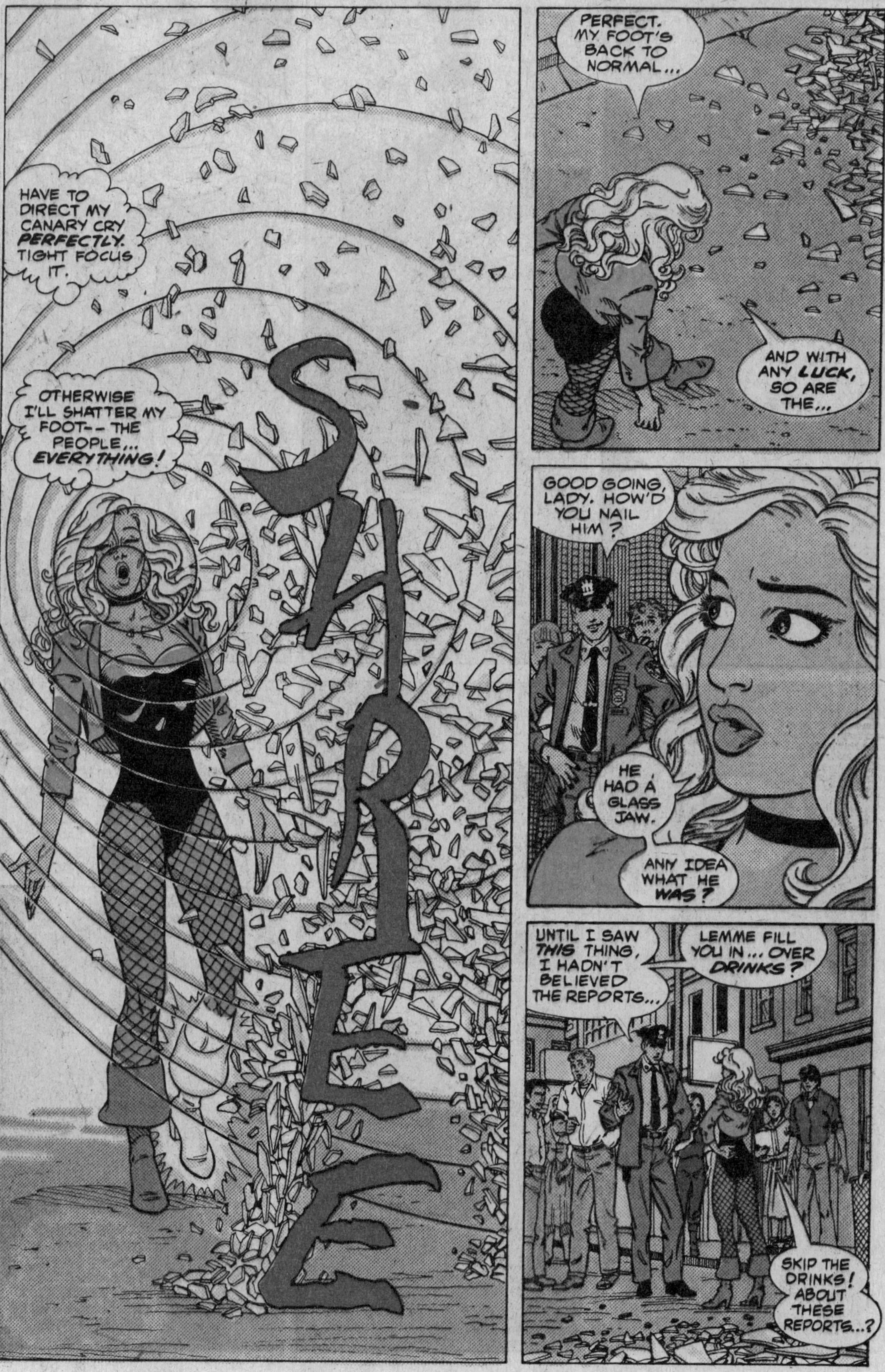
HAVE TO DIRECT MY CANARY CRY PERFECTLY. TIGHT FOCUS IT.
OTHERWISE I'LL SHATTER MY FOOT-- THE PEOPLE... EVERYTHING!
SHRIEEE
PERFECT. MY FOOT'S BACK TO NORMAL...
AND WITH ANY LUCK, SO ARE THE...
GOOD GOING, LADY. HOW'D YOU NAIL HIM?
HE HAD A GLASS JAW.
ANY IDEA WHAT HE WAS?
UNTIL I SAW THIS THING, I HADN'T BELIEVED THE REPORTS...
LEMME FILL YOU IN... OVER DRINKS?
SKIP THE DRINKS! ABOUT THESE REPORTS...?

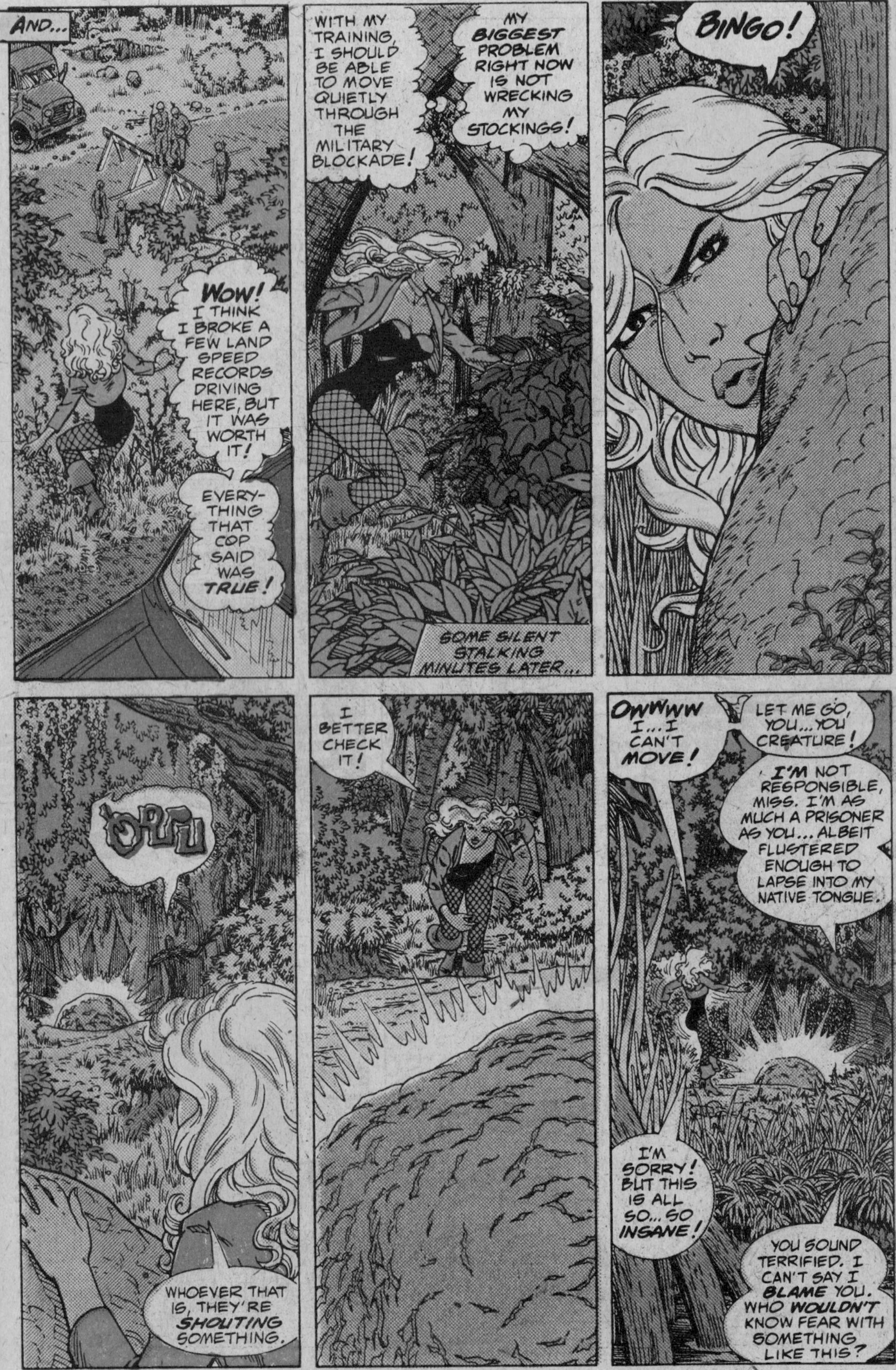
AND...
WOW! I THINK I BROKE A FEW LAND SPEED RECORDS DRIVING HERE, BUT IT WAS WORTH IT!
EVERYTHING THAT COP SAID WAS TRUE!
WITH MY TRAINING, I SHOULD BE ABLE TO MOVE QUIETLY THROUGH THE MILITARY BLOCKADE!
MY BIGGEST PROBLEM RIGHT NOW IS NOT WRECKING MY STOCKINGS!
SOME SILENT STALKING MINUTES LATER...
BINGO!
WHOEVER THAT IS, THEY'RE SHOUTING SOMETHING.
I BETTER CHECK IT!
OWWWW I... I CAN'T MOVE!
LET ME GO, YOU... YOU CREATURE!
I'M NOT RESPONSIBLE, MISS. I'M AS MUCH A PRISONER AS YOU... ALBEIT FLUSTERED ENOUGH TO LAPSE INTO MY NATIVE TONGUE.
I'M SORRY! BUT THIS IS ALL SO... SO INSANE!
YOU SOUND TERRIFIED. I CAN'T SAY I BLAME YOU. WHO WOULDN'T KNOW FEAR WITH SOMETHING LIKE THIS?

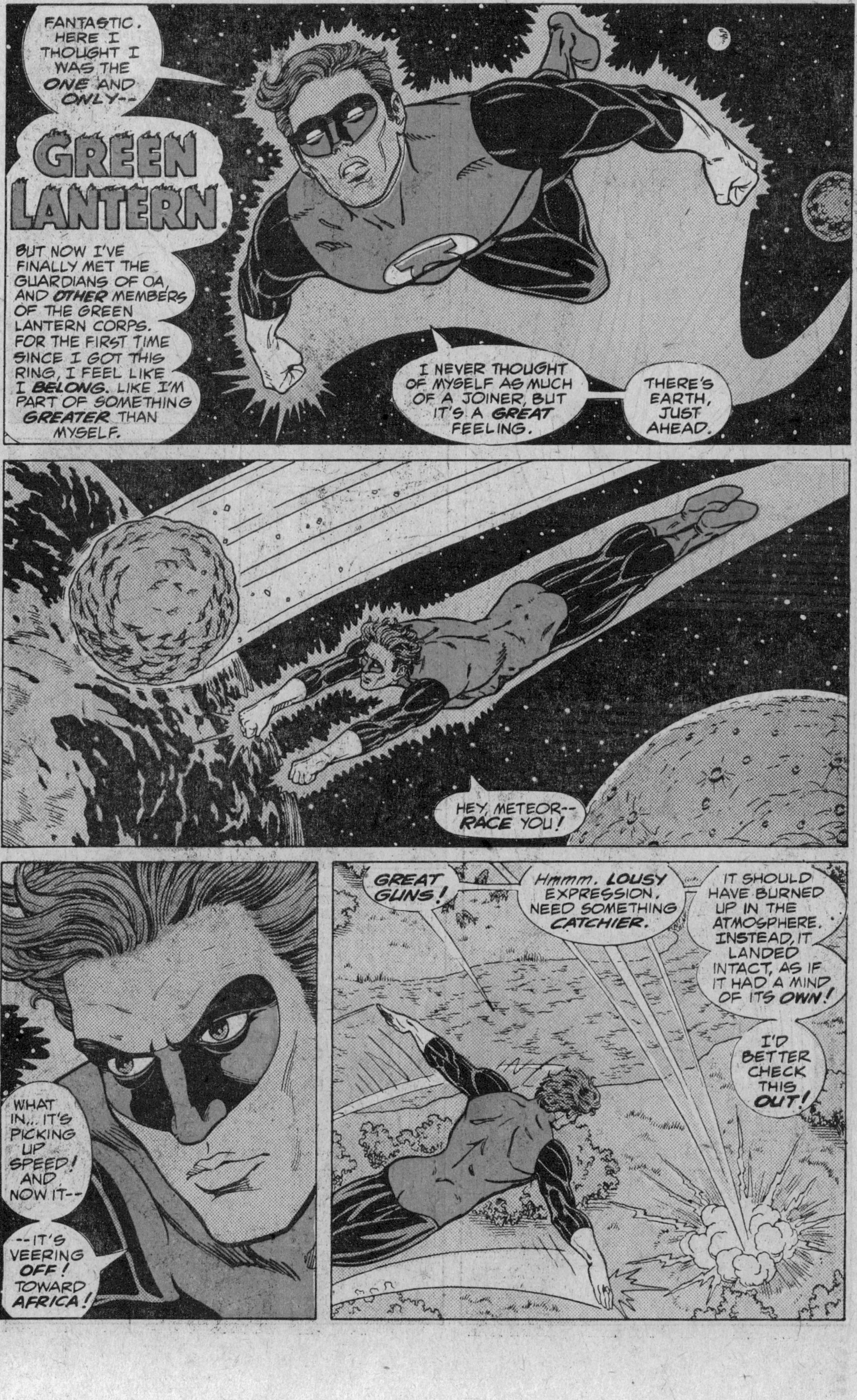
FANTASTIC. HERE I THOUGHT I WAS THE ONE AND ONLY--
GREEN LANTERN®
BUT NOW I'VE FINALLY MET THE GUARDIANS OF OA, AND OTHER MEMBERS OF THE GREEN LANTERN CORPS. FOR THE FIRST TIME SINCE I GOT THIS RING, I FEEL LIKE I BELONG. LIKE I'M PART OF SOMETHING GREATER THAN MYSELF.
I NEVER THOUGHT OF MYSELF AS MUCH OF A JOINER, BUT IT'S A GREAT FEELING.
THERE'S EARTH, JUST AHEAD.
HEY, METEOR-- RACE YOU!
WHAT IN... IT'S PICKING UP SPEED! AND NOW IT--
--IT'S VEERING OFF! TOWARD AFRICA!
GREAT GUNS!
Hmmm. LOUSY EXPRESSION. NEED SOMETHING CATCHIER.
IT SHOULD HAVE BURNED UP IN THE ATMOSPHERE. INSTEAD, IT LANDED INTACT, AS IF IT HAD A MIND OF ITS OWN!
I'D BETTER CHECK THIS OUT!

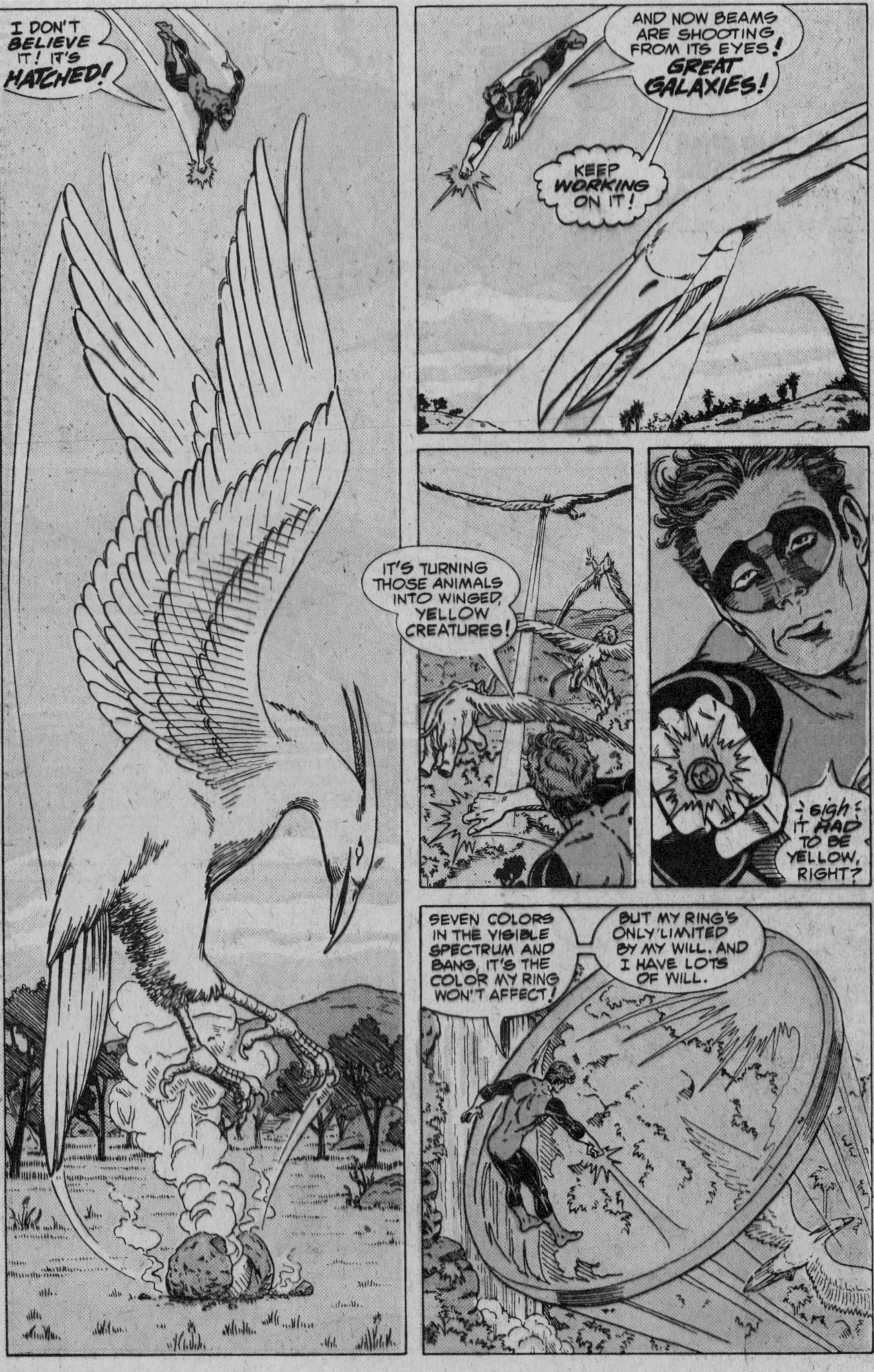
I DON'T BELIEVE IT! IT'S HATCHED!
AND NOW BEAMS ARE SHOOTING FROM ITS EYES! GREAT GALAXIES!
KEEP WORKING ON IT!
IT'S TURNING THOSE ANIMALS INTO WINGED, YELLOW CREATURES!
:sigh: IT HAD TO BE YELLOW, RIGHT?
SEVEN COLORS IN THE VISIBLE SPECTRUM AND BANG, IT'S THE COLOR MY RING WON'T AFFECT!
BUT MY RING'S ONLY LIMITED BY MY WILL. AND I HAVE LOTS OF WILL.

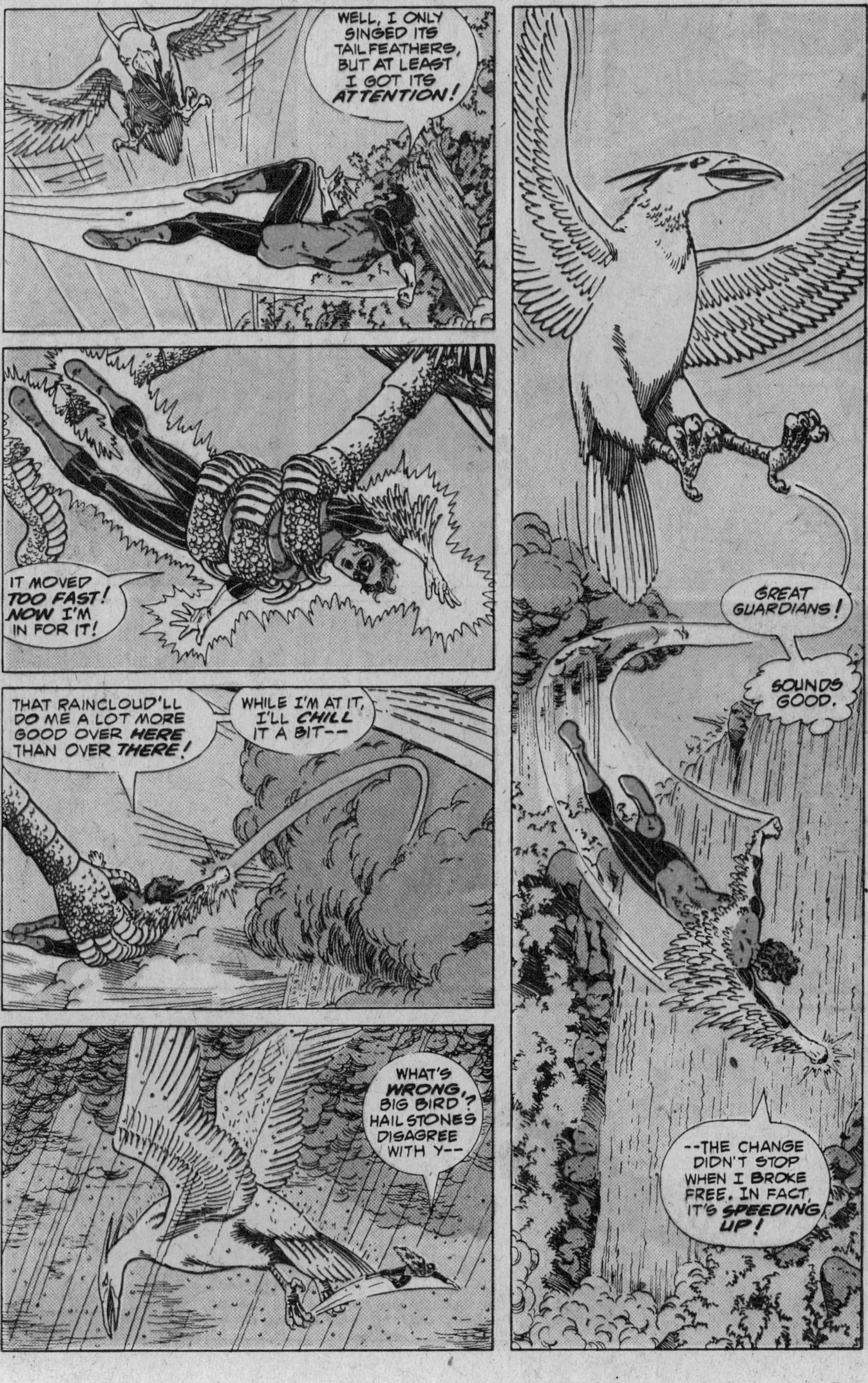
WELL, I ONLY SINGED ITS TAILFEATHERS, BUT AT LEAST I GOT ITS ATTENTION!
IT MOVED TOO FAST! NOW I'M IN FOR IT!
THAT RAINCLOUD'LL DO ME A LOT MORE GOOD OVER HERE THAN OVER THERE!
WHILE I'M AT IT, I'LL CHILL IT A BIT--
WHAT'S WRONG, BIG BIRD? HAIL STONES DISAGREE WITH Y--
GREAT GUARDIANS!
SOUNDS GOOD.
--THE CHANGE DIDN'T STOP WHEN I BROKE FREE. IN FACT, IT'S SPEEDING UP!

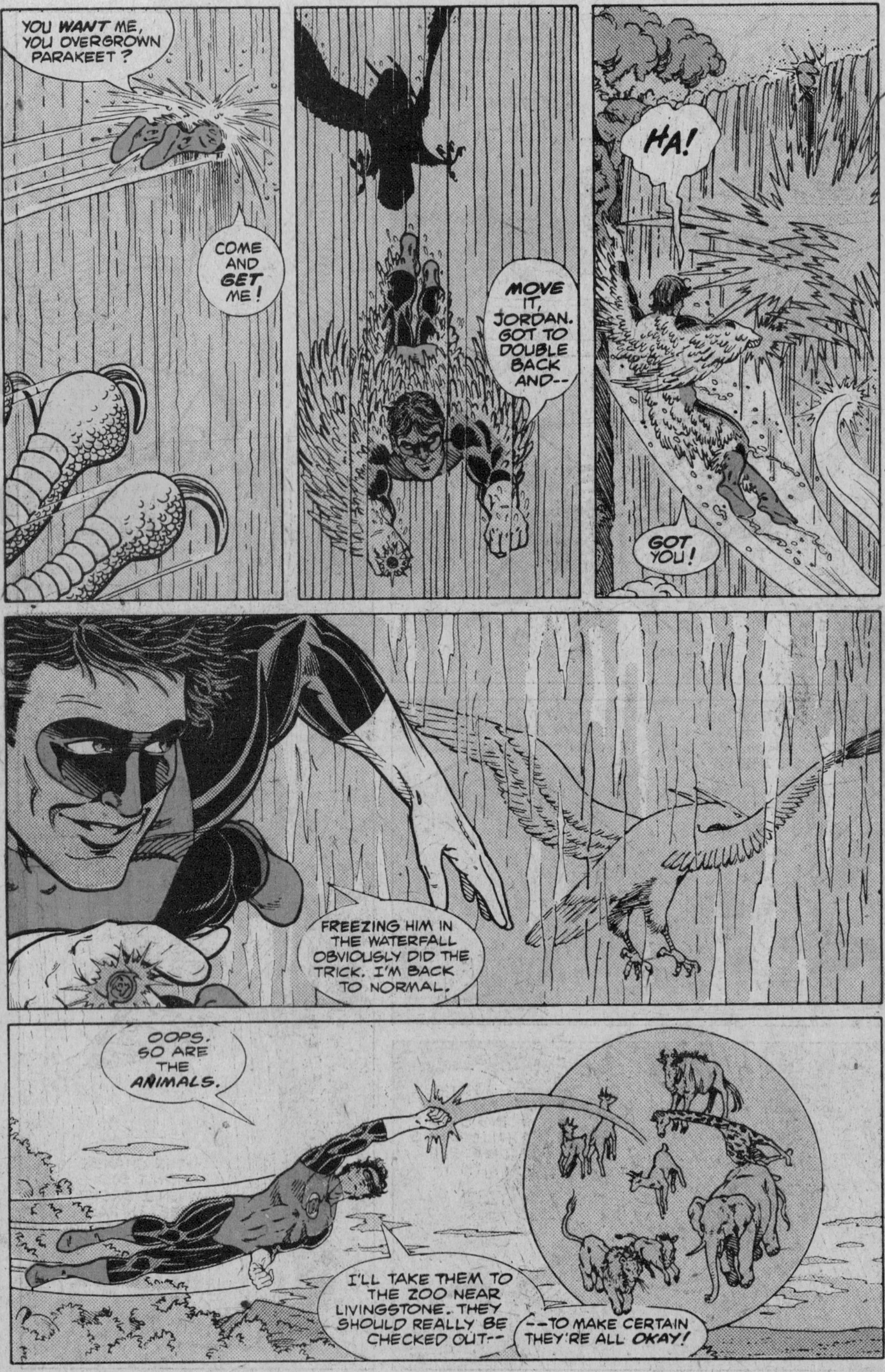
YOU WANT ME, YOU OVERGROWN PARAKEET?
COME AND GET ME!
MOVE IT, JORDAN. GOT TO DOUBLE BACK AND--
HA!
GOT YOU!
FREEZING HIM IN THE WATERFALL OBVIOUSLY DID THE TRICK. I'M BACK TO NORMAL.
OOPS. SO ARE THE ANIMALS.
I'LL TAKE THEM TO THE ZOO NEAR LIVINGSTONE. THEY SHOULD REALLY BE CHECKED OUT--
--TO MAKE CERTAIN THEY'RE ALL OKAY!

AND...

I SHOULD HAVE REALIZED THAT METEOR *WASN'T* AN *ISOLATED* INCIDENT. ACCORDING TO THE AUTHORITIES IN LIVINGSTONE, THEY'RE LANDING AND DISGORGING ALIENS ALL OVER THE *PLANET!*

THE ONLY ONE THEY'VE HEARD ABOUT SPECIFICALLY THAT'S STILL *UN-OPENED* IS IN THE FLORIDA EVER-GLADES!

HOPE IT DOESN'T HATCH ANOTHER YELLOW BIRD. I WAS LUCKY *ONCE*, BUT I MIGHT NEED HELP WITH MORE OF THEM.

THAT'S IT THERE. BUT...

MY GOD!

GET... AWAY... QUICKLY...

IT'S ALL RIGHT. DON'T PANIC. I'LL HAVE YOU LOOSE IN A....

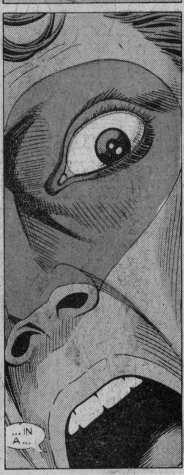

...IN A...

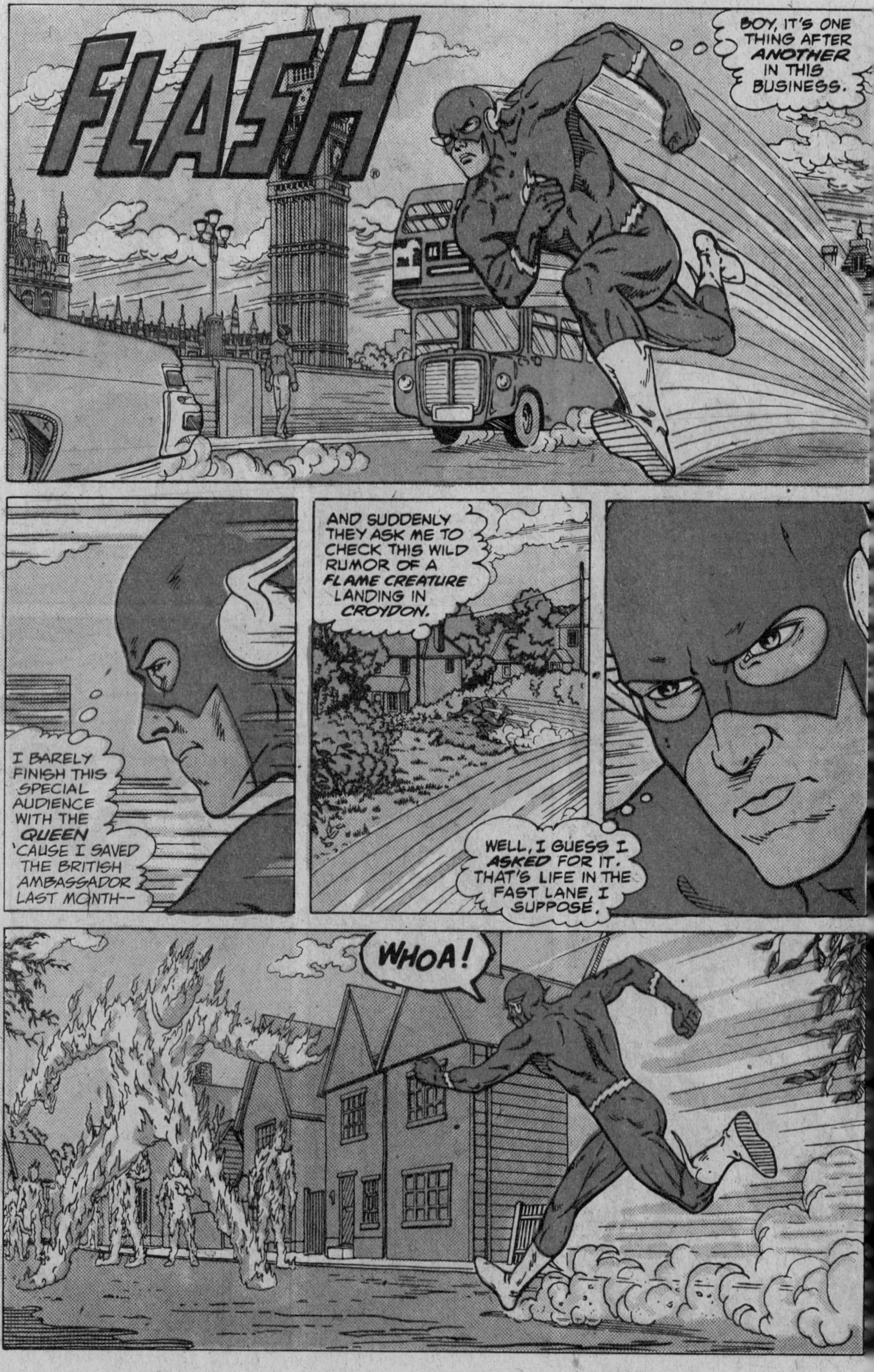
FLASH®
BOY, IT'S ONE THING AFTER ANOTHER IN THIS BUSINESS.
I BARELY FINISH THIS SPECIAL AUDIENCE WITH THE QUEEN 'CAUSE I SAVED THE BRITISH AMBASSADOR LAST MONTH--
AND SUDDENLY THEY ASK ME TO CHECK THIS WILD RUMOR OF A FLAME CREATURE LANDING IN CROYDON.
WELL, I GUESS I ASKED FOR IT. THAT'S LIFE IN THE FAST LANE, I SUPPOSE.
WHOA!

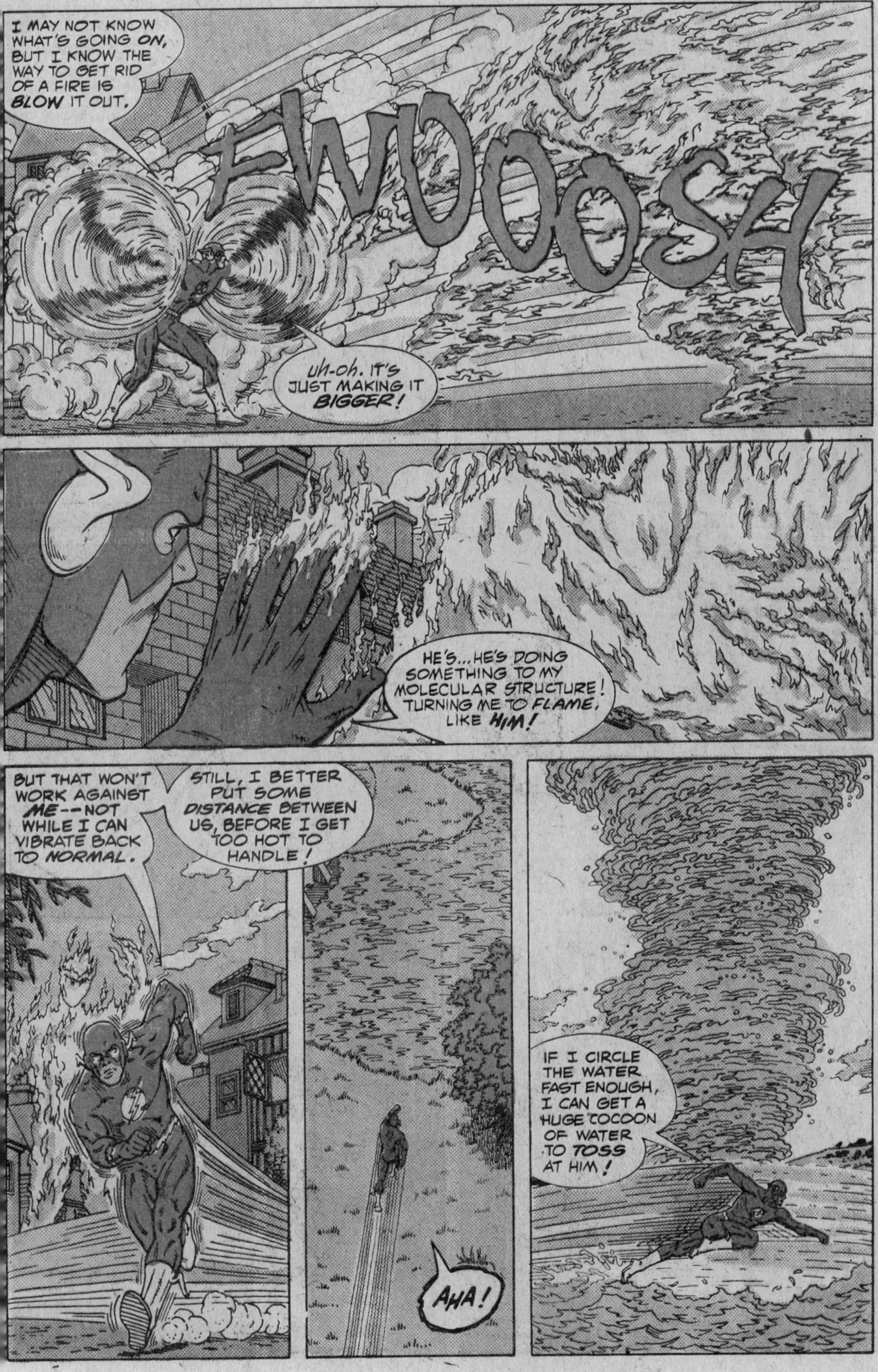
I MAY NOT KNOW WHAT'S GOING ON, BUT I KNOW THE WAY TO GET RID OF A FIRE IS BLOW IT OUT.
EWOOOSH
uh-oh. IT'S JUST MAKING IT BIGGER!
HE'S...HE'S DOING SOMETHING TO MY MOLECULAR STRUCTURE! TURNING ME TO FLAME, LIKE HIM!
BUT THAT WON'T WORK AGAINST ME--NOT WHILE I CAN VIBRATE BACK TO NORMAL.
STILL, I BETTER PUT SOME DISTANCE BETWEEN US, BEFORE I GET TOO HOT TO HANDLE!
AHA!
IF I CIRCLE THE WATER FAST ENOUGH, I CAN GET A HUGE COCOON OF WATER TO TOSS AT HIM!

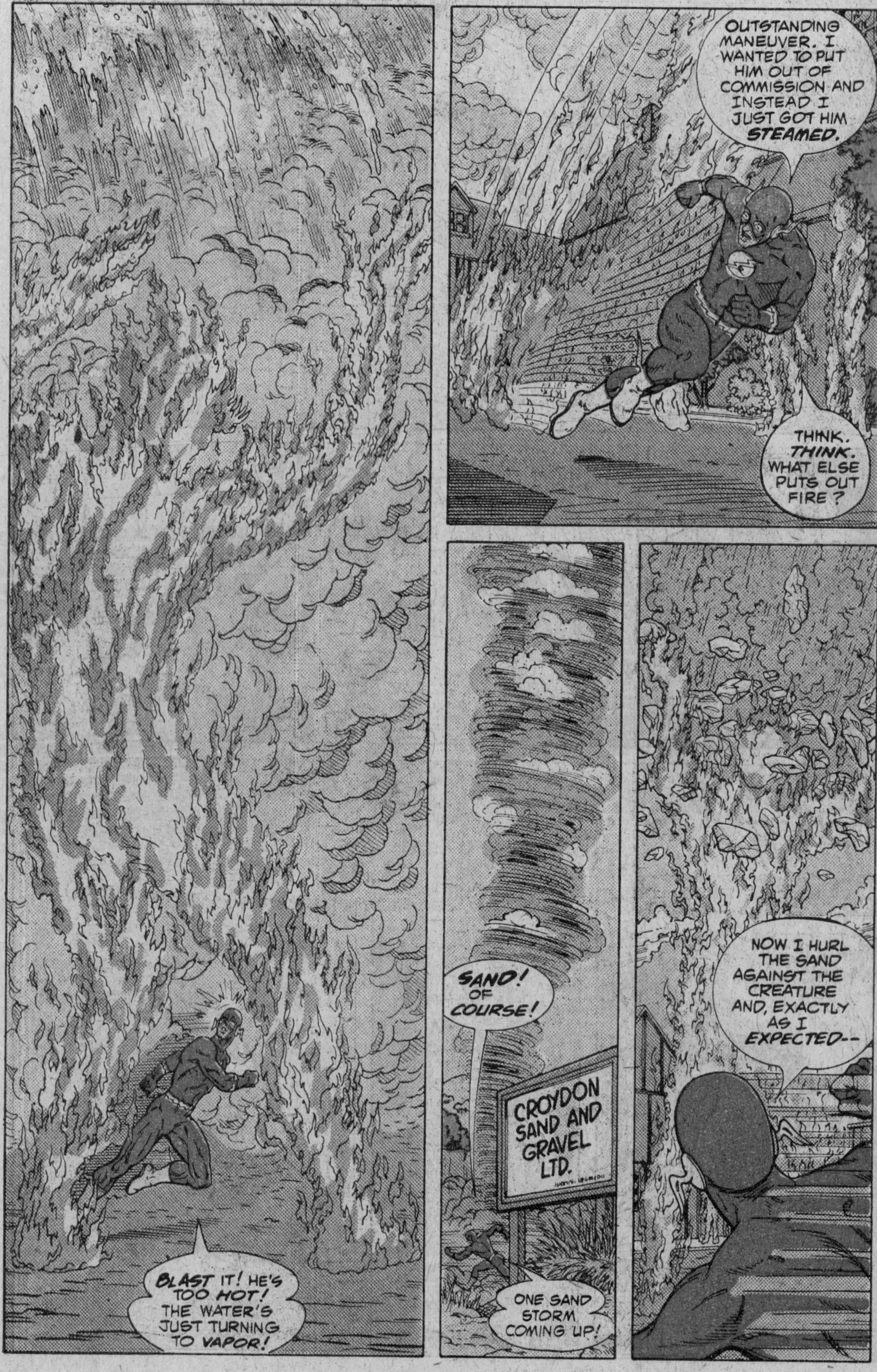
BLAST IT! HE'S TOO HOT! THE WATER'S JUST TURNING TO VAPOR!
OUTSTANDING MANEUVER. I WANTED TO PUT HIM OUT OF COMMISSION AND INSTEAD I JUST GOT HIM STEAMED.
THINK. THINK. WHAT ELSE PUTS OUT FIRE?
SAND! OF COURSE!
CROYDON SAND AND GRAVEL LTD.
ONE SAND STORM COMING UP!
NOW I HURL THE SAND AGAINST THE CREATURE AND, EXACTLY AS I EXPECTED--

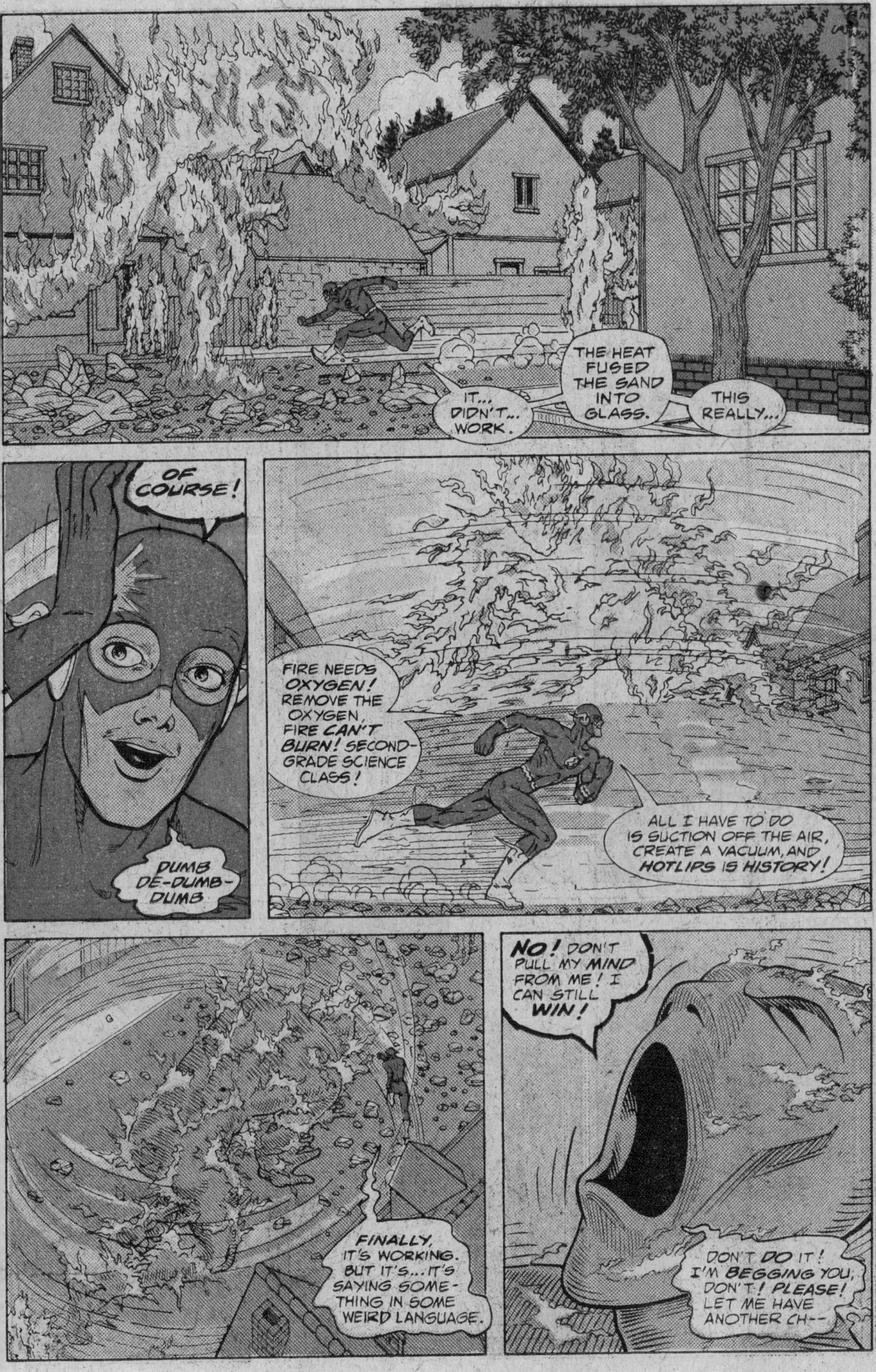
IT... DIDN'T... WORK.
THE HEAT FUSED THE SAND INTO GLASS.
THIS REALLY...
OF COURSE!
DUMB DE-DUMB-DUMB
FIRE NEEDS OXYGEN! REMOVE THE OXYGEN, FIRE CAN'T BURN! SECOND-GRADE SCIENCE CLASS!
ALL I HAVE TO DO IS SUCTION OFF THE AIR, CREATE A VACUUM, AND HOTLIPS IS HISTORY!
FINALLY, IT'S WORKING. BUT IT'S... IT'S SAYING SOME-THING IN SOME WEIRD LANGUAGE.
NO! DON'T PULL MY MIND FROM ME! I CAN STILL WIN!
DON'T DO IT! I'M BEGGING YOU, DON'T! PLEASE! LET ME HAVE ANOTHER CH--

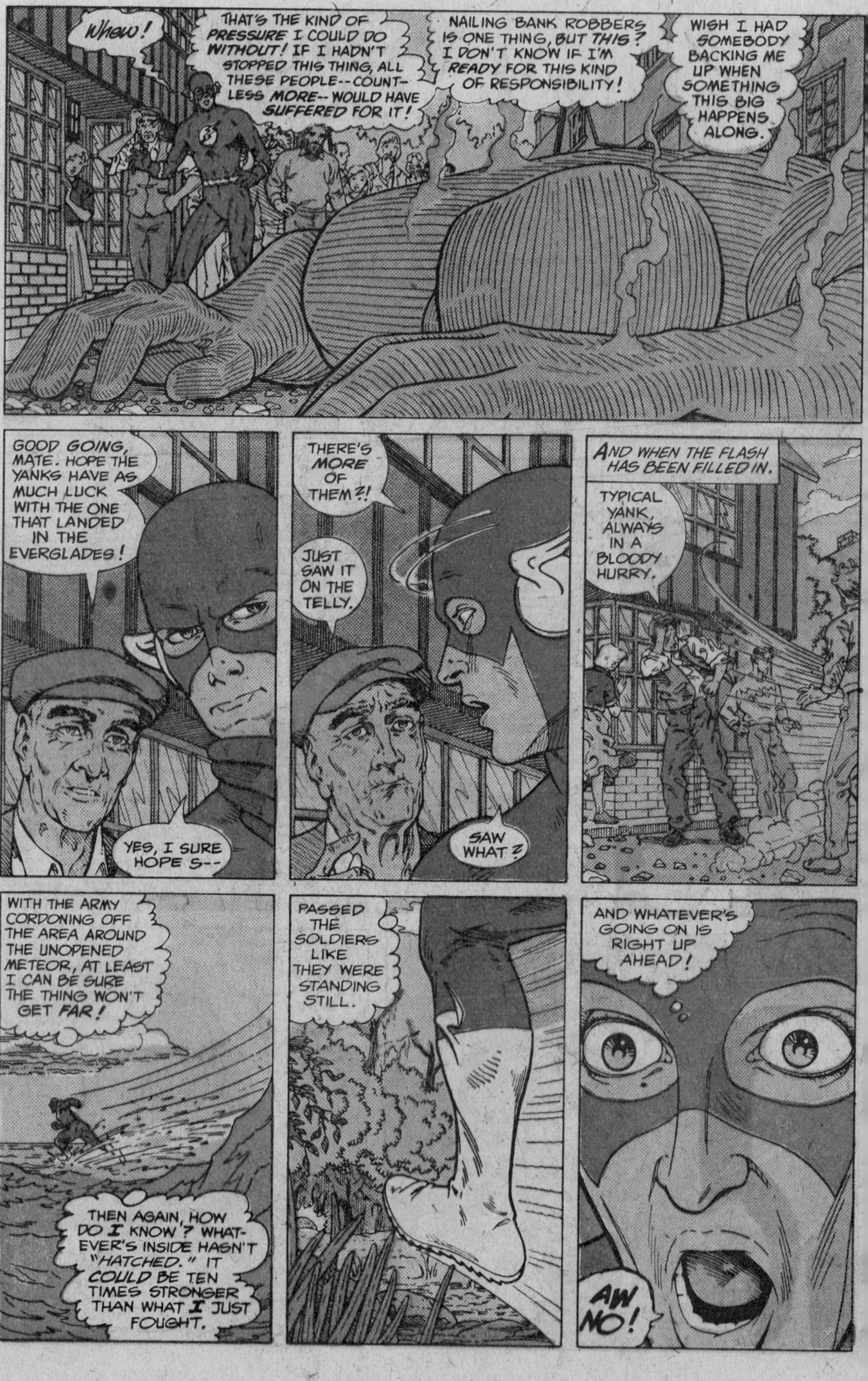
Whew!
THAT'S THE KIND OF PRESSURE I COULD DO WITHOUT! IF I HADN'T STOPPED THIS THING, ALL THESE PEOPLE--COUNTLESS MORE--WOULD HAVE SUFFERED FOR IT!
NAILING BANK ROBBERS IS ONE THING, BUT THIS? I DON'T KNOW IF I'M READY FOR THIS KIND OF RESPONSIBILITY!
WISH I HAD SOMEBODY BACKING ME UP WHEN SOMETHING THIS BIG HAPPENS ALONG.
GOOD GOING, MATE. HOPE THE YANKS HAVE AS MUCH LUCK WITH THE ONE THAT LANDED IN THE EVERGLADES!
YES, I SURE HOPE S--
THERE'S MORE OF THEM?!
JUST SAW IT ON THE TELLY.
SAW WHAT?
AND WHEN THE FLASH HAS BEEN FILLED IN.
TYPICAL YANK, ALWAYS IN A BLOODY HURRY.
WITH THE ARMY CORDONING OFF THE AREA AROUND THE UNOPENED METEOR, AT LEAST I CAN BE SURE THE THING WON'T GET FAR!
THEN AGAIN, HOW DO I KNOW? WHATEVER'S INSIDE HASN'T "HATCHED." IT COULD BE TEN TIMES STRONGER THAN WHAT I JUST FOUGHT.
PASSED THE SOLDIERS LIKE THEY WERE STANDING STILL.
AND WHATEVER'S GOING ON IS RIGHT UP AHEAD!
AW NO!

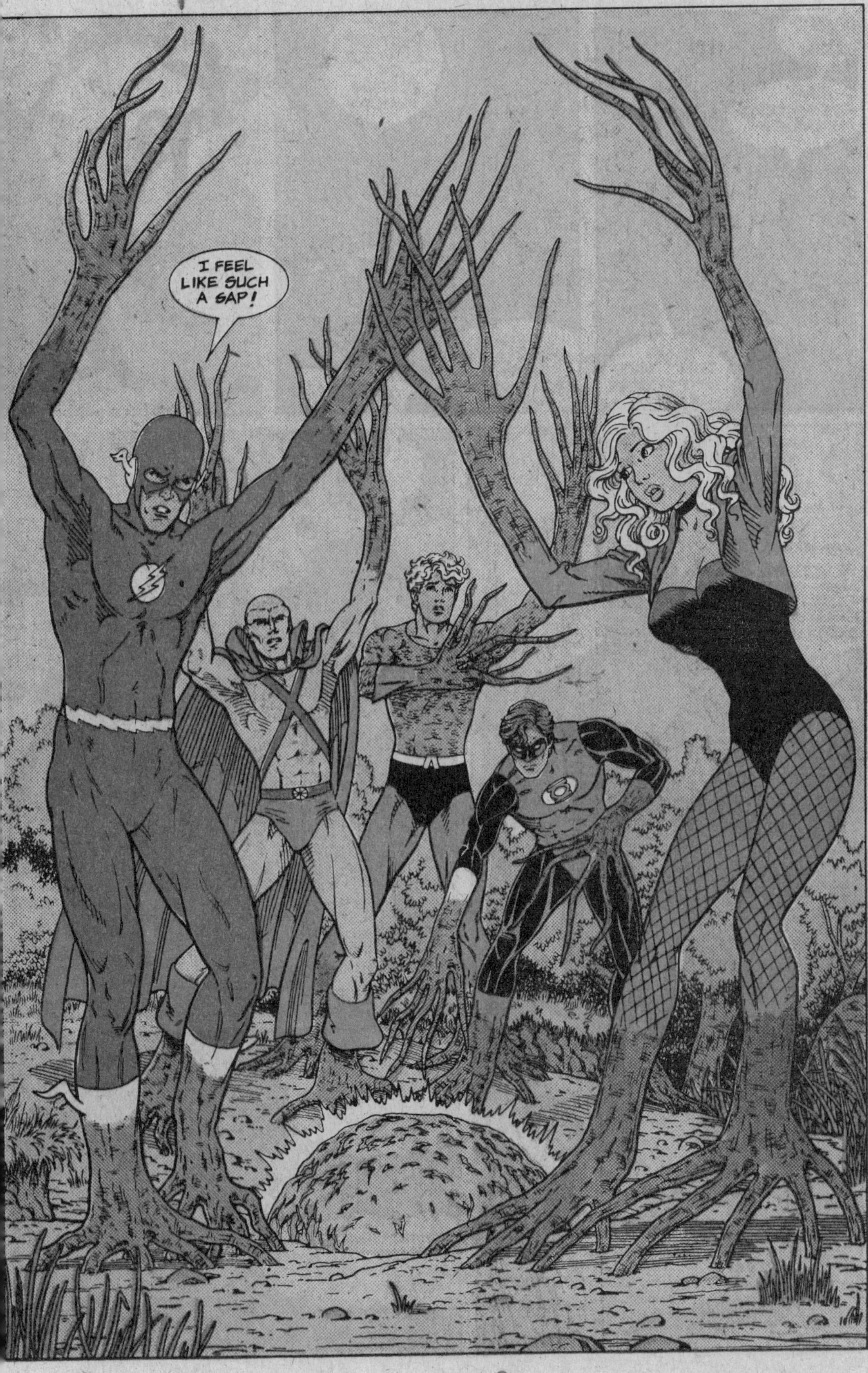
I FEEL LIKE SUCH A SAP!

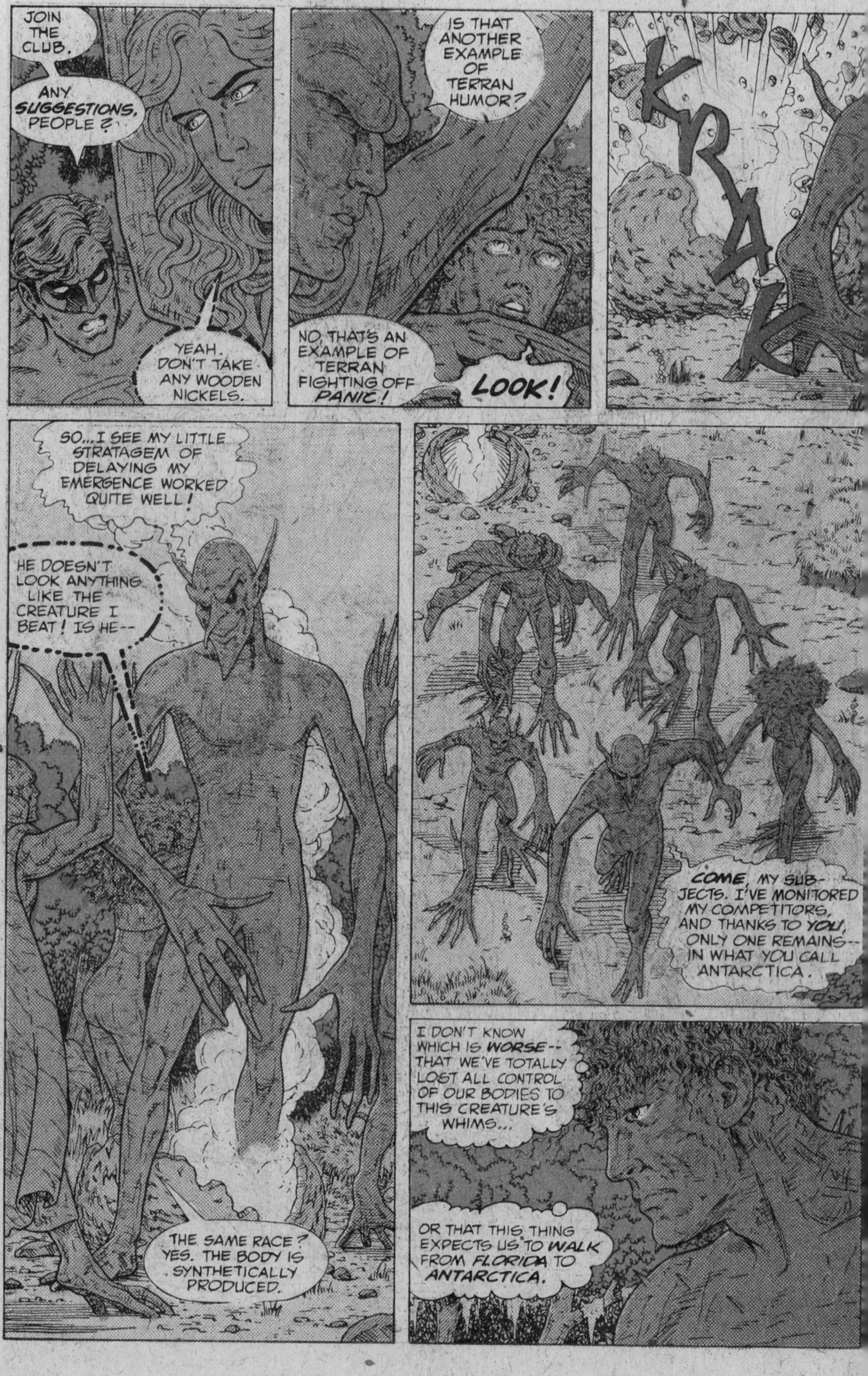
JOIN THE CLUB.
ANY SUGGESTIONS, PEOPLE?
YEAH. DON'T TAKE ANY WOODEN NICKELS.
IS THAT ANOTHER EXAMPLE OF TERRAN HUMOR?
NO, THAT'S AN EXAMPLE OF TERRAN FIGHTING OFF PANIC!
LOOK!
KRAAK
SO...I SEE MY LITTLE STRATAGEM OF DELAYING MY EMERGENCE WORKED QUITE WELL!
HE DOESN'T LOOK ANYTHING LIKE THE CREATURE I BEAT! IS HE--
THE SAME RACE? YES. THE BODY IS SYNTHETICALLY PRODUCED.
COME, MY SUBJECTS. I'VE MONITORED MY COMPETITORS, AND THANKS TO YOU, ONLY ONE REMAINS-- IN WHAT YOU CALL ANTARCTICA.
I DON'T KNOW WHICH IS WORSE-- THAT WE'VE TOTALLY LOST ALL CONTROL OF OUR BODIES TO THIS CREATURE'S WHIMS...
OR THAT THIS THING EXPECTS US TO WALK FROM FLORIDA TO ANTARCTICA.

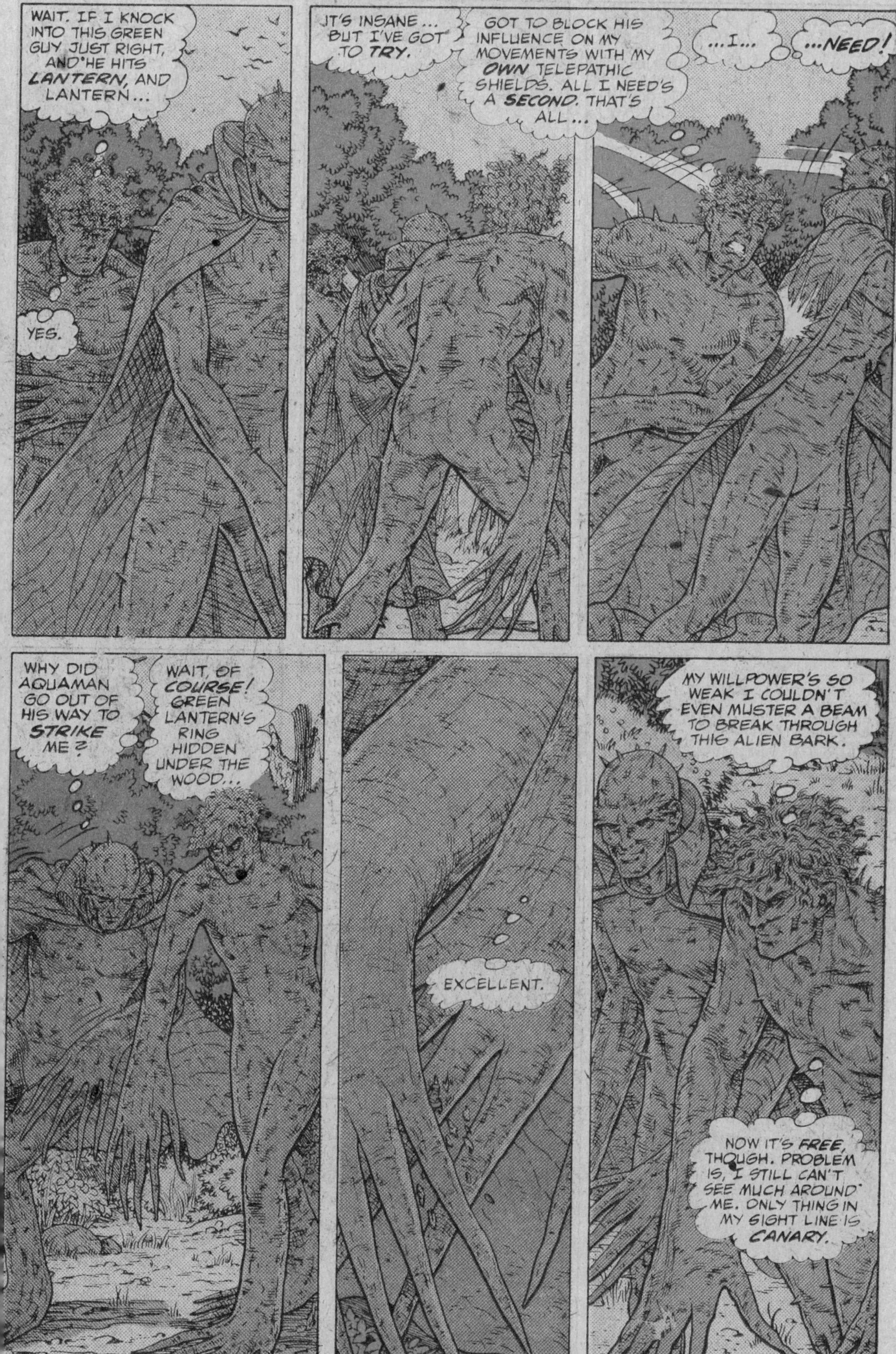
WAIT. IF I KNOCK INTO THIS GREEN GUY JUST RIGHT, AND HE HITS LANTERN, AND LANTERN...
YES.
IT'S INSANE... BUT I'VE GOT TO TRY.
GOT TO BLOCK HIS INFLUENCE ON MY MOVEMENTS WITH MY OWN TELEPATHIC SHIELDS. ALL I NEED'S A SECOND. THAT'S ALL...
...I...
...NEED!
WHY DID AQUAMAN GO OUT OF HIS WAY TO STRIKE ME?
WAIT, OF COURSE! GREEN LANTERN'S RING HIDDEN UNDER THE WOOD...
EXCELLENT.
MY WILLPOWER'S SO WEAK I COULDN'T EVEN MUSTER A BEAM TO BREAK THROUGH THIS ALIEN BARK.
NOW IT'S FREE, THOUGH. PROBLEM IS, I STILL CAN'T SEE MUCH AROUND ME. ONLY THING IN MY SIGHT LINE IS CANARY.

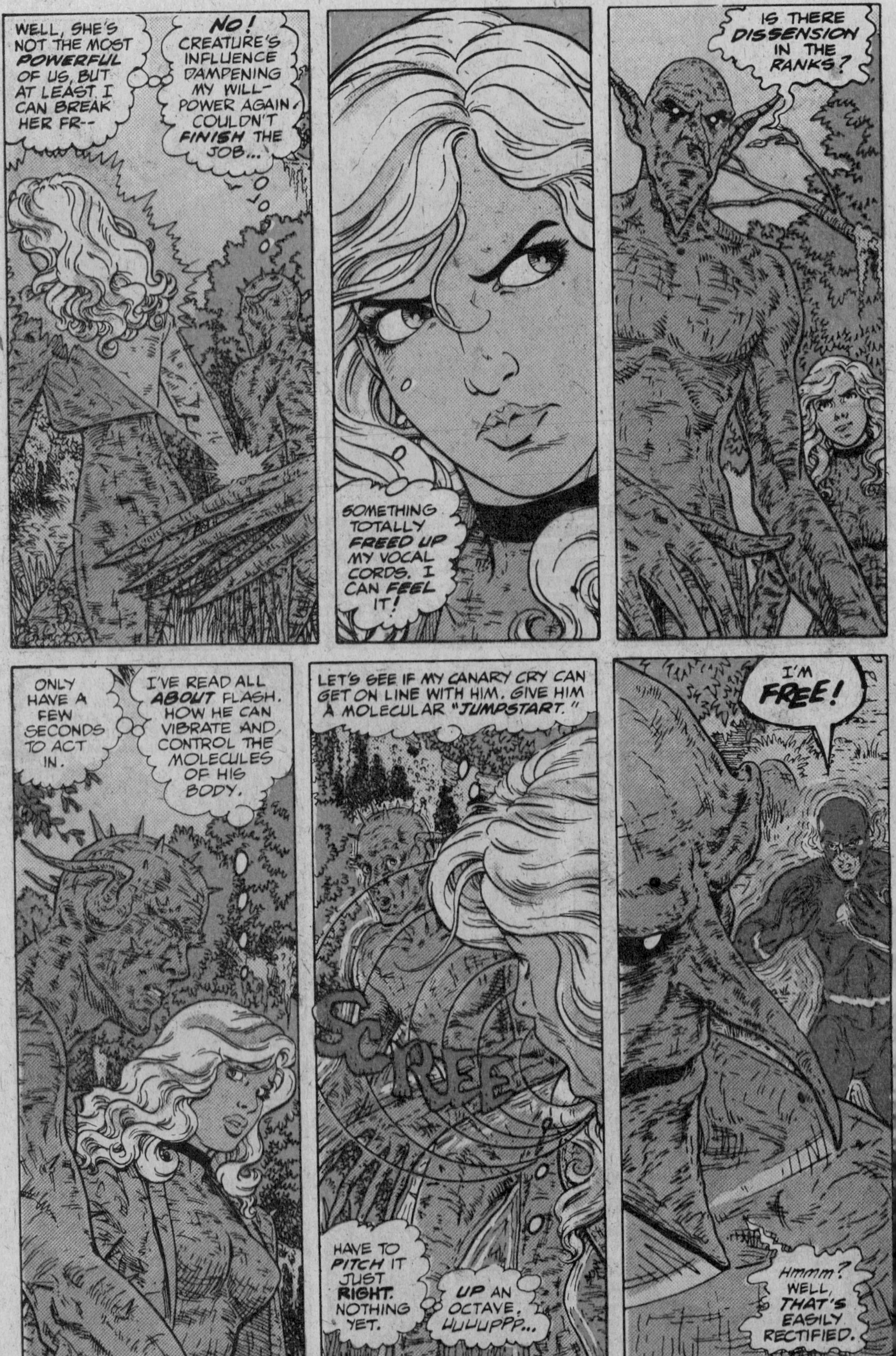
WELL, SHE'S NOT THE MOST POWERFUL OF US, BUT AT LEAST I CAN BREAK HER FR--
NO! CREATURE'S INFLUENCE DAMPENING MY WILL-POWER AGAIN. COULDN'T FINISH THE JOB...
SOMETHING TOTALLY FREED UP MY VOCAL CORDS. I CAN FEEL IT!
IS THERE DISSENSION IN THE RANKS?
ONLY HAVE A FEW SECONDS TO ACT IN.
I'VE READ ALL ABOUT FLASH. HOW HE CAN VIBRATE AND CONTROL THE MOLECULES OF HIS BODY.
LET'S SEE IF MY CANARY CRY CAN GET ON LINE WITH HIM. GIVE HIM A MOLECULAR "JUMPSTART."
SCREE
HAVE TO PITCH IT JUST RIGHT. NOTHING YET.
UP AN OCTAVE, UUUUPPP...
I'M FREE!
Hmmm? WELL, THAT'S EASILY RECTIFIED.

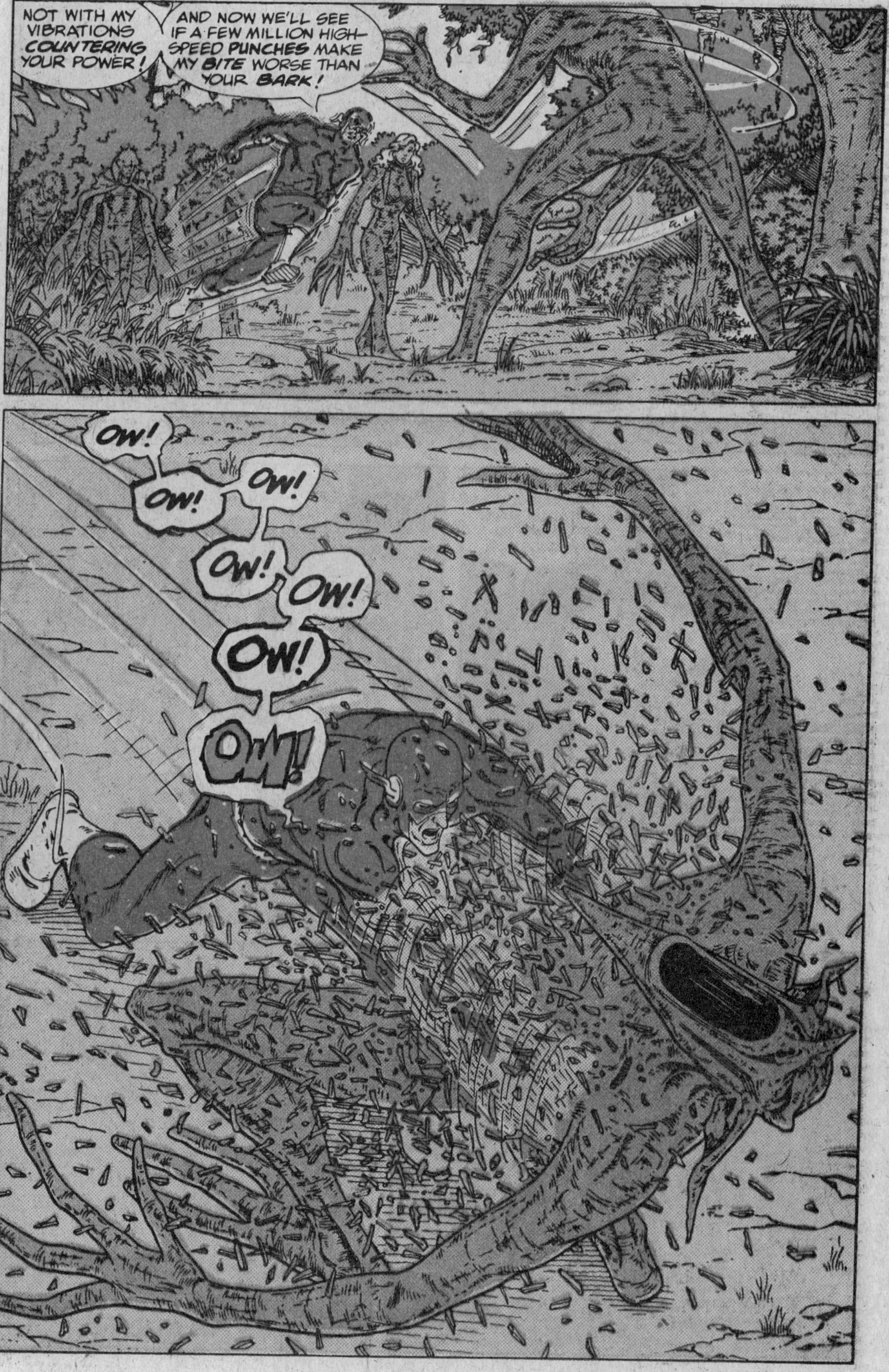
NOT WITH MY VIBRATIONS COUNTERING YOUR POWER!
AND NOW WE'LL SEE IF A FEW MILLION HIGH-SPEED PUNCHES MAKE MY BITE WORSE THAN YOUR BARK!
OW!
OW!
OW!
OW!
OW!
OW!
OW!

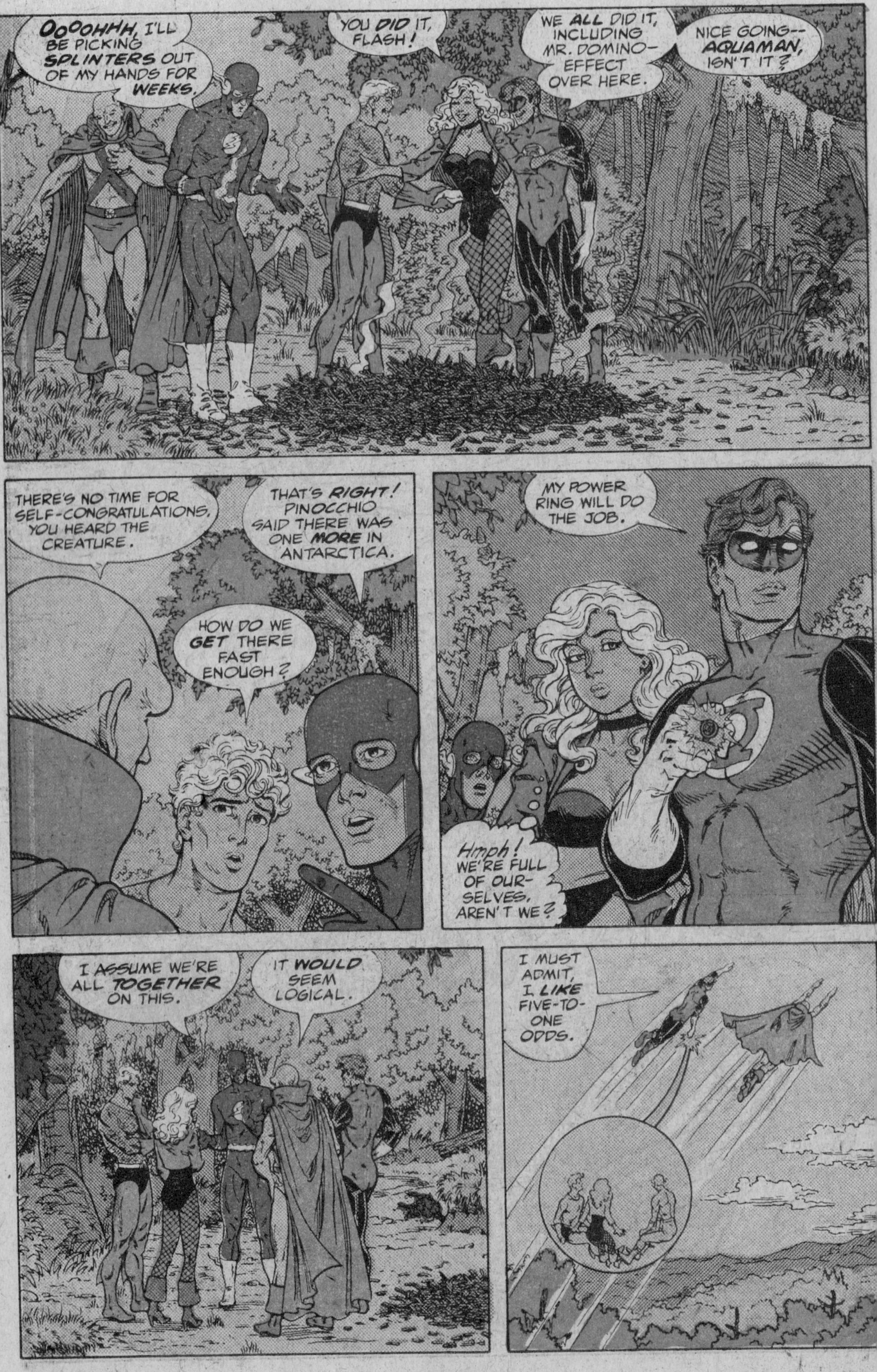
OOooHHH, I'LL BE PICKING SPLINTERS OUT OF MY HANDS FOR WEEKS.
YOU DID IT, FLASH!
WE ALL DID IT, INCLUDING MR. DOMINO-EFFECT OVER HERE.
NICE GOING-- AQUAMAN, ISN'T IT?
THERE'S NO TIME FOR SELF-CONGRATULATIONS. YOU HEARD THE CREATURE.
THAT'S RIGHT! PINOCCHIO SAID THERE WAS ONE MORE IN ANTARCTICA.
HOW DO WE GET THERE FAST ENOUGH?
MY POWER RING WILL DO THE JOB.
Hmph! WE'RE FULL OF OUR-SELVES, AREN'T WE?
I ASSUME WE'RE ALL TOGETHER ON THIS.
IT WOULD SEEM LOGICAL.
I MUST ADMIT, I LIKE FIVE-TO-ONE ODDS.

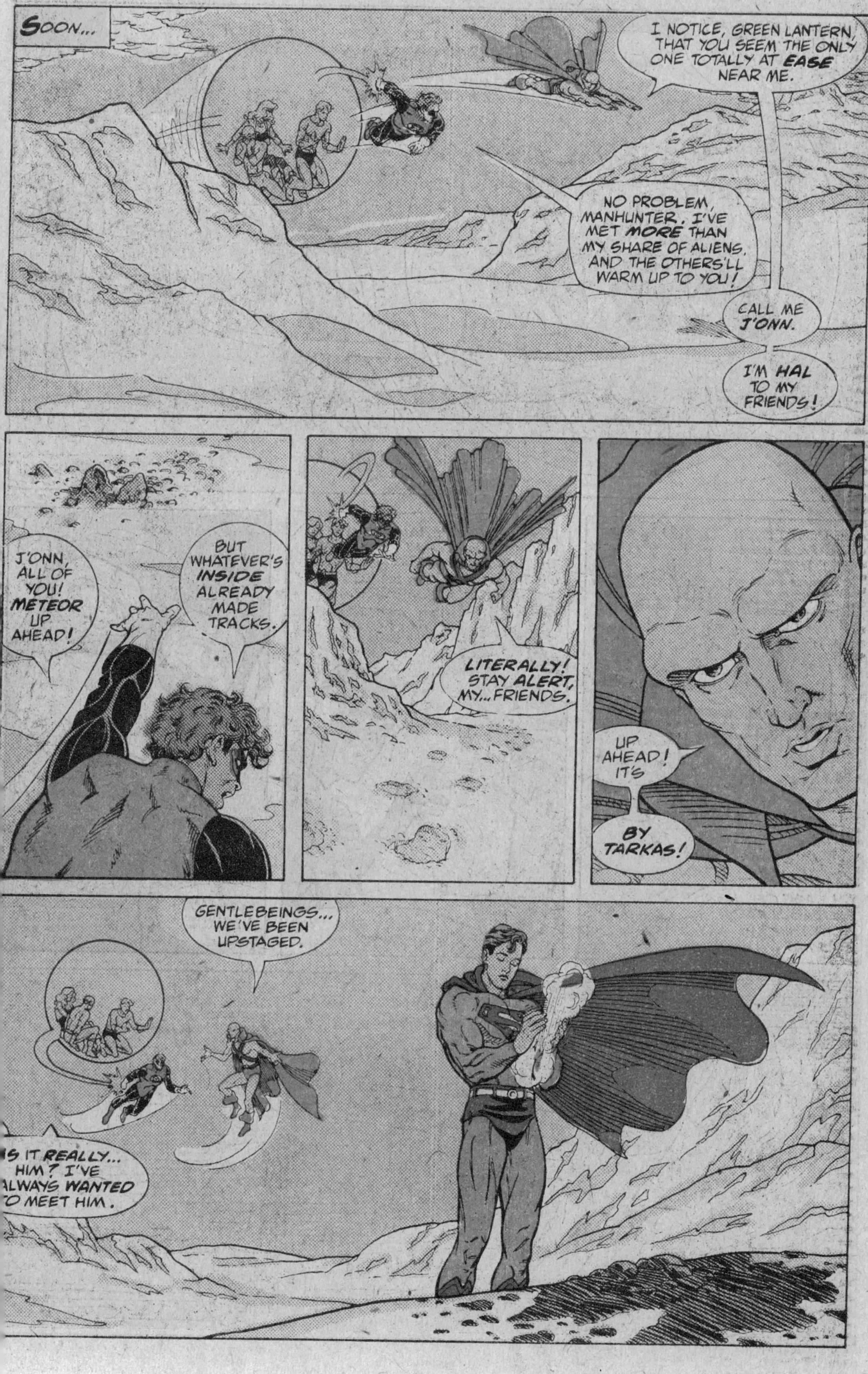
SOON...
I NOTICE, GREEN LANTERN, THAT YOU SEEM THE ONLY ONE TOTALLY AT EASE NEAR ME.
NO PROBLEM, MANHUNTER. I'VE MET MORE THAN MY SHARE OF ALIENS. AND THE OTHERS'LL WARM UP TO YOU!
CALL ME J'ONN.
I'M HAL TO MY FRIENDS!
J'ONN, ALL OF YOU! METEOR UP AHEAD!
BUT WHATEVER'S INSIDE ALREADY MADE TRACKS.
LITERALLY! STAY ALERT, MY... FRIENDS.
UP AHEAD! IT'S
BY TARKAS!
GENTLEBEINGS... WE'VE BEEN UPSTAGED.
IS IT REALLY... HIM? I'VE ALWAYS WANTED TO MEET HIM.

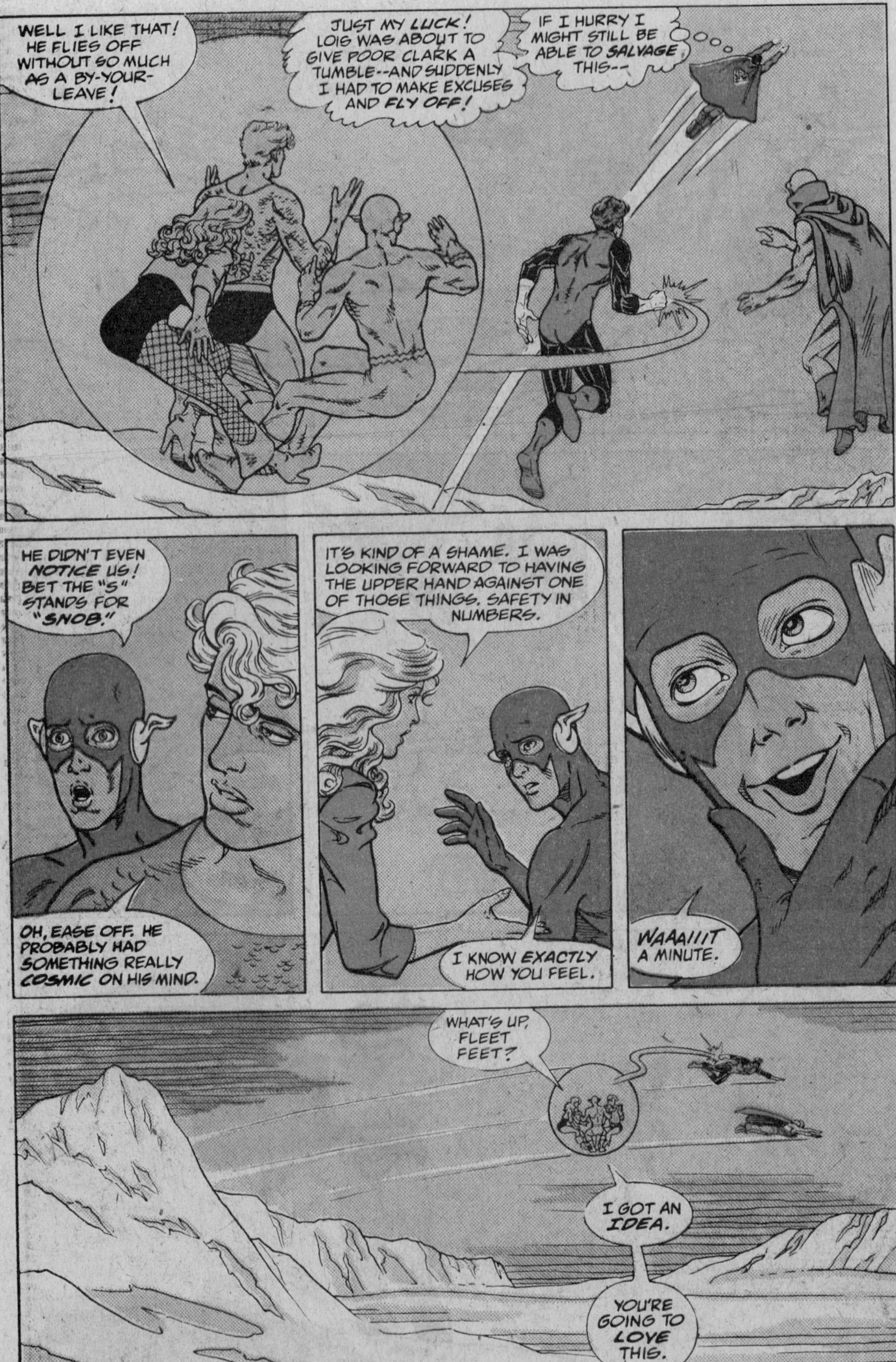
WELL I LIKE THAT! HE FLIES OFF WITHOUT SO MUCH AS A BY-YOUR-LEAVE!
JUST MY LUCK! LOIS WAS ABOUT TO GIVE POOR CLARK A TUMBLE--AND SUDDENLY I HAD TO MAKE EXCUSES AND FLY OFF!
IF I HURRY I MIGHT STILL BE ABLE TO SALVAGE THIS--
HE DIDN'T EVEN NOTICE US! BET THE "S" STANDS FOR "SNOB."
OH, EASE OFF. HE PROBABLY HAD SOMETHING REALLY COSMIC ON HIS MIND.
IT'S KIND OF A SHAME. I WAS LOOKING FORWARD TO HAVING THE UPPER HAND AGAINST ONE OF THOSE THINGS. SAFETY IN NUMBERS.
I KNOW EXACTLY HOW YOU FEEL.
WAAAIIIT A MINUTE.
WHAT'S UP, FLEET FEET?
I GOT AN IDEA.
YOU'RE GOING TO LOVE THIS.

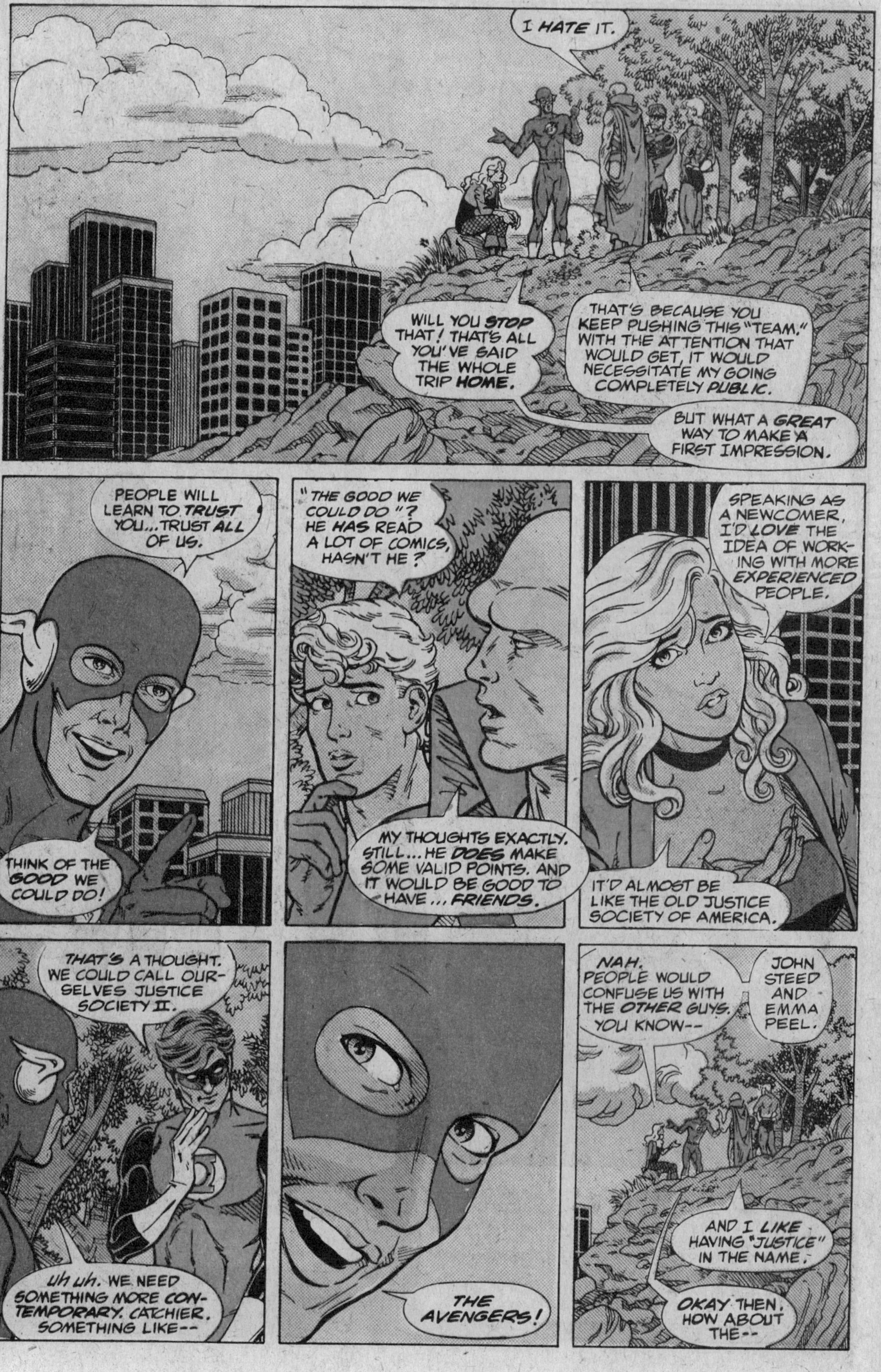
I HATE IT.
WILL YOU STOP THAT! THAT'S ALL YOU'VE SAID THE WHOLE TRIP HOME.
THAT'S BECAUSE YOU KEEP PUSHING THIS "TEAM." WITH THE ATTENTION THAT WOULD GET, IT WOULD NECESSITATE MY GOING COMPLETELY PUBLIC.
BUT WHAT A GREAT WAY TO MAKE A FIRST IMPRESSION.
PEOPLE WILL LEARN TO TRUST YOU... TRUST ALL OF US.
THINK OF THE GOOD WE COULD DO!
"THE GOOD WE COULD DO"? HE HAS READ A LOT OF COMICS, HASN'T HE?
MY THOUGHTS EXACTLY. STILL... HE DOES MAKE SOME VALID POINTS. AND IT WOULD BE GOOD TO HAVE... FRIENDS.
SPEAKING AS A NEWCOMER, I'D LOVE THE IDEA OF WORKING WITH MORE EXPERIENCED PEOPLE.
IT'D ALMOST BE LIKE THE OLD JUSTICE SOCIETY OF AMERICA.
THAT'S A THOUGHT. WE COULD CALL OURSELVES JUSTICE SOCIETY II.
UH UH. WE NEED SOMETHING MORE CONTEMPORARY. CATCHIER. SOMETHING LIKE--
THE AVENGERS!
NAH. PEOPLE WOULD CONFUSE US WITH THE OTHER GUYS. YOU KNOW--
JOHN STEED AND EMMA PEEL.
AND I LIKE HAVING "JUSTICE" IN THE NAME.
OKAY THEN, HOW ABOUT THE--

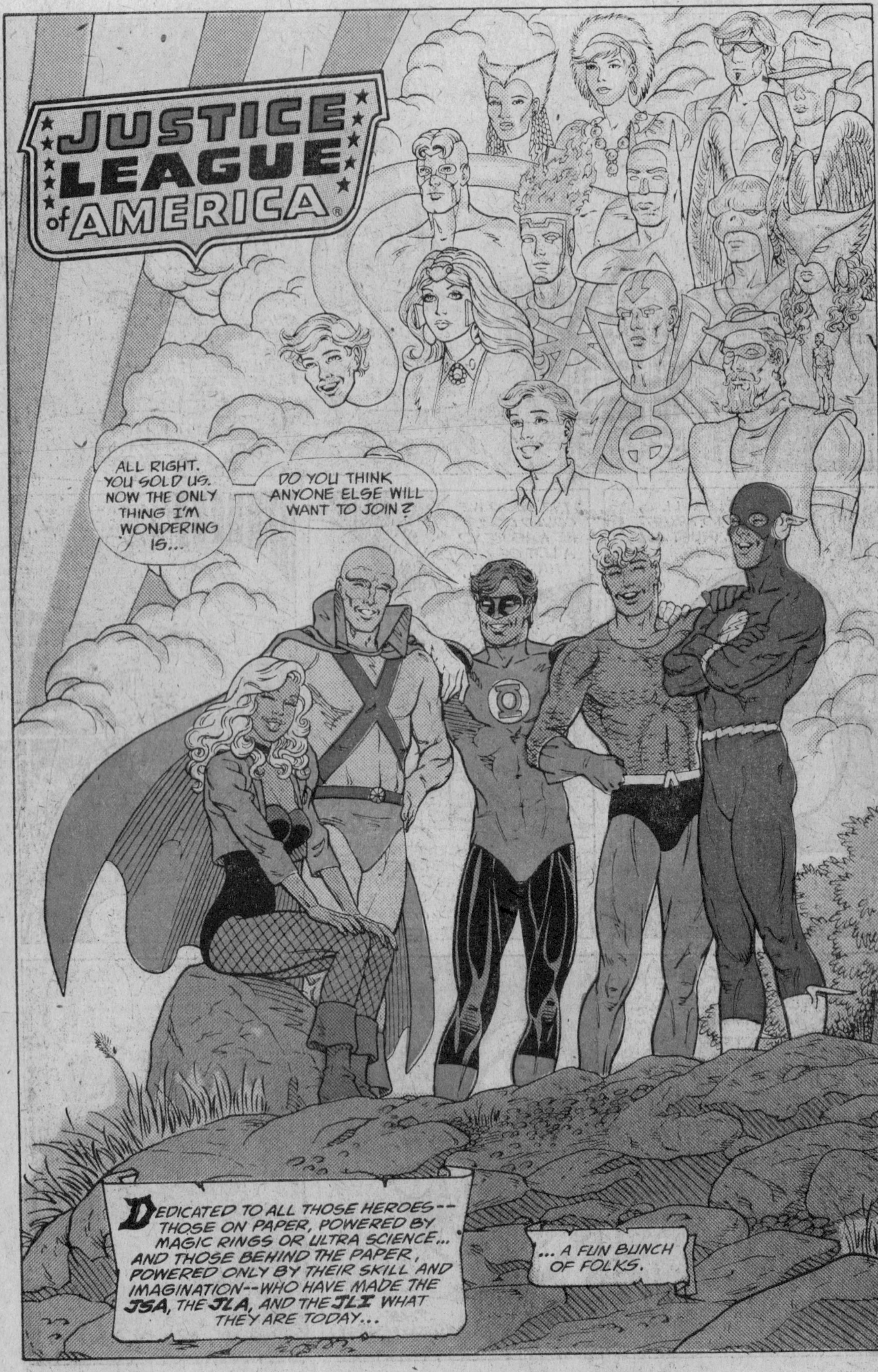
JUSTICE LEAGUE of AMERICA
ALL RIGHT. YOU SOLD US. NOW THE ONLY THING I'M WONDERING IS...
DO YOU THINK ANYONE ELSE WILL WANT TO JOIN?
DEDICATED TO ALL THOSE HEROES-- THOSE ON PAPER, POWERED BY MAGIC RINGS OR ULTRA SCIENCE... AND THOSE BEHIND THE PAPER, POWERED ONLY BY THEIR SKILL AND IMAGINATION--WHO HAVE MADE THE JSA, THE JLA, AND THE JLI WHAT THEY ARE TODAY...
... A FUN BUNCH OF FOLKS.